D1257586

THE LAST TRESILIANS

THE LAST TRESILIANS

by

J. I. M. STEWART

LONDON
VICTOR GOLLANCZ LTD
1963

823.91
S849L

MADE AND PRINTED IN GREAT BRITAIN BY
THE GARDEN CITY PRESS LIMITED
LETCHWORTH, HERTFORDSHIRE

AUTHOR'S NOTE

I HAVE TAKEN SOME liberties with fact in this story. A painting of the date of the White Mermaiden would not be found in Room XV of the National Gallery in London, and Lord Burntisland would have to take a cab (or a No. 88 bus) to the Tate in order to see his first Matthew Tresilian. At Oxford Luke Tresilian's second attempt upon Virgil, *Aeneid*, IV and VI would occur at the end of Trinity Term, and not at the end of the Easter Vacation, as has proved more convenient for my fable. The great staircase upon which one of the "middle" Tresilians hangs is associated in my own mind with a real staircase, but I have transported it to an imaginary college for which I find that I am unable to provide any satisfactory topographical setting. I think of it as adjacent to, and perhaps in both senses looking down upon, the obscure college, again on no real map, presided over by Dr Jopling in a novel called *The Guardians*, published some years ago. There is an indication that Dr Jopling's college lies south of Broad Street. I cannot, although I have tried, come at anything more exact than that.

J. I. M. S.

THE CHARACTERS IN THE ORDER OF THEIR
APPEARANCE

THAYNE DELVER, a professor of the Interrelations of the Arts in the University of California.

CHARLES ROSE, Keeper of Western European Prints in the British Museum.

Lord BURNTISLAND, an elderly ironmaster and statesman.

Sir HECTOR MADRONA, a wealthy man, and patron of the arts.

JANE LANDRETH, an art critic.

BRUNO LANDRETH, her son, an undergraduate.

PHILIP LEECH, a don, Pro-Provost of his college.

KEITH PRATLING, a don.

LUKE TRESILIAN, an undergraduate.

HATTY LANDRETH, a schoolgirl, younger daughter of Jane Landreth.

LUCILLA LANDRETH, Sir Hector Madrona's secretary, elder daughter of Jane Landreth.

ROBIN PACEY, an undergraduate.

JUSTIN PARKS, an Assistant Keeper in the National Gallery, London.

JOHN LITTLEJOHN, Provost of an Oxford college.

Professor FITCH, a very old don.

BRUCE POWDERMAKER, a young don.

BASIL APPLEGARTH, a college bursar.

Lady MADRONA, wife of Sir Hector Madrona.

The Hon. JOHN ALABASTER, a nonagenarian, formerly much in artistic society.

ARTHUR ROUNDHAY, a newspaper editor.

BERNARD LE MESURIER, a Past President of the Royal Academy.

FAITH CRINNIS, only daughter of MATTHEW TRESILIAN, a deceased eminent painter.

ALFRED CRINNIS, her husband, a lighthouse keeper.
Mr SNIDE, a journalist.
MARY EMELEUS, a novelist, once the mistress of Matthew Tresilian.
Dr DOLBEN, a retired physician, Luke Tresilian's guardian.
JANET, Lord Burntisland's parlourmaid.

PART ONE

CHAPTER ONE

THAYNE DELVER WAS a man of buoyant temperament and sanguine expectation. He had brought an umbrella from California to London, but now he had left it in his hotel, convinced that it was going to be a fine day. In fact, rain was falling briefly but heavily, and Delver, head down and coat-collar up, was taking the steps of the British Museum two at a time. His haste was partly symbolical. He couldn't begin fast enough. Never before had he come to Europe at the lure of so rich a hope.

His prospects and the spring shower made him careless. Hurrying beneath the portico and between the deeply fluted columns like a man finding shelter in a petrified forest, he bumped into somebody. He drew back with an apology. Then he smiled and thrust forward a cordial hand. "Say!" he said. "Rose!"

Charles Rose shook hands with proper enthusiasm. An American who, hard upon nearly knocking you down, exclaims "Rose!" and not "Mr Rose!" is, after all, beginning well. Rose doubted whether, had this collision occurred in the Metropolitan Museum in New York, he would himself have remembered to say "Why, Mr Delver!"

"I'm delighted to see you in England again," he said. "Have you been here long?"

"Only a couple of days here in London, although I landed a week ago. At Liverpool, that was. It lets me visit with the folks in Cheshire."

Rose was remembering more about Thayne Delver. He had heard about the kinsfolk before. Delver had explained that they were people in modest circumstances. But they lived in Cheshire. Delver, Anglophil to the core, was proud of them.

"And you'll be working here in the B.M.? Is it Rossetti again?"

Delver shook his head. It was a motion to which he gave the same serious eagerness as to an affirmative nod. "No," he said. "It's something bigger this time. And I can hardly wait to begin.

Still, *festina lente*. Do you know, that's the motto of the Onslow family? If that isn't English humour!"

Even the most agreeable Americans, Rose reflected, are remorselessly informative. With the professors, it must come of all those dreary hours conducting seminars. "You'll be working here through the summer?" he asked.

"No, no. A fortnight in the reading room, completing a general orientation for my project. A few memoirs that I haven't been able to find on the other side. Perhaps some manuscript material, although I don't expect to come on much of that just here. After that, field work!"

"Field work?" Rose wondered whether Delver had taken to archaeology.

"The surviving relatives and friends. A certain delicacy may be required." Delver was looking almost yearningly past Rose at the revolving door of the Museum, at this hour moving like a mill-wheel before the flow of persons sequacious of learning. So Rose was surprised to feel his arm taken in a sudden grip. "Let me tell you about it," Delver said. "Could you put down a pint?"

Rose seldom put down pints, and never round about noon. But the shower was over and he wouldn't get wet. "Yes, of course," he said. He mustn't give this amiable man the feeling that he had been faulted in a knowledge of the native customs.

"The Plough?" Delver asked. "Or the Museum Tavern? That used to be my local in these parts. A first-class bitter there. Or there's the Bull and Mouth. What would that be a corruption of, I wonder? There ought to be a doctoral dissertation on the names of your English pubs." Delver talked rapidly as they made their way through the massive gold-tipped iron gates. He tapped them as he passed. "*Odi profanum vulgus et arceo*," he said. "Wouldn't you say that, to the laity—to what old Dan C. calls *lewede men*—these fortifications of learning must present a forbidding air?"

"I don't suppose they much notice," Rose said. He had been obliged to repress an impulse of disapprobation. How could a scholar, he wondered, refer to Chaucer under that facetious style? Yet Thayne Delver was a sound enough scholar of his kind. And clearly he was well disposed. Above the rattle of traffic in Great Russell Street he was now making Rose a handsome speech.

"As I was saying, not Rossetti. What fun that job was, though! And what an enormous lot of help you gave me! Do you know that you've been instrumental in founding a new Chair? It ought to be called the Charles Rose Chair. At Oxford it *would* be called the Charles Rose Chair."

Rose, who was a man of means and the unobtrusive curator of certain prints in the Museum, shook his head as he caught Delver's warm smile. "I don't see how that can be, at all."

"I couldn't have written that book without your having put me on the things you did. And it happened that the book just turned the scale with our Regents. They established a Chair and appointed me to it. I'm now—don't laugh, Rose—Professor of the Interrelations of the Arts."

"I congratulate you most sincerely. I am quite delighted." Rose spoke promptly. He even remembered that his words must be accompanied by another hand shake.

"Thank you very much. Of course I'm a mere tiro, and miles behind no end of Germans. That's inevitable, since they invented the thing. But the field is going to be a fascinating one, absolutely fascinating. You see"—Delver continued with a sudden switch to intense earnestness such as no Englishman could have achieved —"I'm convinced that in any age there exists a pervasive atmosphere necessarily conditioning the work of every sort of artist. It conditions even artists holding opposed aesthetic or philosophical or political views. That's the major aspect of the thing, as you know. The minor one I was already in contact with in the Rossetti. It's the case of the individual artist expressing himself in several media: Michelangelo, for example, in painting and sculpture and poetry."

"It certainly affords scope."

Like the Museum's over-dieted pigeons taking with surprising lightness to the air, Delver's solemnity vanished in laughter which startled the few people in the bar they were now entering. "That blessed English understatement," he said. "I haven't heard a note of it for years. A pint of best bitter, please. What's yours?"

"I'll have the same." Watching the thick glass being filled, Rose wondered whether, after this chilly drench, his customary tot of rather dry Madeira before luncheon would be wise. He had all a middle-aged bachelor's care in such matters. But his behaviour was irreproachable. Raising his glass, he consulted his memories of hostelries of the character he found himself in. "Cheers," he said.

"All the best, Rose." Delver led the way to a bench in a corner. "If it isn't wonderful to get back! If it isn't wonderful to get away! Not that one altogether manages *that*. We come not single spies but in battalions."

"That was said of sorrows." Rose felt he was expected to show knowledge of Shakespeare. "You wouldn't think of yourselves as that?"

"As headaches, at any rate." Delver made a humorous matter of lowering his voice. "Just look. Foot-loose American professors all around us." There were two or three men in the bar who might be conjectured conceivably to belong to some more than commonly seedy branch of the academic profession, although they were probably employed in the collecting of petty debts. But Delver was delighted with his joke. "Wandering scholars," he said. "The tavern has been their prime haunt for centuries. Let's get them to sing. In Latin."

Rose judged it uncharitable to be irked by this unassuming fun. "It's true that you people do get around," he said. "Your great corporations are wonderful patrons."

"You know they favour one particular category among us?" Delver was continuing on the path of humour. "The bores, my dear fellow! Those of us who are so *intensely* boring that our colleagues are perpetually at work securing us Rockefellers, Guggenheims or any other travel grant that will blessedly remove us from the campus for a semester or more. Of course, this mustn't get too widely circulated. If it did, we'd have bogus bores competing to build up reputations for tediousness in a big way. Do you know Homer Slimbridge of Columbia?"

"I'm sure I don't."

"Boy, if he isn't the real thing! Slimbridge has been in Oxford three years running, on precisely those export terms. And last fall, there in Oxford, he had six invitations from six separate people to dine in the same college on an identical night. He was no end pleased. Of course, it was because the Faculty—the Fellows, that's to say—had been laying wagers with each other as to who should produce the greatest blight of the evening."

14

Rose had heard this story before, although he didn't recall that the victim's name had been Slimbridge. He hoped that he hadn't, therefore, himself looked bored as he listened to it. For Delver was an engaging creature, in whom the great American innocence surely lived on. It would be hard to conceive of a human being, substantially endowed with vitality and pertinacity, less likely to employ these qualities to any harmful effect.

"Every country would like to export its bores," Rose said. "But the sober fact is that Rockefeller and the rest plainly favour your tip-top men. And they're as striking an instance of the survival of the fittest as I know. They emerge from the grim mill of your Graduate Schools, unexpectedly alive, and positively menacing in their erudition. But one wonders how many may have gone under."

"I see you've had a glimpse of our system. And I have to admit there are survivors. You make them sound kind of dangerous."

"Oh, no!" Rose was amused. "Yourself, you know. I was just thinking that you are precisely *not* dangerous, if it isn't impertinent to mention the fact."

"It's wounding." Delver was making a connoisseur's business of holding his beer up to the light. "One would *like* to be a menace."

"Well, I just don't know whom or what you're going to be a menace to. But you *are* one of the survivors, Delver. Nobody could make a mistake about that. Right up at the top of your tree—and drinking bitter and cutting capers, like any sophomore upon whom the shades of the prison house have never closed."

Delver was a man in early middle-age, with bold, mobile features, and a high complexion uncommon—Rose thought— among his galactotrophic countrymen. But he had the true American mouth : a thin line when closed; and, when open, square, like a trap. Over this rugged *ensemble*, and distinguishable even through that colouring, there was now mantling a blush. Rose feared that in a desire to give a foreigner pleasure he had overshot the mark. But then, what he had said was more or less the truth. And he liked, he clearly saw that he liked, the eager pilgrim from California who had succeeded in filling him up with beer between breakfast and luncheon. Rose looked at his glass. He had got two-thirds of the way through the stuff, and his inside felt much as usual. But now a horrible thought came to him. Was it possible that the ritual of compotation required his presently suggesting that they should have a second pint "on him"? At least, he could try distraction. "But the job you've come over for," he asked. "Field work, and the surviving friends and relations. You haven't told me about it. Or about how it hitches on to the interrelations of the arts."

There was a moment's silence. Delver, so out-going and spontaneous, had hung fire. He had been eager to tell about the thing. But now he hesitated. And the reason turned out to be simple. Another Delver had to be brought on the boards for the task—and there had been a moment's hitch, as in a play inexpertly rehearsed. Cosmopolite Delver, determined to be as frivolous, ironic, under-stating as any Englishman among them, must retire into the wings. A more native Delver must take his place.

"Matthew Tresilian," Delver said with grave passion. "I suppose everybody reckons by this time that he was a great painter?"

"Lord, yes. Tresilian is being seen as one of the most important English painters of his age. There's a big exhibition of his stuff coming on quite soon. I have some concern with it."

Delver nodded. "It's like this," he said. "I have some reason to suppose that Tresilian was rather a good writer too."

"Really? Well, some painters—not many—have been able to write."

"Sure." Delver appeared dissatisfied with the effect he had created. "But how would it be if Tresilian's letters proved to be not much behind Van Gogh's?"

"It would be exciting. And a surprise. I don't recall Tresilian's figuring as a correspondent in any of the memoirs of the period. Most painters never so much as send a line to their old mothers. I suppose I'd take it for granted that Tresilian had been that sort."

"Well, I'm reckoning to show you'd be wrong. And there's something more. It seems possible that there's an extant journal of Tresilian's—a journal connected not so much with painting as with his own intimate life."

"I see." Hearing again the confident ring in Thayne Delver's voice, Rose glanced at him before saying more. The keen face now lifted up above the empty glass was that of a man one could rely on. A father had once relied on young Thayne, no doubt, to run a lumber-yard, manufacture more dry-goods, bring fresh drive to marketing real estate. But young Thayne had chosen to go right ahead on another line. He was doing it now. Superficially extraverted and easy, generous in his allocation of time to social uses, an elbow-taker in England and doubtless a back-slapper at home, Delver, like all unaffected Americans a regular guy at one level, would be best likened at another to a highly evolved but rugged mechanism with a keen cutting edge and a good digestion. Rose felt this rather powerfully now. "Of course," he said, "Matthew Tresilian and his intimate life haven't been all that time dead."

"True enough." Delver nodded gratefully, as one who has received words of straight encouragement. "I've an advantage there. There won't be many cold trails. And I have faith in this thing. I believe there's stuff to be got hold of that will set Matthew Tresilian in a far clearer light than he stands in today. I'm going to do the job. And I shall dare to hope that his shade will be grateful to me."

"Yes—of course." Rose was disconcerted by the underlying fervour of this appeal to ghostly sanction. "Although I don't know that shades necessarily relish being set—" He broke off, since there was no point in speaking out of turn. "I wonder," he said—for they were the only words that came into his head—"whether you'd care to have another on me?"

CHAPTER TWO

LORD BURNTISLAND, AN elderly man carefully erect in spring sunshine that had succeeded a spring shower, came down the steps of his club after an early lunch. He glanced across the street, and the long sprawl of pictures again caught and held his attention. It was a small corner of London in which one scarcely expected such things. But demolitions were going on, a hoarding had been run up, and on this the line of posters was displayed.

They were all vulgar affairs. Not, indeed, in execution. As far as immediate pictorial taste goes—he told himself, fair-mindedly —everything of that sort is better than it used to be. It's the underlying assumptions that are so damnably decadent. The nation's economy must expand, we must march with the times— but a sheerly commercial ethos debases things good in themselves. Take travel by air. Many of those old fellows in the club have got into the way of deploring the modern world's senseless mania for speed. I always tell them they're talking rot. To be able to climb into what is virtually a projectile, and be hurled in it from London across the pole to Seattle within a handful of hours, is surely . . . is surely—

Standing on the steps, pulling grey kid gloves over arthritic fingers, Burntisland cast round in his mind for just what the achieving of the jet age so surely was. And, as so often now, he went back to his early reading—that planned course of reading by which, as a simple Fifeshire boy, he had prepared himself to become not only an ironmaster but a legislator as well. That sort of conquest of space is an enlarging of the bounds of human empire—he decided, recalling Francis Bacon. In exchange for the power to do this exciting and near-miraculous thing, you barter a small but definite chance of instant annihilation. What's wrong with that? Nothing at all. But now look at their beastly advertisement!

Burntisland realized that he had spoken words angrily and aloud. It was something he had once or twice noticed himself doing of late. I'll gain a reputation, he thought, for eccentricity —and for senile eccentricity, no doubt—if I don't mind my Ps and Qs. Just at the moment, fortunately, there's nobody about.

The picture dulled and shone again; a cloud had scurried over the sun. A fellow who might be a director of companies sat in front of a little table piled with food. He was gowking at this— the good Doric phrases returned to Burntisland, so long expatriate—like some gormless loon at a Sunday School treat. And gowking at *him* was a ring of three "air hostesses". The girls were tendering trays on which were crowded more of the messed-up concoctions that the fellow already had before him, while in the background, for good measure, a white-jacketed steward was opening a bottle of champagne. The girls, quite as much as the food, were in the poster as objects of sensual appetite. That was where the chief grossness of the glossy spectacle lay. Burntisland felt a wave of anger. It was like a bubble that shot up from darkness to the surface of his mind and burst. A Belshazzar's Feast, he thought, calm again, and remembering his mother's knee. And *hubris,* he thought—for the Humanities, as well as Engineering and Metallurgy, had once claimed his attention in the University of Edinburgh. To take one's concupiscences in one's baggage when tempting fate at six hundred miles an hour is surely a dangerous pride.

Lord Burntisland's inner ear heard the voice of Lord Burntisland delivering this last sentiment before an august assembly. He raised his head in a motion that had been his father's in the pulpit. The result was to transfer his gaze to a second poster.

It's worse, he thought, much worse. The things have been proved as good as lethal. Yet here they are, a hundred times larger than life, and represented as the key to successful courtship. And that's to put it moderately! Seduction would be as fair a word. That girl on her back on the turf, the young man on his elbow beside her, his head poised above her sharply pointed breasts : they're the couples you see in the public parks. In another minute they'll be behaving like animals.

Suddenly uneasy, Burntisland removed his glance from the poster. To any man such things may be an occasion of evil. But he had a duty to consider them. He didn't believe in censorship. But he strongly believed in public vigilance. He was on the council of a body that sought to activate it. So he looked again at the second poster.

No, he decided, the couple are not in a public park. What appears to be round about them is invitingly empty downland. Have they got there on bicycles, in a Mini-minor, in a Bentley? We're not told. A classless couple—the suggestion being that everybody's doing it.

Everybody's doing it, doing it, doing it. . . . For a moment the forgotten music-hall song rang oddly in Burntisland's head. And so they are, he thought, as we all know. Daughters of good families. Sons of God-fearing parents. Copulating in a haze of cigarette smoke, a reek of alcohol, even a fume of unspeakable illicit drugs. He frowned, aware of something in himself that resisted scrutiny. Aware, too, of a physical tremor, as of fatigue, he turned and walked away down the august, gently sloping street, closed by the dark Tudor brick beyond which there now hovered, as if miraged up from Manhattan, the alien lines of the Vickers Building on Millbank. At the first corner he turned and looked back. He might have been taken for a man keeping a look-out for a cab. The air hostesses were still offering their trays and nothing else. The man and girl on the down hadn't moved.

He turned into Pall Mall and walked east. A committee-meeting (of an admirable body, concerned that young people should have free access to the countryside) had fallen through. It was undeniable that he had the rest of the day on his hands. Obscurely, he felt this to be a menace. Idleness didn't agree with him—how should it, after a life like his? Full retirement, supposing he lived to an age at which that became inevitable, was going to be a problem. But at least now, and before going home, he could take a turn in the park. To keep up mild exercise was important for a man of his age, particularly for one who felt that he still had active work to do. He would go round by the Athenaeum and down the Duke of York's Steps. It had been a whimsical notion that had possessed him a few moments ago : the notion that those posters might have stirred into motion behind him. Almost an imaginative notion.

He made his way along the sunny side of the street, slowly but with no appearance of being without an aim. The vista was familiar and even dear to him. The portly façades, if ill-assorted, had long ago shaken down together, like members of a long-established dining club. Only at intervals there intruded some new, young face—fearing its own brashness, aware of nothing warmer than tolerance around it, yet confident that the world would presently be coming its way. Moving through this calm milieu, undistracted by the jostle of a crowd, Burntisland pondered whether, had not industry and politics claimed him, he might have had an artistic or literary career. There had been Raeburn. There had been Allan Ramsay. There had been Scott and R. L. S.

These thoughts (and they were no more than reverie, of which he didn't much approve) were still in Lord Burntisland's mind when, at the corner giving on St James's Square, he ran into Sir Hector Madrona. The man's oddly named, he thought, pausing to exchange greetings. But Hector is probably Ettore. It can't be all that time since these Madronas arrived from Naples or thereabout. Madrona is an industrialist to be reckoned with. But he's also very much a fine arts man. It may be a good idea to have a word with him on this business of undesirable advertisements. He may have a line which he'd be grateful to have taken up in the Lords.

Madrona listened. He nodded with an effect of large if undefined agreement. "Yes, indeed," he said. "But yes, indeed." He spoke softly and in a tone of deference which was entirely conventional; Burntisland had a notion that he could, at need, make a formidable weapon of it. "How much I feel with you, Burntisland." In nose and eyebrows, in mouth, shoulders and paunch, Madrona was a man gently curvilinear. He carried round with him a perpetual air of surprised gratification, as if his inner ear was tuned in to an unintermitted flow of unexpectedly satisfactory intelligence. "Yet there can be no doubt," he went on, "that we are doing much to raise the level of the whole affair—profession, craft, industry, or whatever it calls itself. Poster art is no longer merely on the hoardings, let us say. It's on the artistic map as well. Wouldn't you agree?" Madrona looked at Burntisland as if anxiously awaiting confirmation of a long-cherished hope. "And almost for the first time since Toulouse-Lautrec."

Burntisland frowned. Toulouse-Lautrec, he seemed to remember, had been a degenerate aristocrat—and moreover, like most Frenchmen, a frequenter of brothels. "No doubt, Madrona.

But you mistake me. It's not the aesthetic aspect of the thing that's in my mind. It's the psychological and moral. Particularly the moral."

"Ah—the psychological!" Madrona, who had perhaps heard imperfectly, produced again his large, affirmative air. Burntisland remembered an Edinburgh debating society of his youth, and one interminable speaker who had invariably risen to "homologate" the sentiments of some previous orator. Madrona would make a good homologator. "Fascinating, fascinating," Madrona pursued. "Have you noticed the odd way in which locale seems to be important? Women's stockings and underclothes, now—girdles and brassières and what are called, I believe, foundation garments : why should their advertising be concentrated, as it is, so massively along the escalators in the tubes?"

"Is it?" It was with some promptitude that Burntisland asked this. "I hadn't noticed." He didn't care for talk of the *mundus muliebris* between males.

Madrona raised his eyebrows a shade above their common pitch. "Ah," he said smoothly, "you are probably not an Underground man. But I assure you it is so. Of course, a staircase has powerful emotional suggestions, sexual connotations. You will have noticed it in films. The mounting of a staircase at an accelerating tempo. Most interesting."

"No. I've noticed nothing of the sort."

"You are probably no cinema-goer. But you will recall an interesting piece of German slang. Freud comments on it somewhere."

"Freud?" Burntisland's umbrella tapped the pavement. "Surely all that unwholesome stuff is exploded? It was totally unscientific. I looked into it."

"*Ein alter Steiger*. Again, there is the French *un vieux marcheur*."

"No doubt." Burntisland's only language other than English was Latin, of which he possessed a considerable command. This conversation was not taking the useful course he had proposed.

"So, as we are whisked up an escalator—which constitutes an intriguing variant upon the symbolism of the ordinary staircase, you must agree—we are drawn into a certain unconscious relationship with sexual matters."

"What about when we are whisked down?" It was with no

effect of wit that Burntisland produced this. "I have little interest in these things. I'm simply offended by the various sorts of licence and grossness that commercial advertising battens on. And some other 'channels of communication', as they are now called. Television, most notably. There's a great deal of innuendo, a great deal that's suggestive. Vice *lurks*, Madrona! I become more and more conscious of it. It lurks in media—and there you have another of their newfangled words—sponsored, as often as not, by bodies that ought to know better. Take the British Council. It does the most admirable work. I have a very high regard for it. But it has put out pamphlets, I assure you, on some quite grossly immoral writers. James Joyce, for example. And blasphemous writers, too. I don't believe in the dogmatic side of Christianity, or in a personal God, and so forth. But I won't stand for blasphemy. It's like public impertinence to the Royal Family—a thoroughly bad sign."

"So much of what you say is incontestably true. I respond to it most warmly."

"Well, it's my intention to raise the subject in the Lords. It occurred to me that you might have suggestions for cleaning up the mess."

Madrona made a movement with his shoulders that suggested less Naples than Beirût. "Alas," he said, "but I fear I am wholly inept at these crusades! My dear Burntisland, this is something that preys on your mind?"

"Certainly not." Burntisland was startled. "I'm merely aware of things that prey upon our nation. Cancers, Madrona! There are things going on that ought to be stopped. Otherwise, where are we going to end up?" He paused, conscious of agitation, and conscious also that these remarks were too general to impress. "Take the statistics," he said. "Serving on the bodies that I do, I have access to a great many of the statistics. And some of them are quite appalling."

Madrona nodded. He had the air of a man who, within moderate limits and upon a convenient occasion, is prepared to be appalled. "But you have the comfort of taking effective action," he said soothingly. "It's widely remarked—forgive me —that you do a splendid job on the moral front. And nothing could be more important. I feel a sad dilettante in the comparison, I assure you. I simply want to make things less generally hideous. It's uphill work. I suppose it's absurdly old-fashioned as well. Sometimes I feel like poor William Morris. The more so, of course, because of my socialist principles."

Burntisland said nothing. He had no use for Madrona's socialist principles, which he regarded as a careerist gamble that had failed to pay off.

"But one has a moderate success from time to time. I doubt whether it's a secret from you that I've lately taken up a considerable interest in the development of nuclear power. Well, we're putting up a new reactor station at Grasmere—"

"Grasmere in Westmorland?" Astonishment and horror sounded in Burntisland's voice as he asked this.

"Certainly. It proved to be much the most suitable place, from the point of view of what can be poisoned with tolerable safety, and so forth. And I found that my colleagues were resolved on a purely utilitarian job. Would you believe it? They were prepared to salve their artistic consciences by spattering the walls with a few reliefs hacked out of brick or concrete. I put my foot down. I insisted that the whole thing, lock, stock and barrel, should be by—well, of course, you can imagine. By Leonard Benton Curry."

"I don't think I've heard of him."

"My dear fellow, Leonard Benton Curry is the only really rugged name to emerge in architecture since Frank Lloyd Wright. He's doing this splendid new military prison we're going to have. He can be guaranteed to evolve a tremendous design. His reactor station, believe me, will look like something spewed up by volcanic action out of Windermere, or tumbled down by an earthquake from Helvellyn. That's his line, you see —architecture that seems to be part of the resistless force of Nature herself."

"Will he be all right on the technical side?" It was out of politeness that Burntisland asked this. He had no interest in Leonard Benton Curry.

"Lord, yes! He'll take it in his stride. I've watched him for some time. I have an intense passion, I confess, for this whole problem of industrial design and architecture. Not that it has seduced me from my first love in the arts. Painting is that, as you know. Indeed, most people know. I've taken a prominent part in the movement there." Madrona paused. This time, he seemed himself the object of the pleased astonishment he carried about with him. "Despite, you know, being tolerably active in other fields. And as a matter of fact"—he became confidential—"I've just come from something important now. Question of whether we might get the Queen Mum to open the Tresilian memorial exhibition. Anyway, it will be under pretty august auspices. In fact, it's going to be quite an event. And I feel peculiarly concerned in it. You see, Tresilian was practically my wife's discovery. Or, at least, *middle* Tresilian was. My wife has one of the most important middle Tresilians in her drawing-room now. The Act of Love."

"The *what*?"

"A large, abstract thing. It has something very like Mark Tobey's white writing, although I don't think there can have been any direct influence. It would interest you. You must come and see it one day."

Burntisland grunted. It was as near as he could get to politeness, this time. He regretted stopping to talk to Madrona. As for Tresilian, he had no more heard of him than he had heard of Leonard Benton Curry.

"And, of course, the exhibition itself. You mustn't miss that. You mustn't miss the private view. Everybody will be there."

"I can't say I often go to affairs of that sort."

"Dear me! That means, conceivably, they might fail to send you a card. But I'll see to it. Indeed, I'll make a note of it now."

As good as his word, Sir Hector Madrona produced a small Russia-leather book and inscribed Lord Burntisland's name in an appropriate place. Burntisland looked on in some irritation. It was rather as if the fellow were a policeman. And this struck Burntisland as an unpleasant idea. But he waited, as civility required, until Madrona was finished. Then he said a word of farewell, and walked on.

That encounter—he thought impatiently—was entirely pointless. Nothing will come of it.

CHAPTER THREE

"New para," Jane Landreth said into the telephone. "But what is teasing about nearly all these canvases is a new tentativeness in linear design. Stop. It is something puzzling in an old—no, old won't do; cancel old—in a painter whose full maturity we think of as established long ago. Stop again. The revolution in Mr Ogilvie's painting in the 'Forties was a significant event in its day. Stop. Can this be comma once more comma transitional work—that's with a question-mark. It is an exciting thought. Finish." Jane paused to take breath. "And will you please ask Martin to be very sweet and correct the proof? No, I can't get in this afternoon. Oh, and better take out 'new' in 'new tentativeness'. Good-bye."

Jane—in her later forties, strong-featured, long-limbed and rangy—put down the telephone hastily, and made for the kitchen. It was her son Bruno, now sprawled before the fire, who was the occasion of this perfunctory professional performance. When only her two daughters were at home, a midday meal required no more than an opening of tins or boiling of eggs. But when Bruno was there it was different—and simply because Bruno was a man.

Jane knew that this was absurd, atavic, bourgeois—or at least that it was a consequence of her widowed state. She clung to the belief that the discrimination was something that Bruno had never tumbled to as existing. But it did exist, and particularly when, as now, Bruno had made one of those slightly mysterious dashes home from Oxford. Sometimes he came for the week-end, which probably he wasn't supposed to do. Sometimes it was just a day-excursion. In either event he would find time for a cinema, an institution for which he was supposed to cherish so reticent a passion that, upon returning home, he invariably declined all discussion of his experiences there. Jane didn't know whether or not there was something odd in all this : an indication, perhaps, that Bruno's work wasn't going well, or even that he was suffering from some emotional insecurity. Bruno certainly still did odd things; for example, he still played with Hatty the tiresome game he had precociously invented upon being introduced by a pious relative to the early chapters of *Genesis*. But, after all, his manner on these visits didn't suggest insecurity or any other ill. When not out at his innominate cinemas he sat around in a good deal of self-contentment, subjecting his womenfolk to what it was best to think of as affectionate fun.

"Are you *really* excited?" Bruno asked. He had ceased sipping sherry in favour of the alternative luxury of stretching himself, like an athlete enjoying the prospect of a long and agreeable day. "Or puzzled, for that matter?" It was one of his jokes—one of his young, rather obvious jokes—that art criticism, which for years had kept the wolf from the family door, was a racket. It wasn't a jeering joke. But it couldn't be called amusing.

"I'm interested," Jane said, and disappeared into the kitchen. She continued to talk as she added the Portuguese wine to the *poulet sauté*. "It's a show by a man called Ogilvie. He might be called a descendant, or even a survivor, of the Glasgow School."

"Golly—did they once get round to painting in Glasgow?"

"You're an abominably ignorant young man. Well, Ogilvie's no sort of great painter, and I didn't say he was. But what should make him, in his comfortable sixties, start fumbling after something he can't quite see? So it *is* puzzling, too."

"But not *exciting*," Bruno said, rather tediously.

"Yes, exciting as well." Jane had come to the kitchen door, an oven-cloth in her hand—challenged, indignant, pleased. "Exciting to *me*, if you like. I'm almost that age myself—"

"You're not within twenty years of it."

"Well, I sometimes feel I am. And here's one of my contemporaries—not so eminent as to seem remote and inimitable—striking out, having a bash. That's genuinely exciting. And I don't, as a matter of fact, much say what I don't think—not even over the telephone to a ninepenny paper, and when harassed by the expectations of a hungry undergraduate."

"Why not strike out yourself, Mum? Why not have a bash?"

Jane hesitated. So often she couldn't tell whether Bruno spoke in sympathy or mockery. "So I shall, one day," she said. "You'll see. I'll go to Rome. I'll take up again with people who know what they're talking about. I'll write the Signorelli, after all."

"Meaning after all of *us*—three kids howling for pearls and caviare? You'll manage the real thing?"

"Yes, the real thing, Bruno Landreth. A useful, hard-wearing, decently scholarly book."

Bruno reached for his glass and raised it to his mother in a gesture that made her laugh with pleasure. When he did these things, they were charmingly executed. "Good on you, Mum," he said. "You'll make it." He sipped his sherry. "Do you know," he added gently, "I think I'll come along too."

Jane turned back into the kitchen, having remembered that it was time to add the second half of the *bouillon gras* to the pot. If she went to Rome, she thought, it was very probable indeed that Bruno would go along too. He had a flair for pleasant places and nice times. The last thing he should have been was the son of a penniless archaeologist who had died in the first year of holding a senior university post.

Jane turned down the gas under the chicken and put the opened bottle of wine in the fridge to chill. It was not unlike Chablis. There would be a glass each, and an extra pour for Bruno. Nowadays, when all four of the Landreths were at home together, an effect of celebration seemed to be the expected thing, even if it had to be at the wrong time of day. Jane stripped off her apron, smoothed her hair, returned to the living-room and poured herself sherry. "Half an hour," she said. "And the girls should be home by then."

Bruno, although so lethargically disposed, had taken it into his head to stand up until she was settled. He had bouts of what he called Kensington manners. These consorted oddly with his present clothes. In those tight Levi jeans, and in that anomalous upper garment of American suggestion, he must be indistinguishable in the streets of Oxford from a lad out of the motor works. But then at other times he would turn up fashionably and expensively dressed, for he was a discontinuous creature. Now he was looking at his glass, which was empty, and following this up by replacing the stopper in the decanter with an air of quiet virtue. Jane wondered whether, perhaps, he had overspent his allowance. But it turned out not to be so.

"By the way," he said, "would it be all right if I brought someone back for the week-end at the beginning of the vac?"

"Of course, Bruno."

"His name's Luke." Bruno began to stuff a pipe—inexpertly, yet in a manner suggesting, this time, a full stop. His father had possessed the same trick of indicating a sense that a subject had been explored and settled, so that no more need be said. Yet Bruno's father had died when Bruno was five. Of Jane's three children, only Bruno had their father's round, subtly beautiful head. And only Bruno had the small, clean-cut features, almost impudent but wholly masculine, which so often recalled to her that unknown Roman boy, sharply contemporary and alive among all the puckered emperors and impassive ladies, in the Roman Gallery at the B.M. Jane, watching this head and these pure features poised over the square fingers teasing the tobacco, felt an old pain. She would have liked to say to Bruno that he could bring the whole college if he wanted to. Still, she hadn't been told whether it was to be Luke Somebody or Somebody Luke. "Luke?" she asked.

"It will be just before he goes home to Cornwall. He'd have to spend one night in London, anyway."

"I see. And I'm sure that will be very nice. It's always fun for the girls, meeting somebody who isn't a cockney intellectual. But I don't remember your mentioning Luke before. Is he taking Greats this year too?"

"Lord, no. He's an infant. In his first year."

"A fresher?" Jane was surprised.

"We can scarcely be said to use that word. I'd imagine that, since your happy virgin days at Somerville, it's become what might be called a Redbrick word." Bruno said this with careful absurdity. There were issues upon which he appeared to have no notion where he wanted to take his stand. Vague defensive ironies therefore accompanied most of his references to the English social structure.

"Do the years, then," Jane asked, "mix up quite a lot nowadays?" She was annoyed to hear herself putting a casual quality into this question. Remembering certain complications of Bruno's final year at school, she would have liked him to announce the bringing home of girls.

"I'd say the bloodies do." When his mind was veering one way, this was Bruno's name for undergraduates who had happened to be educated at the most celebrated of English schools. "But that's a matter of social and family connections, I suppose.

Common-or-garden public-school boys like me, and common-or-garden grammar-school boys like Luke, don't—or not a great deal. But that's unenterprising, I'd say." Quick to pick up a tone, Bruno gave his mother a swift, wicked look. "Just like being back at school, where knowing younger boys was a proof of unspeakable depravity."

"Of course it's unenterprising. And what is Luke like?"

"Perfectly beautiful!" Bruno, to whom his mother had so incautiously given a cue, wound further into his favourite rôle as a dark sexual enigma. "He's just over six feet. He plays one of those utterly violent games. Grammar school or not, his hair is short and washed and brushed. He's as fair and pink and white and unpimpled as any bloody in the college. And he has a face"—Bruno paused, thereby naïvely betraying an intended swoop upon anti-climax—"like a bun or bap."

"He sounds quite delightful."

"But a *sensitive* bun or bap." Bruno offered this as if moving on to more refined analysis. "It might be better to say blanc-mange. Because, you see, there's always a slight *movement*. A slight quiver. You know? A smooth pink mug, unmarked by any experience"—Bruno paused, perhaps to consider in his mind's eye his own features as seared by some cataclysmic history—"but rather delicately seismographic, all the same. Luke is always registering slight changes in the chemistry of the world around him. That's it."

"And the pink is perpetually alternating with blue, like litmus paper?" Jane found herself doubting whether young Luke was likely to prove an entirely restful person.

"What I mean is, he's wholesomeness itself. But, at the same time, I think he may develop into the real thing."

"Do you mean that this young man will have to get rid of his wholesomeness before his reality declares itself?"

"Dear old Mum, how clever you are. No wonder Le Mesurier and all the other stuffy R.A.s are terrified of you. Their pencils drop from a nerveless hand"—Bruno had a weakness for elaborating his fancies—"at a first squeak from the pen of the ferocious Mrs Landreth."

Jane laughed, pleased by this absurd remark. "But, Bruno," she said, "what's his other name? Is he Billy or Bobby Luke?"

"No, of course not. His name is Luke Tresilian."

"I see. That's a distinguished old Cornish name."

Bruno registered his wicked smile once more. He never failed to do so when his mother slipped into some attitude or idiom judged to be of an ancestral order. "I don't think," he said, "that there's anything distinguished about Luke's Tresilians—or not in the way you mean. No barts." Jane's grandfather had been a baronet—a circumstance which all her children, perhaps with some insincerity, contrived to find risible. "Of course, they may be people of fallen grandeur, like Thomas Hardy's Turveytops."

"Durbeyfields." Jane's was the reaction of a parent who has had to groom children for scholarships. "Supposed to have been d'Urbervilles once."

"Thank you. I do try to remember those cultural things. But what I was going to say was that Luke's father was a tin miner. Or, at least, I expect he began as that."

"I didn't know there were Cornish tin miners any more. You see nothing but abandoned workings when you wander about there." Jane Landreth hadn't finished this sentence before she put down her glass with a sharp tap. "You don't mean," she demanded, "that this boy is a son of *Tresilian*?"

"Obviously of Tresilian. The point is, of *the* Tresilian. Of *your* Tresilian." Bruno was enjoying this moment. "My young friend Luke—my protégé as it would be fair to call him—is the off-spring of genius, bless his innocent, shining mug. So may he come for a few nights?"

"I've already said he may," Jane replied shortly, conscious that she had been slow-witted. "But listen! There are the girls."

The front door of the flat had been thrown open, and in a moment's succeeding silence a human nose could be heard taking a vigorous sniff.

"Goodness!" a girl's voice said. "Smell *that*. A cooked lunch. *Haute cuisine*."

"Bruin's home." Another girl's voice spoke with excitement and a careful air of being resigned to minor calamity. "No other explanation's possible."

CHAPTER FOUR

Dark, brooding and chthonic, Philip Leech came out from the gloom of Hall. He was among the dons—they might have been called the dissident dons—who chose regularly to lunch there.

The undergraduates were obliged to. Not since before the War had the college been alive at this hour with forward-hurrying, backward-tilted servants, bearing their big baize-covered trays across the rainy quads and up the stony staircases. The young men lunched in each other's company or didn't lunch at all. Leech, now for some years Pro-Provost but then a junior fellow, had opposed the change. And he had opposed similar changes ever since. Although progressive in his academic views, he was passionately attached, his adversaries said, to the idea of undergraduate life laid up in the heaven of the Victorian novel.

Yet no undergraduates had ever caught from him the flicker of an eyelid suggesting that he liked them. As a tutor he was spare of speech, adept in devastating silences, bleakly logical in his analysis of the work brought to him. As a host he was exacting, and perhaps the last surviving man in Oxford to issue regular invitations to breakfast. He was more concerned—or so it was easy to conclude—with his own small, dry contributions to learned journals than with the greater or lesser success of his individual charges in examinations. In all this he seemed to suggest small sympathy with the young. Emerging now from the shadows like a gaunt and reluctant Pluto, he hunched his shoulders self-protectingly as he passed through a shaft of pale sunshine, with a gesture that might have suggested a fear of being jostled by a cluster of youths who were in fact making way for him. Then he paused by the stone balustrade of the great staircase. Sinking his chin on his chest, he stared at the thing spread across the noble wall opposite. He did this nearly every day. He was still taking its measure. It was possible to see it as a vast sea of light, he thought. Yes, you might call it light in the first instant of its creation, pouring out, whorled and convoluted and rearing, into infinite space. It was eccentric, of course, but he was far from believing it to be negligible. After all—although not on the aesthetic plane—he had himself received a sharp enough lesson as to that. Its presence here on the great staircase was oddly bound up with Littlejohn's having triumphantly succeeded to the Provostship.

"Philip, you look like Satan preparing to wing his way through Chaos."

Leech turned to glance at the speaker with a smile. The smile would have been there even if he hadn't owned a sufficiently accurate image of himself to recognize that Keith Pratling's description of him, thus vis-à-vis Matthew Tresilian's painting, represented a passable joke. It didn't mean, however, that he cared for Pratling. He had some contempt for him. To all the practical problems arising from day to day as an Oxford college battles with its job, Pratling's attitude was one of amused indulgence. It was true enough—Leech sometimes reflected—that there were some solemn owls on the Governing Body of the college. But Pratling was a kind of Olympian canary, abundant in chirpings designed to exhibit an exquisite sense of the absurdity of what was going on far beneath him. As this wasn't calculated to win him either influence or popularity, he hadn't greatly to be attended to. Still, in a self-governing corporation he was one of the minor facts of life, possessing the exact weight of a raised hand, an assenting or dissenting voice. Leech, who believed that, with Littlejohn where he was, a long, uphill fight for the traditional intellectual standing of the college lay ahead, was resolved to use every weapon and instrument upon which he could lay his hands. So he was smiling at Keith Pratling now. If Pratling said something soliciting an outright laugh, Leech would manage that too.

"Although, mark you, I have a different private name for it." Pratling was looking across the well of the staircase, down the second flight of which the heads of the last undergraduates were dropping. He was an intemperate man, Leech reflected inconsequently. You can tell them by that revealing trick of raising their glass the moment it has been filled for them. But beneath the too-heavy features it was still possible to see the kind of brightness that produces prize essays and gains Fellowships at an immature twenty-three or twenty-two. Pratling had turned to Leech now with an expression of tolerant amusement. "Yes," he said. "Waterloo."

"Waterloo?" Leech repeated the word amiably, although he saw at once the outline of what must be coming.

"Seeing you standing there, brooding over the lamented Gilstrap's last petty triumph, I seem to see the ghost of a pigmy Napoleon contemplating the field of a peep-show Waterloo."

"A pleasant fancy, Keith." So far, Leech didn't feel that the laugh was called for. Those epithets, he thought, overshot the permissible. Within a few years Pratling would be judged merely impertinent. "And our acquiring the thing was a reverse, I admit, for my notion of what an Oxford college ought to be bothering about."

"There was more to it than that, if I may say so." Pratling now spoke in a tone of whimsical indulgence. "Everybody sees the affair as having been a trial of strength, a real tug-of-war in our dear, delightful flea circus. Littlejohn's election practically followed from it. You were unwary, Philip. You failed to mark the ominous rustle in the stubble as the field-mice mustered." Pratling seemed much pleased with this slight change of imagery.

"Very true, Keith." Leech, although he found particularly jarring the factitious gaiety that Pratling worked up on these occasions, assented with cordiality to what had been said. "I forgot how, in a place like this, it will often be some unimportant issue of taste, some blank aesthetic tomfoolery, that sparks a conflict."

"That was it. How clear-headed you are. You woke up to find the little campaign lost, and certain crucial neutrals taking it as a sign."

"How well you analyse these things." There was a careful exclusion of irony from Leech's voice.

"The episode demonstrated how the balance of power was to be distributed." Pratling, once launched, was prone to these tedious insistences. "And there the thing now hangs." He waved his hand over the balustrade, in a gesture designed to suggest a sophisticated lightness of air. "As a memorial."

"Perfectly true." Leech's amiability was unflawed. "But I don't, believe me, bear any grudge against the picture itself. If it's capable of looking well anywhere, it's against that spread of stone. In putting it there, Gilstrap achieved what he probably called a rare stroke of concinnity."

"Ah, that phoney vocabulary of the old fraud's! One looks back on it with positive affection. Still, you did rather passionately object."

"I felt no passion about this particular painting in itself. Well-accredited people backed it, and I suppose whatever it represents will always have some documentary interest in relation to the present age. Of course, I don't believe it will really last. Nothing odd does." Leech said this with the confidence of a man whose classical education has remained his major intellectual stock-in-trade. "My point was simply that colleges are not museums. We obscure our function, if only ever so slightly, every time we accept another piece of junk."

"It's a purist's view. Naturally, I agree that it would be grossly improper to put our hands in the college's pocket to buy it, junk or not."

"It would be impossible, thank God. Our statutes couldn't possibly be wrested to cover such an abuse."

"Quite so. The painting came to us free. Although I've been told that the donor, having some interest in Tresilian's family, practically insisted that Gilstrap should find a commoner's place for a son or grandson."

"That's absolutely untrue." Leech, hitherto so urbane, had flashed into an anger that made Pratling jump. "The boy in question, Luke Tresilian, was certainly not a strong candidate. But there's a streak of unacademic talent in him, maybe, and he came in on his academic merits, such as they are. Moreover, it was I who thought to discern them and insisted on the place being given. Nobody will judge it likely, I suppose, that I was involved in jobbery?"

"No, no—of course not." Pratling, who had no stuffing, was confused. It was possible to see the muscles of his face going out of control.

"Or in a deal designed to secure that piece of harmless nonsense?" Leech stretched out an arm over the balustrade and snapped a finger.

"I suppose not. I mean, certainly not. I must have been misinformed."

"Certainly you must. I can't think where you can have come

by such irresponsible talk. It would disgrace the obscurest common room. We certainly have no use for it here. As for *that*"—and this time Leech pointed a thrusting index-finger at the big Matthew Tresilian against its background of stone—"I hold it blameless, as I say. But I've seen it come, and I may see it go again."

There was a moment's silence, and then the Pro-Provost nodded and walked away, once more unsmiling and with his habitual air of dark reserve. The smile would come again when required. So would the flash of anger—another, perhaps more genuine, asset, and equally useful when sparingly used. A drift into aestheticism—and the Gilstrap-Littlejohn axis meant chiefly that—was, after all, a mere absurdity in an Oxford college today, something as vulnerable as any other plain aberration would be. To beat it, Leech thought, he had only to hang on. He might even, if he chose his moment well, kill it with a single blow.

Brooding again, he came out under a flat Tudor arch into the First Quad. This year, the great mulberry tree might be in blossom before the end of term. He made a gesture as if gathering about him a gown he happened not to be wearing—an oddity, upon facing sunlight, which his pupils sometimes imitated when in irreverent mood—and moved off, hunched but striding, to his rooms.

CHAPTER FIVE

LUKE TRESILIAN HAD not gone to lunch in Hall. Before cycling to rugger practice, he felt that he must get through so many lines of Virgil. He had failed the Virgil paper in his Preliminary the term before. It wasn't an important part of the examination, and he had done surprisingly well in the rest. But he was disconcerted, because he had never come down in anything in his life. Quite regularly, with Latin and Maths, with French and German, he had slogged himself through in the unnoticeable middle—as, in English, he had always come out at the top. Of course he would cope with the Virgil at his second shot. But Virgil remained a small, ugly worry. If you failed a paper twice, they turfed you out—and that was the end of you.

He didn't want to be turfed out of Oxford, or even out of this incommodious attic room. The room could be fiendishly cold. In fact it was chilly now, and he had been obliged to choose between the faint warmth of the sun on the window-seat and the faint warmth from the feeble object they called an electric fire. He had chosen the window-seat and had successfully curled up his long limbs on it. He had two bananas and a bag of chocolate biscuits. There was something pleasantly domestic about that, as indeed there was about the whole place.

His rugger things, despite the protests of his scout, were tumbled untidily in a corner. Above them, very suitably, there was a photograph of his school's First Fifteen. In this Luke himself was occupying, cross-legged and hands on ankles, the position prescriptive for a scrum-half. Anybody would have said he was too big for a scrum-half. But in fact he played there rather well. On the opposite wall there was a photograph of the Piazza della Signoria in Florence, a distant spot which Luke had visited on a bicycle. At one end of the chimneypiece there stood a tobacco jar, embellished with the college arms. When Luke was feeling that he couldn't care less about all these people and their snobberies, he turned the jar arms outward, thereby announcing himself a youth of lowly station, unaware of what one bought and what one didn't buy upon coming into residence. When he was feeling that nearly everybody he met was a nice chap, and that in Rome he'd better conform with the Romans, he turned the jar with the arms to the wall. It was so turned now, and had been for some time. On the other side of the chimney-piece sat a Teddy Bear in venerable age. This creature kept its station proudly unaltered, regardless of moods or visitors. Between bear and jar hung a watercolour sketch. It was an affair of small, luminous, rectangular washes which didn't keep quite still as you looked at them. If you went right up to the sketch and examined it, you found, pencilled lightly on the mount, the words, "Sketch for Lyonnesse No. 3". Last term a smooth character had called on Luke and offered him a hundred pounds for the sketch, there and then. Luke, who had been warned that things of this sort were going to happen, had turned the man out.

As he ate the last chocolate biscuit, he heard the college clock chime half-past one. He had a good many lines still to do—still to do on this promising new system. He had bought a fresh plain text of *Aeneid IV*. As he went over it, he underlined in lead-pencil any word or expression over which he had to pause, and in red any word or expression that beat him flat. He also had a green chalk, and with this he put a cross in the margin wherever he came on a passage that looked a likely gobbet.

From rooms somewhere below him, there floated up the voices and laughter of girls. Somebody was giving a midday party. It couldn't be his recent acquaintance Bruno Landreth, because Bruno had gone to see his people—if it was to see his people—in London.

Absorbed, anxious, happy, Luke Tresilian worked on. He made some more red marks. But the only real risk—he thought, comforting himself—was of going off your rocker, as it seemed rather fashionable to do when examinations came round. And that wasn't his style.

CHAPTER SIX

SITTING OPPOSITE HIS mother, Bruno served the chicken with precision from the casserole. As usual, he finished the job by providing himself with the two drumsticks. As usual—since this helping, if abundant, represented the coarser part of the dish —he reserved for himself, by way of compensation, the two largest mushrooms. He poured the Portuguese wine with gravity.

"The reactions of our seniors are unpredictable," he said. "Their processes of mind, although doubtless powerful and mature, are unclear to us. I propose to befriend a simple youth, obscurely lurking in an attic on my staircase. I plan for him a small peep at metropolitan culture. But—simply because his name is Luke Tresilian—our mama is faintly disapproving. In her protective, foreboding heart she fears that I have gone tuft hunting, or lion hunting, or worse. She would have me make my friends, not merely among the obscure, but among the obscurely fathered as well."

"Rubbish!" Jane Landreth said. She was conscious of the annoyance often roused in her by the grain of truth in Bruno's most extravagant talk. She would like for Bruno not the world she had been obliged to make her own way in, but some solid world such as her husband's had been : a world of dons, schoolmasters, administrators. And she supposed that Luke Tresilian, bun-faced but seismographic, must be, at least in embryo, what they used to call an aesthete.

"Isn't Bruin foul!" Jane's younger daughter, Hatty, who was in her last year at school, looked at her brother challengingly across her wine glass. "Isn't he affected! Honestly, he gets worse every time. Oxford must be a frightful place."

"Bruin, do you mean that this Luke Tresilian is a grandson of Matthew Tresilian?" The elder daughter, Lucilla, asked this. Although only a year older than Bruno, she was already in a secretarial job.

"Just a straight son, as Mum knows."

"But is that possible?" Hatty asked. "Matthew Tresilian was painting ages ago. We've had a talk on him."

"Then your talk can't have had a biographical slant. Tresilian made a second marriage late in life. Luke resulted."

"Tresilian would be about eighty," Jane said, "if he were alive today. And he died fifteen years ago. So Luke, like yourselves, didn't have a father for very long."

"Has he a mother?" Lucilla asked.

Bruno shook his head. "He had a mother for a shorter time still."

"Then he's an orphan!" Hatty made this discovery with interest. "Perhaps he has no proper home at all. Of course Bruin must bring him. We'll make friends with him." Her eager expression clouded. "But won't he be tremendously rich? Like those awful bowler-hatted Madrona boys?" Sir Hector Madrona was Lucilla Landreth's employer. With all his family, he was frequently the object of Hatty's rapidly generated indignation. "Bruin, is Luke in the gravy?"

"What a gross expression. He shows no signs of being rich at all. And he's been at a very unassuming school. Perhaps Mum can explain."

"I don't think it takes much explaining," Jane said. "Tresilian was already quite famous during his lifetime. But, for most of his days, he was a thoroughly English painter—very avant-garde in some ways, but essentially in the English lyrical tradition. It's something the continent has never understood or had much use for. And that keeps even home prices down quite surprisingly. His international reputation is quite recent. I think it sprang from two things : a big splash made with him at a Biennale in Venice, and the rather belated coming into notice of the work of his very last period. His final paintings change hands at tens of thousands of pounds now. But his heirs mayn't benefit in any very large way."

"You mean to say," Hatty demanded, "that one's father's pictures can be sold for tens of thousands of pounds, and one can be quite *poor*, all the same?"

"Yes, of course. The pictures can sell like that, and one can still be quite safe from the fate of the Madrona boys. They may all have been acquired by dealers long ago for tens of thousands of shillings or tens of thousands of pence."

"How absolutely rotten."

It was clear, Jane thought, that when the unknown Luke arrived he would have an established sympathizer in her youngest child. "But I don't suppose," she went on, "that Tresilian's family can be anything like desperately poor, even if he himself was very improvident during his life. Money must be coming in quite substantially in various ways now. It's not likely that this young man is painfully short of it. Even what Bruno says about his unassuming school may be a matter of a family way of thinking, or of some instructions that his father left. Matthew Tresilian was a working-class boy, and I believe he remained very critical of the rest of society."

"Like Lawrence," Hatty said, naming her current passion. "Bruin, is Luke like Lawrence?"

"Not remotely, I'd say." Bruno showed amusement. "Your blessed Lawrence was a chattering, giggling, agitated, bad-tempered little man."

"He was nothing of the sort!" Hatty's hand had moved ominously on the table. One could still not be certain that she wouldn't, upon these occasions, hurl a spoon or plate at her brother's head.

"Relax, child, relax. Luke is large and plays rugger. And, except when something comes over him, he hardly ever utters a word."

"What do you mean—when something comes over him?" Hatty made a characteristic switch from indignation to urgent interest. "He doesn't get disgustingly drunk, as you do?"

"He doesn't even get pleasantly so. He chants things. And he gets excited and shuts himself up with a typewriter. I expect he has a lot of his own poems locked up in a drawer. At eighteen, simple types often do."

"Why did Tresilian's last paintings come into notice only belatedly?" Lucilla asked. She had a trick, part of her professional competence, of reaching back through a conversation to some significant point which had passed unexplored.

"They were painted in a period of seclusion, I believe," Jane said. "And they remained unexhibited for some years after his death. It sounds slightly mysterious. But I'm not up in it. I'll have to get a grip of Matthew Tresilian—and not just in order to say the right thing to Luke. There's a Tresilian exhibition coming along."

"As for mystery," Bruno said, "I'm not sure that Luke hasn't a whiff of it. Do you know, he arrived in college at just the same time as one of his father's whacking great pictures? There's a theory that Luke was the last of our late Provost's packaged deals."

"Sometimes I think I'll go to Oxford," Hatty said, "just to see if it's as mouldy as Bruin makes out."

"The college has a Tresilian?" Jane asked. "But you never told me! Where?"

"On the great staircase. You go halfway up, look across the well of it, and there the thing is. Flush on that great spread of stone, and with hardly any frame. It's almost *like* the stone. Its life begins where that of the stone leaves off. Something like that. All in a cold, restricted palette. But it's terrific."

"Do you mean," Hatty asked, awed, "that whenever Luke goes up to dinner in Hall he passes something tremendous, and which was painted by his father?"

"Obviously I mean that, you idiot. We needn't start being moved by it."

"But why didn't you show it to me when I was up last term?" Jane spoke quickly. Children, she knew, should be let quarrel when they felt like it. But in Bruno's and Hatty's quarrelling there was often a quality she didn't care for. "I had no idea it existed."

"I don't remember any suggestion that I should take you sight-seeing, Mum. After all, you're an Oxford man yourself. But don't forget to see it next time."

"Does your new Provost," Lucilla asked, "have those up-to-date artistic interests?"

"Yes. Littlejohn's pro, and the Pro-Provost, Phil Leech, is anti. Or so chaps say. The Tresilian was Gilstrap's last score over the other older dons—Leech's lot. Gilstrap was all for youth and art, the deluded old man. Two areas of illusion, are they not? Of course, some wealthy former member paid for the Tresilian."

"Do many of the colleges," Lucilla asked, "go in for art-treasures in a big way?"

"I don't really know. Christ Church, if you can call it a college, is said to have stacks of drawings by Old Masters. New

College has Epstein's Lazarus in the ante-chapel. Keble, the place up by the Parks, has an earlier religious monstrosity—a nicely shampooed Jesus called the Light of the World, by Holman Hunt. But we never had much until old Gilstrap got going."

"I'd like to know more about Matthew Tresilian," Lucilla said. "Lady Madrona has one of his pictures."

"When they built him up, they took care to plant him in the strategic drawing-rooms, I don't doubt." As she said this, Jane caught her son's grin. "All right," she added. "We all produce cynical cracks at times."

"But Matthew Tresilian is *really* good?" Hatty asked this anxiously, and it was obvious that already she couldn't bear Luke Tresilian's father to be other than first-rate. "Apart from those horrible dealers being clever with him in drawing-rooms, he was a great painter?"

"Most of the dealers who count are tolerable citizens, as a matter of fact. Don't get it into your head, Hatty, that all commercial people are horrid, and that all artists and egg-heads are angels."

"Our Mum," Bruno said, "becomes a stauncher and stauncher square every day. It's a reaction from all those cocktail parties with the long-haired lot."

"Yes, it is!" Jane, who had spoken with a flash of Hatty's vehemence, laughed at herself. "But about Matthew Tresilian. He was always a good painter. And near the end of his life something happened to him that made him a disturbing painter as well."

"What?" Bruno asked.

"I've no idea. Just something."

"Oh, come, Mum! You're not saying that something has to *happen* to an artist—to the artist just as a chap, who gets up and shaves in the morning, and goes to bed with his wife at night—before some radical change can come over his painting, or whatever it is?"

"No, I'm not. But it can be like that. And I've an impression that with Tresilian it must have been that way. It's only an impression, though. I see I know very little about the actual facts of his life."

"Perhaps it was his second marriage," Hatty suggested. "Perhaps there was something wonderfully romantic about that." She frowned, feeling that she had made an outmoded remark. "Or something deeply and darkly sensual."

"That dreary Lawrence!" Bruno said. "The stuff he puts into a nice girl's head! All that jazz inspires artists only in rotten novels. Tresilian, I'd say, just found something new—like a Glasgow painter Mum was talking about earlier."

Jane Landreth shook her head. "At least," she said, "it wasn't on the same scale or plane as little Ogilvie's commendable restlessness, at all. It wasn't really as if Tresilian found something new. It was as if something new found Tresilian. Mind you, he was a significant painter, and one with a long development behind him, before this happened. Latterly, he had been doing abstract things in a big way—animating large canvases in a fashion that really makes him the pioneer of abstract expressionism, if the jargon must be used."

"Ruth Madrona's Tresilian is like that," Lucilla said.

"And ours in college." Bruno looked inquiringly at his mother. "And then?"

"And then, as I said, Tresilian had some period of retreat. Out of it there came his last things—and they are quite different. If you want an explanation, and don't feel it can have lain in his personal life—or not in his personal life, narrowly regarded —then you might try Zen Buddhism. That's a favourite all over the place, nowadays."

"Buddhism!" Hatty was indignant. "What could a painter have to do with smelly old Indian or Chinese monks?"

"A lot of modern painting seems to borrow a metaphysic or underlying philosophy from Buddhist sages. And Tresilian's last paintings are disturbing rather in the way that a book about Eastern thought can be disturbing. They seem to be about the total elusiveness of the world. Yet they're not resigned or passive. They're urgent."

"Are there people and things in them again?" Hatty asked.

"Yes. They're figurative—in a broad, impressionistic way. Things are happening, people are in action, drama is being created. But key passages are blurred, so that the effect is ambiguous and mysterious."

"Do you mean," Bruno asked, "that these paintings leave unusually large scope for subjective response or conjecture?"

"Yes, I'd say they do. Just described like this, it all sounds a bit literary, as well as conceptual and philosophical. The painter is saying 'The harder we look the less we see', or 'Only what's peripheral can really be observed'. Perhaps that's Buddhism—I don't really know. Certainly the effect is teasing and disturbing—almost sinister. Too much so, perhaps, for the greatest art."

"Our abstract one in college is a bit elusive too," Bruno said. "You might say protean."

"And so is Ruth Madrona's," Lucilla said.

"That's something you get in Tresilian all through," Jane said. "He was rather fond of simple optical tricks. Something happens to the composition as you look. It's only what happens to a chess-board or to the bathroom tiles, when for a moment they suggest one three-dimensional structure, and the next moment another. His first important work was a series of Cornish seascapes. They're almost straight impressionist things, and very much a matter of *poesie*. Some even have tags of verse attached to them. But already there's something of that protean effect. The thing doesn't stay put. I've known it make people quite angry."

"I want to *see* Luke Tresilian." Hatty spoke vigorously and inconsequently. "I don't believe Bruin has described him at all well. I try to imagine him, and there's a blur right in the centre —just like the pictures you've been talking about."

"You'll see him," Bruno said. "You'll have a brief, enchanting glimpse of him."

"I hope he'll stay some time. We could show him all sorts of things in London. It must be exciting—to be the son of a great painter. But difficult, somehow."

"What do you mean—difficult?" Bruno now spoke as if he resented the sudden vivid quality of his sister's interest.

"Well, if his father has been dead a long time—"

"*Your* father's been dead a long time," Bruno said brutally. "Do you find that particularly difficult? A father's a complication in a girl's life, as a matter of fact. He mixes her up."

"That's mouldy rubbish. I mean that Luke's father has been dead a long time, and that he left behind him, as his last works, paintings that seem to be elusive or mysterious. Isn't that right? Well, Luke must find it rather haunting, I'd suppose. Like just failing to catch the words of somebody who's going away for ever."

"*That's* mouldy rubbish, if you like. You'll find Luke's just a nice, simple lad who plays rugger. So if you start romanticizing him, you'll be disappointed. Besides, I won't have it."

"Shall we make some coffee?" Jane Landreth asked.

"I won't have you whoring after other men." As he said this, Bruno, who had ignored his mother, lowered his eyelids in a melodramatic way and stared broodingly at his younger sister from beneath them. It was the most tiresome of his acts. When Hatty played up to it, as she sometimes did to the effect of a perverse charade, Jane hated it.

Jane rose from table now. "I look forward to meeting Luke Tresilian," she said. Hatty, she was thinking, was intolerant of the young men—mostly Lucilla's young men—who came around. They left nothing to the imagination. Luke Tresilian did.

CHAPTER SEVEN

STANDING ON THE kerb, tapping the pavement with the ferrule of his umbrella while waiting to cross the street, Lord Burntisland went over his unsatisfactory interview with Sir Hector Madrona. Madrona was a fool—but perhaps he had given the man a false impression, all the same. He was himself by no means neglectful of the arts. And one mustn't be narrow about these things. The mischief he saw in all this publicity and advertising and entertainment wasn't merely in its flouting morality in a restricted sense. Equally deplorable was its being so inane. The fellow on the poster, for example, settling down to guzzle in a jet : he was meant to exemplify the satisfactions that attend success. No need, perhaps, to see more in the thing than that. And the young couple on the down : they were annoying as proposing a falsification of human experience. For what, to a young man and woman properly and honourably in love, was the difference between one make of cigarettes and another?

And all this falsity—he told himself—is concurred in and exploited by men quite as contemptuous of it as I am. That's the thing that's really damnable. Fellows who take pride in their clear heads, their taste, their code of personal honour : where do they really stand? They don't give a damn how they debase the mob, provided they outsmart each other in collecting the mob's pennies. There's no end to the cynicism it breeds. You end up with Madrona and his socialism.

Arrived at the end of Pall Mall, Burntisland directed a sightless gaze upon Florence Nightingale on her pedestal. He was trying to conjure up those posters before his inward vision. Already they were a little vague at their centres—at the "punch passages" as he had heard them called by some fellow who had been conferring with his advertisers. Burntisland could no longer distinguish whether the air traveller was intent upon the flavour of his caviare or the charms of his female attendants.

He went down the steps and crossed the Mall. There was

green in the plane trees, and one could imagine a brief warmth in the air at this early afternoon hour. In the park itself people were behaving as if a sympathetic magic might bring summer on. Some, as they ate their sandwiches on the benches lining the paths, were trying basking in a warmth that wasn't really present. And already there were others scattered on the grass : lovers here, furtive peepers at lovers there, and elsewhere comfortably defeated men in braces, snoozing on a newspaper or a grubby coat. But that morning there had been a letter in *The Times* about the pelicans. Lord Burntisland threaded his way among a sprawled humanity, resolved upon ornithological investigation.

A child dived in front of him, recovering a ball. Two girls went past with laughing, vivid faces—and for a second the accident of their glance suggested that they were joined with him in some purpose or perception. They were followed by three Guardsmen : bucolic, gigantic, with peaked caps grotesquely occluding their gaze, their thighs and buttocks gripped in khaki beyond any seeming possibility of flexure. Burntisland found himself thinking of Frederick the Great. But the context was a dubious one, and he returned to what he had read about the pelicans. They were a blameless subject. Cabinet Ministers took an interest in them.

His umbrella was rolled. His dark town overcoat sat snugly on his spare figure. His bowler hat was firmly on his head. So nothing had much suggested to him that there was a breeze, and he was on the middle of the bridge before becoming conscious of it. It came to him as a scurry of shadow on the water, and when he looked up he saw the sky flecked with sailing clouds. The clouds had no concern with St James's Park, but their shadows on the lake seemed a parcel of the place; they might have been Queen's Messengers, hurrying on small occasions from Buckingham Palace to Whitehall. For it was a west wind. It was a wind, Burntisland realized, trailing the skirts of spring across London. The pelicans were unimpressed, but the lesser fowl were responsive. So was everything that grew in this fenced and placarded, this jaded and democratized royal park. Everything was stirring, starting into life, moving on through its cycle.

Burntisland turned back, and walked swiftly through things suddenly grown disturbing to him. There seemed to be even more people—sitting, lying around. Faded men on benches, almost as old as himself, in strained hopeless colloquy with other men's faded wives. Couples like corpses—corpses that had been shot down aslant each other's bodies. A Jamaican and a white woman half under a bush. A knot of lads and girls, tumbling together in dirty horseplay. He could remember a time when all this would have been incredible; when nothing but decorum overtly obtained in this part of London.

An obscure but urgent horror rose in him. He had a sensation as if some incredible thing were about to happen : something catastrophic and irreversible. *Star-scattered on the grass,* he heard his inner voice say meaninglessly. *When you and I shall pass.* It was FitzGerald's poem, which he had committed to memory when fourteen. It had brought him, perhaps for the first time, certain voluptuous sensations. Now, a lonely man, he no longer possessed any context in which these words were significant to him. *Turn down an empty glass,* he said to himself.

Upright and looking straight ahead, his craggy features set, Burntisland made his way out of St James's Park as he had come. Back in Waterloo Place, he turned towards Trafalgar Square. He was not wholly himself today, but he needn't betray anything of this to anybody. Unless to his doctor—and he had an impulse to take a cab and drive to Harley Street. Some contemporary had recently murmured to him how often the first intimation of organic disease takes the form of a generalized nervous disturbance. But that was nonsense. Real senescence came with giving way to such notions. He walked on, with a brisker intimation of some responsible occasion in his stride. He walked past George the Third : the Mounted Madman, he had heard the statue called.

That talk with Madrona—he thought, yet again. I was the man with a grip on things. Madrona may be younger, but he's gone slack. Madrona may have taken up nuclear energy and God knows what. But I'd carry more weight in a board room any day. And don't they say that the fellow's a loose liver? That still counts against a man in decently conservative circles. Thank God for it ! If licence didn't carry its penalties, where should we all be? Everything mustn't be left to the Last Judgement, particularly in an age when it isn't only advanced thinkers who don't

believe in any such occasion. With the decay of dogma it becomes more essential than ever that Society should impose its
own temporal penalties. Otherwise—to put it bluntly—what are
the chances of virtue? And if decent living isn't honoured in the
state, where's the reward of half a lifetime lived in tormenting
abstinence, so lived until only some small, impotent flame flickers
in the ash?

The fountains were dry in the Square, and the dead, grey
paving round them was splashed with pigeons' droppings and
littered with blown paper. But far down the vista of Whitehall,
stiffly on its tower, the big flag flew.

Confidence rose in Lord Burntisland. He squared his shoulders
as he waited for the small street sign that should say *Cross* and
so set him on his way to the House of Lords. Then he caught
a woman's startled glance. He realized that he had once more
spoken some word, or words, aloud. With a plunge into unreason,
his mind seized the notion that his exclamation might have been
maniacal, obscene.

He turned, and in a moment was hurrying up a flight of
steps. He passed beneath a portico, went through a swing door,
and was within the refuge of the National Gallery.

CHAPTER EIGHT

ONCE MORE ASCENDING the steps of the British Museum, Charles Rose proposed to himself a cordial but firm leave-taking of the serious scholar still pacing beside him. The cause of Anglo-American friendship had taken its toll alike of his digestive processes and of his morning's routine. By the time he had finished one or two necessary tasks, only an uncomfortably late lunch hour would be possible. He would accompany Thayne Delver, therefore, to the doors of the reading room. And there, beside the Column of the four Great Miracles, he would shake hands and take his own route through the endless muted corridors as briskly as his unwonted freight of best bitter would allow. It would require a fifth Great Miracle—he thought morosely, as he fingered the tightened waistband of his trousers—to get two pints of hops and water into his stomach again.

But Rose's manoeuvre of disengagement didn't succeed. This wasn't, he had to admit, because Professor Delver was a barnacle. It was because of the influence of the place.

Only unslumbering intellectual curiosity makes the British Museum a tolerable habitat. Without that, it is a vast morgue existing simply to overawe tourists, a gargantuan lumber room, or at best a womb in which one may slumber only in the most uneasy way, oppressed by a nightmare detritus of cultures, continents, millennia. But intellectual curiosity was something that Rose possessed, and he never re-entered the B.M. without feeling the passion quicken in him about something. It had enabled him to master his own niche in the place; it prompted him, too, to sporadic excursions, day long or year long, into remote departments, unfrequented galleries, tenebrous uncatalogued dumps of forgotten learning, superannuated cabinets of rarities, casual oddities. He never paused at the foot of the broad, shallow staircase and glanced up at Hoa-Haka-Nana-Ia against his alarming purple background, without a sense of the enchanting oddity of a universe that could produce both Chartres Cathedral and Easter Island.

And—for that matter—could produce painters like Matthew Tresilian and scholars like Thayne Delver who went in pursuit of them. About this particular learned quest, moreover, there seemed to be something that invited a second glance. It hadn't come to Rose in their conversation that Delver had much to go on. Yet he seemed as full of confidence as of determination. Research in the humanities, even when one has become a professor of the interrelations of things or whatever, was becoming more and more of a rat race, Rose reflected. The ability to convince oneself—he slightly switched the image—that there was really a square meal at the end of the maze must be an important factor in the survival of Delver's sort of learned person. And Delver seemed almost irrationally certain that there was a sizeable refection waiting for him in Tresilian—in Tresilian in a new character as a writer.

Rose, the amateur and man of private fortune, was conscious of something unbecoming in these reflections. Prompted to amends, he paused by the publications counter. Instructed schoolchildren were queueing for reproductions of pink granite lions, green granite beetles, the Mausoleum at Halicarnassus, Ta-Urt the hippopotamus goddess, the Rosetta Stone.

"I wonder," he said, "if I got you right at one point? You've really never set eyes on anything significant that Tresilian wrote?"

"Never—and that's the fascination of it." Delver's glance, as shrewd as it was ingenuous, caught Rose's in a confident demand for agreement. "You see?"

"Yes, I suppose I do. But aren't you taking a good deal on trust?"

"Sure. But, boy, what trust!" As his manner was when excited, Delver momentarily grasped Rose's elbow. "How would you rate Wyndham Lewis as a critic?"

"Tough and bad on painting; tough and good on writing."

"Tough's the word. And, you see, it's not as if the two men were in any close association. Tresilian was no Vorticist. In fact, you'd have to call him a romantic at that time—and romanticism was precisely what Lewis, T. E. Hulme, and all the French crowd were gunning for. But there, as I told you, was the reason why

Lewis was late for the first *Blast* dinner. Tresilian had let him read this journal; he'd got lost in it; and he spoke of it to Etchells that very night in the words I've told you of. I've gone into Etchells. A thoroughly reliable man."

"Very well." Rose was thinking that he himself had presumably been gone into, much as by a detective agency, at the time of his providing Delver with material for his Rossetti. "I accept that, when Tresilian was in his mid-thirties, there did exist a manuscript journal of his which was judged by one of his distinguished contemporaries to be of high interest or excellence. That's a start. But you haven't much reason to suppose the thing—or a successor to the thing—still in existence now. Tresilian seems to have been an elusive person—as some of his painting is, for that matter. It would be my guess that his 'remains', as they used to say, won't prove altogether lacking in the same quality."

"And just there's the fun!"

"I can see that too." Rose found that his elbow had now been relinquished, but that they had turned back, as by an agreed plan, and were pacing the Roman Gallery as they might have paced the terrace before a Palladian house. Frowning emperors and their inexpressive consorts regarded or disregarded them. Halfway down, on the right, was the unknown boy who reminded Rose of Jane Landreth's son Bruno. And then they were among the Graeco-Roman things, with Athenians and Amazons tussling in sharp diagonals. "But what you tell me about letters," Rose said, "is surprising. I'm bound to say I find it daunting that you don't yet know of a single surviving example of any interest."

Delver nodded. "It's not so much daunting as queer. Tresilian can't have written round asking his friends to destroy or return his letters. An action of that sort gets on the record. But I figure the explanation's simple enough. No letters have turned up, because none have been asked for. There's been no memoir of Tresilian of any pretension—nothing, on the personal side, except fugitive articles and casual mentions in books."

"In his private character he seems to have kept well out of sight. You haven't asked for letters through the Literary Supplement of *The Times*?"

"No, no—that would be premature." It was the shrewdness that for a moment predominated in Delver. "I've no standing,

53

you see, so far. There are children to approach, and executors and trustees. My first chore is to see how the land lies. But there *must* be important surviving letters, Rose, if only because I'd be so darn mad if there weren't. Of course, with some artists there are none. There have been painters, as you more or less said, who wouldn't so much as put pen to paper to give directions for their old mother's funeral. But Tresilian *did* write letters. And notably to Marrot. Of course, the Marrot tragedy is irreparable."

"Marrot possessed a long series of Tresilian's letters?"

"It seems so. But I haven't told you how I came on that. You know about Texas? Academically, if you want to strike oil now, you go to Texas. They have all the modern manuscripts that were ever written, more or less. They even have a bunch of letters by this unimportant fellow Aidan Marrot. How would you characterize *him*?"

"As not in the least like Wyndham Lewis. Marrot was a dry art historian, who happened to take some interest in contemporary painting. A measured and cautious person, with the next thing to impeccable taste."

"Fair enough. Well, Texas have a little bunch of Marrot's letters to Tom, Dick and Harry, which it must have been just worth somebody's while to get around to buying up. When I was vacationing there last year, I got to turning them over. And here was this letter, written by Marrot to some Cambridge professor—whose widow no doubt raised fifteen dollars on it."

"With a reference to Tresilian?"

"With a reference to Tresilian. Marrot had been one of Tresilian's few intimate friends. And he tells this Cambridge worthy that the letters he's had from Tresilian over the years constitute an aesthetic credo of remarkable interest." Delver paused. He was looking, Rose thought, absurdly solemn. "What you might call a stuffy form of words. But—from the pen of a measured and cautious person—striking enough. When I read that letter, and it clicked in my head with what Wyndham Lewis said about a journal, I knew what I had to do."

"I'm sure you did." Rose felt depressed. Perhaps this was because, having taken several unregarded turns, they were now in the Egyptian Sculpture Gallery. It was a place full of curiosity, but it couldn't be called inspiriting. It held only a scatter of visitors, but their footsteps and their voices, blending with those in other galleries nearby, produced an unceasing, stammering murmur as of distant waves breaking upon rock. It was true, Rose thought, that there was nothing in the place that hadn't been chipped and hewn and heaved about by human skill. Yet in the context of all this massiveness—they were just passing a monstrous granite arm and clenched fist, fifteen feet long—human life seemed too feeble and fleeting to be squarely looked at. And the ceaseless polyglotic sibilation of the cowed wanderers and gapers made a dismal enough threnody.

"The date and postmark are pretty ironical."

"The date and postmark?" Rose had lost the thread of Delver's remarks.

"That letter to a Cambridge friend, you see, happening to mention Tresilian's quality as a correspondent, was the last that Marrot ever wrote. The bomb fell on him, and on all his possessions, about six hours after he posted it. Tresilian's remains, as you call them, may be elusive. Marrot's—in another sense—were just too scattered to be brought together for burial. And, of course, no scrap of paper survived the conflagration."

"Too bad." Rose nodded soberly. They had turned again and were confronting, far away and closing the long vista of the brutish gods of Nile, a coy Capitoline Venus preparing to enter the bath. Her gesture of pudency seemed premature at such a remove. "There were considerable losses to learning in privately owned collections." Rose was remembering the days when all except the most intransportable chunks of this circumambient junk had been scattered in derelict mansions, remote tithe barns, disused mines and workings over the length and breadth of England. "So your hope is really this : that Tresilian went in for circulating aesthetic credos in a big way?"

"I hope that he covered the same field of interest with at least one other correspondent."

"A purely hypothetical correspondent, at the moment? You've no line on an actual person?"

"Well, I'm working on the problem. I can't say more than that."

Rose wondered what precise sense Delver's last remark was meant to bear. He wondered, too, whether there was not some reserve behind Delver's candour, with its large air of being as wide as a prairie. "As I see it," he said, "you have a notion that Tresilian wrote about his work, and so on, in letters, and about his life in a journal?"

"That's about the size of it."

"His private life?"

Delver in his turn was silent for a moment, as if feeling that this term required definition. "Perhaps not all that private," he said presently. "A *journal intime*, say, in Amiel's manner. Although, indeed, it may have been much less speculative, and much more personal in the ordinary sense. That's what I'm going to find out. Every darn thing's to find out."

"And that, as you say, is the fun." A random memory had come to Rose; it was of a crowd of reporters who had once besieged him when a certain matter of artistic forgery had been, for a brief space, big news. Sleuths, a colleague had humorously called them. But there was a debatable territory between sleuthdom and scholarship. And Rose didn't favour it.

Feeling that he had by now heard enough of Delver's plans, he looked around for distraction. But in their present surroundings there was nothing to talk about, for they had strayed into the old Elgin Room. And all the immortal marbles had vanished; the pedestals were empty; where the Panathenaic Procession had marched and curveted there were great weals of raw brick. They might have stumbled on the aftermath of such an art robbery as had never been. The explanation was unalarming—and as Delver appeared unperturbed he presumably knew about it. The sculptures of the Parthenon had moved next door, into the more splendid gallery provided for them by the munificence of the late Lord Duveen. But here an effect of spoliation and outrage remained, and would continue to remain until the wrecked hall was appropriated to new purposes. Meanwhile, and as on several previous occasions, it made Rose obscurely uneasy—and the uneasiness, with an equal obscurity, prompted him to say something more. "I suppose," he went on, "that what you ultimately aim at is a biography of Tresilian?"

"Well, I want to publish any considerable body of his writing that I can dig up. After that, a biography of sorts does tempt me, I must say. Really, a book showing how his life and work hung together."

"But at present, I gather, you know nothing about his life, or

nothing worth speaking of. So it's rash to conclude—isn't it?—
that it ever hung together with anything else or not." Even as
he spoke, Rose regretted a flash of asperity which might impair
the amiable interest in which he had consumed all that beer.
"I mean—" he went on, and paused for some softening expression. But this didn't come. They had now entered Lord Duveen's
austere temple, and Lord Elgin's trophies were around them.
It was at least sufficiently a temple to produce a disconcerting
feeling that here was a sort of ghost of the Parthenon turned
inside out. Looking up at the sheet of light constituting the
ceiling, Rose had a yet more disconcerting feeling of being in a
covered swimming pool turned upside down. But this was a
notion so absurd that he was constrained to wonder whether all
that beer had affected his head. It had affected his limbs, for
he had only to look at the youth of Athens, poised above the
intricate arabesque of their horses' legs, to feel unusually earth-
bound and heavy-footed. And this—together with the presence
of all these anonymous, battered, triumphant things—didn't
make him incline to the gracefully accommodating.

"I mean," he said, "that a man's life is one thing and his work
is another. I grow more and more convinced of that. Using works
of art as documents in a case is just one of the wrong ways of
using them. And it leads you straight into nonsense, as often as
not. I came across a fellow the other day who reckoned to explore Henry James's personality by studying his use of Christian
names. A very clever fellow he was, too. But think of it! Look
at Dionysus there—the one they used to call Theseus. Look at
Athena and Poseidon at the other end, with their missing olive
tree—isn't it?—between them. Who wants to know whether the
sculptor could, or couldn't, go to bed with a woman?"

"I couldn't agree more with much of what you say. There
surely are a tidy number of inept ways of busying oneself before
artistic productions. But when it comes to the origins of things,
when it comes to working out just what made a particular
poet or artist tick the way he did—"

"Then you go right ahead, and the fun begins." Rose, aware
of having dipped into the portentous, said this lightly enough.
But Delver remained serious.

"Don't imagine," he said, "that I haven't registered the difference between Matthew Tresilian and, say, Leonardo da Vinci.

It's a difference of four hundred years. Nobody minds whether Leonardo had two mothers—which I seem to remember was Freud's notion. But it might still affect people—a son or daughter, say—if one discovered that Tresilian had two wives."

Rose laughed. His sense of irritation with Delver had left him. "But he had, hadn't he? He made a late second marriage, I seem to have been told."

"Sure. But the ladies were decently successive. So that of mine was just a manner of speaking. For wives substitute family skeletons. If they begin to rattle as the research proceeds, don't think I won't be discreet."

"I do feel that even the dead are entitled to their privacy. But that, you know, was only part of what I was thinking of."

"You were thinking of the viciousness of getting art wrong. And that's a large field. I guess it could be pretty variously illustrated."

"No doubt."

"And the folks in chief peril are the artists themselves."

"The artists?" Rose didn't follow.

"You and I—scholars and critics and historians—can make fools of ourselves in front of art. We can even create a certain amount of extraneous mess or confusion—by imagining the wrong influences and derivations, or by shouting for the censor here and a Nobel prize there. But you and I can't, strictly, misuse art. It isn't vulnerable to us; it isn't malleable to our hammers, pliable under our fingers. But the artist can do what he likes with it. Wouldn't you say? *He* can do some goddam wrong thing with art. It's at risk with him, as it isn't with us. Don't you agree?"

They had passed from Athens to Ephesus and thence to the Archaic Room, and were thus at the junction of two long galleries. And Rose was aware that some acoustic quirk in the place was making their decently modulated voices oddly resonant, so that what they said seemed, just for the moment, to be carrying a long way.

He had made no direct reply to Delver's question. Delver's seriousness now was of a kind he could respond to, and the topic had substance. But the hour was scarcely apposite for its discussion. "Don't you," he countered on a lighter note, as they moved back towards the Main Hall through the Roman Gallery,

58

"rate yourself as an artist, after your own style? Your Rossetti seemed to me to have all the signs, if I may say so." Seeing the flush of pleasure on Delver's face, he judged that a felicitous moment for parting had come. Besides, much of the beer seemed now to have reached its ultimate destination within his system. "I must go back," he said. "But I hope to hear more about Tresilian."

Delver shook hands vigorously. "I won't, if I can help it," he said, "let either of you down."

CHAPTER NINE

THE MEANINGLESS PANIC had subsided in Lord Burntisland and his pulse was back to normal. He had heard that people known in Society made assignations here, secure in the knowledge that they would encounter nobody of their acquaintance not similarly implicated in a clandestine occasion. It was a consciousness that didn't trouble him. Even if satyrs profaned this place as they profaned the park, his anger would be unaccompanied by perturbation. There was security here. Lord Burntisland had a powerful sense of the elevating and fortifying character of true art.

He had not been brought up in any severe puritan distrust of the arts. His father, a minister of the Kirk, would have referred to a Virgin Enthroned, even to a Descent from the Cross, as an object of false devotion. But there would have been a circumspect irony in his voice, since he was a scholar, and had known his Virgil and Horace quite as well as his Calvin's *Institutes*. Nor had his father ever taken exception to the Sistine Madonna —decorously truncated so as to remove any suggestion of an Assumption, and reproduced unsensuously in a sombre presbyterian sepia—that had hung above his wife's bed in an austere oak frame. Burntisland had looked up at it a moment after the doctor, leaning forward in his stiff frock-coat that smelt of ether and iodine, had closed his mother's eyes. Afterwards, on his first visit to Rome, and before his intellect had been obliged to acknowledge the sombre truth of the human situation revealed by science, he had seen in the full picture the emblem of his mother's soul, soaring upward to its appointed place. Before pictures of that sort he had liked occasionally to place himself ever since. This small, pious habit—of which the piety had so long since ceased to have to do with religion—stood unconfessed to anybody. His wife, from whom little had been hidden during her undarkened days, had never known of this unimportant predilection which there had been no rational occasion to conceal. Had Hector Madrona come into the National Gallery now, and so witnessed the latest of these devout occasions, Burntisland would not have been embarrassed. But he would have been displeased.

The diffusedly lit, faintly echoing place soothed him. When he had passed through the heavy glass valves and was pausing before Giovanni Bellini's Madonna of the Pomegranate, he found himself breathing more freely, as if secure of an uncontaminated air. In a literal sense there was something to this, for he remembered having been told that in these inner rooms the atmosphere was purged of London's grimes and acids, so that the unglazed paintings could hang without danger on the walls.

At first he moved about indecisively. He knew from experience that an interval of time must elapse before he began to draw spiritual sustenance from the masterpieces around him. He had to get the "wave length", as the young people said. Initially he could even feel in himself a certain incomprehension or indeed hostility before works of evident beauty. For example, the Bellini wasn't, at the moment, impressing him. He studied it, conscious of nothing that he could presume to be artistic pleasure. Why had the painter set that green cloth behind his Virgin, when he could have had a wider Italian landscape, a larger Venetian sky? Why did it seem to be tied at its upper corners to something that wasn't there? And there was the same artist's Madonna of the Meadow nearby. *That*—Burntisland found himself reflecting, perhaps because of his recent preoccupation in the streets—*that* might be an advertisement for some sleeping tablet. The Virgin was just dropping off. And so, in another sense, the Holy Child was, too; precariously slanted, he might tumble from his mother's lap at any moment.

Curious down-and-out types came in here. Next to Burntisland an old man in rags, and with a ragged beard, was studying Cima's little St Jerome in the Desert. The effect was bizarre, as of a decayed Narcissus peering into his pool, and Burntisland moved away from it. There had been, he noticed with disapproval, a great deal of changing things round. But presently he found the Ansidei Madonna, and sat down in front of it.

There were certain barriers to overcome. Of Niccolo da Tolentino's particular claim to sanctity he knew nothing. And he didn't take to him much, here on Raphael's canvas. Mitre and cope, alb and cassock, made up too large a part of him for anything that Burntisland could conceive of as holiness. Niccolo da Tolentino was just another of the higher clergy, and Burntisland's latterday association with prelates had been far from tempering his hereditary aversion to episcopacy. The book to which the saint was giving professionally benign attention was presumably a missal, and there was a Romish and tasteless absurdity in the notion of reading the infant Christ a divinity lesson. Nor did Burntisland greatly care for the Baptist either; a sumptuous red mantle might be reconcilable with a hair-tunic, but at least an ascetic had no business with such a gewgaw as an elongated crystal cross.

The woman with her child was another matter. Here—Burntisland told himself—no amount of decorative elaboration could obscure the simplicity and purity of the artist's conception. It's true that Mariolatry has been a prime prompting in the production of such things. It's true, too, that behind Mariolatry lurk persuasions yet more superstitious. Roman Catholics believe that the Blessed Virgin, alone among mortals, was not conceived in original sin. Anthropologically regarded, however, she's a Magna Mater. She's simply another Great Goddess, with an ancestry in rites and practices of the most scandalous sort. Any intelligent man who has read the authoritative works on comparative religion must be clear enough about all that. Yet don't these scientifically attested facts bear witness, after all, to the centrality, for the human consciousness, of woman in her maternal character? And doesn't Raphael give expression to this in paintings of the utmost refinement, paintings purged of any hint of gross or sensual suggestion?

Tranquillized and edified, Burntisland sat for some time in front of the Ansidei Madonna. Then he looked at the pictures recently hung on either side of it. On the left there was a St Catherine, also by Raphael, and on the right Andrea del Sarto's Madonna and Child with St Elizabeth. Remembering that Andrea had been called the perfect painter, he rose and inspected the surface of this work closely, in an effort to determine in what the unique perfection consisted. But he got no particular light on the matter, and turned to the St Catherine. As far as he could recall, this Alexandrian lady, unlike her formidable namesake of Siena, was as legendary as the miracles attributed to her were improbable. It was curious and slightly discreditable that the Church had made of her so important a figure as it had. But next on the line was another Raphael : the Madonna of the Tower. Burntisland had to move up close to this to check on the tower; it proved to be far in the background and not easy to distinguish. The Madonna, indeed, evinced once more an elevated and ideal conception of womanhood. Unfortunately the whole surface of the picture appeared abraded.

Burntisland was about to turn away from these paintings—conscious that on this occasion they had a little failed him—when he found himself, quite suddenly, in a new relation to Andrea's work. There was no mystery about this. The posture of St Elizabeth—that was it—had opened some spring of memory in his mind. St Elizabeth, the mother of the Baptist, had become his own grandmother.

For it was just like *that*—he remembered now, as a whole scene swam up strangely before him—that his grandmother had sat on the drawing-room sofa, with one hand, veined and wrinkled as here, clasping his own childish shoulder, and with her head turned upward and away. His grandmother's skin, like St Elizabeth's, had been leaden with age. Remembering this, Burntisland saw with what a beautiful tact Andrea's painting was composed, for St Elizabeth's face was so shadowed that the touch of time upon it was recorded with a compassionate reticence. He was much moved. And now the external world faded from his consciousness so that he saw, within that sheltering arm, a small boy in his Sunday kilt, reading aloud. He could distinguish the very page, smell the leather binding, of Professor Henry Drummond's *Natural Law in the Spiritual World*. For his father —too able a man, Burntisland thought loyally, to have ended his days in an obscure Fifeshire manse—his father, abreast of the times, conscious of where the new doubts lay, had early required his son to make the fortifying acquaintanceship of the author of *The Ascent of Man*. And there in the background of the picture, this picture of his own creating, and beyond his grandmother, his mother remained seated on the piano stool, although turned towards her son as he read. When the reading was over, when his father had gravely commended or criticized his manner of accomplishing it, she would touch the keys again. And the family would sing together their favourite metrical psalm, *Unto the hills around do I lift up my longing eyes.*

The Marquis of Lorne's words, set to their dragging, melancholy air, sounded in Burntisland's inner ear. *Oh whence for me shall my salvation come, from whence arise....*

Lord Burntisland sat in the National Gallery in London, staring sightlessly at Raphael, at Andrea del Sarto.

"From scenes like these," he said, aloud and surprisingly, "old Scotia's grandeur springs."

CHAPTER TEN

Luke Tresilian glanced at his watch and saw that it was later than he had supposed. But at least he had got Dido and Aeneas into their cave. Good luck to them, he thought, and made a perfunctory attempt to visualize the amorous scene. But Virgil wasn't interested in that. The affair was supposed to be disastrous. The Nymphs were crying aloud on the topmost height. That was a bad omen, it seemed. "The whole of this fourth book", his Notes said, "is full of omens of dreadful import". Luke was afraid the omens might prove just that in his own case. For he found he couldn't remember any of them—except that somewhere there was a "solitary owl". That must be an omen, and it could hardly be a good one. Perhaps he had better get up the omens of dreadful import. He could imagine a question about them in the examination paper : *Illustrate Virgil's handling of omens EITHER in Book IV of the* Aeneid *OR in the* Aeneid *as a whole.*

He glanced back over a few pages. The red pencil marks were disappointingly numerous. He felt a flicker of alarm, and countered it by pitching the book casually into a corner and beginning to whistle. Then, standing in the middle of the room, he grabbed his sweater and with a duck and twist of his shoulders, a wriggle of his hips, was naked. Still whistling, he scrambled into his rugger togs and slung his boots round his neck. These things had a very good smell. He looked round the room as if making a roll-call of the tokens of his proprietorship of it. They were unimpressive. But then it was only people given to throwing money about who moved into college rooms in a big way—and they were often the people who had to get out again quickest. Luke had a reasonable amount of money, and he had lately been told that at twenty-one he would have quite a lot. But his habits were frugal, in the same fashion that his conversation was sparing. The Teddy Bear (he now gave it a nod) and the tobacco jar (he picked it up and shook it), the rugger group and the shelves untidily overflowing with textbooks and paperbacks : in these there was a sufficient reassurance that here he was. And there was the watercolour.

Luke went over to the fireplace and examined it. *Sketch for Lyonnesse No. 3* : he read the faintly pencilled words with attention, as if they were unfamiliar to him. By what had the appearance of some necessary association of ideas, he turned away from it and walked to his desk. It was a desk with three drawers, one of which could be locked. Luke made sure that it was in fact locked. Then he went back for a moment to the watercolour. His ruddy face changed slightly, as if taking its cue from the impression of subtle movement given by the painting itself. In a low voice, which took no risks of being heard by anybody else on the staircase, he spoke aloud :

> "When I set out for Lyonnesse,
> A hundred miles away ..."

It wasn't the piece of poetry that his father had used. But it was as good. He frowned. He had forgotten how Hardy went on. His memory wasn't up to much, as his struggles with Virgil had been telling him. But another part of the poem came with a rush, and this time he spoke the words out carelessly, and they excited him. He crossed the room, flung open the door, and ran down his own attic staircase and the statelier flights beneath, chanting :

> "Nor did the wisest wizard guess
> What would bechance at Lyonnesse
> While I should sojourn there."

Perhaps a thunderstorm, a cave and a woman of magical beauty, he thought, as he hurried across the quad. This was a new turn to an old fantasy. One day, the fantasy ran, he would go home to Cornwall as usual, and find not Cornwall but Lyonnesse instead—a protean region which took now one form and now another in his mind. Yes, perhaps a thunderstorm rolling down from Wales, and a cave deep in Beeny Cliff. *Insequitur commixta grandine nimbus.* He might write a poem called *Dido in Lyonnesse.* Or a bawdy play called *Aeneas in Spelunca.* He had a vision of himself sitting in the Examination Schools and offering the examiners not the severely literal translation they demanded but the crucial passages from *Aeneas in Spelunca.* He would be sent down from Oxford and become a legend—like Spender or Isherwood or Auden or somebody, who had answered an examination paper in sonnets.

The idea wasn't the less amusing because that sort of gesture wasn't him. He ran down the ramp leading to the basement in which undergraduates kept their bicycles. It was a bit of a *spelunca* itself, and his footfalls reminded him that it was temptingly resonant. Quite recklessly, he shouted the last lines of the poem :

> "When I came back from Lyonnesse
> With magic in my eyes!"

"With straws in your hair, if you ask me." A large young man, also dressed for the rugger field and in no way very distinguishable from Luke, spoke out of the murk of the basement. "Have you been to lunch with the Provost, or something? Are you going to stagger about the field in wild inebriety, you silly bastard?"

"Hullo, Robin." Luke was pleased, judging that these last words represented an advance in friendly intimacy on the part of the second-year man before him. "It might help, if you ask me. This college couldn't field a worse rugger team dead drunk than it does dead sober."

"Too true." Gloomily in the gloom, the other large man—whose name was Robin Pacey—shook his head.

"So it might improve matters if we went screaming round like maenads. With the idiots on the touch-line shouting 'Io, io!' instead of 'feet, feet!' We might get somewhere in Cuppers, don't you think?"

It was some time since Luke had uttered so many words on end. Pacey, who had several times sat silently beside him in Hall, peered at him dubiously in the crepuscular light. "Maenads?" he said. He was a person of literal mind. "Weren't they females?" He gave a tug at a jumbled pile of bicycles, extricating one at random. "We're bloody late, aren't we?"

"I suppose so. But, with me, it wasn't the Provost. It was Virgil."

"Prelims?" Pacey was at once sympathetic. "Aren't they the devil? When my father was up, you were never rusticated for ploughing examinations. Or not for ages and ages. Only for seducing barmaids and throwing dons into the fountain. Those must have been marvellous times."

"But now you can seduce barmaids pretty well for free. So I suppose it evens up."

"Can you really, do you think?" It was with quickened interest that Robin Pacey asked this.

"Yes, of course. But there's still a tabu on dons in fountains." Luke, in his turn, rummaged for a bicycle. "Unfortunately, I don't want to seduce a barmaid. I mean, not just at this moment. I want to be shot of Virgil. And I find it damned hard. I've got a thing about him. Wasn't he believed to be a magician? He puts some sort of evil spell on me, all right."

"You have to keep your nerve," Pacey said seriously. Side by side, the two young men wheeled their bicycles up the ramp. Sideways, and as they reached daylight, Pacey glanced anxiously at Luke. It wouldn't do to lose this large creature who, so unexpectedly, was a first-rate scrum-half. "It doesn't oppress you, does it?" he asked.

"I think of shooting myself, from time to time."

"It doesn't do to get like that." Pacey, who was fiddling with his machine, didn't see that Luke was grinning at him. To his fatherly manner there was now added a touch of authority. "In point of fact, you just pass the things, as soon as it becomes really vital. But, beyond that, and if the worst comes to the worst, you have to tell them that their examinations are bloody rot, and that they can jolly well bugger off."

"Yes, of course." Luke felt that this was thoroughly wholesome counsel, and expressed in thoroughly wholesome English—which he didn't himself, however, stand much in need of. "Unfortunately," he said, "that's what *they* tell *you*. Bugger off. Clear out."

"And it's what we'll be told now, if we don't get on to that ground soon. So push along."

Luke nodded and vaulted into his saddle—an accomplishment he had taught himself at some danger of instant castration. Pacey, seeing that it could be done, did the same. Pedalling hard, they said no more. But at Carfax, Luke, cornering brilliantly on a stationary policeman, tossed at him the last lines of Hardy's poem once more :

> "When I came back from Lyonnesse
> With magic in my eyes!"

CHAPTER ELEVEN

AGAIN THERE HAD been some stranger's startled glance. But, this time, Burntisland, although aware of having spoken aloud, was not discomposed. Old Scotia had never, it was true, been celebrated by painters of the Umbrian School. To one un-provided with a key to the matter his ejaculation must have appeared inconsequent. But the masterpieces before him had directed his mind to his own most sacredly regarded past. That was as it should be. To evoke elevated states of feeling was surely the function of art—and what was more elevated than a strong impulse of family piety?

Moved and gratified, Burntisland looked again at the paintings before him. This time, they seemed to be blended together in a single statement. The feeling which had welled up in him when St Elizabeth's posture had carried him back to a scene of child-hood now seemed to be flowing between himself and the pictures. He was no longer aware that these august figures inhabited separate worlds; that there was green damasked wallpaper be-tween the Ansidei Madonna and St Catherine, the grey marble frame of a bivalvular door between St Catherine and the Madonna of the Tower. He was in communion with the whole group of these ennobled women, drawn within their protection. Nothing catastrophic, irreversible could happen while he enjoyed the ambience of these presences, these divine embodiments of the purity and sanctity of womanhood. Some Italian paintings, he remembered, are called Holy Conversations. It was in something of the sort that, for this precious moment, he was engaged.

O whence for me shall my salvation come, from whence arise? The reverie had returned, the piano was slowly tinkling and his grandmother lightly stroking the boy's hair, as Burntisland stood up and walked from the room. Such experiences must not be tempted too long. Following an uncertain start, he had, after all, enjoyed an artistic revelation of a high order. It was most satis-factory, and must be accounted equally to his own credit and to the credit of art. To the credit—he reflected—of *great* art. I've always maintained—he told himself—that the National Gallery is an institution deserving generous support. The place has a duty to hold up and vindicate true genius, to assert the timeless standards. And a particularly exigent duty it is, in these days of decadence and near madness in poetry, novels, painting and so forth. The next time there's any question of governmental stinginess towards the N.G., I'll take a strong line. It's unfortunately true that oceans of nonsense is poured out about art. That fellow Madrona is plainly a perpetual cistern of it. But art represents a great spiritual heritage. A thing isn't damned because fools make much of it.

Those men are fortunate—Burntisland reflected with sober satisfaction—who are susceptible to the influence of art, who can seize its message. And one may be susceptible, one may have the deepest experiences before masterpieces, without pretending to be any sort of connoisseur. In which case, of course, one has a clear duty. One has a duty to uphold the true values in that sphere, to ignore the ephemeral, to expose the spurious, to root up. . . .

The habit of public eloquence accompanied Lord Burntisland down the first flight of steps within the National Gallery. Before the second flight he paused. There were moments when age had to be admitted as having got some grip on his body. He paused, marking the treads upon which he should set the guiding ferrule of his firmly retained umbrella. (An attendant had tried to deprive him of this dangerous weapon, which a madman might employ so disastrously upon ancient canvas and brittle pigment. But he had said merely "I am Lord Burntisland" and walked on.) He paused—and in the pause some freak of fate brought Hector Madrona into his recollection again.

What was the name of the painter of whose work a memorial exhibition was to be held—an exhibition for which he, Burntisland, was to receive a card which he would probably toss into the waste-paper basket? Perhaps one ought to keep an open mind about such things. Yes, one had a duty to keep oneself informed.

He glanced about him in search of an attendant. Some of these fellows, he had found on previous occasions, knew a lot, and some didn't feel it their business to know anything at all. But now his alert eye had distinguished somebody who was neither attendant nor visitor : a young man in elegant subfusc clothes, walking with an air of politely dissimulated authority through the Gallery. He must be an Assistant Curator, Keeper, or whatever the term was. Burntisland made a gesture which was at once unobstrusive and peremptory. The young man came to an attentive halt.

"Will you kindly tell me, sir, whether the Gallery has any-thing by—" Burntisland was obliged to hesitate, for the name mentioned by Madrona had again slipped his memory. "I am thinking of a painter with, I recall, a Cornish name, of whose work there is shortly to be an exhibition in London."

"Matthew Tresilian?" The young man put this interrogatively, but it was evident that Burntisland's question could have only one answer.

"Tresilian, to be sure. Can he be viewed here, or should I have to go to the Tate?"

"You'll have to go to the Tate to see much of him. But we have one picture here, in Gallery XV. It belongs to the Lyon-nesse series."

"Thank you. I'll take a turn in that direction." Burntisland pointed with his umbrella. "Through there? You seem to have been doing a good deal of moving things around." Conscious that there might appear to be a note of censure in this, he added : "Very happily, to my mind, in some instances. The Ansidei Madonna, for example. That has been given an admirable setting."

The young man appeared properly conscious that this was an authoritative commendation. "I'll guide you there, if I may," he said. "I think you'll find Tresilian's painting worth looking at."

"Thank you. I shall be most grateful. Your Director has been known to me for many years. You must let that be my excuse for troubling you so far." Burntisland, who had a fondness for com-bining old-world dignity with old-world courtesy, paced carefully by the young man's side. "Am I to understand, then," he asked, "that Matthew Tresilian was an animal painter?"

"An animal painter!" The young man looked puzzled. Then, most unfortunately, he emitted an indecorous sound suggestive of laughter. "Oh, I see," he said. "Monarchs of the Glen and Lords of the Jungle? No, it wasn't that sort of lioness that Tresilian was interested in. He was a Cornishman, don't forget."

"An absurd misapprehension on my part." Burntisland, who had been expecting something in the style of Sir Edwin Landseer, didn't pretend to be amused. There had been an engraving after the Monarch of the Glen in the dining-room of his father's manse, and he had never seen why it should be a work treated with levity. He wondered whether this young man, passing through Trafalgar Square daily on his way to work, paused to jeer at Landseer's lions round the Nelson column. And the young man, because he had a childish sense of humour, would certainly tell this story round to his friends. He might even identify Lord Burntisland, which would serve to make the story funnier still. Burntisland, recently so in harmony with Raphael and Andrea del Sarto, now felt a potential hostility towards Matthew Tresilian. "I take it," he said accusingly, "that Tresilian's is a modern manner?"

The young man, who was perhaps conscious of having behaved badly, received this question respectfully. "Well, sir, this is, of course, an early Tresilian. Early, I mean, in his career as an established painter. I think I'd venture to call all his paintings of that period straight romantic. It's known that they were painted much under the influence of Tennyson—of Tennyson as himself a great landscape artist, that is."

"Indeed?" Burntisland's prospective attitude to Matthew Tresilian veered again. "I have myself a great love of Tennyson. But I'm told that he has been unfashionable for a long time. I'm surprised to hear of a painter of the present century being interested in him."

"I don't think that Tresilian much bothered himself about fashion."

"I'm glad to hear it. An artist has little hope of attaining the first excellence if he makes himself subservient to the vagaries of taste." Burntisland said this instructively and for the young man's benefit. Despite his high regard for art, he had no great opinion of people who went in for this sort of dilettante career in galleries and museums. But the young man had at least offered himself as a guide, and it was fair to give him the advantage of mature views on these matters. At this moment, Burntisland realized that he was standing still, and that a medium-sized painting was in front of him. "Is this it?" he asked.

"Yes, this is it."

In order to be perfectly fair, Burntisland advanced a foot or two nearer the canvas. "I can't see," he said, "that it has much to do with Lyonnesse."

"Well, sir, I'm not sure whether that mightn't be called rather a Cornish kind of sea."

"A sea?" Burntisland pointed. "Then, I suppose, these would be sails?"

"Sails? Well, yes—I think one may take them to be sails. They invert and reverse the cloud-forms—if they are cloud-forms—above."

"And *that*? Would it be a human figure?"

"The title of the thing is the White Mermaiden. So that may well be a human figure, as you say—or approximately human. You notice how it gives a strong vertical, cutting the picture-space dead through the centre. Piero's Baptism is the only equivalent thing in the Gallery. From quite early on, Tresilian could get away with these utterly simple things."

"No doubt." Burntisland, who found the comparison just advanced to be one singularly ill judged, was brusque before this jargon. "And *those*—they'd be human figures too?" He advanced yet farther upon the canvas. "I can't at all see," he said suspiciously, "what they're up to."

"I'd say they might be singing." The young man spoke in distinguishable long-sufferance now. "If, that is, one must get a little drama out of it."

Burntisland said nothing more. This was partly because he judged that silence would best convey a certain disapprobation which he felt the young man should be made aware of. But—oddly enough—it was partly also because he was finding it necessary to give close attention to his own sensations.

A moment before, what had been visible in the plain wooden frame in front of him had been no more than a number of irregular rectangles of pigment—some opaque in suggestion, but most of them diaphanous—with here and there an ambiguous form such as had just attracted his questioning finger. Now some of these rectangles had advanced, others had withdrawn, and a few had pivoted as if upon a vertical hinge. The effect of this manoeuvre—if it might be called that—was to create light. Where there had been daubs of paint on a flat surface there were still daubs of paint on a flat surface. But, at the same time, there was a large luminous world of cliffs and promontories and glittering sea, stretching in perspective to a horizon which was at once molten and dim.

Moreover, although this highly impressionist creation—for that was, no doubt, the word—seemed to arrest in perpetuity something which, in nature, must have been filled with momentary accidents of light and shade, nevertheless it contrived to suggest more of present and actual movement than could readily be squared with the fact that here were simply so many fixed areas of paint on canvas. Burntisland felt that this must be animadverted upon—and not favourably. "It's a fluid sort of thing," he said. "You can't pin it down."

"To my mind, it's precisely *that* that makes Tresilian so interesting—that makes him so fascinatingly a pioneer. You know those people in Zagreb—the Nove Tendencije chaps?" The young man was speaking with a new degree of interest. "Have you been in Paris lately? Have you hit the Groupe de Recherche d'Art Visuel? What do you think of Le Parc? Or, for that matter, of Morellet or Yvaral?"

"I've heard of none of them."

"Well, of course, the names are of no importance. It's the idea of the instability of the image that matters. I'm no enthusiast for mere optical tricks: all those mirrors and slotted screens and currents of air. But in Tresilian there's a related thing, legitimately achieved, and with far more subtlety and tact."

"Most interesting," Burntisland said. He was only vaguely aware that the young man was still talking some technical jargon. Tresilian's painting itself continued to absorb his attention.

For a moment Burntisland was obliged to conceive himself as actually within this mysterious creation. Nor was he so only in terms of what might be called optical illusion, because something related to the sense of touch was also involved. It was as if he had fingers that reached out to explore the texture of the farthest curtains of light in the painting.

"And it's Tennyson that's on the frame." The young man, who appeared to have regained an awareness that Burntisland was not a crackpot modern art fancier, resumed an air of polite boredom as he offered this information. And Burntisland saw that on a small panel beneath the picture there were reproduced some lines

74

of verse. "A habit dear to Victorian R.A.s," the young man added indulgently. "Tresilian revived it, rather amusingly, for the whole Lyonnesse series."

Burntisland again said nothing. But he stooped and read the lines :

> All down the lonely coast of Lyonnesse,
> Each with a beacon-star upon his head,
> And with a wild sea-light about his feet,
> He saw them—headland after headland flame
> Far on into the rich heart of the west:
> And in the light the white mermaiden swam,
> And strong man-breasted things stood from the sea,
> And sent a deep sea-voice through all the land.

"This is the third of the Lyonnesse paintings," the young man said. "You can see the second at the Tate. There's a mermaid there as well. But the association is quite different. Some Christian legend, I think. The mermaid, as having a double nature, is regarded in typology as a symbol of Our Lord."

"Is that so?" Burntisland thought this a foolish notion, and didn't give it much attention. His glance had gone back to the painting—rather reluctantly, because his experience of it had been disturbing. It had been an entirely different kind of experience from that which he had enjoyed in front of the Madonnas. Now—only seconds later—the experience wasn't there at all. He could still see that all this apparent confusion of pigments in fact created a seascape of remarkable depth and luminosity. But something that had happened as he first looked wasn't happening again. He felt tired and irritated. "It's undoubtedly clever," he said to the young man—speaking only because it was civil to say something. "I must keep an eye open for Tresilian in future. Meanwhile, I'm obliged to you, sir. Good afternoon."

Pointing his umbrella cautiously at the polished floor in front of him, Lord Burntisland turned and walked away. He hardly supposed that he would really keep an eye open for other works by the late Matthew Tresilian. This had been an idle day and an unsatisfactory one, redeemed only by that brief encounter, before Raphael and Andrea del Sarto, with the art of painting in its true operation.

As for the young man with whom he had just conversed, it

was surely disturbing that a public servant should have his head full of freakish activities in Zagreb and Paris when he ought to be attending to what he was paid for : studying and helping to preserve the masterpieces of the past. Places like this—Burntisland reflected, as he passed once more through the swing doors of the National Gallery and surveyed Trafalgar Square—cost a mint of money. The Tate, the B.M., the V. and A., all those semi-governmental Councils and so forth that had sprung up of recent years : one had a duty to keep an eye on them.

Burntisland's glance travelled down Whitehall. On Victoria Tower the flag still flew. It was a matter—he thought, going down the steps—that he might raise in the Lords one day. Something of the sort—he couldn't remember precisely what—had been in his mind quite recently. It would be a thing to do urbanely, in the fashion those old fellows liked, and without too heavy a hand. He could manage an amusing passage on the young man who had harangued him about Zagreb.

Smiling at this idea, turning a phrase or two in his mind, Lord Burntisland walked to the corner of the Square. The little street sign said *Wait*. And he waited, being the most law-abiding of legislators.

PART TWO

PART TWO

CHAPTER TWELVE

Faculty of General Humanities

From: Thayne Delver   *To:* Dean Donald J. Totland
Dept: Art Relations   *Dept:* Graduate School
         Subject: Tresilian *et al.*

St James's Hotel
Albemarle Street
London

My dear Don,

I find myself with quite a heap of this familiar printed stuff, frugally thrust into the bottom of a trunk, so I can start off as if these thoughts were coming to you from straight across the campus. And perhaps you will take my screed to be so far official as to say a word on the strength of it to key people on the Research Grants Committee. For I see that Tresilian is likely to keep me moving around some, both on the continent as well as here. Only this morning, he has sprung another surprise : to wit that—all unremarked, so far as I can discover—he managed to spend the greater part of 1912 and 1913 in Germany. Those were the first and most vigorous years of the *Blaue Reiter* group. If I can trace some association with Kandinsky at this time, I may be able to make better sense of one turn in Tresilian's development.

Meanwhile, it's Tresilian on his domestic front that I'm chiefly going after. Here, he's certainly virgin soil ! Read the column and a half in the *International Biographical Dictionary of the Plastic and Graphic Arts* and you know as much about him as the world knows at this present moment. Add to this what I've told you about the prospect of rustling up quite a lot of his *writing* and you'll understand how keen I am. I don't expect, and shouldn't welcome, scandals or sensations. But—do you know?—the other day I was left wondering whether somebody else did!

Have you ever met Charles Rose of the British Museum? He's a good scholar, who gave me a tidy lot of help when I was working on the Rossetti papers. But when he and I got yarning a week ago, and I told him I planned some research into Tresilian's life, he looked down his long Bloomsbury nose and pretty well made a lecture out of the theme that the recently dead have the same right to privacy as the living. And Tresilian, mark you, died back in 1947! Tell an Englishman that you are proposing some research into the life of a man who might have been at school with his father, and at once he has a lurking feeling that you're up to something impertinent—like it might be inquiring whether that same father passed bad cheques, or whether his grandmother went to bed with the coachman. I yield to no one in my liking for British reserve. But it's being carried too far when exercised on behalf of persons of public note who might have been cooed over in their baby-carriage by Charles Darwin or invited to dinner by Queen Victoria.

And now I shall put a sheet of carbon-paper in the machine and so get down, both for myself and you, a summary of where this part of my project stands. Who was Matthew Tresilian, and what is his story?

He was born in 1882 (twenty-two years after both Steer and Sickert, and four years before the foundation of the New English Art Club). His birthplace was at Gwennap, near Redruth in Cornwall, and his father was a tinner—by which, of course, is meant a tin-*miner* in this quarter of the globe. There were no family ambitions nourished for young Matthew, his parents having no other notion than that he should become a tinner too. As a lad, indeed, Matthew had a spell at mining, but only during some temporary breakdown of his determination to be an artist. That determination came early.

I'm just back, as it happens, from a first week-end foray in the Stannaries—if the formerly metalliferous moors of Cornwall should still go by that name. For life has drained away from the mines, whether tin or copper, and was already so doing when Tresilian was a boy. I see this as important for his developing visual imagination. He grew up on a battlefield.

Tin mining (unlike copper mining, which came much later) is immemorial in those parts—and on a large scale. Until the discovery of tin in Malacca and South Australia, Cornwall supplied the world. So the Duchy is honeycombed with workings. It must a little strike an American imagination that for some centuries our nearest British, as distinct from Irish, neighbours were tinners toiling in submarine mines near the Land's End. (Yes, you are right. I've forgotten the Scilly Isles. But the image remains attractive.) In those workings, it's said, you can hear the reverberation of the waves breaking on the coast—and even, right overhead, the harsh grating of rocks rolled to and fro on the sea-bed by the Atlantic swell.

But I spoke of a battle. It was between the diminishing economic return from the mines and an advancing industrial technology. Steam was brought in in a big way—literally in a big way, for in the seventies engines capable of pumping from depth, and so on, had to be gigantic affairs. These things were rising on the moors, therefore, at the same time that older and smaller contrivances were falling into disuse, and when many of the mines were "knocking" or being abandoned. But the life-span of the new machines, in turn, was short. Although highly productive, they weren't productive enough, so that the larger mines in which they had been installed fell into the same desuetude as their humbler neighbours. Many still have, today, the appearance of being quite recently evacuated, as if some tide of war had swept over the region in our own time. And there is more to suggest this than the abandoned engine-houses and "dressing" sheds and cottages. This kind of mining had thrown up for centuries what are known as the "deads"—conical heaps, some large and some small, of slaty poisonous rubbish, which might suggest sometimes the tents of an encamping army, and sometimes what a rural prospect may be like in the post-atomic age.

So here is what the young Tresilian was first aware of : a very special sort of industrial landscape. Imagine him not merely roaming about in it but *clambering* about—when quite small. Can't one see in the abandoned pumps and boilers, the tumbling furnace chimneys, the rusty windlasses and broken cogwheels and sprawled and coiled cables—can't one see, in the whole littered complexity of hard metallic surfaces, precisely what would one day come home to him as familiar in the world of

Curvilinear Cubism and in the improbable machinery of Léger? This is an idea that has just come to me. I must follow it up.

But that's not all. If one drives around—as I did the other day across Bodmin Moor to Liskeard—there's plenty of this sort of thing. But there's also, as both the map and the sky-line tell one at once, an astonishing density of prehistoric remains : camps, barrows, tumuli, and what-have-you—the what-have-you including cromlechs, dolmens, logans, quoits and hurlers. It's another little universe of strange, bleak, eroded forms. And here I may mention at once one of the few reminiscences of Tresilian's childhood that I've turned up so far—not from any great depth of research, since it is simply something he confided to that excellent anecdotalist, Will Rothenstein. It being supposed that he suffered from a weak back (a serious matter in a future tin-miner), he was taken to the Mên-an-tol, or Crick Stone, at a place called Lanyon, and constrained to crawl nine times through some orifice in this stone-age antiquity. I wonder, now, what it would be? Something massive but anthropomorphic, with a hole punched through its chest, like a Henry Moore? Or the archetype of one of those whorled voids within a void created by Barbara Hepworth? Whatever it was, or is, the small Matthew Tresilian crawled through it as required—and was a good deal surprised, he told Rothenstein, at being given a new sixpence for his pains. Later, he realized that this wasn't family generosity but an essential part of the magic. One wonders to what the coin may have corresponded in whatever pagan initiation this needle's-eye business descended from.

But my point here, of course, is the significance, for a developing artistic sense, of a region upon which the remains of one epoch of human culture were beginning to be joined by the remains of another : the abandoned engine-houses and water-whims and the rest merging with the stone circles and hill castles. For an intelligent child they would at first be all of a piece—and then there would dawn, one imagines, the amazing fact of the aeons of human life between them. And for the artist, simultaneously, they would continue to hang together—to hang together as both of them things first shaped by the hands of man, and then left to be resumed at leisure by a vast neutral unregarding universe.

Alongside this must be set the fact that, in Cornwall, man has created very little else of an impressive or shapely order. Great houses are few. Domestic architecture of the middling and humbler sort is, as in Wales, charmless and mean. The churches, although some are of high antiquity and many are not without architectural interest, have very little that is striking either in scale or embellishment. The Cornish themselves, I am told, sometimes speak of their region as affording an ugly picture in a beautiful frame.

The frame is certainly beautiful if one takes it to indicate the sea coast—and, even more, the sea itself. Tresilian was to celebrate the former in his magnificent Lyonnesse series. Do you know them, Don? Only Kokoschka (and once himself in a Cornish picture : the Polperro now in the Tate) has got anywhere near these things, in which light comes like a bridegroom, or like an epiphany, to the earth.

But the sea itself! To describe it in all its variety would require a long digression—and the talent of a John Ruskin into the bargain. But I'll just mention one more or less relevant experience of my own. Finishing my jaunt with a night on the north coast, I walked out on a promontory called Trevose Head. There, and from a considerable height, I found myself looking straight down into a rocky basin in which the surface of the water lay entirely under a thick foam. Here and there this rose in spray, so that there was spindrift in the air about me : iridescent clustered globes of the stuff as if a race of juvenile giants were blowing bubbles from the mouth of some cave below. But it was the pulsing surface of the sea that was the thing : an incredibly rich impasto as of the thickest cream in ceaseless movement : a perfectly unified intricacy of arabesques without hint of repeating motif. And, looking at this natural phenomenon, which mysteriously afforded the most intense sensuous pleasure, I suddenly realized that I should come with a fresh eye to certain kinds of contemporary action painting concerned to create effects of afocal space and to eliminate the notion of the compositional centre. Now—you know—Tresilian's penultimate paintings (for example, the big one at present somewhere in Oxford) do remarkably look forward to that sort of thing. Was it conceivable, I found myself asking, that he had arrived at them by himself looking backward to some boyhood's experience like this one? For in his boyhood he did find the sea. That's the next thing.

After Gwennap, that's to say, it's the next significant topographical fact. Tresilian was removed from that whole dreary, bare, rubbish-strewn prospect, and sent to live at St Ives. Despite the episode of the Crick Stone, this wasn't because of anything wrong with his own back. It was because of something that happened to his father's. For Luke Tresilian (as his name was) had suffered, it seems, a disabling accident which prevented his ever again undertaking other than light work "at grass"—by which is meant above-ground. It was still customary, at that time, for a boy to enter the industry more or less as an apprentice to his father, with whom he would share a "pitch" or section of a working. Matthew's prospects were thus impaired by Luke's misfortune, and he was therefore sent to lodge with an aunt—the inducement being the very moderate one that in St Ives he might get employment running messages, with some further prospect of work in a drygoods store later on. He had already, indeed, been in a regular job at the rate of threepence a day—the business of cobbing, picking, jigging, bucking, buddling and splaying the ore being largely entrusted, in Victoria's golden reign, to the female and juvenile sections of the tinners' community.

You may know St Ives. In the early nineties it must have had something of the charm of a Breton fishing village, and it was beginning to be a good deal frequented by painters. Presently it is rather more "ye olde" than is likely to be agreeable to a sophisticated taste, but an artists' colony in fact flourishes to the present day. And you see how curiously fate arranged things. The small working-class boy from Gwennap, setting out to join his aunt in this unknown place, and to run his messages in its two or three steep, narrow and tortuous streets, was not only escaping from the blind, troglodyte life of the mines, which must surely have quenched his artist's vision for ever. He was also, without at all knowing it, coming among his own kind.

It might have done him little good. There are stories in Vasari's *Lives* of youths in humble station dramatically making their talents known among their natural peers. But most of what we know, or think we know, about the English social system would incline us to give long odds against little Matthew Tresilian's contriving to do so. Yet we'd be wrong. Miraculously, if you like, the boy didn't get from St Ives the kind of dusty answer that

Thomas Hardy's Jude got from Christminster. He hadn't been there a month when he came within the friendly regard of a well-reputed artist in the town. The boy was idling on the pier, scratching a piece of slate with a stone, when this stranger paused beside him, noticed how the lines were forming themselves under his hand, and took him straight home to his studio and gave him paper and chalks. I hurry on to say that this story is without satisfactory provenance at the moment, since the *Biographical Dictionary* gives it without any reference. I guess I'd be proud to authenticate it.

But however it may be with the particular yarn, there can be no doubt about the general fact. Young Matthew delivered his groceries, or whatever, up and down St Ives—very much up and down—until duly promoted to measuring out linen and calico as a clerk in one of the modest stores in the place. Probably he liked the first employment a little better than the second, and at one point he made a bolt to something manlier than either. Just outside the town were the St Ives Consols, one of the largest tin concerns in the country—and back he went for a time to follow the trade of his forbears. He may still have been at that (I'm far from having the record clear) when they got together the money to set him to the regular study of art.

For that's what happened. And it wasn't, so far as I can distinguish, a matter of some wealthy man putting a hand to his billfold and handing out easy money. It was a matter of a few practising painters, far from well-off themselves, simply deciding that this thing had to be done for this boy. They were, I suppose, unspectacular and by no means very lavishly talented people, traditional marine and landscape artists, just letting themselves be cautiously touched by the new Impressionism (to use what was then a derogatory term) from across the Channel. For the time-lag was considerable, it has to be confessed, among our English friends. It wasn't till the late eighties that Steer discovered Monet's work. So although Tresilian had been born in the year of the seventh of the eight famous Impressionist Exhibitions, I think we can figure that those provincial painters who discovered *him* were still in a first dubitating excitement about the new movement. These chronological points are aside from my present purpose, but they suggest something that I hope to develop elsewhere. Tresilian was *loyal* to Impressionism. To the end he accepted *Let there be Light* as the archetypal creative command, and everything that came after in his own art he subsumed within this obedience. I have a notion that in this there was operative a kind of fidelity to his first instructors—those unspectacular painters, cautiously tinging their shadows with complementaries and experimenting in the strange new world of optical mixtures.

But go back to the situation. What they had on their hands was a plebeian lad of powerful and original genius. And they taught him all they could, they encouraged him, they coped with the various troubles that one may be pretty sure beset such a boy's adolescence, and finally they got the cash together and sent him off to London, where they secured his entry to the Slade. All honour to them, says the present writer.

Of Tresilian's student days I have, so far, nothing to record. Legros had departed from the Slade, and Frederick Brown and Tonks reigned in his stead. There was still the better part of a year to be spent in the Antique Room, but whereas the students had formerly used, for the most part, red or black Italian chalk on Ingres paper, they now used charcoal on Michelet, and were not positively forbidden that useful chunk of bread. This sort of thing, however, is not my present business, nor will it much amuse you. Matthew Tresilian was the best draughtsman of his year—and would have been the best in a generation, had not Augustus John been at the Slade only four years before him. The prizes and scholarships came his way, and duly transported him in succession to the several parts of Europe in which an assimilative sojourn was appropriate. But he seems to have been very loyal to his roots. And here I see the possibility of an illuminating comparison and contrast with Stanley Spencer, nine years his junior, and probably the next superlative draughtsman that the Slade produced. Spencer was perhaps the more original of the two men—but what he did with his originality was to exploit very great technical skill in fabricating a sort of one-man folk art making virtually no acknowledgements to the major European movements of his time. Tresilian, although you can never find him merely scampering after the latest things, accepts and absorbs far more. His specifically intellectual endowment is more powerful. (This is going to appear—believe me, Don!—when I run his *writing* to earth.) But he has a similar salubrious tenacity in holding to his origins, and he seems never to have made his way very intimately into circles thoroughly remote from these.

And now—but "now", my dear Don, means a couple of exciting days after typing the above—comes something *big*. Ironically, it pretty well contradicts the last sentence I got down before breaking off !

Here, then, I offer you a discovery—and one not twenty-four hours old. At least it's that so far as I'm concerned. And I can say pretty confidently that it has never appeared in print. But this doesn't mean that half England hasn't known it for quite some time. Perhaps my friend Rose knew it when I had that chat with him in the B.M.; likely enough it was what was in his mind when he put over that line on the dead and their privacy. England, as you know, is a country I feel pretty well at home in— but every now and then I get a kind of disoriented feel. Is something a sacred confidence, or is it current in a small, closed circle, or is it known to everybody living in the big, square block? I'm left guessing, often enough. And I'm left guessing about Mary Emeleus. About how many people, I mean, know that she was Matthew Tresilian's mistress. For that's yesterday's discovery.

Don't get thinking, Don, that I'm developing the interests of a cub reporter on a tabloid. Don't suppose I'm not keeping a grip on the artistic and aesthetic side of my project. But of course I admit to being interested in the man himself. He tucked himself out of sight, and—frankly—I'm going to have a peep. And, over and above that—*above* that, do you hear?—I have faith, within due bounds, in the genetic approach. How did a man who had remained essentially an Impressionist while absorbing Cubism— a remarkable feat—come to bury himself for a while in the world of Mondrian? What shoved him on—or back—from his pioneer Abstract Expressionism to what is virtually the *straight* Expressionism of those final extraordinary semi-figurative things? Was he influenced by this or that trend in some of the other arts? If so, through what agency—or whose agency—did this come about?

Now Mary Emeleus, you see, as well as being one of the leading novelists of the time, was very much part of the Bloomsbury crowd. And Tresilian, at least up to the period of this association with her, had been rather a lone explorer. He *must* have been

that, or I'd know far more about him by now! And I suspect—
as I've rather indicated—that the simplicity of his origins made
him a shy fellow. His first wife (whom I've skipped in this
account under the excitement of my new discovery) was from his
own class. So I see the Emeleus *liaison* as bringing him into a
new relation with circles familiar with advanced thought in the
arts. Can't you imagine her—this Mary Emeleus—finding with
astonishment that her lover hadn't read *Le Neo-Plasticism* and
had never heard of *De Stijl*? All sorts of exciting possibilities
can be glimpsed through this first chink in the blanket of
Tresilian's private history. It would take more than Charles
Rose to stop me taking an honest rummage! In addition to
which, mark you, I have my faith in Matthew Tresilian. Not
merely in the art, but in the deep salubrity of the man. It must
be a faith, you may say, since I admit to knowing next to nothing about him. Very well, Don, and be it so. It's my guess that,
simply as a man, he'll turn out to have inches.

Now, how did I get on to this? Well, in a way that—to be
frank once more—I'm a little uncomfortable about. There was
a shadow of false pretences about it. But you shall hear.

I went to a party at our Embassy, given by the Cultural
Attaché, Nick Dallow. It seems that Dallow was raised in Big
Chimney, W. Virginia, and that this has given him a wonderful
start towards knowing everyone in London, and no doubt everyone in Paris and Rome as well. I hadn't been the guest of the
Government of the United States for more than five minutes—
hadn't so much as chosen between the champagne and the
tomato juice—before Dallow was introducing me to John
Alabaster.

Well, that was a legendary moment. The man had known
Whistler. I guess I looked at Alabaster as if I was supposing he
had been resuscitated for the occasion, although I can't say I'd
ever positively opined him to be dead : only as belonging with
things come and gone a long, long time ago. But here he was—
silvery as to the yet abundant hair on his head, and golden as to
the knob of the stick with which he assisted himself about the
room. He had a great air of courteous attention, together with
a smooth line in American reminiscences which he presumably
kept specially for occasions like this. He had first visited New
York, he told me, in 1895, and he added with a charming air of

88

confession that it had been entirely for a lark. He had gone on to Washington, and Secretary Lamont had taken him to call at the White House. The President and his *entourage* were delightful and unaffected people (Cleveland, it must have been, heaven help us!) and there was a great deal of hospitality.

And so on and so forth. I talked to the old man rather with the sense that I was managing a courteous turn of my own : helping an ancient aristocratic automaton to go on ticking. It simply didn't cross my mind that he—or it—would make anything of what I said. Otherwise I mightn't have started in with what is no doubt my thoroughly boring line as the student of Matthew Tresilian.

But I'd got Alabaster wrong. And Nick Dallow, who has us all card-indexed and knows just whom to pull out for whom, had got him right. "Ah, yes," Alabaster said. "You interest me intensely, my dear Professor." He said this with a beautiful air of polite fabrication. "For, of course, I knew Tresilian too. You remember that wonderful laugh?"

Now, Don, I confess! There *was* a split second in which I could have said that I *didn't* remember that wonderful laugh. But I didn't manage this. What I did manage to say was that, sure, Tresilian had a wonderful laugh. That's a trait that has already been talked into the scanty record.

"But did it ever occur to you that it a little belied his nature?" Alabaster didn't give me a chance to reply to this. "Tresilian struck me as a large man, but by no means as a bold one."

"He was a bold painter," I said. (No fake credentials there.)

"Ah, yes—indeed !" Alabaster said this in an acknowledging sort of way, as if we were two profound fellows, and I the more profound of the two. "How right you are there. It was at once his strength and weakness. How many of his pictures are insufficiently considered, and seem heading for disaster in consequence. And how often with some bold, even hazardous, stroke of craft or imagination does he not notably save the situation, transforming by some happy improvisation failure into success. Hazardous, I say, because it grew to a dangerous facility, and occasions can be pointed to when he overreached himself."

Alabaster's is the high-pitched voice of age, and for a second I was aware of these critical remarks as carrying farther than was intended. I almost expected to see all heads turned towards us. But of course it wasn't so. And being reassured as to this, I had leisure to remember that John Alabaster has given evidence in print of being the possessor of a formidable aesthetic intelligence. Here wasn't the right emphasis to put upon Tresilian's work, I thought, yet the old man was far from simply talking in the air. He was giving me something to think about. And he did this again, and to quite a different effect, only seconds later.

"Not," he went on, "that Tresilian was without what might be called phases of personal enterprise. It was during one of these that he became known to me other than as a name on a canvas. Perhaps you recall it? I mean the curious time in the early forties when that talented child Mary Emeleus was his mistress. She used to bring him down to my place occasionally during those years. I forget whether you sometimes visited us at Fallows then?"

Do you know that, for a moment, I was less struck by this accession to my knowledge of Tresilian than puzzled about just how it was coming to me? Alabaster might be taking me for some sort of intimate of his circle simply because he was old and crazed. Or his question might be a sort of flattery : he knew very well I'd never been to Fallows; he wouldn't welcome me there now (and why should he?) if I walked up and rang the bell; but it was gracious to conjure up just for a moment that I had the *entrée*. And—mark you—all laborious and slow as I am, it didn't escape me that there was another explanation still. Back in the Victorian twilight, urbane malice had been very much young John Alabaster's note. Perhaps he was bored by this party (he must have seen enough parties in his time to make it difficult for him to be anything else), and perhaps it had occurred to him as amusing to set a solemn American professor, adding to the tediousness of the occasion by a prosaic enthusiasm for Matthew Tresilian, on a quest that might produce an embarrassing rediscovery of forgotten scandal. What the old fellow had said might be prompted by any of these motives.

Still, he'd said it. The ball was bouncing in my court, and I had to decide whether to take a smack at it or let it go by. Deciding to play, I felt I'd better time my stroke carefully.

"Mr Alabaster," I said, "would you figure it to have been a deep and elevating attachment?"

The English like to hear, you know, what they imagine to be our familiar locutions. And they like the note of naïve moral earnestness to sound in our speech. And, sure enough, the old boy gave a high, pleased laugh. "One would suppose," he said, "that hell and heaven were both rather behind Mary by that time—wouldn't you say? Of course, fornication may have been formidable earlier on. A cradle cat, remember."

I must have looked blank, for I could see a flicker of amusement on Alabaster's face. Then, in the way that happens at parties, some small movement by our neighbours carried him away from me. I was left wondering whether a cradle cat was a kitten, or whether there had been some joke about the kind of affair that children make on their fingers with baling twine. Not that I hadn't better questions I'd have liked to put to Alabaster. And I did have one further moment with him before he left. He came tottering the length of the room for it. "When you next see dear Mary," he said, "—and please *do* see dear Mary— tell her how very much I am still her devoted servant." And at that he gave me what used to be called a quizzical look, patted me on the shoulder, and went away.

Now, how would you describe this affair, Don? Would it not be among the "giftes of Fortune", as old Dan Chaucer calls them? And was I to reject the gift—even if there was mischief somewhere lurking in it? I couldn't, after all, reject the *information*. I now *knew* about Tresilian and Mary Emeleus. Mightn't I try to extend that knowledge? Consider what—from whatever motive—the old fellow said. "Please *do* see dear Mary." Wasn't it a command, or the *viva voce* equivalent of a letter of introduction?

I've written to the lady: the elderly lady, as she must be. I confess to it. I own up. I've said that Mr John Alabaster has charged me with good wishes to her, and I've asked if I may call in order to present them. It may only make her mad. If I get no reply—and I'm telling myself I've only a slim chance of one—I shall feel a little relieved as a moral being. But oh, how disappointed as a researcher!

Don, I hope you're breathless for the issue of this. I'll write again when it's mine to communicate. Meanwhile, all the best !

THAYNE

P.E. *Eureka*. For *cradle cat* read *cradle Cat* : one born into the Roman Catholic faith.

CHAPTER THIRTEEN

COLLEGE MEETINGS WERE held in the Old Library—a noble vaulted chamber which, although it housed some thirty thousand books, was seldom entered for any other purpose. The books were folios and quartos in ancient serviceable calf, but many ran to spines sufficiently tooled and gilded to contribute handsomely to the general effect of sombre splendour aspired to. Their contents were understood to be, for the most part, eighteenth-century theology of a pastoral and unrewarding sort. In recent years they had been disturbed only by a single wandering scholar from the Pacific School of Religion in San Francisco. After a week or two even this pertinacious inquirer had gone away discouraged, and the place's slumbers had been resumed. Only nine times a year it came alive, when the Governing Body of the college met. More precisely, six or seven times a year it came half-alive, while well-modulated voices conducted unexciting business with one eye on the clock that should bring crumpets and éclairs at four p.m. On the remaining two or three annual occasions—and it was for these that some of the Fellows lived—indescribable animosities would quicken into being. The surrounding divines, locked in their sermons and theodicies, their Laudian decorum and their Erastian calm, had to be supposed as listening appalled. The afternoon sunshine, striking in thin shafts through the high Gothic windows, caught a million motes which might have been the dust of battle rising from the long, baize-covered table below. But in fact the motes were there whenever the sunshine was—whether beneath them were dons courteous, dons acrid, dons phrenetic, or no dons at all. The motes, like the tree in a neighbouring quad according to Ronald Knox's limerick, were always there since observed by God—or at least by God's bishops, deans, canons and vicars in surrounding leathery conclave.

The minutes of the previous meeting had been read, and the Provost was signing them. One or two Fellows, tardy of entry through having paused to gulp another glass of Hock at the luncheon table in an adjoining room, were huddling awkwardly into their gowns. Old Fitch the Egyptologist had reached for the pile of writing paper upon which he would prosecute his unending and mysterious epistolary correspondence throughout the meeting. Keith Pratling had assumed the expression of tolerant boredom he favoured on these occasions. Philip Leech was taking a quick, dark look round for absentees. People were casual about apologies, and before now he had been caught out through not holding a preliminary mental roll-call.

John Littlejohn had turned to the agenda and was holding his pen poised above it. "I would like your permission," he said briskly, "to add one item below the line. As it stands, the last item is Twenty-two : Report of the Committee on Additional Accommodation. I should like to add Twenty-three : Question of a possible Bequest. Agreed?" Littlejohn had looked rapidly round the table, ending up, as was his custom, with a glance of particularly courteous inquiry at his principal adversary, Leech. "Pro-Provost?"

Leech nodded. He had thought this one out quickly. Although most were very trivial, twenty-three pieces of business meant a long meeting, and by the end of it people would be getting impatient for their tea. But it seemed hardly likely that "Question of a possible Bequest" could conceal one of Littlejohn's fast ones. And it was elementary strategy to avoid as much as possible the appearance of obstructivness or of suspicion. "Agreed, Provost," Leech said.

"Then may we take the first item? Report of the Committee on a proposed Election to an Honorary Fellowship. The report has been printed and is before you."

With the exception of the smoothly scribbling Fitch, the Fellows fumbled among their papers and scrutinized the one thus brought under notice. They knew its contents perfectly well, but it was still possible that a grammatical solecism or a misspelling might be detected in it. Oddly, it was Fitch who spoke. He did so without pausing for a moment in his writing.

"In the first line," Fitch said, "there appears to be a full stop after the word 'Sir'. I confess that this usage, in relation to titles of honour, has been entirely unfamiliar to me hitherto. I speak under correction."

A majority of the members of the Governing Body produced indulgent smiles. Fitch didn't have to look round to collect them, since he knew they must be prescriptively there. He turned over a sheet of writing paper and went on with his letter.

"Then we omit the full stop between 'Sir' and 'Hector'." With proper patience, Littlejohn made this correction on his own copy of the report. "So we read : 'The Committee recommends that Sir Hector Madrona, K.B.E., M.A., former commoner of the college, be elected into an Honorary Fellowship.' Agreed?"

"Provost, may I simply seek a modicum of information?" It was Bruce Powdermaker—a young, pallid, bespectacled man with bulging forehead and receding hair—who had spoken. He scarcely had the air of one who simply seeks information. So patently was he bottling up indignation, indeed, that his head seemed liable at any moment to depart from his sloping shoulders, like a violently extruded cork, into the murky vaulting above him.

"Most certainly." The Provost gave Powdermaker, whom he thought of as Leech's inept apprentice, the cordial smile he deserved. "I will try to answer any questions with what I understand to have been the sense of the committee. Other members of the committee can correct me. And, of course, the recommendation is open to the fullest debate, should it be required. Mr Powdermaker."

Powdermaker took a covert glance at a note. Then, with what was no doubt considerable courage, he crumpled this up and dropped it on the floor beside him. He heaved himself upright, with his hands clasped in his lap—like a schoolmistress, Leech thought, determined to keep her head in a trying situation.

"May I refer, Provost, to the manner in which our statutes define the classes of person to be considered eligible for this, the highest honour which it is in the power of the college to bestow? That definition speaks—and I am sure members will correct me if I am at fault in this—of persons of high distinction in learning, in the arts, or in public life. I should like to ask, in the first place"—with this last phrase Powdermaker made, implacably, the point that he was in for a substantial innings—"whether the committee felt no uneasiness here? It is plain, I suppose, that no claim is made for Sir Hector Madrona either in learning or the arts—"

"I'm not quite assured as to that." Littlejohn had interrupted with an air of good humour. "Madrona is at least a very notable patron of the arts. He has been both a discriminating and a munificent patron. And, in these days, that's something—believe me. And I venture to say 'Believe me' because here we are on my own humble and unassuming ground, after all."

Philip Leech stirred in his seat, a motion he hadn't cured himself of making when there came to him a first sense that a manoeuvre was in the air. But he didn't speak. His instinct was against Madrona, and he had debated with himself speaking against his election. He would certainly not speak against it now. For Madrona was as good as in. What young Powdermaker had said, and still more what he was plainly going on to say, could have no other consequence. Powdermaker was, of course, fundamentally sound. He knew that they were here to get on with a job—the job of advancing and communicating knowledge. He knew that nine-tenths of this Honorary Fellowship stuff was pompous nonsense, anyway. Unfortunately he knew it, and a good many other things, with a nervous intensity which would be more appealing if he didn't seek to dissimulate it behind a pedantic manner. The patient instructiveness of an impregnably well-informed governess—which was the effect towards which Powdermaker gravitated—would never carry the Governing Body in an affair like this.

"I am very sorry. I fear I must stupidly have missed the argument. Am I to understand, Provost, that Sir Hector Madrona is, in fact, recommended to us as a person of high distinction in the arts? To me, I own, your remarks seemed to establish merely that he deserved well of them."

Somewhere down the table somebody sighed heavily.

"But isn't it abundantly clear," Keith Pratling asked, "that what you have said, Provost, bears directly upon the real point at issue? If Sir Hector works in the interest of the arts, that is one aspect of his service to the public life of the country. Or am I wrong?" Pratling looked whimsically round his colleagues. Inviting them to see this or that as abundantly clear was his favourite formula for asserting his role as one indolently and effortlessly perspicacious.

"Mr Pratling," Powdermaker said, "very kindly returns me to my original question. Did the committee, in fact, carefully

95

consider what may be held to constitute high distinction in public life?"

"Yes. It did." Littlejohn snapped this out with a sudden change of manner which achieved its object of disconcerting Powdermaker for a moment. But the young man held on. Only the effect of the precariously corked bottle increased—as did his air of anxious reason directed towards persons of kindergarten age.

"Then, Provost, I must own to being surprised. Granted that Sir Hector Madrona is an old member. Granted that he has been, in various ways, whether appropriate or inappropriate, a generous old member. Granted that he is an important and successful person, as the world commonly reckons these things. Granted all this—must we not yet ask : Have we really got anywhere towards vindicating him as a man of high distinction in public life, at least as public life ought to be conceived here, and by us? Eminence in politics or government, or long and distinguished office in the highest reaches of the Civil Service, are surely types of the sort of thing we have in mind. Sir Hector Madrona, so far as my information goes—and I am open to correction, Provost, I need hardly say—Sir Hector Madrona is merely a successful industrialist. I would not wish to be thought to speak in a dyslogistic sense—"

Again the heavy sigh was heard from down the table. Powdermaker flushed as he heard it.

"I mean that I am far from disparaging industrialists. I am prepared to admire them. But I don't see them as self-evidently eligible as Honorary Fellows of the college."

"Quite right!"

Everybody turned in surprise. For it was old Fitch who had spoken. He had actually raised his pen from his writing paper. He had done this to point it at Powdermaker across the table.

"Quite right!" Fitch repeated. "Madrona? I can't say I've never heard of him. He was an undergraduate when I was Junior Dean. But I don't recall him as belonging to any of the clubs. I don't recall him as even successfully tagging on to any particular set. So I agree with that young man." Fitch was still pointing his pen at Powdermaker; he had long since ceased to know the names of most of his colleagues. "These Levantine persons have been infiltrating all over the place. Into parliament, into the hunting field, into the manor. To my mind, the late monarch was largely responsible. Let us hear no more of this Madrona."

There was a moment's silence. Some of the older Fellows realized that by "the late monarch" Fitch undoubtedly meant King Edward the Seventh. And Fitch had now returned to his correspondence.

Littlejohn produced a strained smile. He was known to be allergic to Fitch's senilities. "I am bound to point out," he said, "that Professor Fitch's reference to Levantine persons has no sort of appositeness. I must presume that it is directed at Sir Hector. Sir Hector, in point of fact, is of Italian extraction. His family—although this is utterly irrelevant—was, I believe, a distinguished Neapolitan one."

"Wop or Wog, Provost—what does it matter?" A red-faced man at the far end of the table bellowed out these startling words. "Isn't it the fact that this fellow is damn well off? Let's have him in, I say, and get on to other matters. We can do with anyone who's up to his ears in the lolly."

Littlejohn tapped his teeth with his pencil. Numerous members of the Governing Body looked down their noses. This on the part of their Estates Bursar Basil Applegarth—a former rowing Blue—was a tolerated turn. Nobody really liked it. And it gave Powdermaker, as he thought, a chance to pounce.

"Precisely!" he said. "Our Bursar, with his customary acumen, has penetrated to the heart of the matter. I wish I could believe that the committee had been as genuinely persuaded of Sir Hector Madrona's public distinction as they were indubitably apprised of his impressive prosperity."

Leech tried to catch Bruce Powdermaker's eye for the purpose of giving him a stony stare. For the young man had certainly made a false step. To bellow out the slang of undergraduates, as Applegarth had done, or to put on a phoney Old Guard charade like Fitch : these were held innocent, if tiresome, eccentricities. But openly and at a formal meeting to accuse a committee of something like corporate venality didn't do at all. Powdermaker's stock would be low for a long time. His utility—his utility to Leech in crucial matters when they came along—had been halved by a single speech.

97

The election of Madrona went forward. It was proposed and seconded. Powdermaker, fighting on, proposed an amendment to the effect that the whole question of any election to an Honorary Fellowship at this time be referred back to the committee. Littlejohn, having taken courteous note of the precise terms of this, looked round for a seconding voice. Nobody spoke. Leech's supporters glanced at him cautiously. Powdermaker looked at him in open hurt and indignation. Leech moved no muscle. You reinforce success, not failure. The substantive motion was put. Powdermaker, coming to his senses, did no more than abstain. So Madrona was elected *nem. con.* Nobody was surprised to remark that Professor Fitch had paid no further attention to the proceedings.

The afternoon wore on. Across the curve of the great terrestrial globe standing in a window embrasure there crept a shadow as of advancing night. From some suburban distance the voices of young men could be faintly heard, shouting or cheering. Nearer at hand, just beyond the olive-wood doors of the Old Library, a pleasant chinking told that the tea equipage of the Provost and Fellows was being set out by the careful hands of female servants. Professor Fitch, having finished a letter, picked up an envelope and addressed it. There was a theory that all Fitch's letters were directed to Buckingham Palace—and the colleague sitting next to him, perhaps for the purpose of settling a wager, was trying to check on this now. But as Fitch never addressed an envelope except beneath a tent-like structure ingeniously contrived out of the sleeve of his gown, the attempt was unsuccessful. The college, dealing with Item Twenty-one on its agenda while in fact concentrating upon this comedy, somewhat unnoticingly sold a couple of farms and invested the proceeds in the manufacture of certain common objects of domestic utility. It was all nearly over.

"Number Twenty-two," Littlejohn said. "Report of the Committee on Additional Accommodation. As members of the Governing Body will have noticed, there is no printed report. The committee wishes merely to report progress, and hopes to bring definite plans—together with drawings and a model—before the next meeting.

Now Leech spoke for the first time. His exclusion from this particular committee had been one of Littlejohn's most striking improprieties. Leech therefore had to be careful to begin on a note of not much more than casual interest.

"Does this not mean," he asked, "that we shall be a little rushed in the final stages? Perhaps I got it wrong, but I thought the architects had everything buttoned up." On these occasions Leech's idiom was apt to be as self-consciously colloquial as Powdermaker's was pedantic. "The only trouble seemed to be that the site and the money were both a bit tight. May we know if anything else has blown up?"

"One or two matters have had to be referred back to the architects." Littlejohn, all candour and courtesy, glanced at the Library clock. It had been going since the year 1708, and must have assisted at many such nice calculations as the present one. "Shall I enter into them, Pro-Provost? The hour is growing rather late."

A smell of buttered bun at this moment came through the doors of the Old Library. It made no appeal to Leech, who believed that the imbibing of afternoon tea was proper among vigorously exercising undergraduates, but ought thereafter to be confined to old women. Old women, however—according to his definition of the term—now surrounded him. One of these—the man given to sighing heavily—was sighing now.

"Perhaps," Leech said, "we might have this important matter —as it certainly is—rather early on, next time?"

"Thank you. I am most grateful for that suggestion." Littlejohn made a brisk scrawl with his pencil. "Below the line, number Twenty-three. Question of a possible Bequest. I must apologise to the Governing Body for something not wholly accurate here. I hope I may be forgiven." Littlejohn, who was a man in vigorous middle life, looked round the meeting with just the faintest suggestion of helpless age. He had a flair, Leech reflected, for these cosy pantomime gestures. They were meant to endear, and they did, which was enough in itself, Leech judged, to set humanity in a sombre view. "Or rather," Littlejohn was saying, "this is incomplete. There *is* a question of a possible bequest. But there is also the offer of an immediate gift. Both are from the same individual, one of our Honorary Fellows."

The Governing Body woke up. Most of its members looked surprised, and because of this Keith Pratling's face took on an expression of fulfilled expectation. "It being self-evident,"

Pratling said, "that the Honorary Fellow in question is Sir Hector Madrona?"

"I don't know about self-evidence." Littlejohn was urbanely amused. "But it is certainly Sir Hector who is offering us a gift, and who has also advanced the possibility of a bequest only a little later on."

"Good show, Provost!" The red-faced Applegarth produced this in his customary tow-path shout. And he looked cheerfully round his colleagues. "Quick work, eh?"

This time there was effort in Littlejohn's smile. "I fear the Bursar—" he began.

"Provost!" Powdermaker had interrupted on a note of agitation which was almost a squeak. But he quickly caught his usual patient note. "It must be admitted that our Bursar has again touched the heart of the matter, although I cannot believe that his tone very faithfully reflects the feeling of some of us. For here, surely, we are confronted by a strange, an excessively strange, concurrence of phenomena. Is it possible—is it, I ask myself, conceivable—that any member of the Governing Body could have divulged to Sir Hector Madrona a matter so utterly confidential as that of our proposing to debate the electing of him into an Honorary Fellowship? Could there even have been—I hesitate before expressing myself perhaps brutally—some faintly hinted, utterly unspoken ghost of a *bargain*—"

Littlejohn raised a hand. It was a thing he did so seldom that Powdermaker, disconcerted, stopped at once.

"May I interrupt—simply to save Mr Powdermaker from embarking on unnecessary speculation, which might even prove embarrassing to him? There is, of course, a point of delicacy involved in the business before us. The offers which I shall presently describe were made to me by Sir Hector, verbally and informally, a few weeks after some of us here had begun to consider—on our own part verbally and informally—the possible propriety of doing Sir Hector the honour which we have in fact done him this afternoon. I can assure the Governing Body that, so far as I know, neither of these discussions or proposals has stood in any relation of cause or effect to the other. They have been purely coincidental. Nevertheless, as I hope the Governing Body will realize, the coincidence has put me in a position of some difficulty. I felt strongly that our electing Sir Hector, if we did elect him, should be demonstrably an act of general recognition, and not have the appearance of an act of specific gratitude for what would be, in a cold light, merely a rich man's putting his hand in his pocket."

"Hear! hear!" The Fellow who had so far contributed only two heavy sighs to the afternoon's proceedings produced this vociferation with surprising vigour.

"It appeared to me highly desirable, therefore, that the Governing Body should proceed with the proposed election while yet unapprised of Sir Hector's intended benefactions. When in due course I should inform Sir Hector that this had been the state of the case, I hoped that he would regard it as a matter for enhanced gratification. And that is the reason why I arranged today's agenda paper as I did. If I acted wrongly—and perhaps Mr Powdermaker would like to address the Governing Body in the interest of that contention—I am, of course, very ready to accept the Governing Body's rebuke."

Murmurs of deprecation and commendation broke out all round the table. There was nothing these people relished more—Leech reflected—than the feeling that they had acted, or had somebody act on their behalf, in a highly correct and edifying manner. Heaven alone knew what had actually passed between Littlejohn and this fellow Madrona. But a ticklish piece of business was ending—largely thanks to Powdermaker's repeated clumsiness—with the Littlejohn faction cock-a-hoop.

"I observe," Leech said, "that we are all in a rosy glow. Would it now be possible, Provost, to switch for a moment to the cold light you spoke of, and hear just what this rich man is fishing out of his pocket for us?"

"Certainly." Littlejohn stroked his chin, which was his habit when he felt that a good thing was coming from him. "The answer, in the first place, Pro-Provost, is coins. So you see our figure of speech is a wholly apposite one. Sir Hector's late father was a keen, if amateur, numismatist. His collection is extremely comprehensive. Dr Bunter of the Ashmolean Museum tells me that, for some of the Hellenistic kingdoms, it is the finest that has ever been formed. It is also peculiarly rich in medals of the *cinquecento* and the *seicento*."

There was an impressed silence.

"And this is to come to us at once?" Pratling asked.

"Certainly—subject only to certain arrangements about housing, display, insurance, and so forth."

"Display?" Leech was on top of this in a moment. "Surely the Ashmolean itself is the right recipient of any collection of antiquities which it is desired to display publicly?"

"I agree that the coins and medals might very properly go to the Ashmolean. I have little doubt that the Ashmolean would be very glad to have them. But the position is quite simple. Sir Hector Madrona is an old member of this college, and he wants the things to come here."

"We are to sterilise space in order to set up some rather large coin room?"

"I appreciate what is in your mind, Pro-Provost. But there is no question of alienating space from its proper academic purposes as I understand you to conceive them. I am assured that the Madrona Collection will be of great utility to our own undergraduates in their classical and historical studies."

"Thank you." Leech always gave up a weak point at once. "And may we now know about Sir Hector's further intentions?"

"They are even more munificent. He wishes to donate to us—and within the next two years, if possible—his own collection of modern paintings."

"Modern paintings?" Professor Fitch addressed another envelope. "Turner and Constable and people like that?"

"More modern than that, by some way. It is, in fact, preponderantly contemporary. And, although not extensive, it is probably the most valuable collection of its kind in England today."

There would certainly have been another impressed silence, had not Leech spoken at once. "May we know," he asked, "what is meant by 'not extensive'?"

"At present I understand that there are about sixty paintings. But they are without exception superb."

"Surely such things now change hand for fantastic sums of money? If sixty of them are to be scattered about the college, the problem of security will be a very grave one. And there could be no question of insuring them, unless there were an endowment with them for that specific purpose. You may remember, Provost, that Provost Gilstrap ran into some difficulty there when we accepted the large aesthetic object now gracing the great staircase. The Tresilian was said to be worth several thousand pounds—whether hung one way up or the other. Perhaps, Provost, you could satisfy my reserves on these points?"

"There would be no difficulty about insurance. The endowment would be there. As a matter of fact, it would cover more than insurance. It would cover the emoluments of a Curator at about Fellowship level. What I have in mind is a Research Fellowship in Fine Art, tenable for five or ten years, and carrying with it the duties of Curatorship."

"This hopeful young scholar would come prowling round to make sure that none of us had flogged any of the pictures?"

"There would be no question, Pro-Provost, of prowling round. The pictures would not, in fact, be dispersed about the college. Sir Hector would insist that they should be permanently housed together. And he would put up the money for a suitable building. I cannot stress too strongly how much he is prepared to do for us. There will not be the slightest question of our having to divert any of our own resources to purposes which, in a narrow view, do not further learning, education, or piety." Littlejohn smiled as cordially as if in "narrow view" there had been no intended barb whatever. "Perhaps I have said enough to make the position clear in a preliminary way? Sir Hector's formal offer will no doubt reach me in time to be placed before you at our next meeting. And now, as the hour is somewhat advanced—"

"Does it come to this"—Leech had no intention of seeing the meeting closed at a point where Littlejohn had been making all the running—"that the coins and so on come to us more or less unconditionally and immediately, but that for the pictures we have to negotiate the putting up of a building and even the creating of a fancy Fellowship?"

"I must take a little exception to the term 'fancy Fellowship'. Otherwise, that is the position, more or less. And now, I think we may—"

"Perhaps, Provost, before we break up, you will give us some idea of where this monstrous white elephant is to be accommodated?"

"That, of course, must be thought of. But, no doubt, a way will be found for availing ourselves of Sir Hector's princely offer."

"If this building is to go up, it is clear that another must come down to make way for it. I am inclined to suggest it be the Provost's Lodging."

"But *must* something come down?" With a great air of moving tactfully in to smooth over the quarrelling of children, Keith Pratling broke a startled silence with this question. "We have a committee in being for the purpose of planning to build under-graduate sets on our one remaining site. Earlier this afternoon, we were told that this committee had found it necessary to refer certain matters back to the architects. Isn't it sufficiently obvious what that means? Wouldn't the Pro-Provost, if calmed and re-collected, see the point? Provost, is it terribly indiscreet to ask whether the Committee on Additional Accommodation has been entirely in the dark about the proposals of Sir Hector Madrona? Is it in fact seeking to modify—or perhaps even to curtail—its plans for undergraduate quarters in the interest of the great Madrona pachyderm? Or oughtn't I to inquire? Have I even let the elephant out of the bag?"

Littlejohn stood up, reached for his square, and planted it firmly on his head. "We can't possibly," he said, "go back to the affairs of the Committee on Additional Accommodation now. It would be most irregular. I declare the meeting closed."

CHAPTER FOURTEEN

Hatty Landreth, running down Luke Tresilian's staircase with Luke behind her, stopped at a window. "What a lot of dons!" she said. "And all in gowns. They look like crows. Or vergers. Or mutes. Hired mourners, I mean. Some countries have them still. Are they going off to give lectures?"

Luke stood beside her. This had all happened quickly. He had been giving a lot of thought—you might say a lot of fantasy—to meeting this girl when he went to stay with the unknown Landreths at the end of term. And suddenly Bruno Landreth had banged on his door and tumbled Hatty in on him. She had come up for the day with her mother. But her mother had some function to attend at which Hatty would be a nuisance, and Bruno had an essay to write for his tutorial next morning. So Luke was to take charge of Hatty, and make what he could of her.

"They're coming away from a meeting," Luke said. "But only after they've had an enormous tea."

"A meeting? What do they talk about? Is it marks and examinations and things?"

"I don't think it has anything to do with us—with undergraduates, I mean. They have a world of their own."

"They look as if they had. And they look as if they'd been quarrelling in it."

"Probably over whether to buy another pipe, or something like that."

"Another pipe? Would they quarrel over as small a thing as *that*?"

"Not that sort of pipe." Luke blushed, and shifted his weight from one long leg to the other. "The sort of pipe that is an enormous barrel of port. They buy enormous barrels of port, and" —casting round in his mind for something else they might buy, he was assisted by memories of Edgar Allan Poe— "and casks of Amontillado."

"Who's the one that's scowling?"

"That's Leech, the Pro-Provost. He's my moral tutor."

"Doesn't he look grim?"

"Oh, he's all right. He hardly ever sees me. I don't think he regards me as much of an ornament to the place—or even feels that I should have got in."

"He must be a stupid old man."

"I don't think he's that." Luke was alarmed rather than flattered by the vehemence with which Hatty had spoken. "He's the one who wants to push up the intellectual standards of the college. He thinks it's gone all social and arty under this Provost and the last one."

"He wants more Firsts in Schools, and that sort of thing? But that's all rubbish. Bruno says no decent writer has got a First in English since Aldous Huxley. You're going to write, aren't you?"

"To write?" Luke, who was having difficulty in remaining collected in Hatty's company anyway, was thrown into entire confusion by this. "Why should you think that?"

"You say you're not going to be a painter, and that you can only listen to music. So you must be a writer, mustn't you?" Hatty seemed unaware of anything odd in this logic. "There's somebody coming upstairs."

"It's Leech. His rooms are on the first floor."

"Then let's hurry down. You must introduce him to me."

Luke was equally staggered by the substance and the form of this command. But as Hatty was already running down the next flight of stairs there was nothing for it but to follow. And there was Leech, looking even more severe than usual, and just unlocking the door of his rooms. "Sir," Luke said, all on a breath, "may I introduce you to Bruno Landreth's sister?"

At least Leech didn't look surprised. He shook hands as gravely as if Hatty had been the wife of the Vice-Chancellor. "I am delighted to meet a sister," he said with a bleak smile. "It recalls my own undergraduate days. The men still had sisters then, and the sisters still came up to visit—and, having visited, went down again. We all took pleasure in the irruptions. Nowadays, ladies encountered in college are seldom anybody's sister, and seldom about to catch a train. Tresilian, have you a sister of your own?"

"No, sir—or only a much older half-sister."

"Then Miss Landreth supplies the other half." As if disliking this pleasantry as he uttered it, Leech paused, frowning. "And how," he asked in a different voice, "is that rather elementary Latin getting on?"

"Not too badly, sir. But it's a little elusive."

"H'm. You will be well advised to trust in God—and take your hands out of your trouser-pockets. Good afternoon."

With a bow to Hatty, Leech disappeared into his rooms. Luke had flushed scarlet. "But I didn't!" he said. "I didn't *have* my hands in my trouser-pockets!"

"Neither this one nor the other one." With a swift movement, Hatty had taken hold of Luke's right hand. She didn't let go as they went down the last flight of stairs. "But you got it wrong. He didn't mean it the way you think. I don't think he *is* a stupid old man. It's just that he's awkward. And so are you." She smiled at him with a mixed mockery and warmth that made him slightly dizzy. "It was some college joke that he expected you to know about. Something that some old Provost said to somebody long ago. Don't you have to pass an exam in all the folklore of the college soon after you arrive?"

"Of course not." Luke was amused.

"Perhaps that's only at schools. They do at Eton. It's called a Colours Test. And at Winchester, where it's Notions. They—"

She had broken off. Glancing at her, he saw that she was giving a quick bite to her under-lip. He realized that it was because he might be thinking she was parading a snobbish familiarity with the places she had mentioned. He suddenly felt amazingly happy. They were out in the quad, and the day's last sunshine was in the upper branches of the mulberry tree, and they were holding hands still. Oxford was full of young men and women going about holding hands, but it was something that Luke, somehow, hadn't got around to. Now it didn't disturb him that he was doing it with a girl he had first set eyes on a couple of hours before. He was aware of new facts about duration. He saw that there could be aeons within an afternoon.

"Yes," he said, "I expect you're right. Leech was doing his best with some corny college joke."

"And you're wrong, too, about his not thinking much of you. He's rather chilly, just because he thinks rather a lot of you.

He's repressing a kind of protectiveness. Father-substitute stuff."
She looked at him mischievously. "He thinks you're rather vulnerable, Luke."

"Protectiveness . . . vulnerable?" Luke rejected some proposal rising sharply within him to be wounded to the quick by this suggestion. He looked at the girl. She was smiling at him in a way that reminded him of her brother Bruno. But she was smiling at him from below the level of his shoulder, and he saw that she was relying upon the mere evident fact of his young giant's physique to purge what she had said of Bruno's sort of wickedness. "Leech thinks," she went on, "that you should be kept in wood wool, and just unpacked on the rugger field. I mean—"

She had plunged on with this gay speech, but now finished it stumbling, so that he knew the next moment would find her biting her lip again. He remembered that she must be at least a year younger than he was; that she was therefore liable to be painfully clumsy; and that the clumsiness must be much *more* painful just because she was so clever too. Suddenly he felt more protective than Leech could possibly do. They were still holding hands, and now he swung his arm and hers. He felt that, if the sky were really a lid, his scalp would be getting badly scraped. "What would you like to do?" he asked. And then he added : "Hatty?" Doing this made his heart thump. He remembered that, only the night before, he had involved this girl, still unknown, in libidinous reverie. The memory was so horrifying that he dropped her hand abruptly—and just had the presence of mind to move a step backwards, as if it had been his intention to take a challenging look at her. "Where to?" he said.

"To see your father's painting, of course. Mummy will have seen it already. When is the big exhibition?"

"In about a month. Or perhaps six weeks. I've got a card about it." Luke felt this vagueness to be awkward. "I'm always getting dates wrong," he added. "And forgetting tutorials and things." It struck him as he spoke that this wasn't particularly true. In fact he was talking at random. He must sound a clot. But he still felt that quite new sort of happiness.

"Do you remember your father?"

"No, not at all."

"Or your mother?"

"No, she died even earlier. We go through this archway." Luke felt himself mumbling, and going stupider every minute. Hatty's evident determination to get him clear in her head scared him.

"So you don't really know much about your parents?"

"I know some things." He saw her look at him in sharp surprise, and realized that he had spoken in a new voice and unwarily, with a quick passion and pride. "*Your* father died a long time ago too, didn't he?" He didn't have to ask this, because he knew it already from Bruno. And he didn't want to ask it, because he had a shyness about such questions which Hatty Landreth evidently didn't share. He had spoken out of some need of diversion. "Here's the great staircase," he said. "We go halfway up." He was mumbling once more. And he was aware—as he was hardly ever aware—of a probable effect of uncouthness in his lingering West Country accent. "I think you're wonderful," he said.

She looked at him in complete surprise. He was confused at his own words. But, strangely, his perceptions were sharpened, and he saw that her surprise was not at the outrageousness of his speech but at the judgment it had announced. And he had just seen that she had flushed and that her lips were trembling when she turned and was running up the staircase before him. To keep up with her he had to do no more than take long strides on the treads. But he was almost breathless when he came to a halt beside her. It was rather as if he had brought off a touchdown from behind his own twenty-five.

"*That's* wonderful!"

She was breathless too—yet her exclamation, as she gazed at the picture, hadn't at all the effect of a gasp. And he understood that she had somehow bound up in one single experience what he had said to her and her seeing his father's big painting.

"You like it?" he asked. It was something he had never asked anybody before.

"Very much. And I like it *there*. It was a marvellous idea of somebody's."

"It's rather public." Hearing himself say this, Luke was afraid that imbecility was again descending on him.

"You can begin anywhere in it and leave off anywhere. And yet it doesn't leave you where it finds you."

"No . . . I suppose not." He was back with the mumbling. He remembered that Hatty's mother was a professional art critic, so Hatty was no doubt used to a prompt verbalizing of responses to pictures and things. "I'll tell you," he said, "who *doesn't* like it. Leech. I quite often see him standing and glowering at it."

"Leech?" She had to think back. "That don on your staircase? I don't think he'd have feelings about it, one way or another. Not, I mean, as a painting. I was rather sorry for him."

"Sorry for Leech?" This was an idea that Luke found he couldn't at all get hold of.

"He'd had a bad meeting. They'd decided to buy what isn't his sort of port. Invalid, perhaps, instead of Old Tawny." Hatty didn't seem to offer this as a joke. "And then I had that bitchy idea of making you introduce me. And he was very decent but dreadfully awkward—as people seem to be, round about here."

"Yes," Luke said humbly.

"And he made those pitiful cracks about visiting sisters, and so forth. And then he crawled into his rooms, feeling that he just isn't with it. That the young elude him."

"I see." It struck Luke that he had to *do* something, if he was going to stand up to so much swift clarity on the part of this girl that he so much wanted as his. "You do seem to be in the know," he said.

"What do you mean—the know?" She was bright-eyed and indignant.

"A Socrates in pig-tails—that's you." As he said this, he made a grab at the hand he had so ineptly relinquished in the quad. This movement ought to have been the crowning clumsiness of the afternoon. But unexpected rewards attend the frequentation of the football field, and the operation went as neatly as if he were gathering the ball from the heels of a rapidly wheeling scrum. "Let's do a Meadow," he said. "There's time. Then we have sherry till your mother gets back. And then you catch the train that Leech so much approves of. The train that takes all one's friends' sisters safely back to London."

For an instant she hesitated, so that he realized that here was a point of crisis. She had said he was vulnerable, and he had fought a battle in a moment. He had said that about pig-tails, and she was doing just the same thing. And suddenly she squeezed his hand—his great ham of a hand, as he suddenly felt it to be—in an entirely juvenile manner. "Yes, please," she said. "I don't know what doing a Meadow is, but let's do it."

They went down the Broad Walk. A straggle of rowing men

was coming up from the barges, some amorphous in track suits, others all naked limbs and enormous scarves. Hatty observed them with interest. "Does Bruno do anything like that?" she asked.

"Good Lord, no!" The idea of Bruno Landreth as any sort of rowing hearty amused Luke.

"Do you like him much?"

"Yes, of course." Luke found the question disconcerting. "But perhaps I'm chiefly in awe of him. He's very senior to me. He wouldn't even have rooms in college any more, if he hadn't got himself elected secretary of the J.C.R."

"How did he manage that?"

"Not by doing anything in an athletic way. Just by going round and being agreeable."

"Being agreeable?" Hatty seemed to find this explanation surprising. "Of course I know he's senior to you. He calls you his young rugger tough."

"That's just what I am." Luke felt that this was a fair return for Socrates. "Bruno says that he's anxious to bring me forward."

"Bruno says things like that. He's rather foul, really. But I oughtn't to pan him—because I am, too. The two of us have always been tied up together. We're rather a tiresome couple, as a matter of fact. It's a good thing that Mummy has Lucilla. Lucilla's normal."

For a moment Luke said nothing. He was discovering in himself a feeling which—absurdly enough—could only be jealousy. He scarcely thought of himself as having a family. And he saw that, if you do have a family, you are not merely part of it but it is very much part of you. Some part of what he had come (in two hours) to think of as Hatty Landreth *was* Hatty's relationship with Bruno, and with a mother and sister he hadn't yet met. Subtract one of these people, and Hatty would be different. "Look," he said, "if we go over this bridge, you can see the new boat-houses. And we've just got time."

They crossed the little humpy bridge and walked in silence. He had a sudden acute—and surely reasonable—fear that he had been imagining things; that this was an entirely casual occasion, in which he was simply helping a visitor to fill in time; and that all that would ever happen again would be a second encounter, almost equally casual, when he spent perhaps a couple of nights with the Landreths in passing through London. And in London, of course, Hatty Landreth must have a host of friends. She would scarcely notice him.

They were walking past the boat-houses—undistinguished structures subserving a moronic activity. But she probably thought that, as just another type of athletic moron, he was calling on her to admire them. Recklessly, helplessly, Luke plunged into speech.

"About writing—how did you know? Bruno doesn't know. I've never told anybody. Probably it's all nonsense. Probably twenty other people in my college think they're going to be poets and novelists. I want it to be a secret for a long time. I haven't even tried to get into *Isis*. . . . But you *knew*."

"I didn't, really. It was just—" She checked herself. "But tell me what you're writing now."

He hesitated. She might still be a schoolgirl, but she was growing up into a society in which people were perpetually chattering to each other about what they were writing or painting or composing. They did it—Luke knew—at cocktail parties, shouting and screaming to make themselves heard above the din. So now she was just putting on a social turn. And he couldn't respond to it. He had made a dreadful mistake in this rash bid for intimacy. He found that he was standing still, tongue-tied, staring stupidly at the empty river.

"Tell me!"

Her tone was vehement, imperious—so that he turned and, looking at her quickly, saw that he had been entirely wrong. Social chit-chat was out. It was so much out that he remained as helplessly dumb as before. And she waited only a second without herself tumbling into speech again.

"Have you read Lawrence's *Sons and Lovers*?"

He looked at her in bewilderment. "Yes—in the last vac."

"I think you're just like Paul Morel."

It was unexpected and—in this first moment—extremely comical. Fortunately he was too astonished to laugh, and in a second moment he had seen there was nothing to laugh about. For one thing, Hatty's announcement had been essentially a child's, so that he had again to face the fact of her being very young indeed. But more disconcerting was the obvious truth that he wasn't at all like Paul Morel. Hatty, to the extent that she believed he was, was imagining a Luke Tresilian who didn't exist, who was as imaginary as the fabulous creatures—griffins, he supposed they must be—on the coat of arms on the boat-house by which they had halted. He saw that, with a terrifying abruptness and unexpectedness, the afternoon was introducing him to things he had never before given a thought to. He saw that two people falling in love might each be falling in love with somebody who wasn't really there. Ever so neatly as you collared the ball when it came to you, it might be no more than a phantom ball that you carried triumphantly up the field. When they said love was a tragic thing they didn't necessarily mean deserted queens in caves or heroes compelled to seek another shore. They meant that it had its birth in illusion, and disenchantment as its end.

And now he did laugh, taking both her hands as he did so. "What nonsense!" he said. "Nobody is like anybody in a book. Nobody wants to be. You wouldn't like me to see you as something out of *Wuthering Heights*, would you?" He waited in suspense, but quite certain that illusion ought to be tackled head on. "You wouldn't want me," he added, "to mix up Cathie and Hatty, surely?"

For good or ill, he saw that he had taken her with unexpected precision at the knees. If there had been turf under them Hatty Landreth would be sprawled on it. The image wasn't elegant, but it was accurate. He remembered some sage contemporary assuring him that women, in a fashion almost unknown to men, bring themselves up on day-dreams fed by books. Catherine Earnshaw had been very much in Hatty's dream. She was looking at him in a shaken sort of way. He realized—with inexpressible joy—that for her the afternoon was perhaps as bewildering and alarming as it was for him.

"Listen," he said. For he realized that he had to go on talking; that he had to establish something real in place of this shattered fantasy. "Your Paul Morel was going to be a painter and a genius, which I'm not. His background was straight working class, which mine isn't. But these things were true of my father, as you probably know. That's what put Paul Morel in your head. *And* Paul was all messed up with a mother when he ought to have been making a decent lover for what's-her-name."

"Miriam."

"Yes, Miriam. My mother died when I was just eighteen months. So at least I haven't got a complex of that sort." Without calculation, yet as he had seen others do, Luke, walking with Hatty on his right side, took her right elbow in his right hand. And he saw why people did it; it was a very good way of walking along. "When Paul was small," he went on, "he hung around with the girls. When he grew older he had that tremendous flame of genius, and so on. But he was a bit weedy, wasn't he? And he was seduced by a married woman, and then went out of his way—that's how I remember it—to let her husband beat him up. Then he got all chummy with the husband." He turned his face to her, laughing. "I just don't see myself having a destiny like that."

"No—I suppose not." Hatty was subdued and, again, childish. But he felt, with the same strange joy he had felt before, that there was fight in her and that there were whole battlefields before them. And a flash came from her now. "Do you mean," she asked, "that you're not even Matthew Tresilian's son, not an artist, just another muddied oaf at the goal?"

"I'm Matthew Tresilian's son, all right." He laughed at her again—for confidence and happiness were taking great strides in him. "I don't know about being an artist. I'd like to write. It's fun. But I think it will depend on whether enough happens to me. I don't want to be a little man cooking things up."

"I know *them*." Hatty spoke with her quick vehemence. "They come about our house. Mummy has to see a lot of them. But she doesn't like them. She admires about three living writers and three living painters. The people she really gets on with are professors and scholars. She'd be happy in Oxford."

Luke felt that the relevance of this was, in part, of a submerged kind. "Will she like me?" he asked.

"Yes, she will." Hatty paused. "She might like you quite a lot."

The words were harmless. But beneath them there sounded something so artless—it was a naïve and primitive jealousy—that Luke was overthrown entirely. They had reached the head of the Broad Walk again, and the hundred Gothic windows of Christ Church's queer Meadow Building were poised above them. So it was an odd place to do what he did. He swung round, he swung Hatty round, and he kissed her. She drew her head back, but didn't draw herself out of his arms. She kissed him swiftly in return. And then she did break away. They stood staring at each other, very much astonished.

"Turn right . . . this way." Luke was reduced yet again to shameful mumbling. "We can get out by a place called Rose Lane." He said "get out" as if the two of them had fallen into some dire trap together. "We're rather late, I suppose."

"Are we? I'd have thought our pace was pretty good." Hatty on her part was far from mumbling. Her voice had risen so that it reached a couple of old men sitting on a bench and feeding the squirrels. "Romeo and Juliet themselves didn't make anything like it."

"First Paul Morel and then Romeo Montague! You do have a booksy mind. It's not what these things are for: dreaming yourself into. Imagination—the artist's thing—is magic, you know. You mustn't exploit it, you mustn't even explore it, in the wrong way. Weave your circle thrice, and stick to holy dread." Struggling with something which, this time, he had thought about, Luke's voice too rang out sharply—so that neither Hatty nor the old men and the squirrels, but rather persons invisible, might have been his auditors. "And now I want to know things about *you*."

"One at a time. We finish with Luke Tresilian first." Hatty was walking with her hand once more in his, and only a heightened colour spoke in her of their incredible act. "Do you feel that you're like the other people here? Or do you feel that you're different?"

The question was again something coming from a child. But it had a child's cogency. "Whichever you like," Luke said cheerfully.

"No—I want to know."

"I mean that I can sometimes feel the one, and sometimes the other. Most people do, I expect."

"Do you feel that what moves about visibly among all those dons and undergraduates is just the tip of an iceberg, and that underneath there's a perfectly enormous other you?"

Luke laughed. He thought this a highly romantic notion, and that he had better respond to it by talking careful sense.

"What you're really trying to get at," he said, "is whether there's much to me. Perhaps you should ask my tutor." He swung Hatty's arm by way of taking any bite out of this. "But I can tell you just what he'd say. He'd say I'm the kind of boy who comes up to Oxford and finds his level. That's what he said to *me*, after I'd been here a week. 'You'll be out of your depth at first,' he said, 'but you'll find your level.' It was a mixed-up image, but what they call kindly meant. A boy up from a dim school, where he's quite shone, and so come to the mistaken conclusion that he's unusually clever. At Oxford he meets his really high-powered contemporaries, and finds out his mistake. It's upsetting. But if he takes it well, the place will decide he's a nice chap, provide him with a reasonable degree, and write him a chit recommending him for honest employment when he goes down."

"How filthy! Don't you think Oxford filthy? I have—ever since Bruno began talking about it."

"Oh, no!" Luke was distressed that he should be supposed to have sounded a complaining note. "I like it. I like it quite terrifically."

"After having found your level?" This time, Hatty spoke mockingly, as if continuing to feel that he was showing a poor spirit. "Or haven't you yet?"

"Well, again, it's sometimes the one thing and sometimes the other. It's true that I just haven't got the brains of the people who get effortless Firsts, and so on. Nothing like. I'm not good at working things out in any sort of logical way. I can follow abstract things a little : the sort of stuff people talk who are reading philosophy. But it's all gone vague in my head next morning. And I'm no good at debating topics with dons. I lose the thread. I can see them looking patient and encouraging."

"It doesn't sound as if it worries you." Hatty's continued to be a critical note.

"Oh, no. I hope it wouldn't, even if it was the whole picture. But I don't feel that it is. I don't honestly feel I do quite belong with the simplest chaps. It may be that I imagine things, just because my father was a great artist. But I don't think so. I have a kind of instinct for feeling on a level—" Luke broke off. "I'm talking awful rot," he said.

"No, you're not. You mean you believe you can do as well as the brainiest people in the place."

"Well, yes—that's it. It sounds just plain arrogant. And I've never said it to anybody before. But I'll be any good only in my own way, which isn't theirs a bit. It's queer. Either I have to be quite alone, and moping and brooding around like an absolute moron. Or I have to be suddenly and tremendously excited. And then something slides off my mind like a lid, and off I go."

"On paper, you mean?"

"Yes, on my typewriter—in a kind of trance, for hours."

"And that's being a writer." Hatty was now triumphant.

"Oh, no—it isn't. I used to think it was. But it's not. It's only a basis. I used to think a writer worked like that—*in furore*, as they say—and then used what wits he had to polish and tidy up afterwards. But I've decided it's not nearly so simple as that. There has to be a balancing intellectual activity *all the time*." Luke was aware of himself as comically solemn. But he didn't falter. "So I just don't know whether I have what it takes. I *can't* know yet. And I tell nobody these things." He paused, staring at Hatty almost in blank surprise. "*Nobody*. You see?"

"You haven't told anybody yet. Not just *anybody*, I mean. Only me."

They were in the High, and at a crowded hour. But he halted on the pavement and took both her hands again. "This is awfully strange," he said.

She nodded, large-eyed, and with parted lips. "It's out of the blue," she said.

He knew that, without at all knowing it, Hatty was not, in this, speaking the truth. Irruptions of such knowledge were, after all, simply among the inconveniences of having the kind of mind he had been describing : an unreliable but sporadically intuitive instrument. He had been like Paul Morel for Hatty Landreth long before she had set eyes on him. She was a schoolgirl—to put it coldly—who had made a day-trip to Oxford with the expectation of discovering romantic feelings about the son of Matthew Tresilian. But that, in a way, was for Luke Tresilian all in the day's work.

Every now and then, he had noticed, the father of whom he preserved no recollection was a factor in the particular sort of relationship which people struck up with him. It was like that— still at this moment it was like that—with Hatty. This made what was between them fragile if not tenuous. But as Hatty in her own simple identity—and certainly not as anybody's daughter or sister—had somehow in a brief afternoon transformed herself from a nocturnal figment to a real person pulverising every defence he possessed, it was simply up to him to cope. *He* had to become a real person to *her*. And he was sure he could do it. He had a genuine self to offer. It is one of the few advantages of having an instinct for story-telling that one can shed some of one's own falsities into the queer sort of truth that fiction is. If one is lucky, something tolerably honest is left behind.

"No," he said, "it isn't quite out of the blue, really. Before we met, I was imagining things about you."

"Tell me," she said eagerly.

"No, I certainly won't tell you. I was just being silly. But you were doing some imagining about me, too. And even if what you imagined was accurate, it isn't the whole story. Your idea of me has been like the trailer, not the whole film. And the trailer can be quite glamorous, and the whole film quite boring. For goodness' sake forget about the heir of genius, and the young writer business, and so on. Love me for myself alone, and not my yellow hair."

She looked quickly up at his head, nearly a foot above hers, and this misguidedly literal way of receiving his words set them both laughing. "That was a quotation," she said triumphantly. "So who's being booksy now?"

"All right. It was. But I don't even know yet what put into your head this business of my trying to write."

"It was Bruno. Bruno *does* have a notion of it, whether you've told him or not. He said something about your having a drawer with poems in it. And, of course, I saw."

"Saw?" Luke glanced at Hatty sharply.

"When we were coming out of your room. You tried a drawer in your desk, just to make sure it was locked." Hatty returned Luke's glance candidly, happy in her own acuteness of observation. "I'm sure it's a habit: something you do without being aware of it. You'd hate—"

"That's complete nonsense!" Luke had turned on Hatty with a sudden impatient resentment which had them both pale and shaken in an instant. "I'm sorry," he went on. "I'm being idiotic. But there's no writing of mine in that drawer. Anything I write I just shove into a cupboard. Of course I feel rather private about it, but I have the sense to know that nobody is likely to be interested."

"I see," Hatty said. She had flushed now, and she spoke while looking straight ahead of her. "I'm sorry to have been spying."

"Don't *you* be idiotic. You were quite right about what you saw—in a way. I do have that nervous trick with that drawer, although I hardly ever open it. There's something rather important in it. I'll tell you about it"—he hesitated—"one day."

"Thank you very much. I'll count the minutes." They were drifting down the High; somebody shoved his way between and past them; as they came together again he saw that there were tears in her eyes. They were—he told himself with lucidity in the midst of confusion—angry and mortified tears. They ought to be disenchanting. But he looked at her and knew that he was in love. When she spoke again it was to say, "God, I'm an awful little bitch!" And this overthrew him finally.

"You're creating," he said. "The bus drivers are goggling as they judder past. I love you. What's in that drawer is something written by my father. For me. And left sealed up when he died. I was given it when I was sixteen. Nobody knows about it, except some lawyer who handed it over. And now you. You must read it. I want you to. Hatty."

In the High at the moment there were more than juddering buses. There were two enormous lorries loaded with what seemed to be sheet iron. The clangour of these succeeded upon Luke's *staccato* utterance in rather a useful way. When it had faded Hatty was able to say, "Please—I'd like to. But only after you've had a second look. At me, that is." She glanced at him rather wanly. "Luke," she said, "I didn't mean quite all this."

"You've got more than you bargained for, all right." He returned her glance almost grimly. "I promise you that you have."

"All right. But I'm a terrible mess. I've done frightful things." She looked at him tragically—and with heaven knew what, as he clearly saw, childish nonsense in her head. "Luke—isn't life *frightful?*"

"No, it isn't," he said. "And, for you and me, there's one simple and marvellous fact about it. That there's *masses* of it. To go on through. To grow in. To transform and glorify. Hour by hour, for thousands and thousands and thousands of hours. And this is just the second on our clock."

A third lorry went past as Luke Tresilian spoke. It drowned his words. Its object being simply to shunt certain chunks of the physical universe around, it naturally had no regard for the sort of thing he was trying to say.

CHAPTER FIFTEEN

"CHARLES ROSE WAS at the opening," Jane Landreth said. "And he's going back to town on this train."

"Charles Rose?" Hatty asked dreamily. And she added, "Oh, your old flame."

"Yes, my old flame. He was on the platform—but staring carefully into vacancy. He knew he had a first-class ticket in his pocket, and guessed that we had second-class ones. It bothered him."

"So much for old flames."

"Oh, no—Charles is giving the situation careful thought now. In about ten minutes he'll stroll along the corridor, glance through the door, register delighted surprise, and come in and chat."

Hatty made no reply. She was sitting in an unaccustomed stillness in her corner.

"Charles is the next thing to a gentleman of leisure," Jane said. "As for us, we haven't an hour."

"No—we haven't an hour." Hatty had glanced at her mother swiftly, and with the small, secret smile which made her, at times, so like her brother Bruno. "Not an hour," she repeated.

"Paddington at eight-five, home in a ruinous taxi, sardines or the Lord knows what, into whatever clothes those sort of people wear at that sort of party—Lucilla will have an idea—and then off Lucilla and I traipse. And you have home-work. I'm sure you have home-work. It's a hard life."

But Hatty had again lapsed into silence, so that her mother looked at her sharply. The mention of home-work ought to have produced some brief utterance in Bruno's disparaging manner. It had produced only the same secret smile. Nor was Hatty's silence a consequence of the presence of strangers—a circumstance that so often strikes dumb the self-conscious young. Luke Tresilian—a boy whom, as Bruno's latest friend, it had been satisfactory so quickly to approve—had found them a compartment to themselves. He had, indeed, been ingenuously surprised that they were travelling second, so that Jane had to suspect Bruno of feeding him with a most inaccurate notion of the metropolitan grandeur of the Landreths. But Luke had acted promptly in getting them thus comfortably accommodated. In fact he had acted, Jane reflected nostalgically, rather as male undergraduates used to act on that particular railway platform long ago, and as they had now noticeably ceased to do. There was, of course, a special reason for this, a reason that her mere ten minutes' glimpse of him—of Hatty and him—at the station had been sufficient to make clear. But he would be a decent lad in any circumstances.

"Did you like Luke Tresilian?" Jane asked. "Was he a satis-factory young man to be handed over to for the afternoon?"

"He's quite nice."

Jane checked an impulse of annoyance by reflecting, very justly, that her question had been as disingenuous as Hatty's answer. She had known very well that Hatty had accompanied her on this expedition to Oxford because she had formed a romantic notion of the unknown Luke Tresilian. She now knew equally well that—against reasonable probability—there had been a rapid and substantial sequel to this mere impulse of fancy. No more than two or three hours had passed, and here she was with what looked like a full-scale boy-and-girl affair on her hands. It was just one more thing, and might well call for tactful handling over a period of weeks or even months. Hatty's "A" levels were coming along. She must be coaxed across those fate-ful stepping-stones to the higher education. She must be got into a university. She must "qualify", as they said, to earn a living in some way. If one was a parent and penniless, it was irresponsible to admit any other thought. For husbands of the most reliable-seeming order were constantly being killed on mountains, drowned in lakes, incinerated in jets, seduced by secretaries, even stricken with disabling non-lethal diseases. That every woman ought to be equipped to earn her keep was some-thing which after all Jane had learned in a pretty hard school herself. But once let a young girl become seriously—

Jane pulled herself up. Here was morbid anxiety again, that occupational hazard of widows.

"Yes," she said, "I thought Luke nice, although I saw him

only at the end of the afternoon. Perhaps, when he comes to London, he'll stop a little longer than Bruno has planned. You could show him round."

"Yes—I suppose so."

From the Thames valley which was now flowing past the window Hatty had moved a composed gaze to her mother's face. And now she was again gazing impassively outward. It would have been impossible to glimpse or guess in her the vehement child she commonly was. Perhaps, Jane thought, she was being one of the female persons—they could scarcely be called romantic heroines—in the particular novels and plays which were at present her chief means of interpreting the world. Probably it was Lawrence again. It would be tiresome to have Hatty, when she ought to be improving her French irregular verbs, concentrating upon the potent dark stream of her own blood, and bringing the sensual sub-consciousness to meals with her three times a day. But you must put up with that sort of thing—Jane told herself—if you insist on having literate children. Young people, when facing new and disturbing experience, are entitled to whatever masks and roles and make-believes may help them to cope. If Hatty was Ursula Brangwen today and Beatie Bryant tomorrow, that was simply a manifestation of what psychologists called (she seemed to remember) the identity-crisis of adolescence. And at least, as a parent, she was accustomed to it. Both Hatty and Bruno had done a good deal of their growing up—if it *was* growing up—in terms of more or less conspiratorial imaginative projection. There was an occasion, for instance, upon which they had been Borgias for weeks on end. Or some Egyptian prince and princess, unmentionably related.

"Was your expedition a success?" Hatty asked. She had turned back to her mother and spoken absently.

"Entirely so. The Oriental Gallery is really remarkable. I'm going to write about it next week. All sorts of things have happened at the Ashmolean since I first knew it. And of course I enjoyed seeing the big Tresilian. I expect Luke showed you that?"

"On the staircase? Yes, I saw it."

"Does Luke himself have anything of his father's?"

"He has a water-colour. Of some cliffs. And a bear."

"Cliffs with a polar bear?"

"No, of course not. They must be Cornish cliffs. I mean that there's a bear perched up beside the picture."

Jane laughed. "That sounds very domestic. And bears must have come in again. They were rather fashionable among undergraduates a good many years ago. It had something to do with a novel by Evelyn Waugh."

"Luke's bear certainly hasn't *anything* to do with a novel by Evelyn Waugh."

Hatty had flashed this out with unwary scorn, so that Jane laughed again and had to check herself hastily. "Has the bear a name?" she asked.

"Of course." Hatty was now looking at her mother disapprovingly, as if seeing no occasion for levity. "It's Ambrose."

"Did Luke give you any other family information? Bruno doesn't seem to know much about his people—apart from his father, that is. Does he live with relations?"

"I don't know at all. I didn't ask him. He has a half-sister. But it wasn't me he told that to. It was an old don we met on his staircase. Luke must have a half-sister, much older than he is, because his father was married to somebody else before he was married to Luke's mother. It doesn't sound anything very exciting, a half-sister. Luke sounds rather alone, actually." Hatty paused, as if she had detected something unguarded in her own voice. "It must be quite nice, to be that. I mean, if you have friends and things."

"No doubt," Jane said, and wondered whether she herself was really so oppressive a parent.

"But you were quite right." Hatty had glanced past her mother and into the corridor. "Here's your beau."

And there, certainly, was Charles Rose. He had his umbrella; he had his bowler hat; he had his indefinable air of being a scholar and not a business man, all the same. Jane, even while her heart really warmed to him, went through the necessary fiction of welcoming surprise. For Charles was insisting on looking surprised. Yet he knew very well—Jane thought—that she knew that he knew himself to have been observed on the platform at Oxford. "Charles!" she said through the glass. "What fun. Come in and talk." Perhaps it was fair enough to call him a beau. But Hatty had been asserting that her mother's days of love-liking lay in a past as dim and faded as a drawerful of *carnets de bal.* Somewhere in Hatty's head—so strange children are—was a determination to share Luke Tresilian with nobody.

"I wondered whether you'd be coming up for that little occasion," Charles Rose said. He shook hands formally. For Jane his expression held the faintest air of reproach, and for Hatty of incredulity. It was a protest against the stealing on of time. "We might have lunched together, if we'd known we were both going to be involved—and shown Hatty whatever Oxford has to show in that way nowadays." Rose paused, perhaps to be given a good mark for this prompt inclusion of Jane's daughter. "But the George, you know, has vanished. It's too sad."

"We wasted a lot of money there, if you ask me." Jane often found herself reacting rather briskly to the elegiac note which was so apt to tinge Charles Rose's conversation.

"I'm sure we did." Charles, who had sat down beside Hatty, nodded humorously. But Jane could see that he was instantly wondering whether circumstances still constrained her to think about money rather often. So she reacted again.

"But tonight," she said, "aren't we both going to get something for free? Champagne and a dab of caviare on a biscuit?"

"Yes, of course." Rather touchingly, Charles's face had lit up. "I met Lucilla the other day, and she said she was insisting on your going to the Madronas'. You've never been to their house?"

"Yes, we have. Sir Hector believes in being properly affable to his secretary's mother and sister. But I haven't been there on a grand occasion, with everything on show."

"There are two awful young men," Hatty said. "They wear—" Her glance fell on the seat opposite Charles Rose, and she could be seen searching rapidly for a substitute for "bowler hats". "They wear absurd status symbols," she said, not much improving matters. And she turned her head once more towards the outward scene, as if she regarded her contribution to the conversation as having been made.

"I don't know that Madrona himself is a bad fellow," Charles said tolerantly. "And he possesses either taste or the means to hire it. He's got together a lot of things that are well worth seeing."

"That's why I'm going to the party," Jane said. "Not really as a substitute for a square meal."

"You can always get one of those off me." This time, Charles had tried for a broadly humorous note. But the feel of it seemed not to please him, since he added rather hastily : "There's somebody else on the train who's going to the Madronas'. I've just been talking to him. John Littlejohn. Isn't he Bruno's Head Man?"

"Yes. He became Provost in succession to somebody called Gilstrap. But I haven't met him."

"You may tonight, Jane. He's sitting in the dining-car now, impressing the waiters by being in tails and a white tie. He says he wouldn't have time to dine at his club, and that he's hungry enough, after an abominable college meeting, to eat whatever British Railways set before him. And he's uncommonly pleased with himself. He has news for Madrona, he says, and the fact that the Madronas are giving a big do tonight is a felicitous coincidence. It seemed to me that 'felicitous coincidence' was some dim academic falsehood." Charles Rose shook a solemnly indulgent head. "Well do I remember those minuscule dons' intrigues."

Charles—Jane recalled—had been at one time a Fellow of All Souls. He now rather enjoyed the air of belonging to a larger world. All Souls, he seemed to feel, could appositely be tucked into a corner of the British Museum one day. A benevolent industrialist—perhaps a super-Madrona—might donate a special gallery in which to exhibit it.

"I've gathered that Littlejohn is interested in the arts," Jane said. "And so was Gilstrap before him. Gilstrap got the college its Tresilian. I saw that today. And so did Hatty."

"Did you, indeed?" Charles tried to collect Hatty's interest with this question, but failed. "I've been on the committee, by the way, for the Tresilian show next month. But something else put him in my mind recently. Ah, yes—Delver. Did you ever meet Thayne Delver?"

Jane shook her head. "I don't think I ever heard of him."

"Rather a nice American, with whom I had dealings of a sort some years ago. They've made him a professor of the inter-relations of the arts, or some such jargoning thing. And he's back in England now, breathing down the late Matthew Tresilian's neck. He's got it into his head, you see, that Tresilian was as notable a writer as he was a painter. So there were two Tresilians, you may say, and Delver is going to interrelate them."

"Will he succeed?"

"He's very pertinacious. I gather he proposes to make a start by investigating Tresilian's life. Presumably Tresilian did have a life. It's only a minority of us, after all, who don't."

Jane put out a hand and patted Charles Rose on the knee. It was a sufficient response to that wry remark. "Tresilian had a son," she said. "Hatty has been spending the afternoon with him. He's a college friend of Bruno's. They're on the same staircase."

"Then Delver will be tramping up it in no time." Charles again tried to canvass Hatty's attention, and again failed entirely. "Or rather, in a rather precisely calculated time."

"When Luke Tresilian isn't there, you mean?" Hatty had attended after all; in fact she had swung round in a sudden indignation that was both surprising and alarming. "Snooping and stealing?"

"Nothing quite as bad as that, I'm sure." Charles Rose was entirely tactful in his manner of correcting this childish misapprehension. "Thayne Delver is a perfectly honest person. He's even full of the best American highmindedness. He has a luxurious conviction that anything he discovers is certain vastly to edify the world. But he does feel that knowledge has to be surprised; that there's some moment of advantage for making this or that raid upon it. Whoever the surviving Tresilians are—this young man you've met, and any other—Delver has them on a time-table."

"It still sounds pretty nosy to me."

"I rather agree with you, Hatty, as a matter of fact. But not on any very rational grounds. If biographies and such-like are to be written, the job should be done early, and on the strength of first-hand inquiry."

"That doesn't mean that this man ought to go spying into secrets."

"Secrets?" Jane asked lightly. She had an impulse to mitigate the rather sultry impression her youngest child was giving. "At least Luke Tresilian can hardly be a repository of family secrets. When his father died, he was no more than—"

"We all have secrets," Hatty said. "They may be large and tragic." She lowered her eyelids in Bruno's best enigmatic manner, and from beneath them looked broodingly at Charles

Rose. "Or they may be futile and quite small. But they're secrets, all the same, and we're entitled to preserve them."

There was a moment's silence. Charles, Jane thought, was disconcerted. Being a careful bachelor, he was unattuned to these juvenile wave-lengths. Nevertheless he was looking at Hatty kindly. He had always wanted to lend a hand with the children; he had never very effectively brought it off. And again Jane's heart warmed to him.

"Charles," she said, "we'll have all our champagne and caviare together. On a *tête-à-tête* sofa behind a magnificent Chinese screen. And we'll talk about old times as if we never had new times in our heads."

CHAPTER SIXTEEN

Lord Burntisland drew the broad silk ribbon over his head, wrapped it round the gilt and enamel star and—as the cab came to a halt—thrust these insignia into his coat pocket. He disapproved of the casual modern habit of failing to wear decorations when legitimately commanded or invited to do so; he disapproved still more an equally casual nocturnal wandering round in them.

It had been something to get away from his dinner at an early hour, but in doing so he had not thought to plead to anybody that he was going on to Lady Madrona's. It had been Bernard Le Mesurier who had pleaded that, and it now occurred to Burntisland that Le Mesurier might have been prevaricating. In which case he would himself be making Lady Madrona a bow to no good purpose. For what had come into his head was that Le Mesurier might be a useful man to talk to, and that the fact of this woman's having sent him a card afforded an immediate opportunity. Whether Le Mesurier were a good painter or not was no great matter. You met his portraits in every board room —and, as often as not, in any drawing-room you let yourself in for. He was a Past President of the Royal Academy. He would be a powerful ally in the campaign Burntisland was envisaging.

It took only a couple of glances to see that the Madronas' London life was conducted on lavish lines. Their house was of the order one finds only at the corners of these great squares— possessing, down one of the adjoining streets, an extra depth which admitted of the carving out of apartments of considerable grandeur. It would afford, Burntisland reflected, a whole Corporation with what is nowadays called prestige accommodation. But no private individual gained prestige by living in this way now—or not in London. In an age when it was so much the thing discreetly to disperse your luxury—tucking it away in unobtrusive flats, in country houses, in yachts, in enclaves of opulence on bread-line Caribbean islands—you only got sniffed at for this sort of living in style. Nor, it seemed to Burntisland, did footmen in livery, and all this mass of hothouse flowers flanking a marble staircase, very clearly accord with socialist principles. Nevertheless, as he himself mounted between these presences and proliferations, he was impressed. He was impressed, not at all by the expansiveness and expensiveness on view, things that his career had long rendered him immune to; he was impressed simply by a certain doggedness which—whether in Madrona or his wife—must go to the asserting of so Edwardian a vision.

And there they were at the top of their staircase—and exactly like those earlier specimens of their kind celebrated by Sargent in the Tate. (Lord Burntisland's mind had been running a good deal on painting lately.) Madrona was more than ever curvilinear; he was a knight, it struck Burntisland, who, if armed, ought to carry a scimitar. And his mannerisms were accentuated upon this grand occasion. He was not merely a host taking pleasure in receiving his guests; he was one to whom these guests, whatever their actual conversational range, were mutely communicating perpetual accessions of mildly astonishing and wholly pleasing news. But if Sir Hector Madrona was thus largely receptive of gratification Lady Madrona was correspondingly lavish in dispensing it. She was a good-looking woman, curvilinear to different effect from her husband, and she got away very well with a certain air of viceregality. She knew instantly who you were—even if this were the first time she had summoned you she knew who you were—and she would point out in her initial, perhaps her sole, remark to you that there did in fact exist some small thing upon which you could reasonably take your stand. Encouraged in this way, you bowed over the diamonds beneath which her fingers presumably lurked and moved on to take a glass of champagne. And it was not champagne of the sort that prosperous but prudent persons normally dispense to large promiscuous companies.

Lord Burntisland—automatically and from experience that had accrued some decades earlier in his life—divined all this as he moved rather stiffly up the final treads of the staircase. On the last occasion that they had met, he recalled, Madrona had talked some nonsense—indecent nonsense, surely—about staircases. But he was not here for more of that, or even for the Madronas' collection of pictures, celebrated though it was said to be. When handing over his coat he had noticed with satisfaction, among fifty others, the unmistakable broad-brimmed hat of Bernard Le Mesurier. The painter had in fact come on to this showy affair. Burntisland would seek him out, sound him over what he had in mind, and take himself off to bed.

"Dear Lord Burntisland," Lady Madrona said, "how delightful of you to come. Hector tells me you are interested in our Tresilian. Look at it *now*, by all means. But, later, let us look at it *together*. I should so value your impression. There is often such stimulus in an opinion from *outside* our small artistic world."

"And Burntisland's a very keen observer," Madrona said. "When we last met, we had some interesting talk about Leonard Benton Curry. I'm sorry that Leonard Benton Curry can't be here tonight. He cables that he's in Brazil. It's a country in which things are happening on precisely his scale. Wouldn't you say?"

Owning no opinion on this point, Burntisland offered none, and moved on. There was a crush of people in a vista of rooms quite as spendid as he had expected; an eddy among them as he looked revealed, ominously and at a distance, some rows of chairs and a group of music stands. At present however the visual arts held sway. The Madronas' pictures were on the walls, their sculptures were dotted about, and their guests were engaged in the main in inspecting what was thus expansed to view. It was an activity generating a great deal of noise; the women in particular, Burntisland noticed, appeared to regard animation as the best means of asserting an aesthetic nature. The sight wouldn't much have pleased him at any time, for he thought poorly of going round a private house with more than a polite modicum of admiring and gaping. He had learnt certain attitudes long ago, when a raw young man having much learning of that order to do, and they were with him more inflexibly now than conceivably they were with persons brought up in a different sort of nursery. So he would have walked around, anyway, with a slight sense of alienation, a forbidding conviction that it was all pretty vulgar. But this was pointed, in the particular instance, by the further fact that the art on view was distinctly not of the sort he responded to. To put it mildly, there were no Raphael Madonnas here.

Lord Burntisland rounded, at a respectful distance, an attenuated male figure constructed out of barbed wire. The movement brought him up against another male figure, also attenuated, but alive and supporting itself on a gold-headed cane.

"What the devil are *you* doing in this galley, my dear Burntisland?"

"Not proposing to stare at all this stuff, Alabaster, as you may guess." Burntisland, as he spoke, gave Alabaster the kind of appraising look that an old man does give to a man yet older. Anyone speaking brutally, he supposed, would describe Alabaster as a weird old death's head. He was amazing, all the same. Once more to confirm this gave Burntisland real pleasure. He had no doubt that Alabaster's career had been variously reprehensible. But the man did hang on. And he did it on his own terms, asserting his own style. There was something to be said for that. "I came along," Burntisland said, "because I want to have a word with that fellow Le Mesurier. I'm disturbed by the way that artists, of a sort, lend themselves to all this squalid and immoral advertising. It occurs to me that they might be given a lead from the top. If a man is competent at a craft—and I take drawing and painting to be that—it's shameful that he should bend it to the production of dirt and twaddle."

"So it is, Burntisland. But then so many things are shameful in this inexplicable—but fortunately beautiful—world. Persons like yourself can scarcely know where to begin."

"To my mind, it doesn't much signify. See *something* veritably to be done, and do it."

"Do you know, I too have found inspiration in Thomas Carlyle in my day?" Alabaster said. He gave a high-pitched, quavering laugh, which made even some of the animated women turn from their aesthetic studies and stare. "At the moment, I'm a good deal occupied with Sartre."

"No doubt there is much to be said for keeping up."

"Nothing whatever, my dear fellow. Or nothing whatever, in my case. In fact, I regard it as a burdensome faculty that I happened to be born with." Alabaster gestured with quick elegance around him. "All this, for example. I'm quite 'with it', as the children say."

131

"But isn't most of it rubbish?"

"Dear me, yes. But so has been the greater part of what has passed as art in every generation. In much that these good people have on view here, however, the authentic principle of aesthetic delectation does flicker. Here and there, and in queer enough places, it positively flares. No doubt you will think me dogmatic in the assertion. But it's again a matter of being born with something : a specific but regrettably sub-creative sensibility in face of these things. I know."

"Does Le Mesurier know?"

"An enchanting question. Let us seek him out and inquire."

"I'd have thought it odd that *he* turns out in this galley. He does at least paint what he sees in front of him." Burntisland made a gesture, brusquer than Alabaster's. "I'd expect him to keep clear of all this."

"I see your point." Alabaster paused for the purpose of acknowledging a tap on the arm from the lorgnette of a passing dowager. "But you're mistaken in supposing Le Mesurier to paint what nature presents to him. It's true that his portraits of all those worthy gentlemen are built up from photographs. It's true that there's a meticulous representation of city clothes and various forms of fancy dress. It's true that there are often graphs on the wall, and impressive industrial processes seen transacting themselves through office windows. But what, on Le Mesurier's canvases, is the one constant fact intimated about these tycoons, as they say? That they've merely dropped in. They've dropped in from tramping their estates and commanding their regiments. You will forgive me, Burntisland, but I find the spectacle of that particular social underworld perpetually fascinating."

"No doubt," Burntisland said.

"Then take the women. But, my dear fellow, let us promenade. There are one or two things I might point out to you." Alabaster took Burntisland's arm with his free hand, and the latter felt himself constrained to cautious locomotion. "Whereas the men —I speak again of Le Mesurier's concoctions—have dropped into the city from the country, the women have dropped into the country from the town. No mere itinerant lady's maid could have achieved that complexion and. *coiffure*. Both have been created somewhere off Bond Street a couple of hours ago. Yet there the enchanting creature is, with a whole country house and part of a walled garden behind her. And don't think, again, that Le Mesurier is painting what he sees. He has perfected a pseudo-archaic trick of ignoring aerial perspective. So there is the great house, too, in a foreground of its own, with every lintel as hard-cut and distinct as the locks on the lady's head. Those, I assure you, are Le Mesurier's two working formulas. We can't, how-ever, check up on them here, since our host, to his aesthetic credit, has nothing of the sort on view."

"It makes it odder that he should have Le Mesurier himself on view."

"Madrona is becoming a major patron of the arts. And I've reason to believe that he is very wealthy *indeed*." An unwonted tinge of respect had come into Alabaster's voice as he mentioned this. "So Le Mesurier comes along, and salves his dignity by being a Grand Old Man. He is courteous, tolerant, whimsical in front of it all. When alone with Lady Madrona, he no doubt confesses that she owns a little something—in the way of the finer artistic vibration, that is—that he himself hasn't got. Event-ually he will achieve a portrait of Madrona painted at the ex-pense of his tenantry. And it will be hung in some shire hall or other where our worthy host is regarded as a bit of a grandee."

Burntisland made no reply to this. He was beginning to find Alabaster's talk less astringent than carping. They had paused together in front of an enormous sphere of wood which had been variously hollowed, tunnelled, waxed and polished. "Per-haps," he asked, "you can explain *that* to me?"

"Certainly. You begin by nourishing in yourself the habit of seeing the nude human form as landscape. At the same time you nourish the habit of seeing landscape as a nude human form. So far, it's plain sailing."

"Is it, indeed?" Burntisland said, and felt irritation rising in him.

"Then, perhaps, you conceive of yourself as *being* whatever in the nature of things makes these perceptions or imaginings possible. And *then*"—and Alabaster concluded his exposition on a sudden note of mockery—"you take your chisels and go right ahead."

"And *here*, I suppose"—Burntisland had moved on—"you begin with the habit of seeing the nude human form as a badly blitzed dovecot?"

"Ah!" Alabaster looked delighted. "Here a high connoisseurship is required, I confess. Higher, I feel, than it would be modest in me to lay claim to. Let us coax our hostess into the presence of this thing, and have her expatiate upon it."

They were looking at a structure of irregularly contrived pigeon-holes in plywood, such as might have been achieved by a pertinacious if not particularly well-endowed six-year-old. Into each of the orifices thus constituted there had been inserted some small object of diurnal domestic use : a door-knob, an egg-cup, an ink-bottle and the like. And then everything had been painted over in a mat black paint.

"Most amusing," Alabaster continued. "That is what one says in front of this. Most amusing. And one passes on."

For a moment Burntisland refused to pass on. "But look," he said. His voice had risen a little. "Oughtn't responsible people to *behave* responsibly in front of this sort of thing? It's nonsense. Since it is offered as a work of art, it's offensive nonsense. It's the intolerable degradation of something that counts, or ought to count, in civilized life. It ought to be stopped." His voice rose another shade. "The whole thing should be come down on."

"I appreciate your point of view." To an effect that was half of amused malice and half of sympathy, Alabaster shook his finely silvered head and glanced sidelong at his companion. "But are not you and I—it's something to canvass confidentially between us—just a little old to intervene? We might find that we had become not much more than grotesque exhibits ourselves. We might simply be exploited for our amusement value, as they say."

"Good evening to you both."

"Good evening, Roundhay." Burntisland, turning to the man who had interrupted, spoke without much cordiality. Fleet Street was not a part of London he had any great notion of, or troubled himself to carry any very detailed information upon. And Arthur Roundhay he simply knew as some sort of power there— a principal henchman, perhaps, of one of the grand monarchs of the Press. He was large and florid and his manner was genial; his greeting, indeed, had been to Burntisland's taste more abounding in this quality than the degree of the acquaintanceship between them at all called for.

Alabaster, on the other hand, appeared to have no impulse towards reserve. "My dear Roundhay," he said, "let us hear some new thing. It's your *métier*, is it not?"

"Certainly it is—and I am happy to oblige you. You see the middle-aged chap vigorously admiring the Picasso—the one in the ill-fitting tails and the tie making its way towards his left ear?"

"We see him," Alabaster said. "But he is, in fact, vigorously admiring a Braque."

"Yes, yes—something of that sort. And what would you judge to be his walk of life?"

"A scholar," Alabaster pronounced. "He's undoubtedly a scholar."

"Correct. His name's Littlejohn. He's the Provost of Madrona's old college at Cambridge—"

"Oxford," Burntisland said. If it was clear that Littlejohn was a scholar, it was equally clear that Roundhay was a journalist.

"You may be right. Well, this don has just told our host that he has been made an Honorary Fellow of the college. The word is going quietly round. In the course of the evening we shall all take occasion to murmur a word of congratulation, eh? And a small inner circle, much without ostentation, will no doubt forgather in a corner for the purpose of drinking a toast. Nothing is involved, I suppose, except the gratifying of a little harmless vanity. And some dressing up. Madrona will be able to wear a splendid scarlet robe when he next visits the dear old *alma mater*."

"Well, at least you will be able to report that he has done so," Alabaster said, with amiable irony. "But now give us your opinion on a graver matter. Burntisland and I, prompted by our surroundings, were just initiating a discussion on the morality of art. This is a topic, no doubt, within the province of some at least of your numerous public prints?"

"Certainly." Roundhay appeared delighted with this antique manner of referring to newspapers. "There's no doubt that art should be kept an eye on. Models, for instance. Perhaps it's a respectable profession in a small way. But when parliament brought in that Act clearing the tarts off the streets—well, every one of them became an artist's model overnight. Advertising in shop-windows, you remember, complete with vital statistics and spicy bits about special poses. A shocking scandal. We made a big thing of it."

Alabaster nodded appreciatively. "My dear fellow, I'm sure you did."

"And then there are all the nude shows. 'Artistic spectacle' is a term to keep your ear open for, I can tell you. As a matter of fact, I've got a couple of very clever girls who've managed to get themselves hired as strippers now. As soon as one of them really makes the grade—gets into the top hot stuff—we're going to blow the roof off in our Sunday. Revelations running for a month or six weeks." Roundhay turned to Burntisland. "You're specially interested in that sort of thing?"

"No, I am not."

"Ah—but then there are the picture postcards. You notice how fond modern painters are of pubic hair?" As he produced this question with something of a shout—for Lady Madrona's party was growing steadily noisier—Roundhay stepped back to admit the passage of a startled young woman between Burntisland and himself. "Well, it gets by on canvas. The courts seem to have made up their minds about that. But it's a different matter on a fourpenny coloured postcard after Modigliani or some such chap. Any lad can send such a thing to an innocent girl through the post. And that's corrupting, wouldn't you say? Every now and then it has to be exposed."

Alabaster considered this. "Why?" he asked.

"Why? Doesn't the Press live by exposure, as some famous old fellow said?"

"Perhaps he said indecent exposure?"

Burntisland frowned. This was a totally disagreeable conversation; he was disgusted with it; in fact he was disturbed by it. He saw no reason why, so far as he was concerned, it should continue. He therefore transferred his gaze to the middle distance, gave a sudden smile of recognition to an imaginary acquaintance, and walked away. As he did so he congratulated himself that he had more or less kept his mouth shut before Roundhay. These fellows could be valuable allies at times. But you had decidedly to choose your moment for inviting them into conference.

"*Dear* Lord Burntisland, how *very* sweet of you to recognize me!"

His manoeuvre had landed him, he found, with a young woman he was not conscious of ever before having set eyes on. There was no need, he judged, to elicit her name, since within seconds she would probably drift away again. But in this expectation he proved mistaken. The young woman was of the literally clinging sort, and she would certainly have kissed him had he not been unbending as well as tall. "You dear, dear old thing!" she said. "Come and look at the new ones." She turned rapidly— so that her dark hair, which was long and unconstrained, swung about her neck—and gave Burntisland a tug that almost brought him down on Lady Madrona's unyielding parquet. "Did you know Herbin?" she asked. "Did you ever meet him in Paris? *He* was such a dear old man, too. And look!"

Burntisland looked. Before him were two paintings of the most geometrical sort, executed in bright, flat colours, such as one sees on constructional toys. He conjectured obscurely that they were perhaps designed to brighten some opulent nursery, since they might represent boxes of building bricks intended for the play of Brobdingnagian infants. Anyway, they seemed harmless enough, and didn't precisely offend him. He thought therefore that he might stretch a point in the interest of civility. "Most amusing," he said, remembering Alabaster.

"Amusing?" The young woman was horrified. "But you dear, dear creature, they're masterpieces! Was there ever anything so utterly exempt from the contingent and the accidental?"

Burntisland, who in his leisure time was inclined to philosophical reading, thought poorly of this use of language. He therefore moved on in silence to the next painting.

"White," the young woman said.

"Ah, by an Englishman."

"No, no—it's *called* 'White'."

"It's not all that white," Burntisland said, not intending wit. He was becoming confused—as a man may do who has been thrust into some experimental chamber contrived by psychologists and forced to question the reports of his senses. Burntisland's senses told him one thing quite clearly about the canvas he was now inspecting. It had been left out in the rain, and that was all that had ever happened to it. But here it was—much good money having undoubtedly been paid for it—and these were presumed to be rational beings around him. He made an immense effort himself to say some rational and moderate thing. "It appears to me," he managed, "to be somewhat lacking in incident."

"Yes, isn't it?" The young woman, thus joining enthusiastically in commendation, swung him round again. "And here's the Madronas' new Nicolas de Staël."

This time Burntisland was abruptly shocked. The large areas of pink and purple and yellow meant nothing to him. But there could be no mistaking the ghastly crimson splash and spatter that obscured their point of convergence. A road accident sometimes produces that amount of pulp, that effusion of blood. Burntisland turned away—he couldn't complain of lack of incident here—in search of something that should at least be undisturbing. Perhaps the very next exhibit could be classed as that. It was large; it had presumably been executed with brushes and paint; but it was indistinguishable from what he understood to be called a "dress length", and as such might have been selected by a widow of sombre tastes. And next to this again was something of roughly the same order : a slab—surely—of that sort of speckly mosaic flooring still to be found in older and drearier public lavatories. Finally on this wall—and there was quite a crowd of the Madronas' guests congregated before this one— there was a six by four foot chunk of dried mud.

Standing in front of this, Burntisland felt for a moment only a sharp technical curiosity. How could it be done? How, having chosen a section of cart track, could you excise it, rear it up, fix it so that it shouldn't flake and crumble? It wasn't even in a frame. There, on the wall, it simply *was*.

"What do you think of it, Lord Burntisland?" Because of the crush, the young woman had been obliged to let go of him. It was perhaps a resulting sensation of regained freedom that prompted his reply.

"It seems," he said, "rather to be asking to be called muck."

He heard somebody giggle. But what he chiefly heard was a silence that appeared to have fallen in his immediate neighbourhood.

"It's by Dubuffet, you know," the young woman said. "It's done in papier maché."

"Whatever it's done in, it is not, in my opinion, a work of art." Burntisland spoke, he believed, quietly and even casually—

138

giving what was no more than the personal opinion of one not much interested in these things. But perhaps his voice had risen, for there was undoubtedly a stir around him.

"But it's by Jean Dubuffet!" The young woman sounded almost frightened. "It's *raw* art!"

Burntisland wished that, like John Alabaster, he had provided himself with a walking stick. He was feeling insecure on his feet and there was something gently swimming in his head. He seemed to hear the name "Dubuffet" being repeated many times against a background that was either laughter near at hand or merely the general babble of the whole party. He looked around him and saw only one individual face with distinctness. It was the face of the young man who had conducted him to the Tresilian in the National Gallery. He thought the young man was laughing. But perhaps he was only smiling. Then he saw a second face—florid, but with eyes that were narrowed and speculating. It was the face of a journalist he had lately been talking to, but he couldn't recall the man's name. This failure of memory was vexatious. More than that, it told him that he wasn't very well.

But he could still walk. And he was looking for somebody. He was looking for Bernard Le Mesurier. He turned about and walked stiffly, a little blindly, to another part of the room.

PART THREE

CHAPTER SEVENTEEN

THE ONLY PICTURE on Bruno Landreth's wall was a sketch
by Lawrence Toynbee of a three-quarter line in action. This and
a rather unusually splendid machine for making coffee had both
been important in the early stages of Bruno's establishing his
position in the college. The coffee machine had been in request
for various societies and temperate private occasions, and Bruno
had been let come along with it, since he alone knew how to
operate it. The sketch, being the representation of an athletic
occasion authentically hand-painted by an artist of name, had
been in effect an ingeniously contrived simultaneous bow to
divided and disparted worlds. And it had been the occasion, only
quite recently, of Bruno's extending the privilege (as it now was)
of his acquaintance to Luke Tresilian—Luke in his first weeks
having glimpsed it through an open door and subsequently ventured upon a shy and respectful murmur to its proprietor when
encountered on their common staircase.

Bruno possessed other and less extraneous recommendations.
His public character was commonly that of a debonair *désoeuvré*
negligence, but occasionally he would emerge as a man of action
in matters which he had observed undergraduates to judge important. His apparent indifference before the approaches or
withdrawals of important people had been unflawed, for he had
a very good nerve. In private he discovered, after a diffident
fashion, a simple and spontaneous warmth. The number of
people believing that, at bottom, Bruno Landreth was their best
friend must have been very considerable. But what was perhaps
chiefly impressive in him was his evident immunity from the
slightest hint of *Angst*. His few enemies said that he was merely
rubbery. The general belief was that, as a consequence of
abundant and precocious sin, he had been psycho-analysed
by an eminent practitioner and thus endowed with a deep
emotional maturity to which was due his buoyant nervous tone.
So Bruno was prospering and ought to have been pleased

with himself. Socially, he could at last feel well on the way to the top.

"I've noticed again and again," Bruno was saying now, "that only a sound liqueur brandy is safe after those curried prawns."

"Why curried?" Luke asked. "The question answers itself as put."

"Exactly. So have another tot now, both of you." Sprawled on his sofa, Bruno managed to point an elegantly slippered toe at the Armagnac. He was an impeccable host.

"I wonder," Robin Pacey inquired, "whether one could tip off the public health authorities to inspect the college kitchens?" He reached out for the bottle. "Thanks, I will. They'd find the most appalling things. The prawns are from barrels sunk by enemy action in the First World War. Kaiser Bill's patent gut-rot prawns."

Bruno smiled indulgently. The wit of this rugger-moron Pacey was somewhat random. "You too, Luke," he commanded. "Spin the bottle. No heeltaps. As to skylight, liberty hall."

Luke shook his head. He didn't propose to drink more brandy. "Do you know," he said by way of being reasonably convivial nevertheless, "that Wordsworth has a line in the *Prelude* saying that right underneath him the college kitchens made a humming sound less tuneable than bees? The sound our kitchens ought to make, symbolically at least, is an unintermittent succession of—"

"Enough!" Bruno interrupted. "Enough of this windy suspiration of whatever. If my mother had stayed up I might have cadged a square meal for both of you poor devils. But she had to go back to some glittering party, it seems. And my sister Hatty has had to go home and read *Polyeucte*."

Luke found it hard it imagine Hatty doing this. He found it hard, too, not to blush. Happily he remembered Dryden. "*Polyeucte*," he said oracularly, "is as solemn as the long stops on our organs."

Supposing this to be a bawdy joke, Robin Pacey laughed automatically.

Bruno eyed him with a benign tolerance. "Do you know," he said, "that simple, sterling Luke has fallen in love with tempestuous, teen-age Hatty? What shall we do?" He reached for the brandy. "How does an anxious and foreboding brother handle such things?"

"It's difficult, no doubt." Pacey was uneasily humorous. He would have said that this sort of talk about a sister wasn't on. But Bruno Landreth must know. "I'd suppose," he ventured sensibly, "that Big Brother's best plan is just not to speak out of turn."

"That's a true word." Bruno grinned happily at Luke, who had been thrown into confusion, and at the same time stretched his limbs luxuriously on the sofa. The movement was finely expressive. It indicated that one man, at least, had attained to simple wisdom, a wise felicity, and that his friends too would presently discover how effortless it all was. "Only before it ends happily," he went on, "there will be the appearance of vast complications for poor Luke. In the vac, you know, he is going to be received into the *intimité* of the Landreths—the poor bastard."

Luke, who was sitting with both his long legs cocked over the sloping arm of Bruno's wicker chair, slewed round and put his feet on the ground. "You and Robin," he said, "seem to be the proper people to have a cosy gossip about this. I'm going to bed."

"I'd better be staggering across the quad myself." Robin Pacey got to his feet. He clearly felt that, whatever this might be about, he wasn't with it and didn't want to be.

Bruno waved him back into his chair with authority. "These things are best touched upon lightly," he said, "and in the presence of a well-disposed outsider. Luke falls in love with Hatty. He comes home, and he encounters my mother. You can see why this is significant. Look at him. Consider the stage of his emotional development. Consider how much *he* wants a mother. Almost at once it will be the older woman he is dreaming about, and in ways that will trouble and confuse his chaste mind very much. I suppose you know, Robin, that there are many young husbands who find their mothers-in-law more attractive than their wives?"

If Robin didn't know this, he didn't quite have the courage to admit it. "Oedipus and all that?" he said. "I suppose so. But it's a bit corny, if you ask me, all the same."

"You know, too, that many men come to feel that they have made the wrong choice between two sisters? That's why the business of marrying the deceased wife's sister made such a shindy. Enormous charges of repressed guilt were touched off by it.

Now, to return to my family situation. I have another sister, several years older than Hatty, who is called Lucilla. She is sexually attractive. And in temperament she is very close to my mother. So the touch of the maternal, you see, will appear to be there. Luke—or Luke's unconscious, I should say—will compromise with Lucilla. They will be married at St Margaret's, Westminster, and we shall all be very happy ever after."

There was silence. Both Bruno's guests were on their feet.

"All right, all right," Robin said. "Rely on me to turn up at any wedding that's going." He moved to the door. "But we've drunk too much brandy and been talking rot, I'd say."

Luke moved to the door too. It didn't seem to occur to him to speak. Bruno rose, and looked from one to the other of them charmingly—the wise youth who has certainly been condescending to talk rot, but who has inevitably let it be touched by his own deep knowledge of the heart. "Must you go," he said, "and the night still so young? But one shouldn't detain the parting guest." He moved to his outer door and opened it. "Good night, good night," he said, and watched them pass through. *"Soyez heureux, mes enfants; vous êtes encore jeunes."*

"Good night." Speaking and moving awkwardly, Robin Pacey lumbered down the ill-lit stairs.

"Good night, Bruno." With even longer strides than usual, Luke departed for his attic. Within seconds there floated down the sound of his firmly slammed door.

Bruno closed his own door and went back to his sitting-room. He corked the brandy and put it away. He caught a glimpse of himself in the big, flawed looking-glass which the college for some reason provided over the chimney-piece. He had his wicked smile. He pottered about, still with this smile. Then it faded.

"Damn!" he said. "Damn, damn, *damn!*" He gave a vicious kick at the waste-paper basket, and then disappeared into his bedroom. A few minutes later he came out again, in his pyjamas. He prowled around, frowning. He stopped and listened. He went over to a corner of the room, where there was a golf-bag. He thrust a hand down it and brought out a cane. With this he gave several experimental whacks at the arm of a chair. It sounded disagreeably loud. Nevertheless he crossed over to his writing-table, shoved his head under it and tried to beat himself. With a certain flick of the wrist one could do something, but it

146

didn't come to much. With his buttocks mildly stinging, he flung the cane across the room. Then he went after it, retrieved it, and put it back in the bag. He dug deeper and produced a cricket stump. He thrust this between the seat and side of the chair so that it stuck out parallel with the floor.

Bruno went back to the bedroom, took a bottle of pills from a drawer and swallowed two of them. He went to another drawer and got a large handkerchief, and to a third drawer and got some stout string. He returned to the sitting-room, sat down on the floor, and used the handkerchief to tie his ankles together with a firm knot at the heels. He took the string and tied one end of it round his left thumb. Then came the difficult part : binding the two thumbs tightly—really tightly—together. Using his teeth, he did it so that he hurt both teeth and thumbs. He bumped himself over to the chair, pushed his legs up between his arms, and with a single strong deft movement rolled sideways on the cricket stump so that it thrust itself beneath the crook of his knees. He tumbled over helpless. He still possessed the *Children's Book of Indoor Amusements* in which two boys in Eton jackets were depicted trussed up like this for something called cock-fighting.

He had got himself, with very little labour, into bonds from which it would take great labour to escape. He was already sweating by the time that he even got himself upright and poised on his bottom again. Then came the business of knocking, edging, wriggling out the stump. The first part was easy. A sideways bumping against the chair drove the stump further through until its head was flush with his elbow. Then it became difficult. If there were only a little play its own weight would help to jolt it out. But, even in his thin pyjamas, there was none at all. He was getting a good deal thicker-set than he had been as a boy, and that made a big difference. The room seemed suddenly to have got very hot, and his head was swimming. Perhaps it was swimming in the direction of blind panic, so that he would scream and scream. And, of course, since he had swallowed those pills, there would presently be sleep to contend with. That was one of the hazards. He would fall asleep, be discovered in his bonds next morning, and inevitably be carried straight to an asylum.

The stump tumbled out with a small clatter, his knees shot

away, and he fell back flat on the floor. He felt vast relief and a small sense of disappointment. But, of course, he was only half through. He flexed and unflexed his stiff arms several times. His thumbs were hurting, so that he bit them hard in order to get a different sort of pain. Then he got to his feet, hopped to the light-switch by the door, and turned off the light, so that only the glow of his bedside reading lamp was left. He turned and hopped towards the bedroom. But his exertions, or the pills, had made him unsteady; he lost his balance and came down helplessly and heavily on the floor. He was terrified. It had been a terrific bump, and Leech's rooms were directly below. He lay still, awaiting the end. But nothing happened. With a small sense of anti-climax he got on his feet again, gained his bedroom and tumbled on the bed.

It was of course possible to pick up a pair of scissors, hold them gripped between his knees or teeth, and work the string gently and doggedly against a blade until it gave. But he was a prisoner not accommodated in that way. It had to be teeth alone. He started gnawing. The cord was very tough and it was monotonous work. He felt sleepy, and bored, and then *very* sleepy. But this in turn produced terror once more; if his scout found him in this state in the morning, it would be as fatal as if he had been lying trussed on the floor. He drove his mind to find a stimulating fantasy, and to elaborate it as he gnawed. But waking fantasies are boring things; they have none of the punch that dreams derive from their involuntary character. Bruno drove his mind, drove his teeth; his whole body was sweating and tensing; at the same time, he was so drowsy that his eyelids were like magnets wanting to click together.

Then, quite suddenly, it was over. The cord gave, his thumbs came apart, his loins and his whole body shivered and relaxed. He managed to bend forward; he managed, although his fingers were almost as nerveless as his thumbs, to untie the handkerchief from his ankles and toss it away.

He lay back and stared into the hopeless darkness until he fell asleep.

CHAPTER EIGHTEEN

JANE LANDRETH FOUND herself enjoying the Madronas'
party. It was coming at the end of a good day. Going back to
Oxford—sometimes so frustrating—had been a success on this
occasion. The Ashmolean was delightful. Bruno—who came before the Ashmolean, after all—seemed to be behaving responsibly; it was certainly an excellent sign that he had not exploited
her visit to get out of his tutorial or whatever it had been. As
for what had appeared to blow up with such disconcerting speed
between Hatty and the Tresilian boy—well, it was much less bad
than it might be. One of her current anxieties was lest Hatty,
so easily kindled, might discover an adolescent passion for some
impossible youth with neither morals nor manners. Luke's
manners, she thought, were of the not very prevalent sort from
which decent morals may be inferred.

Light at heart, she glanced around her again. The Madronas
must be credited with having contrived a brilliant scene. She
had only to close her eyes ever so slightly—she told herself maliciously—to imagine that here was one of the great vanished houses
which she had glimpsed, already in their decline, in the days
before her marriage. Indeed, from that world one or two ghosts
still walked. There was John Alabaster, for instance. Having discovered that Lucilla was a mere employee of his host and hostess,
he had settled in to wandering round with her—"distinguishing"
her, as people used to say—for the rest of the evening. There was
amusement in that. But there was more amusement in the fact
that he was thus paying court to Jane's daughter on the strength
of having been a friend of Jane's grandfather. And Bernard Le
Mesurier, who was advancing upon her now, must be nearly as
antique; he had been one of the fashionable portrait painters
of the day while Jane was still in the nursery.

"Ah, the formidable Mrs Landreth!" It was with perfect
cordiality that Le Mesurier greeted her, although the printer's
ink could scarcely be dry on her last joke about him. "How much

you must be in your element in this treasure house! Let us look at everything together. You will open all these mysteries to me. You will admit me among the *adepti*. And first, let us look at *this*."

The old man had chosen well, Jane thought, if he was proposing to get his own back. He had paused before a metallic object fashioned out of hundreds of three-inch nails. These had been compacted together, heads outward, into the form of a huge egg. And a segment had then been cut out, presumably in order to show what it was all about.

"A hedgehog?" Le Mesurier ventured. "A hedgehog which, having passed through the fourth dimension, must henceforth make do with being permanently inside out?"

"Something more uncomfortable even than that, surely," Jane said.

"I agree with you." Le Mesurier now regarded the object with sobriety. "If it's our business to give symbolic expression to ghastly states of mind—and perhaps you will tell me that it is—then we might reasonably go to this chap for a tip or two. And you mustn't suppose that I dismiss all this. You mustn't even suppose that I don't think about it. I'm grateful to our host for having brought together such a body of experimental stuff. I'm for keeping an open mind. Perhaps the other fellow is right, after all. Take André Masson, now." Le Mesurier, who was a short man, raised his perfectly trimmed white beard towards Jane's face. "He'd be one of your crowd?"

"Yes—more or less."

"Well, he thought he had a better notion of Mont Sainte-Victoire than Cézanne had. You can see him indulging this perfectly legitimate conjecture any day you care to drop into the bowels of the Tate. And why not? People have to poke around. So good luck to them." Radiating vague good feeling, Le Mesurier took Jane's arm and steered her across the room. He brought her to a halt, with what she sensed was premeditated design, before a large, hot canvas to which she didn't, for the moment, much attend.

"On the other hand," he said, "I must confess to having reserves. Like the Bank of England, I have substantial reserves. But perhaps you wouldn't think much of them. Often they are mere paltry matters of good taste. Is it in perfectly good taste, for example"—Le Mesurier's free arm shot out at the painting before them, and as it did so his voice became charged with venom—"meticulously to exhibit upon canvas a cluster of excised cancers awaiting incineration?"

"But that doesn't seem to be what the painter had in his head," Jane said. "It's called 'Polymorphs in Desert Sand'."

"Excellent! The next time I'm prompted to express myself on the walls of a public lavatory I'll remember to add 'Polymorphs in Desert Sand' underneath." Le Mesurier moved on. "But don't think that I adopt a moral stance. Artists don't readily do that, even if they're only old Burlington House dotards." He gave Jane a fatherly pat on the arm. "But, by the way, there's a chap here whose morals *are* outraged. Do you know an eminent ship-builder, or manufacturer of bath-tubs or some such, called Burntisland? He's been after me to lead some sort of crusade against naughty and suggestive pictures on public hoardings. And apparently, he's been behaving oddly. In a little room off this great place there are some calligraphic sketches in Chinese ink. Perfectly harmless, but the genius who has achieved them has labelled them 'Mescalin Drawings'. One often sees that sort of proud claim. Well, this fellow Burntisland—he's in the Lords, you know—has made Madrona a speech, telling him that to lend any sort of kudos or prestige to such things is to encourage the young and susceptible in the persuasion that it's smart to take dope."

"I'm inclined to think he's right." Jane felt interested in this crusading figure. "Is Lord Burntisland still here now?"

"Impossible to tell in this shocking crush. But it seems that, earlier on, he also behaved oddly in front of the Madronas' pet new piece : a big Dubuffet. Quite disturbed the worshippers. Would that, by the way, be what they call *Art Autre*?"

"There are various names."

"Including Anti-Art. I'm very interested, you know, in being *against* art. Saying, quite frankly, that you hate it in your guts. Did you know Willie Yeats?"

"The poet? No, I didn't."

"A talented chap—with a nice old father, whom I met once in New York. But that's by the way. One of Willie's poems says that hatred of God may bring the soul to God. A hard saying, eh? But what about hatred of Art bringing the soul to Art?

151

Express such a hatred with concentrated artistic skill and devotion. Labour to bring into being from out of the void something that a starved cur wouldn't take a second sniff at on a rubbish dump. Cover a big canvas with the contents of a tin of paint, and then take means to make it flake and crumble so that it looks like the outside of a slum-dwelling in a French industrial town. Is one bringing the soul to Art? It's an interesting question." Le Mesurier again patted Jane on the arm. "My dear," he said, "how's Signorelli?"

She was startled that he should know or remember about this. "Not much to the fore, I'm afraid."

"Of course, he isn't easy to make little jokes about. Not like the poor old R.A. Still, get thee to Orvieto. And quickly too. Farewell." He made a bow and moved away. Then, for a moment, he turned back. "And in thy orisons," he murmured, "be all my sins remembered."

She thought of Orvieto. She saw the city on its incredible crag, foreshortened as one bumped up in the alarming little funicular. She saw—for a moment in amazing detail—the Cappella della Madonna di San Brizio. She remembered her first time there: the guide-book that said "locked; opened by sacristan on request", and herself looking for this functionary, with "Dove la Cappella Nuova?" carefully formed on her lips. She tried to recall the musculature in the small of the back of one of those splendidly human devils. But at this the brief mirage faded, and she was looking at another painting on Sir Hector Madrona's wall. In sepia and sinopia the artist had delicately evoked what might be the wraith, the phantasmal form of a mastodon's vertebrae. Then he had loaded his brush with white pigment, stood well back, and lashed out as with a whip in the direction of his canvas. Jane felt a sudden horrible despair. It wasn't that she blankly failed to understand the thing, since it did exist for her as the instrument of a vestigially controlled communication on the part of the man who had contrived it. It was rather that she had no means of viewing it in any intelligible relationship to the frescoes she had just been recalling. She could, upon challenge, put up a decent show in four hundred words. In those brutally splashed diagonals—she would say—was concentrated all the vapulation of Signorelli's hell. Her readers, having consulted their dictionaries, would be impressed.

But it would be nonsense. Jane turned away, seized for the moment by what she was accustomed to call satirically the myth of the capacious masculine intelligence. You did have to have that, you did have to be one of the big synthesists—a Hildebrand, a Wölfflin, a Riegl—authentically to see history turning and returning upon itself in the mirror of art. As this thought went through her mind she saw Charles Rose approaching her.

Charles's, she thought, wasn't a capacious intelligence, but it was an acute one. It could work so successfully on the basis of small and fugitive indications that you could easily be persuaded that his mental operations were of an intuitive sort. They weren't in the least. But he was uncomfortably good at prediction—a sort of genuinely intellectual Sherlock Holmes. Perhaps, basically, this was what had frightened him, made him one of those who seldom speak out. How to lose friends and cease influencing people, Jane thought : have a clear view of what's coming to them.

"Not a Chinese screen in sight," Charles said. "But all too much champagne." He lowered his voice to that effect of a prim propriety which was never far from him. "Odd sort of crowd, aren't they?"

She took his hand for a moment. "But I'm enjoying myself," she said. "Or I was until I had a go with old Bernard Le Mesurier. He did all the scoring, and has left me doubting my vocation. It was the more impressive because he amiably confessed to doubting his. He went off murmuring a prayer that I should forgive him all his naughty pictures." She broke off, remembering something. "Do you know somebody called Lord Burntisland?"

"A rocky but crumbling old person? I glimpsed him a few minutes ago, talking to Bruno's Provost Littlejohn."

"It seems he has ideas about naughty pictures, too."

"Then their perpetrators had better look out. He's a hyperethical type, and quite capable of denouncing Tachisme or whatever in the High Court of Parliament. It was very nice"—Charles made one of his periodic retreats upon the dimmest convention—"to see Hatty in the train this afternoon."

"Was it? I thought she behaved in the most unlicked way."

"Ah, yes—that. I think it likely that Hatty will—" Charles broke off. "And Lucilla looks amazingly well," he said.

Jane was amused. "Lucilla? Yes, she's in rude health."

"No, no. She looks amazingly *well*. And it isn't just that she has that pseudo-Regency rake Alabaster to go round the room with."

Jane followed Charles's glance. "I see. Yes."

"Pallas Athene in that straight back and arrogant head."

For a moment Jane only thought it odd that she should have the same poet quoted to her twice at one party. Then the possibility of a much larger—and an alarming—oddity dawned. In the train Charles had said something about having seen Lucilla lately. And the tribute he had just delivered had been in the very grandest style : too grand for the real Lucilla, although she was a good-looking girl and certainly carried herself well. Charles had taken to seeing her through a gauze of his own devising. And wouldn't it be fatally like him to do just this thing? Lucilla, surely, would no more think of marrying Charles Rose than she would think of marrying John Alabaster himself. Jane had a sudden bizarre vision of Charles, old and white-haired and stately, making an offer of marriage to Lucilla's daughter—and in terms abundantly declaring the doubly retrospective character of the proposal. It was absurd—and it was something more. For the second time that day she had experienced a small shock of relegation; of seeing herself mirrored in a mind that no longer thought of her as being in the running. First Hatty comically warning her off the nice child Luke. And now Charles making her—with a profound unconsciousness, despite all his cleverness —this hint of a valedictory nod. It was like being in the first chapter of a sophisticated modern novel, where it is darkly intimated that everybody is to be amorously permuted with everybody else, to the enforcing of the dire truth that we all inescapably exist.

Jane looked over Charles's shoulder at what was undoubtedly a piece of *Art Autre*. Somebody had taken a length of two-by-two raw timber, cut it into cubes, and fixed these on the lid of a packing-case in roughly parallel lines. It might have been an abacus invented by some prehistoric genius. But it had nothing to do with how people behave to each other. Jane found that she liked it.

"Let's look at things," she said. "There's a Tresilian, for instance. Let's find that."

"Then we'd better hurry up." Charles set a measured pace

which she supposed must be his notion of decorous speed in a gathering like this. "I believe there's to be a string quartet. It will be interesting to see what sort of music the Madronas judge to be congruous with their exhibition. As for Tresilian, how old-fashioned he's likely to seem. And how the *vie des styles* gallop nowadays. It must make a collector's life very hard. As a matter of fact, I hear a rumour that Madrona intends to give most of this away. He intends to try something different."

"Something quite different? Philanthropy? Pedigree cattle?"

"Not at all. Nothing less than Italian painting of the *cinquecento*. He seems to believe that it can still be done. His wealth must be approaching the fabulous. He is, of course, very shrewd. He has pushed himself into notice with all this modish stuff. Now he's going to settle down to getting his money's worth." Charles came to a halt. "There's the Tresilian," he said cautiously. "But a kind of party within the party seems to be going on in front of it. Perhaps we'd better come back later."

"Not a bit. Lucilla's among them. She'll give us the entrée."

"That's true." Perceptibly, Charles quickened his pace, so that Jane was amused by the success of this tiny laboratory experiment. "My God!" he added. "This lot's being distinguished from the common herd of guests by being given *pink* champagne. Can such things be?" He was horrified.

"It's because Sir Hector has faintly Socialist principles. He indoctrinates Lucilla from time to time. You must have her tell you about it. But look." Jane, catching Charles's sharp glance, forestalled anything he might have said. "We're for it. We're being gestured at."

This was true. Their host, having observed them hovering, was waving them into his circle. It was indeed a semi-circle, and the big Tresilian stood behind it. But this seemed fortuitous; the picture was coming in for no special attention; some little ritual unconnected with it appeared to have been going forward. And now Madrona, although he must have welcomed both of them within the hour, was raising his eyebrows in delighted, deferential astonishment. It was as if he had always dreamed that there might be a Jane Landreth and Charles Rose in the world, and as if some enchanter had opportunely waved a wand over his assembly and crowned it by making this fond imagination true. Nor was Lady Madrona laggard, for her genius for conferring favour instantly asserted itself. Halting a servant who was advancing upon Jane and Charles with a tray, she herself picked up two glasses and pressed them, winking and brimming, into their hands. "Dear people," she said—so that Jane could positively feel Charles shudder—"you come at the *eleventh hour*! So please—just *one* sip to the Provost and Hector together."

They sipped in this mysterious interest. Charles—Jane thought —excelled himself in conventional bowings and murmurings. Lucilla, with Alabaster still beside her, stood with what was, for her mother, an irritating air of commanding the comedy. There was a young man, vaguely familiar, whom Jane associated either with the Wallace Collection or the National Gallery. There was an old man, who was being so courteous to the young man that it was plain he didn't approve of him, and who must, she realized, be Lord Burntisland. And there was Littlejohn, interesting to Jane as the Head of Bruno's college, who was being talked to by Arthur Roundhay, and who was evidently at the disadvantage of not knowing whether this was a mere journalist or a not-yet-enobled newspaper proprietor.

The vaguely familiar young man slipped up to Jane. He seemed to take it for granted that he was known to her. "I say, Mrs Landreth," he murmured. "This old chap with the handle— Lord Burnt-Something-or-Other. Are you a chum of his?"

"Lord Burntisland? I haven't even met him."

"Oh, bother! I thought you might put in a word for me. Explain that I read Ruskin in bed every night. I'm in his black books, you see. I think he might get me sacked."

"How dreadful!" Jane knew very well that young men like this cannot be sacked at the instance of offended peers. The young man was putting on a party turn. "What went wrong?"

"It was in the N.G., some time ago. He stopped and asked me about a picture. I took him to it. And he said something funny which I laughed at."

"Well, that sounds all right. But he doesn't look very much of a humorist."

"That's the point." The young man glanced cautiously in the direction of Burntisland. "What he said wasn't meant to be funny at all."

"I can see that that would make a difference."

"Yes—and then something similar happened tonight. A silly

wench was showing him the Dubuffet. And his face was so comical that I had to grin at it. And he saw me."

"Well," Jane said crisply, "you were caught doing something ill-bred. And that's that."

"Oh, quite. And now he's said a few words to me in a freezing manner. It chilled my blood. And there's another thing." The young man looked disconsolate. "I see you don't remember me from Adam. I'm Justin Parks."

"So you are," Jane said, genuinely remembering. "And since we met, you've published a paper on Baciccia."

"That's right." The young man brightened at once.

"Why not send a copy to Lord Burntisland, with the writer's compliments?"

The young man looked uncertain. "Now you're making fun of me," he said.

"It's what you seem to have been doing with this distinguished old person. How would you suppose he'd take a Dubuffet? Propose that one should immediately be bought to grace the House of Lords? All these pluggings of one or another isolated aesthetic quality are only likely to appeal to the sophisticated, goodness knows. But what was the picture you showed him in the N.G.?"

"The Tresilian. I don't know what had put it in his head. It's a lyrical, lovely thing."

"How did he react to it when he saw it?"

"I say! They may hear us." The youth called Parks looked round cautiously. He was enjoying this discreet murmuring with Mrs Landreth. " 'Suspicious', I imagine, would be the word. 'Are you sure this was really done by hand?' That sort of thing. And I think he said he'd keep an eye on Tresilian in the future."

"He doesn't seem to be doing that now. There's a great big Tresilian straight in front of him. And he couldn't care less."

"Oh, but—my dear—he's had it! You should have seen." Justin Parks was cautiously amused. "Lady Madrona showed it to him. No, that's not right. She dowered him with the sight of it. You know? He was a person of more merit than he supposed, and here was his reward."

"And how did he take it?"

"Well, of course, he's not like me. He's one of those perfectly well-bred types, late risen from the people or thereabouts. What new men have got into the way of calling a new man."

"My God," Jane said.

"Yes—aren't we revolting?" Parks cheerfully swept Jane within this condemnation. "But what was I saying? Oh, yes. His lordship was irritated. He was irritated by our hostess and her *empressement*. He was irritated with himself for having come to such a fool party. And he was irritated by this Tresilian, which was incomprehensible to him. But he restrained himself, making courteous noises. Only the next time he sees a Tresilian, I think it likely he'll take his umbrella to it. I can't think why he isn't carrying an umbrella now. He does in the N.G.—with nobody venturing to stop him."

"And now," Jane said, "you must go and talk to my daughter. And send Mr Alabaster to me."

Parks was sufficiently impressed by this touch of grand manner to scurry. And John Alabaster almost scurried too. "My dear," he said, as he came up, "I have been most delightfully improving my acquaintance with Lucilla—as I think it is? A charmer, indeed. And with just a touch of the chilly, you know, to set it off."

Jane saw no need to acknowledge this qualified compliment. "I'm puzzled by Lord Burntisland," she said. "He doesn't seem to make much of an affair like this."

"Decidedly he doesn't. And he looks fagged out, wouldn't you say?" Alabaster put a touch of satisfaction into this question. "He came on a mission—which hasn't, I imagine, precisely fulfilled itself. And now that predatory don, Littlejohn, has got hold of him. He's just made the old boy promise to go up to Oxford for some rude banquet. Burntisland, being a son of the manse, has a vast respect for learning."

"But not, it seems, for the arts—or not for their contemporary manifestations. He doesn't, that young man tells me, take even to the Tresilian."

"Then he's made yet another rash promise. Our hostess has positively engaged him to escort her to the opening of the Tresilian show. I suppose you'll be there? But of course you will. It's a professional occasion for you. And I shall go myself, if only because I knew the man."

"You knew Matthew Tresilian?" Jane was interested. "He seems to have been rather an elusive figure. I'd like to know more about him—partly because he's so very much growing in stature as a painter, and partly because my two younger children have got to know a boy called Luke Tresilian, who's the son of his second marriage. I was talking to Charles Rose about it this afternoon. He told me of somebody who's chasing up Tresilian's life."

"That would be my shrewd American." Alabaster laughed— and it was a sound, Jane thought, in which one heard, like the note of a high, cracked bell, an ancient and inexpugnable malice. "His name—well, I forget his name. And I met him—I'm sure I can't tell you where. But he felt he was being rather clever with me. Perhaps he was. I took to him. Sufficiently, at least, to drop him a hint."

"A hint on how to chase up Tresilian?"

"Yes, and perhaps one or two other people."

"I know about your shrewd American. His name's Delver. And he believes, incidentally, that Tresilian was rather a notable writer. He hopes to chase up that too. No doubt it's exciting, but I feel the pictures are enough to go on with." Past Alabaster's shoulder, Jane could just glimpse the big painting on the wall. "If some of those people would move on, we could have a proper look at this one. I don't think the Madronas have a late Tresilian—one in that strange last manner?"

"I know they haven't. They're as rare, you know, as they're startling."

"Why did he paint them? As you knew the man, perhaps you know the answer."

"You think there is a mystery about it?"

"Well, it was a kind of harking back, in a way. He had gained the freedom of that tremendous, if remote and withdrawn, abstract world. And then he makes a final plunge into what might be, with some difference, the world of Munch."

"Whose most celebrated thing is called, I seem to remember, 'The Cry'. The Expressionists, my dear, painted funk, panic, hysteria—or just shock, bewilderment, despair. There isn't often any great mystery, you know, about what confronts us with these disagreeable emotions. The answer is personal calamity. Tresilian had two children by his first marriage—a boy and a girl. The boy was killed in the war. That's all."

"It was as simple as that?"

"Why not? It suddenly rendered him a universe with sense-lessness as its core. One looks around, and there is this and that :

shapes of beauty and awe and intricate formal design in what seems a divine abundance. One concentrates one's gaze in order to distinguish the central and sustaining principle of the astounding exhibition, the point of stillness upon which the mighty wheel must turn. And there is nothing there, nothing at all."

"I see."

"You might make a little essay out of it." Alabaster's mocking smile had a suggestion, Jane thought, of the strained and mechanical. He was far more fagged out than his younger contemporary, Lord Burntisland, showed any marked sign of being. Only an iron will stood between Alabaster and an already procrastinated dissolution. What propelled him through meaningless social occasions like the present it seemed impossible to conceive.

"Had Tresilian been devoted to the boy?" Jane asked.

"On the contrary, I suspect that he had rather neglected him. And, no doubt, that enhanced the catastrophe. Whether his grief or guilt was assuaged when another marriage brought him another son : that, I don't at all know. You see, he swam into my ken only when he became the lover of a woman that I wanted as a mistress myself. He swam out again when his second matrimonial adventure fortunately—if with a mortifying belatedness—removed him from the scene."

"I see." Jane repeated the words mechanically. An eddy among Sir Hector Madrona's guests had suddenly given her a full view of Sir Hector Madrona's Tresilian. It had, she recalled, some absurd title; there had been a habit in those days of finding, at the height of a studio party, an *outré* nomenclature for new paintings. But the thing itself was majestic. And it was a world of its own. It referred you to nothing beyond itself.

"Ah, we can see it now." Carefully, as if the movement must not be let go too far, Alabaster cocked his head on one side. "What do you think of it? And how does it compare with the picture at Oxford?"

"It's smaller," Jane said. This sort of thing was part of her common round—but she had to take, all the same, a moment before any passable comment came to her. All these people round about, with their champagne whether penny plain or twopence coloured, had become, for the moment, shadowy and insubstantial, their babble shrunk to a papery whisper. And Alabaster was like a revenant in stays and on a stick, mouthing mockery and senile self-confession into a void. But the painting was a gaunt rock, intricate with the gravure of aeons of geological time, from which mist or cloud or sea spray had just fallen back. Standing before it, Jane felt that great chords must begin to sound.

"My dear, the music's starting."

Alabaster had spoken in vexed resignation. She turned, and saw people beginning to seat themselves in rows at the far end of the room, where a man had taken his place at a piano and another was tuning a violin.

CHAPTER NINETEEN

The fog was in the room. It made fuzzier the fuzzy oleographic Good Shepherd on the wall. Yet when the woman opened the outer door it came in like a new thing, an intruding physical presence that drove her back, smothered her breath with its breath, nuzzled at her neck with insistent unwanted lips. She shivered, drew the shawl round her hair, and went out.

Immediately she heard the high, thin note. It was like the cry of a child that had been carried very far away. And it never stopped—never. That the ear continued conscious of it was strange. There had been a time when she had supposed it not to exist, or not in an outer world. When they had come here from overseas three years before, she had taken it, as a disturbing symptom, to the doctor who came once a week to spend a perfunctory afternoon in the room to which the banker also came—but only once a fortnight—to spend a perfunctory morning. (These were the only comings and goings in the village. They were the only comings and goings for miles around unless you counted the rota folk : the man and his wife who came to the otherwise empty cottage next door—the man to tend the shore light when her own man went out for his spell on Carn Braddoc.) About her ears the doctor—a young, worried man—had been believing but unhelpful. But her husband, harshly affectionate, called her a fool for her pains. The high, thin note came from the light itself. It came, for a technical reason she never understood, whether or not the light was flashing. You could hear it at any instant you were prompted to do so. Even when the foghorn was going—as it was going now—the shattering roar, ebbing to a low deep sob and fading away, delivered back the ear to this strange vibration from above.

She moved forward, blindly but with confidence. There was never anything out of place in this constricted universe. Everything had the exaggerated trimness that belongs to a ship ashore.

She knew that, on either side of her, white-painted cable ran from wooden post to wooden post in precise, shallow loops; that ahead of her and at right angles to these the small garden was demarcated by similar loops of the curious chain-work, perhaps ornamental in intention, that takes the form of blunted and harmless spikes; that if she stooped down and touched these they would reveal the texture, the peculiar turn at the edges, of metal objects upon which there have been laid innumerable thin super-impositions of paint. There was a smell of paint now. She caught it even in the blanketed air, and this did for a moment make her pause in uncertainty. She remembered that the flagstaff had been unstepped from its tabernacle for painting, and she was un-certain where it lay. Then she recalled it as set up on trestles parallel to the path. Everything had its place. There could never be confusion. There could never even be small, unexpected discovery. She had submitted to the code and discipline of the service, and in the house there was no drawer or shelf harbour-ing a forgotten shoe-lace, candle end, pencil stump, bunch of keys. Only in the garden sometimes she would find among the flowers some tiny cluster of petals that had appeared in error. And she would take them between her fingers with a clutch at the heart.

She went through the low gate, and heard the muted click as its coiled spring swung it back so that the latch fell. The rough, uneven path began at once, winding down to the cove and then up to the turn of the road half a mile along which ran the scatter of cottages. She still moved confidently, although it was a path scarcely perceptible beneath her feet. She might have been remote in an antique world, so that the blare of the fog-horn suggested itself as wrung from some monstrous creature in a toil. So powerful was this act of her own mind, this projecting of all she knew of pain upon an insensate thing, that she paused and turned to look, almost expecting some looming shape, al-though knowing that there could be only fog. And, strangely, there was in fact a shape, although an unsurprising one. It was the foghorn itself and the rock platform on which it stood, poised in one of those sudden rifts that could make these seascapes phantasmagoric.

She stared at the dully gleaming, elongated metal cone. You could see it as some wide-mouthed beast, baying at the sea, its

hind-quarters crouched and tapered in a convention existing—
she remembered uncertainly—in Egyptian, or perhaps it was
Assyrian, art. For a moment something far down in her mind
caused her to reject this image and to stretch out an invisible
hand to the touch and texture and recession of the glimpsed,
lucidly geometrical thing. Then the machine was engulfed, so
that she turned again and walked on. But it blared again behind
her. She found herself wondering why, in a scientific age abounding in sophisticated signals, these lugubrious noises were still in
demand by mariners. Perhaps they answered some unacknowledged emotional need. Like the need she herself sometimes felt
to let her mind play on such fugitives, idle topics as just this,
interesting only for themselves. But it was a habit she found it not
wise to encourage. She turned her mind to dinner. She saw herself in the vegetable garden sheltered by the big white-painted
wall. She was choosing between winter spinach, broccoli, leeks.
And in the larder there was one thing, in the refrigerator another. On that side, life was far from hard. It might be more
interesting if it was. Were there children, they might have to
take thought. As it was, they had what they liked, so far as
humble material provision went. She walked on.

The fog was nowhere uniform. It was this that made it like
a live creature : hovering, outflanking, biding its time. The scale
of things behaved queerly in its cold embrace. When she came
up to the road the stone stile loomed enormous, like something
only a giant could overstep. Through it she saw the uncertain
outline of the Bethsaida, the nearest building to the lighthouse
and its cottages. She felt a pang—and realized with a kind of
numb wonder that it came of her remembering that she never
went there now. She could still recall the inside drabness that
answered the drabness without; she could recall the unutterable
tedium of the hymns, the prayers, the harangues. But now she
almost wished that she had continued to go alone, at least at
irregular intervals, after her husband had decided to take his
religion through the post.

The next instalment must be here now. But first she stooped
for the milk bottle, since that was there every day. It felt cold
to her hand. She put her other hand in the box above. There
were two letters. She looked at them and saw that neither writing
was unfamiliar, although one she had not set eyes on for many

164

months. She put both in a pocket and turned back. As she did so, voices greeted her from the road.

"Mrs Crinnis! Day, Mrs Crinnis! Morning, Mrs Crinnis!"

She could not tell whether or not she knew the passing children. They had identified her because of the path on which she stood; they were only blurred forms to her. But the voices were friendly, and she answered gently. Yet as she turned away she heard smothered laughter and running feet. She wondered if the encounter had been an adventure for them. She wondered if she was thought to be crazed.

Alfred was sitting in the kitchen. He had brought a lantern in from the watch room and was polishing it. His open Bible was on the table beside him.

"Is it going to lift?" she asked. She tried never to come into his presence without some simple spoken contact. She was in her mid-thirties and he was twenty years older. She feared his disappearing into some total solitude one day. Now he was looking up at her in slow wonder.

"Can't you hear the nautophone at the Zoze?" he asked. "There's no mistaking three hundred cycles to the second. The wind must have gone round three points. The fog will lift."

She nodded, not greatly attending. He knew more of the science of his signals than his work required. It was scarcely a bond between them, although she could amuse him by her ignorance—and even sometimes by her knowledge, as when she told him that the hundred and eighty cycles of his own siren made F sharp in the tenor clef. Now she laid the two letters on the table. He glanced from one to the other, and then raised his eyes to hers again in a long look. He picked up one of the letters and opened it. "It's as I thought," he said. He spoke almost with animation. "Zephaniah."

"Zephaniah, is it?" She glanced at what he had brought out of the envelope. It was the usual cyclostyled sheet, and she knew that it would be full of raving.

"God's severe judgment against Judah," he said. "Howl, ye inhabitants of Maktesh, for all the merchant people are cut down. I wonder, now, would Maktesh be Penzance? And do you think, Faith"—his voice had turned almost wistful—"that we might read Zephaniah together? 'Tis filled with a power o' pregnant matter. There shall be the noise of a cry from the fish gate. There's dark matter must lie in that."

"Together? Yes, perhaps." Faith Crinnis looked at the second envelope, addressed to herself. "I'll be getting the vegetables," she said, not touching it. She picked up a basket and went out again.

She crossed the little kitchen garden without a glance, set the basket down by the wall, and passed through another gate. The high, thin note was in the air—but in a moment the obliterating siren slowly rose, blared, dropped swiftly to the grunt, rose again. There might be pockets out at sea, Alfred had told her, in which the grunt alone was heard, while the remainder of the signal was inaudible. She thought of the prophet Zephaniah, and wondered how Alfred or any man could believe that here too were crucial signals, half lost and to be pieced together by the poring mind. But Alfred believed that the books of the Bible had been written by the Holy Ghost. Perhaps it was not beyond the Holy Ghost to write about Maktesh and mean Penzance. The world had been made to hold much that was crazy and more that was cruel. She halted on the track she was climbing and looked at the sea. The fog was lifting, but there was still little visibility. Far out there was Carn Braddoc. It, at least, was *known* to be treacherous. It took its name from that.

She moved on—climbing steeply, with a long, unhurried stride. She was aware of her own body : of the strength and straightness and elasticity of it, its near youth, its shapeliness that appeared through whatever she wore. She carried these things like a useless burden up and over the headland, not pausing again until she stood on the verge of the cliff.

The place was called the Cauldron. Because the cove took the form of more than half a circle, and because its sides were con-cavities of dark and naked rock, it retained something of the appearance of such a thing even in sunlight and with a blue sea washing into it in straight lazy lines. But in weather like this the illusion was complete. Directly in front of her there might be an answering lip to that on which she perilously stood. And below, because the fog was stirring, eddying, rising up in oblique drifts and sudden vertical spirals, it was possible to believe there lay a crucible in which had just been achieved the first stage of some gigantic sublimation.

She stood gazing fixedly down. The vapour parted farther so that she glimpsed, far below, a white and working surface which might itself have been floating, a great fleece of cloud, high above some remoter deep. But it was the sea. It was a moving texture of unbroken foam. Then, suddenly, it was unbroken no longer, but was chequered with dark patches of circling water. And sounds came up; a chafing brabble that might have been from remote, eager voices; a pulse as of rhythmically moving feet; a sibilation like the brushing of silks. For a moment she saw—so infinitely far beneath—the brilliant assembly, the stately ball. Then a gannet dived—and with so thwart a movement that she felt dizzy and drew back. The Cauldron was there once more, a dangerous and alien place. She turned round and made her way down the zig-zag path and up again, as if with an emptied mind. She retrieved her basket and filled it. She went back into the house.

Alfred had finished burnishing the lantern, and had put it aside. The Bible was still in front of him, together with the cyclostyled commentary.

"You've been a long time," he said. "You'll be catching cold." He spoke gratingly, kindly.

"I took a walk."

He shook his head. But it was over the text before him.

"Woe," he said, "to her that is filthy and polluted." He lifted his eyes to her. "There be those of so superficial a mind they think that to be no more than a sharp reproof of Jerusalem. The prelates have set just such a false gloss at the head of the chapter. Woe to them too, children of Ammon. They shall be as Gomorrah, even the breeding of nettles, and saltpits, and a perpetual desolation."

She wondered—as she had done several times of late—whether he was going mad. Probably not, she told herself quickly. Cornwall was full of elderly men mumbling scripture. Among the people on the lights it might be an occupational disease. After all, their employers called themselves to this day the Brotherhood of the most Glorious and Undivided Trinity. Not, perhaps, that Alfred believed in the Trinity. Perhaps he regarded it as an invention of the prelates.

She checked her idle and devious mind, sat down, took up her letter. "It's from Luke," she said.

"Aye." This time he glanced up only briefly, and after having placed a finger on the page before him, as if to be sure of not losing his place. "Three, eleven," he said. "Mind that."

Often now she could attach no meaning to his words. She opened the letter and read it :

Dear Faith,

We don't seem to see much of each other, or even write. But here's something that perhaps we ought to consider together. As you know, the big exhibition of Father's work is coming along soon, and it seems that interest is growing in him in various ways. Have you had a letter, I wonder, from an American professor, who is interested in his life, and also in finding and (I suppose) publishing anything he wrote? I think he may want to go down and see you. How would you feel?

The man I mean is called Delver. (There may be others, it occurs to me.) He wants to come to Oxford and I suppose he must. Of course I have no memories that could be useful to him. You must have. But I have the manuscript I think you know of. I have sometimes wondered whether you ought not to read it—although I know you feel that my mother's story is not your affair. Anyway, ought I to give it to this man? I have written to my guardian and he has replied : No—neither give it nor mention it. He copied out for me a poem by Kipling called "The Appeal"—which says not to question anything except the books Kipling left behind. But I feel that what Father wrote he did mean for the world one day. It's a question of when—and so I have wondered if you have an opinion.

Won't you come to London for the exhibition, and we could go together? Not to the opening or private view or whatever they call it, but quietly and later, without people knowing us. After all, you and I are the last Tresilians.

I'm getting on all right, although there is some worrying Latin. And I've got to know a lot of nice people—one very nice indeed.

Love from LUKE.

She read the letter once through, with an impassive face. Her husband appeared to have withdrawn entirely into his researches;

he would finish his first study of the new commentary before going to turn off the diaphone. She opened a drawer, took out some writing-paper, and at once wrote her reply :

Dear Luke,

Yes, the man has written to me. But I haven't replied and I won't see him. My life here is entirely of the people, to whom I was returned when still almost a child. I don't propose to recall, even for a professor, other circumstances, other habits of mind.

Since you ask me, I say : Give him your manuscript. It disgraces nobody, I suppose, and may content him.

I hear word of you from the trustees from time to time. And in my own life there are no events. So there is scarcely need for writing.

FAITH CRINNIS.

She addressed and stamped an envelope, and put the letter inside.

"The reply isn't important," she said. "Still, I'll slip up with it to the box now."

"Aye." He nodded. He was incurious. His finger moved again on the page as she passed him.

"Behold," he said, "at that time I will undo all that afflict thee : and I will save her that halteth, and gather her that was driven out."

She thought suddenly that it was she, not he, who would go mad. She opened the door quickly. The fog had shifted, and she could see the long resinator of the diaphone glisten in a shaft of light.

"For God's sake can't you turn it off?" she said. For it was still blaring, still like a creature in pain.

CHAPTER TWENTY

Silence was what chiefly struck visitors to the great elongated honeycomb that thrust its endless storeys into the dull London sky. There was indeed one pervasive sound : a continuous vibration from the air-conditioning. But its frequency was higher than the bat's squeak, so that it was audible only to the young and unimportant. In your thirties—except for one or two news rooms still mounted on the traditional clattering pattern —you passed into a world of almost Trappist silence. And there were other austere continuities. Day and night, the lighting was the same; summer and winter, the temperature never altered. The ventilation had been bought in New York, and would have withstood a heat wave. Were it to fail, hundreds—it was said— would suffocate before they could reach some frangible surface and break through to survival. This story had come from New York too. And from San Francisco came the elevator that ran up the exterior face of the building. It had caught the eye of the proprietor when he was strolling there. But the elevator was only for his top men : chairman, certain directors, editor, managing editor, some favourites of the moment. It also served as a sort of *grande entrée* for distinguished callers. This was why it had brought up Lord Burntisland. Such a manner of ascent had not pleased him. It had been as alarming as the chair-lifts he remembered in Switzerland—and much less rational. People gaped up at you as they went along the street. You had a feeling of having been constrained to lend yourself to a stunt. The thing was, as they said, a gimmick.

Arthur Roundhay, whom he now knew to be the satrap of the moment in this alien empire, had received him in an octagonal chamber, four sides of which were glass. Up here you were at least able to look out on open air, even if you were forbidden any whiff of it. From where he sat, Burntisland saw Roundhay's head as impressively haloed by the dome of St Paul's. On the wall on the left was a large photograph of the proprietor, benignly smiling. Beneath this—and, one would have conjectured, incapable of smiling in any circumstances whatever—sat an underling whose name Burntisland had distinctly picked up as Snide. Snide, it seemed, was present as being the paper's detail man in the particular field of the visitor's concern. "We'll have up the detail man," Roundhay had said, pressing a button.

Burntisland had not come to Roundhay in a hurry. That wouldn't have answered at all. His plan was now formulated, the colleagues who would support him in debate were known, help in various other quarters was marshalled. Now he brought out the names one by one, and had the satisfaction of seeing Roundhay grow yet more genial and Snide sit stiffly on his skimpy chair.

"And I am particularly satisfied," he said at the conclusion, "to have the goodwill of your—" He had been about to add "employer" when it occurred to him that this was not perhaps the right word. Roundhay was no doubt a director after a fashion. "Of your principal," he said, and glanced at the photograph.

"Ah, yes. I have the Chief's note here." Roundhay pointed to a desk which appeared to be unimpeded by a single scrap of paper. "He says we must make a gesture in the matter. I'd say, you know"—Roundhay laughed easily, as a man who is putting something in a merely whimsical way—"that it's pretty well an order. So let's go ahead."

Burntisland was prepared to go ahead, although "gesture" was not quite the word he would have wished to hear. "I look to you for a strong leader," he said. "That in the first place. But the vital thing is to keep up the pressure until we gain our point."

"Exactly so." Roundhay had produced an effect of massive assent. But his eyes were those of a man who is confronted with a problem—and a problem in the shape of another man inconveniently planted in front of him. "Of course," he said, "we'll get nowhere by underestimating the difficulties. And it's tricky work—at this present moment, above all." He turned to his assistant. "That right?" he snapped.

"I'm sure it is." The man who appeared to be called Snide had given a gulp and made a grab at incisive speech. "I doubt whether advertising has ever been in a more sensitive state. There's television a big questionmark, with political upheaval round the corner. There's the tobacco people feeling one breeze and the pharmaceutical people feeling another. Then Lord Burntisland mentioned cinema posters. Of course we must agree they are sometimes the sort of thing one would rather one's daughter didn't pass on the way to school. Still, the cinema industry is having hard work to pay its way. We have to think of all these things. We even have to think twice about those paperback people who turn out everything in suggestive covers. Book publishers are of no importance in themselves. But, nowadays, it's hardly possible to work out who really controls them. So there might be trouble there too."

"There are interests, no doubt," Burntisland said stonily.

It was in the little silence succeeding this speech that he became aware of an unaccountable and disconcerting circumstance. Snide was still sitting directly under the photograph of the proprietor. But Roundhay's head was no longer haloed by St Paul's. Sir Christopher Wren's masterpiece had ceased to be located where it had been. It had changed ground. And Lord Burntisland—whose visual sensibility had existed of late in an irritated state—felt dizzy. He found himself taking a grip of both arms of his chair.

"Ah—amusing, isn't it?" Roundhay was evidently accustomed to callers becoming thus conscious of their untoward situation. "This room rotates on its axis in precisely sixty minutes. A notion the Chief picked up at the World's Fair in Seattle. They had a restaurant like this. Only this is on a different principle. As a matter of fact, we're floating in a bath of mercury. It's like the top of a lighthouse."

"Very interesting." Burntisland was annoyed to find that he was experiencing a slight sensation of sea-sickness. "It would appear to return us to our subject. Such a contrivance is no doubt for advertising purposes. A 'stunt' as the young people say."

"Oh, not in the least!" Roundhay seemed almost offended. "It has never been publicised in the slightest degree. Comparatively few people know about it. The intention is entirely symbolic and for our own inspiration. Again, of course, it's the Chief's idea. A clear, objective glance from a commanding height, sweeping England."

Having nothing civil to say, Burntisland, as was his habit when so circumstanced, remained silent. He noticed however that the nonsense of the thing did not leave him wholly composed; that the sensation of wandering, confused and bewildered, in a world no longer tolerably lucid to his intelligence—a sensation he had been experiencing with increasing frequency of late—had for the moment possessed him. Still, he had made some headway with these people, or rather with the fellow Roundhay, since the underling with the absurd name—which was now temporarily escaping him—was negligible. He had spent many years in negotiation; he knew when he was leaving at least a wholesome headache behind him; Roundhay was realizing that, if only because his boss was grown as old and eccentric as this tiresome visitor, the problem presented would have to be thought about. Naturally enough, Roundhay had his advertising revenue on his mind. Burntisland, a business man, knew very well that business has to be business if a man is going to stay in it. He had no impulse to treat Roundhay *de haut en bas*. Still, he had talked with the fellow's employer on a serious and elevated plane—one taking no account of balance sheets. Roundhay, just as much as Snipe or whatever his name was, would have to toe the line.

"We'll think," Roundhay was saying—and with an effect of being at once grave and jovial. "I promise you we'll think—and then we'll have another conference. Of course, our best tactic mayn't be head-on. A diversionary technique might be worked out."

"Diversionary?" Burntisland said sharply.

"No, no." Roundhay seemed almost confused. "I've got the wrong word. Oblique. Subtle. You know the kind of thing I mean."

Burntisland was not at all sure that he did know. And in Roundhay's glance he had read the look of a man who remembers, or tries to remember, something. There was now, however, no point in prolonging this meeting. Burntisland stood up—refraining, as he did so, from taking another sighting glance at St Paul's.

"I think," he said, "I'll have you send me down in another lift. I came up in one that might be intended to register your soaring circulation. At night, it struck me, you probably pick it out in coloured lights."

"Certainly we do—and it has a coronet on top." Roundhay

seemed struck by his departing visitor's acumen. "You couldn't, I suppose, stop and lunch with us?"

"Thank you—no. I have to keep a dinner engagement in Oxford. And I no longer find it easy to be active throughout a day."

Duly despatched in a more reticent lift, Burntisland plummeted to ground-level, frowning. With his last words he had surprised himself. He didn't commonly say that sort of thing. Such confessions caused people to remark to each other with satisfaction that you couldn't hang on much longer, or with condescension that mentally you were almost as alert as ever. And in fact he was perfectly fit to lunch with one set of acquaintances and dine with another. After the busiest day he would need only an undisturbed hour in a train to prepare a speech tolerably appropriate to an Oxford after-dinner occasion. The simple fact was that he inclined more and more towards solitude, that it wasn't good for him, and that therefore he took up these activities, accepted these invitations.

Turning into Fleet Street, he raised his umbrella at a taxi, thought better of it, and brusquely waved the man on. The street was crowded, and he had an impulse to keep in the crowd, after all. Nobody loitered in this quarter of the city, or had much of an eye for others as they passed. There was a stir and vitality about it that yet didn't in any way impinge or impend or disturbingly beckon. Young men predominated: unattractive young men with poor complexions and postures, hurrying about on other men's petty occasions. It was curious how many people still demonstrably spent their time running messages in the City. There was something unchanging about it. Glancing from the pavement to the street, he could almost be in expectation of the horse-drawn omnibuses of his earliest memory.

Suddenly sunshine struck through the foggy sky. He took off his gloves as he walked, so that he might feel the warmth on his hands. He had a poor opinion of persons who are perpetually whoring after the sun, and who suppose that a business—or a dozen businesses—can be conducted on the strength of an open telephone line from Cortina d'Ampezzo or St Tropez. But he had an instinct for sunshine when it came. Sometimes, even, it would abruptly drive a shaft deep into some sensuous hinterland of his mind, and images would be released on the surface as if on a sensitized paper that responds to heat. Just this was happening now. He was recalling his mission—the mission which, if successful, would have brought him straight home to a seat in the Cabinet. He remembered its failure—but remembered chiefly the lakesides, peopled but not crowded, as the Conference dragged uselessly on through those hot Potsdam days. The young men—he supposed there had been young women too—had hurled the discus and the javelin, had raced and wrestled and dived in splendid nudity. It had been, of course, simply the neo-Graecism that has for centuries haunted the German mind. No more than a few months later Hitler laid his hand on it, and the Pheidian forms disappeared within uniforms and helmets and jackboots.

That had been a long time ago. He paused, and found that he was looking at a paper-stall, hung all over with cheap magazines. The hanging had been done from the top left-hand corner, so that they made an irregular diamond-shaped patchwork, and you had to cock your head to interpret them. Probably Roundhay's organization had a hand in the whole lot. People still bought, it seemed, periodicals instructing them how to do fretwork, keep bees, collect postage stamps. Others were of a kind that had enjoyed no public currency in his earlier years. All, doubtless, preserved in their letterpress a highly respectable tone —even those the covers of which were devoted to exhibitions of nakedness : excessively muscular men and curiously ugly women, posed within certain threadbare conventions of decency. How different, he thought, from the visionary quality of that distant German scene. He turned and crossed the street.

Yes, indeed, a long time ago. He walked on, seeing nothing now, brooding on time and its effluxion. He supposed his life had run within a narrow course. Yet year by year he could trace it, forward or back, and always see variety, the unexpected challenge, achievements that had appeared worth while in their moment. How rich, at least, compared with the endless dropping away of meaningless days at Epping ! Fleet Street had faded. He was aware of nothing but terrible pain.

That morning there had been bad news, although no more than bad news of a familiar sort. She had entered upon one of her phases of violence, and heavy sedation had been required. As she grew older, it seemed, more risks attended this. The medical

superintendent of the private asylum had telephoned, as Burntisland strictly required that on such occasions he should do. But
there was no point in visiting the place. His wife had given no
sign of recognition for years. Sitting at her bedside was like
sitting in the empty waiting-room of some branch-line station
through which trains had long ago ceased to run.

He cried out "Taxi!" in a loud voice. He did this because he
believed himself involuntarily to have cried out something else,
and thought that he might thus cover up the aberration.
Curiously enough, a taxi came at once to a halt beside him. He
climbed into it stiffly but with precision, concentrating on the
necessary motions, so that it was without awareness that he gave
the driver some direction. He sank back in the fusty little space,
wrestling with darkness.

But he had known for more than half a lifetime now that he
would never draw up any of these matters further towards the
light. Elspeth's affliction, when it came, had scarcely moved him
even in common degree, so that he had concluded his marriage to
have been a shallow, as well as an imperfect, thing. But the years
had declared his error. Her affliction became his guilt; he believed—for long with an intolerable force of conviction—that at
some unacknowledged depth of his own being there had lurked
an evil, an obliquity, which destroyed her. His reason rejected
the thought. Yet the abstinence in which he henceforth lived had
been only partly prompted by what could be called the moral
sense, and had been prompted not at all by any religious sanction.
It was, therefore, magical; an endless expiatory act. Only once—
or was it twice?—a brief madness of his own had streaked that
abstinence with momentary behaviour inexplicable to any self he
knew. The private, isolated fact was unimportant, for he was a
man of strong and rational mind. What was important was that
he had let early disaster cripple so much, dictate so many
barriers, proscribe as a region of darkness and danger too much
of instinctual and passional life.

Burntisland braced and squared himself against the jolting seat
of his cab. All this was unprofitable. There was a little that he
had got clear long ago; no wrestling with the shadows would do
anything for him now. He addressed his mind to questions of the
day. He reflected on his Oxford engagement. He had felt doubts
about it. With the university he had very little association, and

with Littlejohn's particular college none whatever. It was one of the most notable of the colleges, and must possess among its own members a sufficiency of eminent persons who could provide it with postprandial eloquence. Littlejohn, then, had some reason for wanting to cultivate him. Some part of the college's investments, perhaps, lay in a field over which Burntisland had a special command. That would be it : something about their portfolio. Not that he had not had a hand in educational affairs; he could speak on them with a very sufficient authority if they wanted that sort of thing. And a night in one of those places had its charm—only the more so for a man whose own education owed nothing to institutions south of the Border.

With reflections of this sort Lord Burntisland calmed himself, and it then occurred to him to wonder where he was going. For a moment his mind was blank, but almost at once he recalled that he had asked to be driven to Victoria Gate. That meant a walk across the Park and being home in time for lunch. It was a reasonable proposal, for the day was turning out fine. Yet for some reason it was now disagreeable to him. He leant forward, tapped sharply on the glass, and gave the driver the address of his club.

CHAPTER TWENTY-ONE

"I GUESS I'D LIKE to get out around here," Thayne Delver said, leaning forward and speaking apologetically. The cab came to what he could feel was a sulky halt, its proposed goal still some blocks away. He stood on the sidewalk and sorted his florins and half-crowns with less than his usual confidence, so that the driver hoped for more than the correct tip he actually got. Delver watched him drive off with a jerk, and then looked round to orient himself. He was just by Notting Hill Gate, so the address must still be some distance off. That would let him stretch his legs, and again try to plan ahead.

There was no doubt that he felt discomposed, and he had a feeling that if he didn't take care he might get rattled. It wasn't that the prospect of Mary Emeleus in itself was all that daunting. He had been round a good many literary monuments, major and minor, in his time. It was rather that the occasion of his calling on her was surely tricky. He couldn't—or so he thought—announce baldly that his interest in her was prompted merely by her having been Matthew Tresilian's mistress. Thus he was forced from the start into a disingenuous role. More than that : it was a disingenuous role that the lady herself would probably be quite acute enough to tumble to.

Further, there was the awkwardness of the hour. She had written that she would be at home on Monday and looked forward to the pleasure of a morning call. It was now eleven-thirty. That seemed good enough—but in the cab Delver had remembered something disconcerting. Mrs Beeton's work on household management, in the edition of 1888, had been among his mother's not very numerous heirlooms, and it had become in childhood—far more than Fannie Farmer's indigenous equivalent—his constant reading when hanging about the kitchen. The first chapter was the most fascinating of all, and it was from the first chapter that his present memory had arisen. "After luncheon"—Mrs Beeton pronounces—"morning calls and visits may be made." Despite misgiving, Delver smiled as he walked. If Miss Emeleus had used the expression in this sense she had been absurdly precious. Could there possibly be people in England who still called the afternoon the morning?

Delver checked this semantic speculation in favour of matters of more pressing concern. That he should call on this woman simply as the bearer of John Alabaster's greetings lacked plausibility—unless it were reinforced by a lively admiration felt by himself for her work. Conscious of this, he had sat up late on two successive nights and succeeded in re-reading a couple of her early novels. He had read *The Rack Dislimns* and *Fenella's Pilgrimage*. They had dated, but they were good in their brittle way. "Delusive" was perhaps the word for them now; Mary Emeleus was a writer from whom more had been expected than it was sagacious to expect. It was probable that she had later paid for this error in estimation. The critics who, in a short-term way, fix literary reputations seldom forgive their own incautious early enthusiasms. Delver hadn't read any of her later books—the books, that was to say, up to about ten years ago, after which she had fallen silent. It might have been wise to tackle one, and dig some merit out of it as a talking point. Writers don't much relish the unspoken premise that they were at their least unentertaining a generation ago. But anything of the sort would only be deepening the disingenuousness of his approach. He must go ahead on whatever terms came to him.

He had no idea of her present circumstances, but the street through which he was making his way suggested that they might be those of a decayed gentlewoman of the most sharply accented sort. She inhabited, perhaps no more than a hall bedroom—or whatever was the British equivalent of that—behind the tattered stucco of one of the dismal houses he had here gotten among. It was pretty well a negro quarter. You could have spotted it, he told himself, even if none of the inhabitants were themselves in evidence; you could have spotted it from the peculiar combinations, subtly disturbing to a white taste, in which they had been painting their doors and windows. But at the next intersection there was an indefinable hint of change. The rooming houses seemed less desperate, and in the window of one he saw a notice pusillanimously reading "Regret no coloureds". Then, halfway down the succeeding block, the buildings of this sort tumbled themselves like a dirty surf against a great red brick cliff that might have been a factory but turned out to be a ten-storey pile of apartment dwellings put up when, in London, ten storeys was an architectural gesture in itself. Consulting a numbered door, he found he had arrived at his destination.

He still couldn't decipher much of Mary Emeleus's condition. The place might represent anything between "model" dwellings for the industrial classes and "flats" just short of the luxury order. An Englishman would gain from a bird-cage, a plant, an ornament glimpsed in a window definitive intelligence which would come to himself only upon more abundant communication. And the interior continued inexplicit. He went up two flights of dustily carpeted stairs—if there was an elevator he had failed to locate it—and down a long corridor off which the apartments opened with a frequency suggesting they could scarcely be commodious. But at the end he came upon one which he divined to be of somewhat superior pretension. It was here he rang a bell.

His first thought when the door opened was that the moment might tell him something new about Matthew Tresilian. It didn't. Mary Emeleus in her sixties was a handsome woman, and when younger must have been a beauty. But it was an orthodox beauty, depending on fine bones and bold planes, such as might have been any artist's choice. Her hair was white. Her pale skin, although cared for, hinted an infinitude of finely criss-crossed lines, like paper smoothed out after having been crumpled again and again. Only her eyes, which were dark and bright, seemed youthful—but something in the manner of her holding her head made Delver wonder whether, invisibly to an outward view, her sight were not beginning to fail. She was dressed, he vaguely saw, in some unfashionable, artistic way. A crucifix of more than common dimensions hung on a dull metal chain from her neck.

"Professor Delver? How delightful! There has been all Mr Alabaster's famous kindness in his having asked you to call."

Her voice, he noticed immediately, contrived to be at once authentically upper class and an affair of deliberate cultivation. It had bold prominences and acclivities moulded to go with her features. The effect of politely muted irony which he had caught came less from its tone than from the finicalness of her grammar. In the circumstances irony was fair enough, he thought—reflection having confirmed him in the view that Alabaster's impulse had been malicious. But it might simply be a pervasive manner-ism natural in one whose writings had been so steeped in various dilute solutions of this attitude or quality.

She led the way into a drawing-room. He saw, in a series of quickly succeeding impressions, that it was unexpectedly large, that it was shabby, that it was old-fashioned in its appointments, and that this old-fashionedness was the consequence of a sophisti-cated cultivation of the Victorian taste. Victoriana were all over the place. But these were put in inverted commas, as it were, through the instrumentality of a scattering of objects which must still, in the thirties, have borne a boldly modern look : a chunky and twisted metal object that might be descended from Epstein's "Rock Drill"; an Etruscan mirror-back of exuberantly Priapic inspiration; a couple of "primitive" paintings of Douanier-Rousseau-like suggestion; some "child art" of the sort, in that decade, much loosed upon the world from Vienna. Over the chimney-piece hung what appeared to be a small water-colour by Cézanne, and to the glass of this there noticeably adhered the remains of one of those small red labels used in galleries to show that a painting is no longer available for sale. Delver, pass-ing close by in order to take the chair pointed out to him, had the expertness to see that the little picture was in fact a colour-print, originally worth perhaps a dollar. He found himself less entertained by this new manner of keeping up with the Joneses than shocked that so minutely absurd a subterfuge could have been resorted to by one who—in the fullest sense—had known Matthew Tresilian. Of the work of Tresilian himself there appeared to be no trace in the room.

"I'm afraid I can't offer you tea." Mary Emeleus said this with an air of politely dissimulated perplexity which was meant, he realized, as an intimation that he had indeed arrived at the wrong time of day. "But perhaps," she went on, "I might offer you a bath?"

He was sufficiently startled to answer quickly. "Wouldn't it be a little early for that too?"

"In London, at least, it is what one ought to offer American guests as soon as they enter one's door. It's a filthy town, and you must all suffer in it acutely."

"You think that, as a people, we set an exaggerated value on cleanliness?"

"It is at least better than setting an exaggerated value on dirt." Mary Emeleus leant forward and picked up a book. "Now, *this* one," she said, handing it to Delver. "Wouldn't you agree?"

It was a recent novel, and quite unfamiliar to him. "I haven't read it," he said. "It's too squalid for your taste?"

"Only *une âme de boue* could produce such a thing. But, tell me, are you an admirer of *her*?" Mary Emeleus had picked up and pushed forward another novel.

This time the writer's name was known to Delver. But he still hadn't read the book. He saw the kind of awkwardness that was approaching. But, for the moment, he temporized. "She's sure been having a tidy little success," he said in his best transatlantic manner. "Only I haven't myself gotten as far as this one. I find it very interesting, Miss Emeleus, that you keep up with these younger writers."

"But listen!" Mary Emeleus had picked up the book again and was leafing through it. "Yes—here: 'The suave, silent Daimler swung down the drive'. Think of it!"

"It's certainly a shade on the alliterative side."

"But *Daimler*, Professor! Surely, in well-bred writing, motorcars, like clarets and diseases, remain anonymous?" She turned over a couple of pages. "And while one character may permissibly, I suppose, think of *possessing* another—of enjoying her, as the old books say—surely he must not, unless of the humblest class, at all entertain the thought of *having* her?"

"It's rather a tenuous difference, perhaps."

"Good writing is largely a matter of tenuous differences. I take it that your main field of interest is the modern novel?"

"Well, no—it's not." Delver was not the less uncomfortable on being cornered simply from having realized that cornered he must be. "But, of course, I'm a reader of novels—of some novels —and I'd like to say how much I've enjoyed—"

"How *very* kind!" Mary Emeleus let a sweet smile of the most freezingly obvious artificiality coincide with this ironically brusque interruption. "But may I ask where your studies *do* lie?"

"Well, Rossetti has been one of my great interests, ma'am." Delver was rather pleased with "ma'am". It seemed to have the right colonial ring.

"How intensely interesting! I knew his brother very well— as a survival from a past age."

"William Michael was certainly that. He was only a year younger than Gabriel, but he lived to be ninety. It would have been something to know Christina, would it not? But she was born in 1830, and died when she was sixty-four." Delver was pleased with all this ready chronology too. It seemed to authenticate him as a scholar well up on the literary side of things. His hostess, however, showed instantly that she was not to be misled.

"Perhaps," she said, "your interest in Dante Gabriel lies in the fact that he was both poet and painter?"

"That is so." Delver saw that he had better at once come clean. "My Chair, you see, was established for the purpose of research into the interrelationship of the arts."

"But how entirely fascinating! Tell me, Professor—would the art of cookery be included? Many writers have wholeheartedly interrelated themselves with that—my own adored Peacock among them. Perhaps you have published something that I ought to know on the flavour of Peacock's prose in relation to his ideas on sauces? Or am I being *stupid*?"

You are being a bitch—Delver thought—but that is as God made you. And you are far from being stupid. In fact, you have taken the trouble to look me up in some reference book. Aloud, he said : "You are only being what I expected you to be. And that is, extremely enchanting." He had some thought that a speech thus boldly out of character might throw her at least momentarily off her stride. It wasn't so.

"I believe I have had as many friends," she said, "among artists as among writers. So I always like to hear talk of them. Who, Professor, has succeeded Rossetti in your interest? Are you in England now to pursue any specific research?"

"Matthew Tresilian's my man at present."

"How delightful! I knew him well. Perhaps it just so happened that John Alabaster had that within his recollection, and so suggested this call?"

"Our talk did turn that way." Delver paused. He had an undiminished sense that the thing was awkward. Yet, now that his concern was out, his simple and respectable hand on the table, he was not without the expectation that Miss Emeleus might come clean. No doubt the former self upon whom at this moment she must be looking back was a sinner in terms of the religious persuasion to which she adhered. But Tresilian had been a great painter; it was only human nature that she should regard herself as being, in her own medium, an artist of similar calibre; these facts should dispose her to rise above mere conventions of decorum and propriety. But perhaps the nub of the matter was the figure she cut in the story and the particular emotion it had left her possessed of. If humiliation was her predominant memory, if it had all simply ended in her losing a battle, she might want to take the whole episode unopened and uncommemorated to her grave. And of course, however she felt about it, she might well be chary of chattering with the first intrusive scholar to turn up. It remains awkward—Delver told himself—however you look at it.

"Perhaps, Professor, you think of writing the biography of Mr Tresilian?"

He marked the "Mr" as a distancing gesture of a decided sort. "That," he said, "is something I've thought about. Perhaps the time hasn't quite come for it. At any rate, it could only be done with proper authority and a lot of collaboration. There are children living, and I gather there are some pretty close friends as well. Any responsible biographical project would require their general good will."

"I don't know that all modern biographers feel like that." Mary Emeleus reached for a small enamelled box beside her. "But I am so terribly sorry! Do you smoke?"

Delver didn't smoke. "Moreover," he said, "anything I myself did eventually write would be published by my own university. In this country it would probably be issued through the Oxford University Press. That's generally reckoned to be a tolerably reputable concern."

"But of course." Miss Emeleus's interest in him, it seemed to Delver, had rather suddenly declined. "So, for the present at least, your concern is with Mr Tresilian's art?"

"Well, yes. But perhaps the plural is more accurate. His arts. Frankly, I'm on the track of something that I believe to be important—and something that seems pretty well unknown. Tresilian wrote a good deal, and excellent judges are on record as believing his writing to be important. It might be *very* important. And I'm after that. I'm even daring to wonder whether you may be able to help me."

"Ah, writing." Miss Emeleus's voice and posture had alike

become almost obtrusively relaxed. It might have been possible to conclude that her interest had now sunk to zero. In those bright dark eyes, however, whether they saw clearly or not, Delver thought he discerned the flicker of some other quality. "Yes," she said casually. "You are quite right. Matthew was a very good writer. But what sort of writing do you expect to find?"

"I've reason to believe that, at certain periods of his life at least, he kept a private journal. And he certainly wrote one series of letters about artistic problems which were unfortunately destroyed during the war. I'm hoping for others."

"And either kind of writing would be, you think, of great interest to the world?"

"Most decidedly. If his stature as a painter is really what it seems now shaping to be—and my own view is that it *is*—then anything of the kind would be of the highest importance."

"I suppose it would." Her manner was now absent, and when she spoke again—which was after inserting a cigarette into a long jade holder—her mind seemed to have drifted away entirely. "I am so ignorant about American universities. Do tell me about yours." She listened while Delver spoke briefly but with some emphasis. "I see," she said. "Yes—I see."

"But," Delver said, "to go back to Tresilian, if I may. You say it is known to you that he was a good writer. That in itself I find exciting. Can you also tell me where any of his surviving writings may be found?"

She was now striking a match—a service which, since he carried none, he had been unable to perform for her. With this she then gave as much attention to lighting her cigarette as if the thing had been a cigar. "Yes, indeed," she said. "I own what may well be all of them." She paused. "And the copyright as well," she said.

He was so astonished that, for a moment, he might have been hearing no more than a bare statement of improbable fact. Then he realized that he was being blandly propositioned. There was really no other term for it. She had been curious about his university because she was curious about his cheque-book. And it was, of course, likely enough that she possessed at least some writing by Tresilian. Tresilian might even have embodied in a legal document—although he certainly hadn't in his will—such a disposition of the copyright in his writing as Miss Emeleus was so queerly and revealingly suggesting. In that case, it seemed, Delver's chance-meeting with Alabaster had brought him at one move dead in front of a major objective. His problem might now be—to put it bluntly—just what the lady would settle for.

Delver didn't resist an impulse to take a swift and more definitely appraising glance round the room. People in the position of Miss Emeleus often formed an exaggerated estimate of the monetary value of such property as seemed now to be in question, and they were more likely to accept a realistic appraisal if their immediate circumstances were such that an unexpected accession of ready cash would be welcome. His present guess was that, if things were really easy with her, Miss Emeleus's surroundings would materially differ from what they were. There was no sign, on the other hand, of her positively eating her way through her furniture. So the results of this ignoble survey must be judged negative. He looked from the room to the lady. He had an embarrassed sense that she understood how his mind had been working. This was the likeliest explanation, at least, of a faint mockery he could detect in her glance.

"I wish," she was saying, "I could with any degree of hospitality invite you to luncheon. Unfortunately I take no more than a glass of milk and a biscuit, and I dine elsewhere. However, I can recommend the Welsh Pony. It is just across the street. Recruit yourself there, Professor, and then come back and let us continue our talk." Before he could find any reply to a suggestion he found so mildly odd—and again mocking—she had risen and was crossing the room. "And take with you," she went on, "some of Matthew's writing. Just a glimpse of it. A foretaste or sample, shall we say?"

He scrambled to his feet, and knew that he was absolutely staring. Meanwhile, she had walked over to a bookcase, and when she turned round what she was holding in her hand was a printed book. He took it from her as she held it out to him—conscious that his stare had become a helpless goggle. It was one of her own later novels, with the cryptic title *Glory Ann Barn*. For a moment he supposed confusedly that Tresilian had collaborated with her in this work, or that in some crazed fashion she had come to believe this to be so.

"Among other things," she said, "Matthew wrote a considerable number of descriptive sketches and autobiographical fragments. He thought they might be useful to me."

"Useful to you?" To his further discomposure, Delver could articulate no more than this idiotic repetition.

"As a *professional* writer, Professor. For Matthew was—it must be mentioned—deeply attached to me, and it was his hope that, one day, I would build at least part of what he had written into something with enduring form."

"I see." Delver did his best to look like one prepared to admire *Glory Ann Barn* primarily for itself alone. "But I suppose the—well, the original material, shall we say, has been preserved?"

"Yes, indeed. For literary scholars will always want it, will they not, for purposes of comparison? How much the learned world would give for Thomas Kyd's *Hamlet*."

There was no reply possible to this, if only because he found himself very far from being able to estimate the extent to which Mary Emeleus was speaking out of a conscious and bitter irony. She knew, she could not but know, that criticism had relegated her to a minor position in its hierarchy of English novelists. She knew, correspondingly, that it was in course of establishing her former lover among the greatest English artists. So what could she really take to be posterity's ultimate verdict on her having messed around with the written memorials of that commanding spirit? Delver just didn't know. It wasn't, however, a riddle there was any immediate need of solving. His present business was every scrap that he could manage in the way of diplomatic dealing.

"I shall read *Glory Ann Barn* with tremendous interest," he said. "Not that I shall be able to do much justice to it during a snack in a pub."

"Oh—but please!" She made a gesture that seemed expressive of diffidence and confusion; and he judged that, if this didn't make much sense in the context of her present comportment, it had borne a fetching appearance forty years before. "You *must* allow me." She took the book back from him and walked over to a writing-table. He watched her inscribe it. When she handed it to him again the words on the fly-leaf were: *To Professor Thayne Delver from the author, he too being a lover of Matthew Tresilian.*

"Thank you very much indeed," he said. "I shall cherish it."

He found himself speaking without awkwardness, for what he said was true enough. Mary Emeleus's life had in some manner dried away into shallows, he supposed; and it did make him uncomfortable, curiously uncomfortable, to reflect that what he was looking for could be in the possession of somebody capable of that silly little trick with the Cézanne print. Moreover she had been long past her youth when Tresilian met her; her character had been fully formed; it must have been distinguishably the woman still standing pen in hand before him whom Tresilian, in one fashion of loving or another, had loved. Delver found himself aware of all these facts, and very aware that in giving him this book she had business relations in view. Yet he remained pleased with it. "And I may come back," he asked, "some time in the afternoon?"

"As soon as you have lunched, if you care to." She was leading him towards the door. "I shall have thought a little by then— about the things you would like to know." She paused and seemed to take a deep breath, so that he suddenly felt something tired and worn in her mockery. "Let us hope they will be the things you would like to hear about."

CHAPTER TWENTY-TWO

It had been entirely like Bruno—Jane Landreth thought with
a vexation she was used to—to act as he had done over Luke
Tresilian's week-end. Luke had arrived alone on the Friday
evening and explained that Bruno would not be home until the
Tuesday, which was the day on which he himself would be going
on to Cornwall.

Luke could fairly be called an ingenuous youth; he was no
hand at dissimulating embarrassment; and Jane had been inclined at first to suppose that the underlying reason for Bruno's
absence lay in some notion of leaving Luke and Hatty a clear
field for their romance. She would have liked to think that
Bruno had judged the time come to close down on the inter-
mittent amusement he called the incest game. There had been
moments when this unsavoury fantasy had alarmed her, and had
perhaps alarmed Hatty too. It seemed possible that Bruno, having pitched his friend at his sister's head with surprising success,
was now absenting himself with the idea of letting them make a
little running together.

But all this wasn't really plausible, and perhaps it was a shade
morbid as well. The truth of the matter must be taken to lie
simply on the surface of Luke's explanation. Bruno had received
an attractive dinner invitation for the Monday, and he was staying up for it. The dinner was of an undergraduate club to which
he didn't belong, and to which nothing in his social connections
entitled him to think of belonging. It was being given by a former
member in some great house in the neighbourhood of Oxford.
Office-bearers were entitled to invite guests, and Bruno, it seemed,
had been invited. It was from such guests that new members
were commonly elected. And Bruno had set himself this goal. For
the time being, at least, he had quite stopped talking about
bloodies.

Luke came out with these facts haltingly but in a manner
Jane much liked. He was loyal to Bruno; he clearly admired him

as a senior who was also almost a sage; at the same time he plainly thought this dinner business held less of seniority and sagacity than of a venial childishness. He seemed to own a naïve persuasion that snobbery could be a foible only of the immature. In this context he had twice ventured on the expression "poor old Bruno". Such a freedom Jane had interpreted, with satisfaction, as intimating a dawning consciousness that a freshman commoner may sometimes be required to talk sense even to a fourth-year Scholar about to take Greats. She was already making plans for Luke's being a wholesome influence on Bruno.

As for the romance with Hatty, there were moments when Jane was inclined to conclude that it had been, after all, an abortive affair. She couldn't suppose that she had imagined it; throughout the week-end there had been something between the young people that didn't square with that. Nevertheless, love wasn't running smooth. If neither of the two hearts involved was, as a consequence, to be broken—and as to that one just couldn't know—then this ought to strike her as all to the good. Hatty was a schoolgirl. It would be several years before Luke Tresilian was earning a living—which one had to accept, in England, as the definition of being grown-up. A love-affair would thus be an untimely thing. Nevertheless Jane wasn't at all sure that she felt pleased that Luke was probably no more than a ship passing in the night. For she liked him extremely. Once, indeed, she caught herself reflecting that he was the son—or, say, one of the sons— she hadn't had. She wouldn't *not* have had Bruno. There was no need for her to assure herself of that. A child is a fact. But Luke would have been nice too. It must be that way that she felt.

Still in some perplexity, she appealed to Lucilla's lucidity. This she increasingly did. Apart from the fact that it was necessarily inexperienced, it was rather the same sort of lucidity that she could appeal to in Charles Rose. Only Charles's had a touch of Hamlet's thinking too precisely on the event; Lucilla's was commonly a preliminary to action. Should Charles and Lucilla ever team up—and lately the disconcerting notion had again several times visited her—it would be Lucilla who eventually ran the show. And now Lucilla didn't seem to take Hatty's and Luke's relationship other than seriously. She had responded to her mother's speculations with the quick but cool impatience that was characteristic of her.

"But can't you see," she said, "that they're children who have run ahead of themselves? They're bewildered—virtually in a state of shock. Each has suddenly been given a quite new part, and doesn't know how the role has to be played."

"If it's play-acting, surely, we needn't bother about it."

"That's not what I'm saying at all. Growing up is largely a matter of observing adult roles and trying out feasible ones. It's a dead serious affair. Hatty's head may have been filled with amorous nonsense, and she may have seen herself playing any number of romantic heroines and tragedy queens. But actually she's a schoolchild who believes that she must pass exams and go to a university and all the rest of it. She's quite as aware that she's not yet eighteen as you are. And yet here's this grown-up thing, or what she feels to be that. It's senseless not to expect her to be bewildered. She may take refuge for a time in being a perfect little bitch to the boy. Or just in odd, awkward withdrawals. Don't you think?"

Jane felt it to be out of politeness that Lucilla had concluded on a query. It seemed to be her own role at the moment to put the questions. "And Luke?" she asked.

"It's even newer to him than to her. Young men don't day-dream much except in a casual erotic way. The business of being in love is something he hasn't had a clue to."

"I'm not sure that boys are as uncomplicated as that." In fact, Jane was certain they weren't. Lucilla's air of standing dispassionately outside the sphere of the emotions and pronouncing upon them at once impressed and disheartened her. "And I'm not sure," she added, "that, in some ways, Luke isn't mature beyond his years."

"As one supposes him to be eighteen or nineteen, that mayn't take us far. Still, I rather agree, and it makes for what I say. It's very serious for him. He's a serious person. For what it's worth, by the way, he's going to possess substantial private means."

"Lucilla! You can't possibly—"

"We've talked quite a lot. The Tresilian estate has been very efficiently handled. It held on to eighteen major things. Six have been sold in recent years for very substantial sums. And a dozen remain for the memorial exhibition. Their chances are pretty good. And it nearly all comes to Luke when he's twenty-one."

"What about the half-sister?"

"She doesn't, for some reason, get much. I don't think, incidentally, that Luke has any idea of setting up as a *rentier*, or that he even has much notion of income and capital at all. Still, I've offered you a relevant fact."

"You mean he and Hatty might really—"

"Why not? He might take a job, and ask to be let marry her on her next birthday. It happens quite a lot nowadays. By no means all next-to-child marriages are shotgun ones."

"I suppose not." Jane was startled by this baldness of statement. "But isn't it the point that things seem *not* heading that way?"

"I agree that Luke is finding it difficult too. Hatty at home isn't quite the same person as Hatty roaming free in Oxford. Luke's sensitive enough to be aware of that. He has to begin again in the new context. And a *strange* context. By the way, how on earth has he been brought up? What's his home like? He seems so oddly unattached. There's a Latin phrase for it."

"*Terrae filius*, perhaps. But I don't think it would pass with a professor. If you're Matthew Tresilian's son the Latin for you is *honesto genere natus*."

"You must tell him so. He's terribly anxious to improve his Latin. He has to go up for an exam in it at the end of the vac."

"Then Hatty mustn't too much distract him, or he her." Jane made as if to end the conversation on this lighter note, but in fact failed to do so. "You think a family is more formidable to him than it would be if he had one of his own? I feel he's shy of us. He's even shyer with me now than he was when he arrived on Friday."

"Bruin would say that's because he's getting you mixed up with your younger daughter."

"Bruno is never at a loss for nonsense." Jane, for some reason, was sharply displeased. "Let's not, for goodness' sake, pick up his habit of talking half-baked psychology of sex."

"We're in no danger of that. But haven't you got anything out of Luke about his home, and so on? You have plenty of opportunity. When he's not out with Hatty he seems chiefly happy shelling peas for you."

"He's certainly much better than Bruin at that sort of thing. But it won't last much longer. Tomorrow's Tuesday, and his train's at eleven o'clock."

"Well, you have a last chance of a long talk now. He's leaving Hatty at her extra French and coming back by himself." Lucilla crossed to the window and looked down. "In fact, here he is."

"Lucilla, could you get him a drink and entertain him for an hour? I'm going to be shockingly late with dinner."

"I had to bring back a lot of papers, I'm afraid."

It wasn't often that Lucilla said this sort of thing. When she did, it was understood to be final. But on this occasion her mother almost rebelled, although it seemed scarcely out of a rational impulse. She ought to get to know as much about Luke Tresilian as she tactfully could. And she liked doing so; in the past few days she had enjoyed talking to him; and particularly she'd enjoyed breaking down that early constraint in him which had been occasioned simply by her being Hatty's mother. Yet now, somehow, it was her instinct to move into the background during the brief remainder of his visit. She found it hard to account for this—although it did occur to her, surely morbidly once more, that he might let slip about Bruno things she didn't want to hear. More sensibly, she could feel that if Luke and Hatty had indeed become seriously attached to each other, it had been within so brief a space that the time hadn't come for anything like family notice to be taken of it. She didn't want to have on her hands a Luke who felt that he must "say something". Perhaps her feeling was no more than that. Whatever it was, it led nowhere at the moment. For Lucilla had disappeared. And Luke, having mounted several flights of stairs with his usual unbelievable speed, had tumbled into the flat and then straight into the kitchen where she was working.

"Hatty has to have an hour and a half."

He made this announcement so much as a matter of moment that Jane found it difficult not to laugh. "She needs it," she said. "Every minute of it. If she's ever to see Oxford or Cambridge, that is."

"I'm sure she'll win a scholarship at Somerville. Just as you did. They'll take one look at her. As they did at you."

"On the contrary, they tormented me for hours." He was still very shy. But the things he said always seemed spontaneous, and she believed that she had flushed with pleasure at his last speech. "Of course it's easier for men by quite a long way, getting into a college."

"Yes, I know." He was at once humble. "Is there anything I can do?"

"About getting decent French idiom into Hatty's head?"

"No, I'm afraid I'd be no good at that. I mean about supper."

She had forgotten to think what he could do. And in her small kitchen he looked enormous. It was hard to imagine that, with all that length of limb, he could so much as turn round without disaster to the crockery. But she remembered that there was some game which he played very well; and in fact he had a precise muscular co-ordination that was the more striking because it went with a deceptive appearance of clumsiness. Luke wouldn't be accident-prone : that was one handle that chance or fate would never have on him. It was something on the credit side of an obscure account; on some other plane he didn't suggest himself as being notably hard to hurt. "Could you peel those apples?" she asked. "I'm going to make a pie. Or would you prefer a dumpling? On their last evening it's a rule that people choose."

"Then a dumpling, please." He was satisfactorily definite about this. "Into about quarters, would you say, or eighths?"

"Some into quarters and some into eighths." She watched him get to work on the plate of apples. "Where did you go?"

"To the Tate. There are postcards of all the Tresilians there now—even of the watercolours. I got a whole set. I'll show you. I think they're rather good. I have a watercolour myself. In my rooms. Hatty's seen it. You must too." He finished peeling the first apple. He had done it in one unbroken spiral. "Do you mind if I try just with this one?" he asked. "You know—over my shoulder."

"Go ahead." He certainly had a flair, she thought, for simple pleasures.

He dropped the peel behind him—the kitchen didn't admit of throwing—and they both turned to look. "It's a J!" he said, and glanced at her with a face full of laughter. Then, rather swiftly, he stooped, picked up the coiled peel and threw it into a basin. "How many shall I do?" he asked abruptly.

"Till the other basin's heaped up. I hope Hatty doesn't forget that cream."

"It was the last thing I said to her when she was diving into

194

her tutor's: *Remember that cream for your Mum.* We'll beat her if she's really forgotten it." Having finished his second apple, Luke looked up. The unremarkable features of his ruddy and wholesome face seemed slightly altered, so that Jane was put in mind of something—probably fantastic—that Bruno had once said about them. "It's been frightfully nice," he said, "being with all of you. I haven't got a family, you know. Which has made me absolutely a victim of families, from time to time."

"A victim, Luke?"

"Awfully decent people have laid on spots of family life for the orphan." His words, she noticed, were no longer quite spontaneous; he was trying to guard himself against what he would think of as sentimental utterance. "But I've never, somehow, quite been with it. The Landreths have been the first to ring the bell."

"I'm glad." She was touched by the awkwardness of his speech, even although the boy's talk seemed to be taking a plunge in the direction she didn't at present want. "You must come back. We'll expect it."

"Thank you very much." Luke peeled one apple in silence, and then another. He worked carefully, neatly and frugally, so that only the thinnest skin came away. "You know," he said suddenly, "Bruno sometimes talks awful rot." He looked at her seriously, and as if the inconsequence of this remark escaped him. "You don't mind my saying that? Of course, I think he's brilliant. Everybody does."

"I hope his examiners will take something approximating to that view." An impulse of irritation—whether with Luke or Bruno, she hardly knew—gave her words a sudden dryness she didn't like. "But are you going to tell me something about how you really have been brought up, Luke? Or shall I have to have it relayed by Hatty?" She had asked the first of these questions, she supposed, to obviate any sense that she had at all intended to shut him up. The second surprised her. It was almost an invitation to him to talk about what she had decided would be best left alone for the present.

"Of course you must know about me, if you want to be bothered. And there's not much to know. I suppose that's the point about me. I'm like the lucky nations that have no history. My parents died before I can remember. In a sort of pre-history, you might say. Since then, I've been cared for, and just let grow."

"Do you mean, cared for—impersonally?"

"Oh, no!" He was amused. "Not like in an institution. Affectionately and with good sense. But with nothing pressing on me or pulling at me. If I wanted—well, an intense relation, I had to imagine it. Am I all wrong in supposing it's been any sort of lucky condition? I do think I've come out fairly capable. And with a lot—well, waiting in me. Forward-looking. I mean, I *expect* a lot. But perhaps I'm not talking sensibly. It's hard to express. I can tell you, though, about my guardian, Dr Dolben. He's a country doctor at Padstow, which is where I live. He was a friend of my father's, so he took me on. It was quite a stout thing for a bachelor to do."

"Decidedly it was, particularly if he was anything like your father's age."

"Well, he's always been rather old." Luke laughed, as if seeing that this was a vague remark. "But I'm sure he's not eighty, which is what he would be if he'd been born in the same year as my father. I think he must be about seventy, because he retired from his practice a couple of years ago. His patients seemed to mean everything to him—that was why I never saw a great deal of him—and I used to think he'd be lost without them. But fortunately, you see, he has this interest in fossils too."

"And did he teach you to be interested in them?"

"Oh, no. I prefer things that are alive. Birds, mostly. Isn't it odd that Hatty doesn't know a thing about birds?"

"My children are all townees, I'm afraid." Jane was finding Luke Tresilian's story a little strange. "Have there never been any women around? Hasn't your bachelor Dr Dolben any sisters, even?"

"I never heard of any. When I was small I had a nurse to myself. Since then, there have been just house-keepers. Very nice women, mostly. You mustn't think I've been what is called deprived, you know. As I was explaining, families were always laying themselves on. Padstow's a friendly place. I was always going out to tea. Rugger most afternoons, back to tea with another chap, and then home to home-work."

"It does sound beautifully uncomplicated." The artlessness of Luke's manner, Jane perceived, was not entirely unconnected with a sense of style. His speech, for all its spontaneity, was something he enjoyed the shape and cadence of. There might even be a poet in him. She watched the delicate precision with which he peeled another apple. It made her—most oddly, she felt—experience a sudden desire to see him on his football field, evidencing the same quality as he gathered the ball from the dangerous heels of the scrum. "But what about Tresilians?" she said. "Uncles, aunts, or whatever? Or relations of your mother's? Don't you ever run up against anybody like that?"

He shook his head. "But you know, don't you, the outline there? My half-brother John was killed in the war. His sister Faith is eighteen years older than I am, and married to a kind of lighthouse-keeper."

"Goodness, wasn't it very romantic having even a half-sister married to a man who kept lighthouses?"

"I hardly ever see her, and I've never seen him. Alfred Crinnis —that's his name—is apparently terribly unfriendly and gloomy. He's always praying and reading the Bible. He's a fanatic. Perhaps that has cut me off from Faith. But there's something else as well. I believe Faith thinks—quite wrongly—that my father ditched or dumped her brother John and herself. You see, *their* mother—my father's first wife—was an entirely simple person. Her name was Ann Jollow. Surprisingly late in his life, I suppose when he was already about forty, my father returned to Cornwall and married this girl, who was of his own original world. Good on him, I say."

"I'm not sure about that, Luke. It's not a thing that always works terribly well."

"Of course, by that time my father was quite well known. And although he seems to have kept to simple habits, and been loyal to his roots in the folk, and so on—still, he'd been all over the place. You'd have to call him *déclassé*, I suppose. Is that right?"

"The French use the word only the other way on. But it's clear what you mean."

"So perhaps it *didn't* work terribly well. Anyway, in about ten or twelve years their mother—John and Faith's mother, that is, who had been Ann Jollow—died. I don't know the details of how my father coped. He doesn't seem to have found a Dr Dolben that time. And then the war came along. I think it's Faith's idea that my father suddenly found a thoroughly upper-class mistress, changed his habits, and just couldn't be bothered with his two motherless kids. He packed them off to Cornwall—and virtually as peasants. But she's got it wrong, Faith has—as I say. My father did have a mistress for a bit. Artists do, as we know. She was a woman novelist. But he wouldn't not have done his best for his children. The essence of the matter was the Blitz—getting them away from that. Of course he may have had some notion too that we weren't going to win, and that if there was an invasion it would be safest to be humbly hidden among the people."

"And Faith has chosen to stay hidden?"

"More or less that. Really, she won't have anything to do with me. I've tried. Only the other day, I had to write to her, and I suggested she come up to London so that we could go to the exhibition together. But I bet she won't. She mayn't even answer."

"And there are no other relations at all?"

"None that I know of—except that I did once go to a family funeral." He grinned. "Yes, that was my nearest approach to family life. Ought I to feel a terrible lack? I can't say I do. Except that I have this notion that Faith and I should gang up just a little, even if she is so much older than me. But there's this silly class feeling. Her husband's what Bruno would call a prole, and her mother was a village girl. And my mother, you see, was a countess." Luke paused. "For what the point's worth," he added hastily.

"I didn't know that." Even having a baronet among one's grandparents has its uses on occasions, and Jane's expression hadn't flickered, although there had certainly been something mildly comical in Luke's manner of coming out with this unexpected information. "Your father's career, you know, has escaped the net of even the most obvious reference books, so far. It can happen with artists, I've noticed, in a way that it can't with writers." Jane thought she detected in Luke a certain gratitude for these unflurried remarks. "But tell me about your mother."

"Not only a countess, but a *Polish* countess!" His face was suddenly alive with joy and fun. "Do you know, I haven't told Hatty that yet? When I do, she'll get me more mixed up than ever with those awful people in D. H. Lawrence."

"You mustn't tell me if you haven't told her." Although Jane said this lightly, she said it quickly. "Or you could tell all of us at dinner. If it would go with apple dumpling."

He laughed. "There's no secret, really. How could there be? Not, I mean, as to the simple fact. Lots of people knew about my father's second marriage. Lots of people must remember about it. I had a letter from an American professor not long ago, showing that he knew at least a little about it and a lot of other things as well. But I know more than anybody else, because my father left me an account of the matter. One day, I shall have to decide whether to publish it."

There was a moment's silence. Luke had spoken these last words, Jane thought, as if he were suddenly an older man. She saw that, buried somewhere in this small mystery, there was something very important to him. That might well be. There was something, too, that he was proud of—and it was nothing to do with any notion that Polish countesses are inherently superior to Cornish village girls. "Publish it?" she said. "You mean, give the information to a biographer?"

"Oh, no." He shook his head. "If I ever manage to write anything, it will be because my father was a writer before me. This about his second marriage—it's a finished and perfect thing."

"Then," she said, "I hope you will decide to publish it one day."

The job with the apples was over. He got up from the stool on which he had been perched and brought her the heaped-up bowl. "Do I pass?" he asked.

She looked up at him, laughing. It would be perfectly possible, she saw, to fall in love with her daughter's young man. She knew people who did that sort of thing. She conscientiously read the more approved novels which made a staple of it. Fortunately —she told herself—it showed up as absurd and even vulgar when measured across the length of one's own kitchen table.

"Yes," she said. "You pass, Luke. I think you always will."

CHAPTER TWENTY-THREE

At dinner Lord Burntisland had sat on the Provost's right, and on his own right had been an Egyptologist of great age called Fitch. Throughout a protracted meal he had given unflagging attention to the conversation of each of these neighbours in turn. In this he had been only the stricter with himself because he had concluded, quite early on, that the occasion to which he had been bidden was a second-string affair. At first its character had puzzled him. The majority of the guests appeared not to be old members of the college—and upon inquiry he was told that a Gaudy for these was held some weeks later. The present company must be described as of miscellaneous notabilities. And Burntisland, glancing round the hall and then examining the table plan which was printed with the menu, had marked with an expertness bred of long familiarity with formal banquets a significant prevalence of brigadiers without brigades, barristers who had mistimed taking silk, P.P.S.s who had become P.P.S.s noticeably late in their parliamentary careers. Long ago Burntisland had been a Minister of the Crown; long ago that day had come and gone upon which, on returning from Germany, he had not been invited to join the Cabinet. He could not fairly be called touchy in such matters. But a sense that he had been invited as a major also-ran to make a speech to a gathering of minor also-rans did exist as a faint irritation in his mind. Professor Fitch also irritated him. More and more, Burntisland was coming to dislike very old men.

He had made, he knew, a good speech. Coming up in the train, he had prepared it with care; into delivering it he had put everything he would have put had he been speaking in the Guildhall itself. Now he was beginning to tire. He wondered when at least the formal part of the proceedings would be over.

From the vantage-point of the dais, Fitch was peering myopically down the hall. The lighting was subdued; the white shirts and red faces floated in cigar smoke. "I do not know how it may be," Fitch said, "but I am put in mind of Bowker's astringent jest."

"Indeed?" Burntisland, who sat the more stiffly upright as fatigue overtook him, leant politely sideways. The port was circulating pretty rapidly in the body of the hall; the din of conversation was consequently rising in both pitch and volume; at the far end, moreover, a group of college servants, perhaps judging that all this had gone on long enough, were contriving to make rather a lot of noise in piling cleared dishes. Fitch had embarked upon an anecdote. It would be civil to try to hear enough to arrive at some notion of the point of it.

"It is a story about beans," Fitch said. "They may have been French beans. They may have been the so-called 'broad' beans. The point is immaterial."

Burntisland nodded his comprehension of the fact that either or any variety of beans would do. As he did so, however, an advancing decanter came under Fitch's hand.

"Ah!" Fitch said. "As you will have observed, Ferreira '45. And Oporto bottled. You may be prompted to hint a criticism. You may judge us precipitate, since it will undoubtedly further develop and improve. But there is plenty downstairs, so we have indulged ourselves." He filled his glass and, it seemed, forgot his story.

Burntisland turned again to the Provost with some relief. He took no interest in the discussion of wine, and almost as little in jests, whether astringent or otherwise. But he had a concern for various problems of higher education, and as Pro-Chancellor of a Scottish University he had standing in the field. On the subject of entrance to the Oxford colleges he had one or two searching questions in mind. Littlejohn, however, was now inviting his attention to a piece of silver plate on the table before him, and Burntisland was constrained to express a civil curiosity about it that he didn't particularly feel. This led to its being up-ended by Littlejohn, the butler and a second servant in order that Burntisland might satisfy himself of certain high authenticities conveyed by sundry silversmith's marks on its massive base. He inspected these with gravity. Having no comment to make, he made none. It was replaced on rather a muted note.

"The fellow to whom these things were offered"—he found Fitch was saying—"went by the name of Withycombe. He had won the Craven and both the Gaisfords. That's the point of the thing, you see. A promising man."

"Indeed," Burntisland said again. A group of guests in an adjacent corner of the hall were guffawing loudly. There was little hope of grasping the thread of Fitch's story. Burntisland debated with himself taking out his watch. At an affair like this it was Littlejohn's business to budge. But there would not be anything improper in a hint from the principal guest. Fitch was continuing to tell his story, but seemed now to be telling it to the man on his right. Burntisland, deferring the operation with the watch, turned again to the Provost. The extent to which the Oxford colleges were evolving a common policy still eluded him.

Once more, however, Littlejohn spoke first. "You will have noticed," he said, "that the portrait over your right shoulder is a John. It's one of the last things of its kind that he did. We are very happy about it, although you may judge it a little high in tone."

At the cost of some discomfort, Burntisland looked over his right shoulder. He judged the painting to be a workmanlike performance. "Is it," he asked, "a faithful likeness of the person depicted?"

"Oh, decidedly." Littlejohn spoke emphatically, but with an indulgent smile. "You mayn't have known the man. He is my predecessor in the Provostship, Lambert Gilstrap. Incidentally, I must be next on the line. My colleagues are already being good enough to talk about it. Some would like to commission Gunn, and some Kokoschka. I wonder whether you have an opinion?"

Lord Burntisland had no opinion. On this occasion, however, he did not mark the fact by keeping silence. "I'd go along to the Academy," he said, "and look around for a keen young fellow with his reputation to make. Another generation may commend your enterprise." He was noting with satisfaction that Littlejohn was disconcerted when he felt a hand on his right arm. He turned and found Fitch peering at him with an air of suspicion.

"You follow me?" Fitch said. "He was on what they call a diet. Rejecting certain dishes and accepting others. All balderdash, you will agree."

Burntisland, who observed a strict regimen and took two looks at anything offered him, expressed no agreement.

"And a poor sort of breeding, too, at refections of a formal sort. Well, here was this fellow Withycombe, who had come to nothing, dining at the high table of his former college. And there were these beans."

"Beans?" Burntisland said. He was recognizing that his fatigue was more oppressive than usual.

"French beans or the so-called 'broad' beans. It is entirely immaterial. Withycombe, obeying some wretched apothecary's behest, passed these beans. You understand me? He declined them. So the servant took them away. It was at this juncture that Bowker produced his astringent jest. 'My dear fellow,' he said to Withycombe, 'you surprise us all. We think of you as one of the might-have-beens.' " Fitch peered at Burntisland, and then down the length of the hall. "I do not know how it may be," he said, "but my present situation puts me in mind of Bowker's astringent jest. It is a story about beans—"

With no misgivings now, Lord Burntisland took out his watch. The senility of this old person must be known to his hosts, and they ought not to have subjected him to it. Moreover it alarmed him, or at least made him uneasy. Probably Professor Fitch was still capable of acute work on his own subject, while being at the same time a social menace whenever he was allowed out. That was one of the formidable aspects of old age; its patchy character. Those poets were surely right who had dwelt upon the profound treacherousness of time. You prepared for its frontal assault. But somehow it managed to come upon you from behind.

"A most delightful dinner," he heard himself saying, and realized with satisfaction that he had brought Littlejohn to his feet. He shook hands with Fitch. "Highly enjoyable," he said, "I shall remember your story about poor Withycombe. Good night."

The main body of guests were now standing about the hall, or drifting out of it. Burntisland, with Littlejohn beside him, threaded his way among them. Every now and then he had to stop to shake hands with an acquaintance, and to listen gravely to polite remarks about his speech. It was a sort of thing he appeared to have been doing for a hundred years. There was the man who had too much to say. There was the man who felt he ought to say something and couldn't think of anything. There was the consultant physician who made jovial remarks while eyeing you like the fellow who undertakes to guess your weight at a fair. There were the vaguely familiar faces with their carefully casual invitations to luncheon and their undoubted designs upon you. Burntisland made his way through all this and found himself at the head of the great staircase that led down to the open quadrangle below.

"And here," Littlejohn was saying, "is something that may remind you of our last meeting." He had pointed over the low balustrade at what Burntisland took for a moment to be an intricate building operation. In fact it was a large painting of the abstract sort. "Our Matthew Tresilian," Littlejohn said. "We are extremely proud of it. But it is now, as you know, merely a herald of what is to come."

"Indeed." Burntisland remembered that the Provost was perpetually talking about one artistic object or another. It was a perfectly proper interest, no doubt, but one which it was surprising to find cultivated in an obsessive manner by a scholar. As for Tresilian, the name found, at the moment, only a faint echo in his head. It had been turning up, he seemed to recall, in a number of rather tiresome contexts within recent months. "Have you had it long?" he asked, aware of silence.

"By no means for long. It was almost the last thing that Gilstrap did for us."

"Then I congratulate you on its acquisition." Burntisland was conscious of making this response in a manner rather too grey and formal for the presumed conviviality of the hour. And he was conscious in the same moment that one of Littlejohn's colleagues had joined them : a hunched and darkly brooding man who had been introduced to him earlier as Philip Leech, the Pro-Provost. Leech, although he gave the impression of having watched the exchange over the Tresilian with an observant eye, did not refer to it.

"Thank you for your speech," he said. "You said things that need saying. I hope they won't all evaporate with the volatile ethers that my colleagues call the 'bouquet' of our doubtless admirable port."

"The port was certainly admirable," Burntisland said with a dry conventionality through Littlejohn's equally conventional laughter. He was aware that he and Leech had exchanged a signal.

"The least we can try to offer you in return is a quiet night. But I doubt whether you will get it. The present crowd won't keep up their jollity for very long." Leech's darkling glance swept the congeries of elderly men now straggling down the staircase. "Unfortunately a number of our undergraduates—the members of a most troublesome club—have stayed up over this first week-end of the vacation to attend a dinner somewhere in the county. The Provost has been indulgent enough to give them uncommonly late leave. If you are awakened in the small hours by hunting horns and what are called, I believe, view halloos, don't suppose it to be an alarm of fire. It will be merely our young barbarians at play."

"I shall try to recall it, even when starting out of slumber." Burntisland, although slumber was precisely what he needed, was momentarily alert again. Able men getting across each other had been part of his environment throughout a lifetime, and the spectacle of it still interested him. This determined his response to Littlejohn's next remark, which expressed a wish that he would spend a few minutes in common room, in which the college hoped to continue the entertainment of its guests. "Thank you, Provost. That will be most agreeable." He turned, gave careful attention to the shallow stone treads of the staircase, and moved slowly down them. As he did so, he remembered that the first occasion upon which he had seen a painting by Tresilian had been in the National Gallery. And the second time had been at Hector Madrona's. It was Madrona who was giving some valuable collection or other to this college. Surely it would be more useful and appropriate to found a couple of Research Fellowships. But not—he thought grimly—so showy. He resolved that, before going to bed, he would have some conversation with Leech about all this. Leech seemed a sensible man. And Leech was clearly in opposition to some of Littlejohn's ideas.

The common room was so crowded that he instantly regretted his decision to enter it. Edged by Littlejohn towards its farther end in the interest of obtaining a drink he certainly didn't want, it struck him that there was something positively indecent in this squeezing and wriggling mass of closely packed males. Moreover there was a quite unbearable din. The common room was a long, low apartment which, continently tenanted, would probably display elegant proportions; and it was just possible to see that it was decorated and furnished with considerable taste. As a drawing-room, many hostesses of his acquaintance would envy it. But only the most rash of them would send out cards aiming at such a crush as this.

Burntisland had on other occasions had cause to remark the ineptitude of the academic classes in matters of this sort. On the whole, he was disposed to condone it as an instance of the unhappiness in practical affairs that is prescriptively supposed to go with the life of learning. But he couldn't condone this racket. Inordinate mechanical noise of the kind one was nowadays everywhere subjected to was bad enough. He had been playing a vigorous part of late on a committee seeking ways and means to combat it. But for raw human hubbub there was no excuse at all. And it was a fact, an undeniable fact, that recently he had been becoming a little prone to hearing tiresome noises inside his own head. It had been explained to him by an eminent aurist as a common phenomenon of early senescence which need occasion no alarm. But it was undoubtedly uncomfortable, and it was exacerbated by exposure to this sort of thing. Irritation mounted in Lord Burntisland. His air of courteous attention to whatever was proposed to him correspondingly grew.

Leech had been drawn away. Littlejohn, made aware of some pressing duty of hospitality, disappeared after introducing him to two men, apparently colleagues, neither of whose names Burntisland had come anywhere near catching. One was young, and the other was in early middle age. Burntisland, although a guest, felt that his seniority obliged him to initiate conversation. "I suppose," he asked, picking a topic at random, "that most of the guests accept your very hospitable invitation to stay the night?"

"The hardier do," the middle-aged man said. "Others get into their cars and drive through the small hours. They remember the sort of beds that Oxford colleges judge suitable for undergraduates. We ourselves have a hundred which a former domestic bursar bought most advantageously from the local workhouse when it closed down. Powdermaker, you must once have had one of them yourself."

"Certainly. I took it over at a valuation, paying thirty shillings." The young man called Powdermaker provided this information with a prim precision which might, or might not, have been humorous in intention. "It depreciated by seven-and-six during my incumbency. But Lord Burntisland, fortunately, is in the guest-set on the Pro-Provost's staircase. It is tolerable, but scarcely does us any positive credit. How unfortunate, Keith, that you were not here when it was furnished." Powdermaker turned to Burntisland. "Pratling," he explained, "is our authority on the minor elegancies. Although he frequently expresses a strong sense of the nugatory nature of nearly all our occasions, he is a great hand at censuring a window-box or choosing a door-knob. When our new building has gone up there will be wonderful scope for the exercise of his taste."

"Our new buildings," Pratling said.

"That is as may be, Keith. Who knows?"

Burntisland had listened to these exchanges without pleasure. His upbringing had given him a respect for learned persons; his later life had made him aware that they have their tiresome side. Powdermaker and Pratling were sparring about something he had no concern with, and he would willingly have left them to it and gone off to bed. But convention appeared to require some further exchange. "The college, then, has a building programme?" he asked.

"Yes, indeed," Pratling said. "Plans—one has to say, as it happens, alternative plans—are well advanced. Only the other day, some quite remarkable models were delivered to us. The Provost plays with them like a child. As it happens, they are in the next room. Would you care to look at them?"

This suggestion appeared to offer an escape from the crush, and Burntisland allowed himself to be edged towards another apartment. It was the sort of place, he thought, that you find in inferior hotels behind a frosted glass door saying "Writing Room". There was a table in the centre. And on the table there stood what he recognized at once as a model of the college. There was even the mulberry tree that Littlejohn had pointed out to him. The scale was given by two or three minute figures in academic dress. One of these was emerging from under the archway leading to the great staircase and the hall. Burntisland was amused. With a cautious movement such as Gulliver might have made in Lilliput, he managed to peer into the model at this point. The staircase itself was really there. There was even some sketched evocation of the big painting by the Cornish artist whose name was again escaping him. It was clear that the college employed an architect with a junior staff which liked this sort of thing.

"We are looking," Powdermaker said, "at the college as it is today, and virtually as it has been for over two hundred years. For it was in the early eighteenth century, you may remember, that large benefactions enabled us to expand and to take what has remained our prominent position in the university. At that time we built pretty well wherever we could. Unfortunately, therefore, there is very little available ground now."

"I see none at all," Burntisland said.

"It is not quite as bad as that. Notice this long, narrow range of buildings." Powdermaker brought an instructive forefinger across the model. "They represent no more than a collection of obsolete offices of various kinds : coach-houses, brew-houses and so on. Without much loss, they can be demolished. So we demolish them." His hand came down and lifted out the buildings indicated. They came away neatly in one solid block. "The oblong space we now see represents our building site."

"So we rummage in the play-box." Pratling said this. He had gone over to a side table and when he came back he was holding another model building. "We fit it in—so. And we are now looking at an additional fifty sets for undergraduates."

"In what promises to be a building of considerable architectural merit," Powdermaker said. "But notice its strong point. It is undoubtedly the long, unified façade. Lord Burntisland, you would agree?"

"So far as I can judge, Mr Powdermaker, it will be a happy solution of a difficult problem. The site is clearly not an easy one."

"You wouldn't, I suppose," Pratling asked, "ever have had occasion to consider the weighty matter of just how young gentlemen should be accommodated while passing a little time at the university?"

Burntisland frowned. This problem, as it happened, was one to which he had been giving his mind in Scotland quite recently. And he didn't care for Pratling's tone. "Certainly I have," he said with some severity. "And there is no single answer to be arrived at. Differing circumstances and traditions must be allowed for."

"Precisely!" It was with a quite new vehemence that Powdermaker now spoke, and Burntisland saw with surprise that the young man had been seized by some strong emotion. "So let us pass from Plan *A.* to Plan *B.*" As he said this, Powdermaker tugged out the part of the model that Pratling had inserted, carried it to the side table, and returned with another one. He thrust it into place. "Plan *B.*," he said. "Accommodation for thirty-five undergraduates—and not in sets, but in bed-sitters."

Burntisland studied the appearance now presented. Part of the same new building was recognizably there. But its length had been truncated—not at all to the advantage, he felt, of its proportions. And this had been done to make room for another new structure, which he found entirely puzzling. It might have been a small gasometer. "May I ask," he said, "what this affair is meant to be?"

"I should describe it"—Powdermaker spoke on an uncomfortably high note—"as a singularly poor crib of the Guggenheim building in New York. It is designed—if designed be an apposite word—for the display of paintings. And we are given to understand that it will be known as the Madrona Gallery."

"I see." Burntisland stared at the thing. "And you yourself would rather have your undergraduates a little more spread out?"

"Certainly. Bed-sitters are simply not part of the tradition of this place. Some centuries ago, two undergraduates often shared a sleeping apartment, but each had a small study to which to withdraw. Later, when social habits changed, the bedroom became a shared sitting-room, and the studies became bedrooms. That is quite a common arrangement still. But quite a different matter"—Powdermaker's finger performed an agitated arabesque over the model—"from *this.*"

"I don't see myself," Pratling said easily, "that it makes much odds, either way. I don't really know why my colleagues are becoming so excited about it. To me the interesting question is not how we put the little brutes up but how we put up *with* them."

"One way to do so," Powdermaker said, "is doubtless to cultivate a vacuous frivolity."

For a moment Burntisland said nothing. It was clear that upon the harmless-seeming toy before him considerable passions were at present focused. He himself wanted to hear no more of them. "May I ask," he said, "if this cylindrical object is by the same architect as the proposed undergraduate building? Or is it possibly by Leonard Benton Curry?"

Burntisland's two companions were impressed. "That's the name," Pratling said. "He's a pet of this chap Madrona."

"And I take it, Mr Powdermaker, that there is considerable opposition to this proposal, and that you yourself join in it?"

"Most decidedly."

"Whereas you, Mr Pratling, take rather a detached view? And would I be right in thinking—if the question is not impertinent—that your Pro-Provost, Mr Leech, is among those against it?"

Pratling laughed. "Leech is against Littlejohn. Put it that way."

"I should myself strongly deprecate putting it in any such fashion." Powdermaker's quiver of indignation was again in evidence. "The matter is entirely one of corporate policy, and indeed of principle. The issue is perfectly clear. We get back to our proper business, which is intellectual discipline, or we decline into an empty aestheticism. It is as simple as that."

"I shall be interested to hear how it turns out." Burntisland said this dismissively, and while moving across the room. In a sense, he supposed, he was Littlejohn's personal guest, and he ought not to listen to this sort of thing. Besides, he was now very tired indeed, and there were some rather inconvenient noises in his head. But at least the night was over; he now had nothing to face but his bed.

Powdermaker opened the door for him, and he had to turn round to say good night to Pratling, who had remained a little behind. The movement brought the model into focus again, and along with it the image of Sir Hector Madrona. Quite against his intention, he spoke a final word.

"It's not for me," he said, "in the least to take sides. But I will say that *that* affair"—and he pointed at the Madrona Gallery—"is an extraneous sort of thing which, to my mind, you'd be better without. But you won't kill it, you know, by getting worked up." As he said this he smiled at Powdermaker —bleakly, in fact, but with the intention of warmth and encouragement. "There are things that you will kill that way, but this isn't one of them."

"That's what Leech himself says." Powdermaker seemed struck by this coincidence of opinions. "He says that what would kill it would be ridicule."

"Ah—ridicule." Burntisland repeated the word almost inattentively. The noise in his head had increased, and he knew that he'd had enough. "You must forgive me. I shall find your Provost and say good night. A delightful occasion." He nodded to them—an old man to his juniors—and walked stiffly out of the room.

CHAPTER TWENTY-FOUR

Later

... AND "LATER", MY dear Don, means not far short of midnight. I've dined—at least I guess I've dined, although I couldn't
name a thing they put before me—and I've prowled these London streets in the dark. I've stood in Piccadilly Circus watching
the lights, but not much considering whether I was in that hub
of Empire or in Times Square. This new situation obsesses me, as
you can well imagine. For it really is a baffling way to have come
upon Tresilian's writing—refracted, one may put it, through the
brittle, shallow crystal of this woman's fiction. And shall I ever
see it more clearly? I'd call her terms—her present terms—a
mad woman's.

But let me clear my head, let me go on from where I left off.
This isn't a noisy machine. If there comes a knock on my bedroom wall, that will just be too bad.

There I was, then, in this Notting Hill pub, with a plate of
cold beef and a pint of beer before me, and *Glory Ann Barn*
in my hand. I think I was already on bad terms with the book—
with the book itself, as distinct from whatever of Tresilian it
might reveal. The title seemed ambiguous in a mannered, outmoded way. Did it refer to a building, or to some female, pictur-
esquely and improbably named? Well, a prefatory note put me
right as to that. Glory Ann Barn exists on the Gloucestershire
map. The writer had often marked it as she tramped the Ridge-
way, had often planned a detour that should inform her what
manner of thing it was. But she had never, in fact, set eyes on it,
and just because of this her imagination had got to work. You
can guess, Don, the sort of stuff. Before I'd started on the novel
itself I was confirmed in the persuasion (which I'd had only from
hearsay) that in her final books Mary Emeleus had sadly gone
off. In her early fifties, this would be, approximately at the time
of Matthew Tresilian's death.

For a moment one seems to see a romantic possibility here :

that Tresilian was her inspiration, and that her inspiration died with him. But chronology makes nonsense of that, unless old Alabaster has been hopelessly inaccurate. He spoke, indeed, of Mary Emeleus as having been a "child" when she became Tresilian's mistress. But he named the period as the early Forties, which must almost certainly be correct. Miss Emeleus was in her own forties then, and Tresilian's affair was with a mature woman who already had nearly all her effective accomplishment behind her. Alabaster's turn of phrase gave a nonagenarian's perspective on it. If anything, her whole *liaison* with the painter must be associated with her decline. Psychologically, that may make sense. She had run into an incomparably more powerful artist, and there might well be something depressive to her talent in that. Alternatively, a great deal of tension that had previously given nervous force to her writing may have been released into the relationship.

At this point I record an impression of the woman as I've twice glimpsed her. Tresilian may well not have been her last lover. I've even picked up from something she said or hinted the notion that he had a successor in John Alabaster himself. It's a macabre and even revolting notion when you consider Alabaster's age, even twenty years ago. But such things aren't uncommon among idle folk. It's a very literal form, you might say, of what the English are calling at the moment the aristocratic embrace. Yet, however this may be, I seem to sense Miss Emeleus as having preserved *some* relationship with Tresilian. Not necessarily an active sexual relationship, but certainly a relationship of affection. There was no rumpus at the end of the run. If I'm right about this, it's a fact at present obscured in several ways. For example, what Tresilian seems chiefly to mean to her at the moment is the possibility of making money out of his manuscripts. Again, her way of talking about and estimating his writing suggests disenchantment. But against this is the fact that among the writings of his that she claims to possess there seems to be some remarkably *late* writing. *Glory Ann Barn* shows that she continued to come by it *after* the "affair" was over—and indeed after the date of Tresilian's second marriage. This is remarkable. But let me tell you something about the book.

Despite the barn in Gloucestershire—which she makes out to have been converted by a sculptor into a cottage and studio—

the book has for the most part a London wartime setting. And the war going on in it, or behind it, is Hitler's war. The mischief, so far as a hurried reading can inform me, lies just there. The Mary Emeleus who wrote the book was still the owner of a sufficiently acute and observant mind. For that matter, she revealed herself only this morning as possessing precisely this. But that war and that London were somehow beyond her.

Although this is no occasion for literary criticism, I suppose I mustn't leave that "somehow" totally unelucidated. A continuum of finely discriminated sensuous impressions is what the woman had evolved a more than respectable flair for evoking. *The Rack Dislimns*, for instance, is a sensitive stream-of-consciousness affair, quite without those effects of tedious rumination often so prominent in fiction of that kind. And it copes with another war, the Kaiser's, very well, distancing it to a muttering thunder, a horizon just perceptibly flickering, the faint shock of saccharin or margarine on the palate, the unfamiliar harshness of a Tommy's uniform brushed against in the dark. But the delicate recording instrument which could make so much of those small, fugitive sensations—which could suggest in terms of them a whole English social order passing away—this instrument shows in *Glory Ann Barn* as choked, jammed and inexpressive when set to record a minute-to-minute consciousness of a London in which death arrives first and the noise of its arrival follows after. Miss Emeleus, to put it quite simply, was making a very great mistake about her range when she elected to display the virtually Edwardian consciousnesses of her typical characters at the receiving end of Hitler's last assaults on London. And this is where Tresilian comes so startlingly in.

He comes in—believe me, Don, he comes in—much as Shakespeare comes in in *Pericles*. You remember? *Thou God of this great vast, rebuke these surges. . . .* It will be fascinating to look up the early reviews of *Glory Ann Barn* and see whether anybody, lacking the clue we hold, took note or offered explanation of what was happening. If the woman had always incorporated her treasure (or loot) *verbatim* and unadulterated, people couldn't —I dare swear—have done other than shout about it. But she commonly tinkered—I can swear to that too—and in a surprising fashion. Briefly, she had had from Tresilian—there on her elegant writing-table—episodes so powerfully realized, and rendered in a prose so masculine, sinewy and direct, that one would suppose she would have seen her only hope of harmonizing them with her own surrounding writing to lie in muting them and toning them down. Instead, she seems to have keyed them up; you might say, to have *melodramatized* them. There can be no doubt of it. And I assert this (let me chronicle at once) in the face of something very rum indeed which you will find me recording the woman as claiming in the course of our second interview.

I mustn't begin quoting now—not if I'm going to get half a night's sleep before breakfast. You'll have to take something on trust. And of course I still have to study the book. Presently, I'll mention just two significant places I came on in my first almost hectic session with it in the Welsh Pony.

First, and done with a masterly economy, there's London under the V2s. These rockets weren't like their immediate predecessors. And it wasn't merely that they arrived unheralded, so that the open sky itself became the menace. They were as odd in their effects as they were lethal. Summer turning to winter in a flash as the blast left the plane trees standing, but stripped of every leaf. A woman, similarly stricken, unharmed but naked in the street. There are several descriptions of such things that are themselves stripped and bare : Tresilian's prose, I'll be bound—and, this time, with no frills added. (It occurs to me, by the way, that the fact of his having ceased at that period to paint in any straight figurative fashion would enhance for him the satisfaction to be gained through his mastery of another craft, that of vivid descriptive writing.) Second comes something quite different. It makes me almost declare there was a novelist in him. But as the evidence comes to me *through* a novelist, it's rather a tricky point ! As you'll learn.

I must say a word about the structure of the novel. It's loosely episodic—and this just in the interest, I'd say, of working in the material from Tresilian's wartime diary (as I suppose it was). One minor character who turns up from time to time is a painter called Arabin. Whether or not he's intended as a straight portrait of Tresilian is something I can't, at the moment, tell. But some of his experiences are certainly based on Tresilian's writing. I say "based" this time, because I feel sure the woman has in several places embroidered her material. Arabin becomes an official war artist (as I do know that Tresilian for a short time did) and witnesses the allied assault on Normandy and the fighting round Caen. As straight description—"war correspondent" stuff according to the older conception of that role—this is splendidly done. Better still, and indicating an even higher order of talent, is the manner in which the strain and strangeness of being commissioned to maintain a sheerly aesthetic consciousness in the face of the tremendous spectacle is grasped and rendered. "Arabin turned over a page and tried again. This time, as he rearranged his corpses, he felt the warmth of the sun pricking at the back of his hand. By noon, he thought, the bodies would be steaming. But he could manage no more than a pencil note of that." Arabin's son is a combatant somewhere on the battlefield, and the implications of this are handled powerfully and at the same time with a most effective reticence. Or they are so handled up to a point. For this episode ends on what seems to me, in the last analysis, a false note.

Briefly (once more), Arabin, who has gone forward where he has no business to be, comes upon a battery that has been wiped out to a man. High explosive has done a fantastic job; there are gunners splayed out over their guns as in some atrocity seen or imagined by Goya. Fascinated, Arabin begins a rapid compositional drawing. But the thing isn't quite right. Again he is prompted to rearrange his corpses. But this time (for at the moment he is quite alone) it is not merely on the page of his sketch-book but *there*—in the spectacle he is going to commemorate. Macabrely, he advances upon one of the bodies as he might do upon a model in his studio to alter the pose of a limb. And the body is that of his son.

You will think, Don, that I ought to write "is, *of course*, that of his son". And certainly that would point the trouble. The thing is just too pat, just too much *like* fiction. But I'm bound to say the handling is astonishingly good. Here—I decided at once as I read—was Miss Emeleus doing what I'd once or twice been certain of her doing before : taking over from Tresilian, melodramatizing, forcing a note. It was a bad calculation from the point of view of the unity of tone of her book. She'd taken over, I repeat, and turned the screw once too often. Yet she'd done it, I was bound to admit, as with a single, strong thrust from the wrist!

But now I come to my second session with the lady.

If my first call on her had been too early in the day, this one was later than I'd promised. Since I'd sat in that pub, with my nose in *Glory Ann Barn*, until the "Time, please!" that concluded its afternoon session, it might be said that I'd given Mary Emeleus ample interval for the degustation of that glass of milk and biscuit. Even so, and although I'd read and skimmed with the concentration of an idle Junior in the last hour before a critical exam, I was far from having got the affair into focus in the fashion that I'd have liked. Still, I had now enjoyed a glimpse —even if so queerly at second hand—of one sort of writing in which Matthew Tresilian had engaged. And if there was something unexpected about it—well, I guess unexpectedness should have been with me precisely the expected thing. What I'd thought of myself as first coming upon was some correspondence like those lost letters to Aidan Marrot, or a journal of a more reflective and inward, a less pictorially conceived, sort than that filtered to me through this goddam *Glory Ann Barn*. And I now had a feeling—I here record—that Miss Emeleus in her dealings with what had come to her, had done no more than (one might put it) meet Tresilian halfway. By which I mean to hint the notion that Tresilian's impulse to write was something more closely allied to the creative side of him than it had occurred to me to imagine. Say that I just haven't thought of him as getting on paper anything that could at all usefully be cribbed by a Mary Emeleus.

But now I was once more on the lady's doorstep, and with my finger on the doorbell I told myself I wanted two things. First, I wanted to talk, and have her talk, straight turkey : how much did she possess, and how much did she *want*? I didn't apprehend much difficulty here. If her figure was beyond *us*, my dear Don (and perish the thought!), it needn't be beyond, say, the boys in Texas. But secondly, I wanted Miss Emeleus to come clean on a lot more. I wanted her—with my usual modesty of expectation, you'll say—to open her heart and memory on the figure of Matthew Tresilian. I wasn't sure I'd believe all I was told, mark you. I hadn't forgotten that shocking little matter I've mentioned : the red tab on the Cézanne print. No woman would play a trick like that who hadn't come rather pathologically to feel that her own worth had ceased to be properly estimated by the world. But only let her *talk*! Judging the reliability of what she said could come later.

"You have given me ample time to reflect, Professor." Those were her first words as she opened the door to me, and she uttered them with so much of what one might call her professional irony that I felt, paradoxically, this *was* turkey, and that the tone represented only a final gesture of defensiveness before she did, in some fashion, speak out. It might indeed be that she supposed me to command a much larger chequebook than in fact I did. But I had—I told myself—another and, it might be, fundamentally more potent advantage. She really is very substantially forgotten. There have been novelists in our time whose reputation has, if anything, been enhanced by their falling silent in what might have been no more than mid-career. But it hasn't worked that way with Miss Emeleus. Perhaps she reckoned that it would. Perhaps that was why, back in the early nineteen-fifties, *Glory Ann Barn* had been her penultimate novel. It didn't greatly matter. What mattered was that, even at the cost of indiscretion, she was now ripe for reasserting herself as having had her place on the artistic map of her time. I heard all this, I say, in those first words with which she opened our second encounter. And that, *you* will say, was just my usual sanguine disposition at work. But, as you'll discover, it was, within certain limits, the fact of the case.

"You want to know about Matthew." We were back in the Victorian drawing-room and she was looking at me with those bright eyes I had guessed were no longer seeing a great deal; looking at me, too, through the still-impressive ruins of what I again discerned had been a notable beauty. "John Alabaster—let us be frank—has scarcely given you a good start with me. He was being malicious, don't you think?"

"Mischievous," I said.

"The difference is rather tenuous, perhaps." She was echoing, I recalled, some earlier word of mine. "Like so many aristocrats, he is capable of occasional utter grossness, too. It would not surprise me to hear of his having told you—a casual acquaintance at some promiscuous party—that he had once caught me on a rebound."

"Indeed, no!" I protested. I was really a good deal shocked. "He said nothing at all like that."

"At least it would have been true." She was looking at me with the mockery that I now knew to be habitual with her. But it was mockery on the part of one who had decided notably to change her ground, all the same. "For a time, you see, I just couldn't rise to what Matthew had done. Particularly when it turned out there was going to be a child. *That*, he hadn't led me to expect would be in the bond."

"The son by his second marriage?" I asked. I was largely in the dark. But at least there could now be no doubt that light was on the way. And I was prompted to acknowledge it, as it were, proleptically. "Let me thank you in advance," I said. "For I know that you are going to tell me a great deal."

"Perhaps a little," she said. "Not a great deal."

"Don't forget that a certain interest I feel in Tresilian's personal history doesn't prevent my being, primarily, a perfectly respectable art historian. I think your coming to know him coincides with his period away from figurative painting—in fact with his developing his middle style. I shall be entirely grateful if I simply learn something about that. I have a notion you may have introduced him to fresh influences."

"I think I did. And it wasn't before time. What you call his middle period—the period of the big, austere, abstract things—is of course not "middle" at all, so far as his life span is concerned. It lasted no more than five years. And within three years of that again"—she hesitated—"Matthew had grown old and died."

"It's the output of those last three years," I said, "that people now get most excited about. The return to the older, representational Expressionism, but with all that elusiveness and haunting ambiguity. But perhaps that doesn't seem his major achievement to you?" I was honestly interested, of course, in her views on this. But I did have the thought that, if I set the subject of Tresilian's purely artistic development in the foreground, the ultimate effect might be to make her more forthcoming about other things.

"I think it was freakish: that last phase. He had, after all, done a freakish thing. It was quixotic; it had its nobility, even; I can see that and praise it now. But it aged and bewildered him, and these last paintings were the result. What *I* call his great work—the middle-period things—grew up in a context I did have some part in creating for him. Matthew was a *naïf*, you know, when I first met him. He knew the Germans. But he didn't understand the *École de Paris*. And he had never explored Significant Form. I don't think he had even heard of the philosophy of G. E. Moore."

I believe I'd have chuckled, Don, if I hadn't known it would be an injudicious thing to do. Not that it mayn't have been in part from the death-throes of Bloomsbury that the penultimate phase of Tresilian's art arose. From the moment the Emeleus *liaison* was first revealed to me by Alabaster I'd seen a genuine field for research in what the new association might have made him freshly or more sharply aware of in the intellectual and artistic currents of the period. There was something comical, all the same, in hearing the old shibboleths preparing to form themselves on this elderly woman's lips.

But in fact she went off on another tack—and it was the personal tack I'd been banking on. "The irony of it!" she said. "That it was I who virtually sent him to Spain."

"It was you?" I asked. In fact I had no notion of what she was talking about. Reflect on that, Don, and you will realize how oddly what ought to be readily accessible facts of Tresilian's life have got themselves tucked into near-oblivion.

"Indeed it was. I had influential friends, and I thought it would be well for Matthew, and for Matthew's painting, if he could be got, if only for the briefest space, out of the greyness of wartime London. And there was this question of a feeler, at the discreet level of an academic and cultural mission, in Franco's Spain. Hardly anybody knows about it, and of course nothing came of it. Or nothing except Matthew's rather absurd, rather gallant act. A woman from a Warsaw ghetto! But she was in some technical way a citizen of Vichy France, and she was to be returned there, where her chances would be slim. Somehow Matthew got her over the frontier into Portugal. Then he managed to marry her in the Embassy there—I suspect because our Ambassador's wife adored his work. That, in turn, enabled him to bring her—this fugitive proletarian Anna with the unpronounceable other name—to England. They buried themselves in his dreary native Cornwall for a time. That was where the child was born : a boy to whom they gave the name of Matthew's father, Luke."

At this point, Don, Miss Emeleus paused for breath, for it had been a long speech. But she was hesitating too. And I thought I saw, for the first time, a faint flush on her cheek. "The child was born," she said, "a bare eight months after that chivalric Lisbon occasion. Matthew must have been performing in a more commonplace role with the woman well before he thought of the Scarlet Pimpernel turn. Still, it's shabby to recall that, I suppose. He might well have ditched her. She was attractive, no doubt, but not all that of a catch. Particularly as she was dying, you know. There must have been something a shade formidable in that."

"Dying!" I said. I was really startled.

"Oh—yes, indeed. She might well have died in a French or German concentration camp. But when she did die it was after knowing herself to have become the mother of an entirely healthy child. It was a triumph for her, one admits." She paused again. "And I myself will admit that it was a triumph for Matthew too. I'm glad that, as a friend, I stuck to him."

You may imagine, Don, the interest with which I'd listened to this extraordinary recital. It left a good deal in obscurity, but I had a sense that Miss Emeleus herself came out of it not badly. And this momentary viewing her in a more sympathetic light put me in mind that I hadn't yet said the decent thing about *Glory Ann Barn*. So I tried to make good this deficiency now. She received what I said conventionally and with reserve. I saw that she very well knew the novel as a whole to be no great success, and this made my task a tricky one. I tried at first not to concentrate on those passages and episodes drawn from Tresilian's writing which were in fact my sole interest in the book. But of course she understood perfectly well that they *were* my sole interest; and keener than her own literary vanity by a long way was probably her desire to know just how my mind was operating in terms of dollars or pounds sterling. So I had to come round to them pretty soon; and indeed I found myself managing not badly some sort of reasoned critical appreciation of the way in which she had worked this oddly prefabricated material in. But presently I got one unexpected reaction.

"Your difficulty," I said, "I can see as having been a necessary changing of what may be called the compositional key, Miss Emeleus. Here was admirable material, but not itself, presumably, in the key of fiction. You go most remarkably to work with it, if I may say so, in the descriptions of London under fire. But I found myself even more interested in the episode of the Normandy campaign as seen through the eyes of the war artist. Tresilian's hand is clearly there—and, of course, yours is too. One might say you go hand in hand through those tremendous scenes." I was rather pleased with this. "But one question I'd venture to ask does concern that matter of compositional key. Just what artistic calculation prompted you to add your own climax to Tresilian's narrative there? I mean, of course, your making your painter walk up to the battery and discover his own dead son."

"You are mistaken, Professor. I have a little heightened the prose. But the substance of that episode is Matthew's own, right to the end."

The woman seemed surprised that I'd got it wrong. But I myself was quite flabbergasted. "I'm not sure that I understand," I managed to say. "I take it that the material entrusted to you by Tresilian was essentially autobiographical in character : a body of recorded experiences while serving as an official war artist, and so on. Am I to take it that he himself actually embodied an element of fiction in his writing of that sort?"

She seemed more surprised still. "But," she said, "don't you know? Matthew had a son by his first marriage. He was called John Tresilian, and he was killed in the war."

"Yes, of course." I agreed the more hastily to this because— as you'll hear, Don—it was a statement I happened to be aware of as requiring sharp qualification. "But," I went on, "that seems no reason why Tresilian should invent so extraordinary an episode. It strains credulity, after all. It strains credulity, Miss Emeleus, even after your mature artistry has done its best for it. I'd call it a perfect example, if I may say so, of the sort of thing that happens only in the imaginations of novelists."

There was a moment's pause. She seemed both disconcerted and offended. "But it was *true* !" she said. "I had it equally from Matthew's own lips. And doesn't it authenticate itself as you read?"

This last question was a facer, and not merely because a negative answer would appear to impugn the art—whether Tresilian's or the lady's—that we were discussing. It was a facer also because an affirmative answer was only by a very small margin not possible. In terms of verisimilitude and conviction that wildly artificial battery episode does come surprisingly *near* to success.

But that it *is* fiction is a matter of *fact*. It's a matter of distressing fact which it so happens I'm in possession of. I haven't mentioned it to you, Don, so far. I didn't mention it to Charles Rose, although there was a point at which I felt it disingenuous not to do so. In a fashion I needn't now detail, young John Tresilian's story is one of the few pieces of family history that, so far, I have unquestionably got straight. A lad of just twenty, he was certainly in one of the Normandy landings. His nerve broke : and I presume it was under fire. No doubt he might have been shot there and then. But he wasn't so fortunate. They clapped him in a psychiatric hospital. Some months later he died by his own hand.

If there wasn't a darn awkward silence ! I had to break it with something. "Did you yourself," I asked, "know the boy? And his sister, who is still alive?"

"I saw them once or twice. But then, of course, they went to Malcar."

"Malcar?"

"Some unspeakably dreary inland place in Cornwall. Matthew sent them there for safety, even although John was already almost of an age to fight. I never tried to see them again. It was slightly awkward. They might feel, I supposed, that a new turn in their father's life had caused him to lose interest in them."

I caught this, and I record it. But I was hardly listening. The woman's claim that Tresilian had put his own son's death into fancy dress was still shaking me. And I guess my gaze was directed above the chimney-piece. If it came to a choice between the probity of one of the greatest artists of our time and the woman who had committed the petty absurdity up there—well, it seemed tolerably easy to decide where to jump. But—Jesus Christ !—what was the woman up to? Whether or not she knew the *truth* about John Tresilian she had herself, I was certain, fabricated the corresponding *fiction*; and now she was maintaining that it was the boy's father who had done so—had both done so and persuaded *her* that the fiction was truth.

Could she have forgotten what the facts of the case really were? It seemed hardly possible. Was she thinking to enhance the value of Tresilian's manuscripts by suggesting they contained matter as richly strange as such a story as this, if authentic, would assuredly be? That seemed too devious and muddled to be tenable either. Tresilian's manuscript itself must prove her to have been talking nonsense as soon as it was produced. Was she off her head? The correct answer here was less important for the moment than was getting away from this whole awkwardness that had sprung up. For I was keener than ever to get past all this *Glory Ann Barn* nonsense and lay my hands on the real thing. What was vital was not to antagonize the woman. And that entailed making some pretty dumb remarks if not positively dishonest ones. I edged into talk of how close they must have been to each other, Tresilian and herself. Two artists with a real affinity declaring itself even through their very different several media. I'll say, Don, not to speak it profanely, that what might crudely be called the professional patter of the Interrelationship of the Arts came in very handy. At the same time I was trying to see, a little more clearly than I had managed so far, what had really been the interrelationship of these two people at a simply personal level. There had been something of sufficient strength, it seemed, to survive that chivalric second marriage—and even its having issued in the birth of a child. But there seemed much that was entirely obscure. For one thing—and this was a fact I ought to have been more clearly aware of before—the chronology of Matthew Tresilian's last years makes a perplexingly crowded period. These years had seen a love affair, this hitherto unsuspected Spanish mission, a strange marriage, the birth of one son, service as a war artist in France, the tragic death of another son, the death of the new wife—and the painting of the last Tresilians. One day, it will all take some sorting out.

Meanwhile, that turkey had to be talked! I won't weary you, Don, or keep myself yet longer out of bed, by attempting to chronicle in detail the comedy (as it no doubt was) of our manoeuvring over this ground. The moment came when she produced her treasure—and not, I was horrified to see, out of any fireproof receptacle either! She produced it, in bulk and tied up in ribbon, and seemed disposed to market it, more or less blind and by the kilo, there and then. When I asked whether I might have the privilege of examining some of it—which was at least a reasonable start—she did in a rather gingerly fashion untie a ribbon or two and let me look, or *peep*. There is no doubt of what's there! And she would, she said, part with the whole lot—under this condition and that. These conditions, incidentally, didn't make much sense, and I concluded that she has very little notion of business, or of what can, and can not, be embodied in a bargain. But at least she was entirely clear about a price. "I don't think," she said, "that fifty thousand would be an extravagant sum."

You can imagine that I was startled! "My dear Miss Emeleus," I said, "we are talking, of course, about a category of things that have, in a sense, no price. I'm sure we are agreed upon that. These are *priceless* papers. But when we come down to the available resources of those likely to be interested in acquiring them, I assure you that fifty thousand dollars is an impracticable sum of money."

"But *not* dollars," she said—and rather as if she was helping me. "Pounds."

Well, Don, I said at the start that her present terms are a mad woman's. You'll agree they certainly are! There is little to be done, that I can see, except to give the matter time, and perhaps coax her into seeking impartial professional advice. I repeat, there's no doubt of what's *there*. Miss Emeleus possesses what may simply be called the Tresilian Papers. Unfortunately— let's face it coldly—the notion that they are of really *major* importance is something confined at present pretty well within my own head. Even if I'm right—and I am!—the world remains to be persuaded. And *that* can only be done if at least some of them are given a currency the lady seems indisposed to at the moment. So I can only sign myself—again for the moment—

Your frustrated
THAYNE.

CHAPTER TWENTY-FIVE

It was nearly midnight, and Bruno Landreth was still intermittently trembling with humiliation and rage. He was also
very hungry. Under the combined prompting of these sensations
his neat features—delicate and all but impudent, like that
Roman boy's—had turned pinched and feral. When he paused
in his caged prowling to look into the blistered mirror (and he
did so at every second turn on his heel, since his instinct remained histrionic even in this genuine agony) he saw lips that
had gone bloodless, eyes that had retreated in dark rings, all
within these few horrible hours.

He hadn't dared to go out to a restaurant. He hadn't dared
even to skulk across the quad and see if anything could be
scrounged from the buttery. Even if he got out of his dinner-
jacket people might wonder about him. Besides, the college was
full of Vile Old Men being given some sort of feast by the
dons.

His dinner invitation had been no invitation at all. What he
had taken for a firm proposal made with aristocratic nonchalance
—and had accepted with a swift assumption of the same tone—
had turned out to be only a vague thought about which its pro-
pounder had promptly forgotten. Nor had anything been done
to repair the misunderstanding during those agonizing moments
in which Bruno's entire lack of standing had been revealed to
him. *Just* how revelation had come—the sheer if undesigned
brutality of its circumstance—he couldn't for a moment let his
mind revert to without an access of resentment and shame and
utter subversion of pride impossible to bear. And now—what
seemed to add immeasurably to the ghastly squalor of his fiasco
—he did quite simply and crudely need something to eat.

But he only continued to prowl. There was nobody, *nobody* in
this filthy college that he could ever face again. For everybody,
even the scouts and porters and kitchen boys, would learn about

his disaster. The fact that he had bothered to make himself a niche in the place, that he had made himself a somebody in the eyes alike of bloodies and trogs, toughs and blacks, aesthetes and hearties and sub-men and proles : this only made it more unendurable still.

He paused once more in front of the looking-glass and tried speaking aloud. "I am a great demon out of hell," he said. But it wasn't any good, for he was nothing of the sort. He tried something else. "I am a pitifully arrested, feebly perverse product of the lunacy called an English education." This time he didn't utter the words aloud. He merely repeated them savagely several times inside his head.

He had tried, of course, his common resource under stress : beating himself while imagining he was beating someone else. But it hadn't answered. It had seemed only silly and disgusting and futile. He knew from experience that when he got *that* response from one or another masochistic or auto-erotic excursion he was pretty well at the end of his resources. Soon he would be on his bed, curled up in a pre-natal posture and blubbing—blubbing as they had made him blub on his first night at private school.

Only he wouldn't, he *wouldn't*. This had at least been so searing an experience that he knew, on second thoughts, he would never weep again. The damned don't weep. You couldn't imagine Hatty's Heathcliffe in *Wuthering Heights* weeping. Or perhaps Heathcliffe *had* wept. Anyway, *Wuthering Heights* was a rotten book. . . . Catching himself in fatuous rumination, Bruno gave a kick that sent his small fireside table in shattered fragments across the room. He uttered a howl of pain. He had forgotten he was wearing only those flimsy pumps.

Footsteps! Nursing his toes and cursing, Bruno turned paler than he already was. Somebody was coming up from Leech's landing just below. It was Leech going to stick his head in and rebuke him with acrid courtesy for the row. Or worse—a million times worse—it was Leech already made aware of Landreth's social misadventure, and awkwardly resolved to do his duty by a pupil by placing the matter in a mature perspective. The thought of this brought Bruno out in a cold sweat. But now as well as footsteps there were voices. The dons could hardly have decided to send a committee. The truth came to him, and he relaxed. Leech was bringing one of the Vile Old Men who had invaded the place up to the guest set on Bruno's landing.

Yes, this was certainly correct. He heard the outer door of the guest set being opened, a brief further murmur of voices saying good night, the door closing, and Leech going down to his own rooms. Leech had been playing the solicitous host to some foul old general or admiral or City tycoon. Both of them gorged and tanked up, no doubt, after a tremendous dinner. The thought sent two distinguishable stabs straight through Bruno's viscera : the renewed stab of simple physiological hunger, and the renewed stab, almost equally physiological in its effect on the gut, of insupportable memory. Among the people who would have to know—it occurred to him—was Luke Tresilian. And Luke, promoted to the status of a family friend; Luke, infatuated with Hatty; Luke, who possessed every asinine virtue a bred-in-the-bone nice chap can be born with : Luke would not merely be generous in shared indignation. He would also—the clumsy clot —be deft and subtle in sympathy. And in the end—Bruno saw in a flash—Luke would edge him, Bruno, into a position in which the tragedy would dissolve by way of cheerfully absurd schemes of vengeance into Rabelaisian laughter. Discerning this, Bruno Landreth—if only for a time—hated Luke Tresilian keenly.

But now he thought of something else. Luke the nice simple chap had a number of nice simple habits : among them a positively childish tuck-box habit. He would sustain himself, that was to say, when absorbed in some private world to which he frequently withdrew, in a squirrel-like fashion out of tins of biscuits and packets of chocolate. It was possible that supplies of these remained in Luke's rooms now. In which case Bruno had only to walk upstairs and find them. Nobody would have thought, here at the very beginning of the vacation, to sport Luke's oak. Certainly Luke himself wouldn't have done so. Ambrose the bear, the Matthew Tresilian watercolour, the mysterious contents of that locked drawer : these would have departed in Luke's luggage. There was nothing else worth twopence in the rooms.

Except, perhaps, something like a half-crown packet of chocolate biscuits. As Bruno visualized this his mouth, which had been dry with his rage, lavishly salivated. He gave a parting kick at his waste-paper basket—cautiously, this time—and went out on the landing. The staircase, as usual, like all the staircases in the college, was murderously ill-lit. The rotten place had been toadying for all it was worth to the Vile Old Men, including the particularly important one, as he must be, who was in the guest set over the way now. But it would never occur to anybody to do anything to prevent their breaking their necks when they went rolling off to bed. For a moment a brilliant notion hovered enticingly in Bruno's mind. He would somehow contrive a large-scale fire alarm in the small hours. In the morning the quad would be piled with corpses.

Unfortunately that wasn't him. He hadn't the guts for it. What he was fit for was purloining Luke's biscuits. He paused to listen. There was still a light under the guest-set door. But there wasn't a sound anywhere—or only from the distant third quad, where some of the V.O.M. were still living it up. It would be at least an hour before any of those bloody bloodies got back from their rotten binge. He'd be back in his rooms with his own oak sported by then.

Bruno paused for long enough to make, very softly, a rude noise outside the guest-set door. He was feeling every bit like that. Then he went cautiously up the winding attic staircase. Sure enough, Luke's oak was unsported. The single feeble light on the landing shone directly on the "Mr L. Tresilian" painted above it. All undergraduates were "Mr" here—those that weren't beastly noblemen, that was. He felt his way into the sitting-room and pressed down the switch.

Luke, in defiance of bursarial regulations and with the connivance of his scout, had fixed things so that two or three cosily shaded lights went on at once. For some reason this disconcerted Bruno. It somehow added to a sense of trespass. But that, of course, was absurd. He had often enough drifted in here in the absence of the owner and made himself at home. And Luke, if he could be aware of the present state of the case, would be eager that Bruno should have not only any provisions that lay about but everything he possessed in the world as well. He felt another spurt of hatred against Luke. It had an ambivalent quality, he found himself thinking. He was far from clear that he wasn't rather in love with Luke. In fact it had been Luke that he had imagined himself caning, which was surely significant. Not that *that* had at all worked.

For a moment he stood still, drawing comfort, a faint return of self-respect, from being the proprietor of this sexual sophistication. He noticed with surprise that Ambrose was in fact still on the chimneypiece, balancing that troggish tobacco-jar and an abandoned packet of cigarettes. Ambrose was looking at him —and as Bruno observed this he felt a curious sensation in his cheeks and forehead. He was blushing.

But Ambrose had been left here because Luke, in London, was busy putting aside childish things. For the second time in his evening's disastrous solitude Bruno spoke aloud. "There's but a dining-time," he said, " 'twixt us and our confusion." Of course he was addressing Hatty, and out of *'Tis Pity She's a Whore*. Suddenly he felt very frightened and entirely honest. What if all that mouldy rubbish that he had made a game of answered to something really in the heart? What, even, if he had nurtured a real spark of it in Hatty? The precocious sexicologist, learned in Krafft-Ebing, found himself shivering. But that was because his stomach was emptier than it had ever been before. He'd had very little lunch. He'd had no tea—only that cautious spoonful of olive oil which was to have secured for him a comfortable margin of calculation during the night's patrician inebrieties. He crossed to the shelf where he knew the biscuits might be. And there they were. An unopened packet of Rich Tea. And a half-pound block of chocolate as well.

He tore off the wrappings, flung himself into a chair, and ate ravenously. He had got to wondering whether he was going to be sick when, once more, he heard footsteps on the stair. He had left the light on in his own rooms below; it must be somebody who had looked for him there and then taken a guess that he was in Luke's rooms upstairs. Perhaps it was Leech again. Or perhaps it was one of those filthy men back from the dinner already. It might be one of them proposing to gloat (Bruno realized with alarm that this notion approached insanity) or (and this would be worse) to do an utterly sweet-natured gentleman turn with a few vague words intended to be sensed as an apology. At the thought of this Bruno decided that he really was going to be most instantly sick, and he scrambled to his feet in panic, made for Luke's bedroom, mistook its direction, and positively blundered across the room again. He was in the middle of this horror when the outer door opened—there must have been a tap at it—and a very old man came into the room. He seemed to move and hold himself stiffly, as if afraid of what might happen if he did not. He was in evening dress.

"Please forgive me. But I see that, as I hoped, I have come upon a fellow-guest, not yet gone to bed." The old man must have been momentarily more aware of Bruno's dinner-jacket than of his youth. "There was a light in the rooms next to mine, but they proved untenanted. I then went down to Mr Leech, but he appears to have gone to bed." The old man (who was, of course, one of the Vile Old Men) had by this time taken in a little more. For he now smiled faintly. "But I judge it possible," he said, "that you were not one of our rather senior company at dinner."

"I haven't been of any company at dinner." Bruno, who was now at least at a standstill and not being sick after all, said this with a savagery that was far from polite. "I'm just a bloody undergraduate."

The old man frowned, and then lifted his chin with the motion of one persuading himself that he has misheard and must try harder. "Then you are Mr Tresilian," he said. "I noticed the name over the door." He paused, and seemed to judge it courteous to introduce himself. "I am Lord Burntisland," he continued, "and the guest of your Provost. The occasion has been a pleasant one, but nobody has provided matches. Seldom smoking, I seldom carry them. It is simply that I must boil some water. The gas-ring was pointed out to me. A small matter of routine."

Bruno felt in his pockets. "I haven't any either," he said sulkily. The threat of vomiting was coming back again. He thought it was because the old man horrified him. What he called his matter of routine must be some revolting medical expedient to keep him quite unnecessarily alive. "But if you'll wait a minute, sir, I'll get you some from the scout's pantry." It was with disgust that he heard the tone in which he said this. Quite involuntarily, his rudeness had modulated into standard public school deference. "Won't you sit down?" he added.

"Thank you. I shall be glad to." Lord Burntisland lowered himself carefully to a chair—and then quite suddenly, and rather alarmingly, he slumped in it. And it wasn't merely his body that lost its stiff poise and went slack. Something happened at the same time to the muscles of his face and the focus of his eyes. Bruno remembered a great-aunt who sometimes behaved like that, and who was then said to be confused. But with this old man, probably, it was just a matter of being tight after his beano. Bruno went out to get the matches.

When he returned Lord Burntisland was again braced and upright. But on being handed the matchbox he did not immediately rise to his feet. "Forgive me, Mr Tresilian," he said. "I feel there is some association I ought to be able to make with your name. You must not judge me impolite if I fail to do so. It is perhaps to be accounted to fatigue." He seemed slightly puzzled by Bruno's silence. "You *are* Mr Tresilian?" he asked.

At this a devil—but at first no more than a small and idle devil—stirred in Bruno. Why shouldn't he be Mr Tresilian? And why shouldn't he be a Mr Tresilian that—fatigue or no fatigue—this old dotard would remember? "Yes," he said, and almost at once brightened a little. "I'm Luke Tresilian."

"The Evangelists." For a moment there played over Lord Burntisland's face the shadow or the ruin of a smile. It prompted no sympathy in Bruno. "Or two of them : Luke and Matthew. Are you related to a painter of whom I have been hearing something of late?"

"Matthew Tresilian was my father," Bruno said. "You've probably seen the big picture by him on our great staircase." Having thus plunged into thumping lies, Bruno found that he was feeling better. But it was still rather a childish and pointless deception. If he could now somehow exploit it in the direction of outrage and nastiness, if he could horrify this old creature and at the same time take some really mean and gratuitous smack at Luke, he would have contrived, he realized, at least a momentary anodyne for his own smitten and ravaged spirit. As he perceived this, as it dawned on him how splendidly Satanic his own nature was, Bruno almost felt cheerfulness breaking in. But as yet nothing really amusing had occurred to him. So he must continue the conversation on exploratory lines. "Do you like my father's work?" he asked.

Lord Burntisland—he had a Scottish accent of a dry and cultivated sort, and it was Bruno's guess that he was a judge—

hesitated. "I cannot claim to be in sympathy with the modern movements," he said. "But I was happy to learn"—he hesitated again, and this was clearly because what he had been happy to learn was momentarily eluding him—"I was happy to learn that I shared with your father a love of the poet Tennyson."

This, although exquisitely comical in a way, was not particularly promising. "Of course," Bruno said, "between that time and his death my father's art changed a good deal."

"So I understand. Indeed, it is something that has been demonstrated to me. And I have been told that your father had a last phase which is particularly perplexing."

Bruno was about to say: "It was the sad result, sir, of his terrible retributive disease." That would at least be wildly funny. But it would almost certainly conclude this strange interview— and what principally *made* this interview strange was the fact that it had been continuing at all. He could see that the old man didn't give a damn for Matthew Tresilian's painting, and was indeed unfavourably and even suspiciously disposed towards it. But towards Tresilian's bogus son—who hadn't received him with much politeness in the first place—he seemed to be rather drawn. Bruno had only to consider this circumstance for a brief further moment before there dawned on him a truth of the most entertaining sort. It was a truth about this ageing creature which the ageing creature might himself be largely unconscious of.

"I must not keep you up by this intrusion." Lord Burntisland still showed no sign of moving. He had glanced around the room and was now looking at Bruno again. "It is a pleasure to glimpse your life in this informal way. I myself was a student at Edinburgh, and I have no children. My contacts at Oxford have been only with the elderly, I am afraid."

Bruno listened and watched. The old man's features were of the craggy sort, and it must be their natural tendency to compose themselves somewhere between the severe and the grim. But at the moment they had softened. It would have been simplest to say that, in a cautious fashion, he was looking at Bruno with kindness. He is looking—Bruno thought, amused—at the son who never turned up on him, and whom he would have sent here or to New College or to the House and sometimes visited like this. Probably that idea is going through his head now. But, at the same time, he's ever so faintly puzzled. The son who might have been doesn't quite cover the attraction he feels. And he will take alarm at a breath. The fun—Bruno said to himself —is to see an obscure uneasiness slowly mount in him. I have to be fetching, but I have to be pure as driven snow. And I'm a great demon out of hell, after all.

Bruno had been sprawling on Luke's sofa in the attitude of a relaxed Ganymede. He now unobtrusively corrected this posture, sat up, and put his knees and toes together as he had seen nice girls do. And if he couldn't be Ganymede he could at least be Antinous. He had only to turn his small Roman head *so*, and drop his delicately chiselled chin *thus*, and the effect was achieved. Even if—he added to himself, at once picking up the idiom of his role—I look a perfect *fright* after all that passion about their filthy dinner.

"Did you ever know my father, sir?" he asked respectfully. It would be as well to make sure of his ground here. He mustn't say anything about Matthew Tresilian that would give him away.

"Far from it. I am afraid I heard of him only recently. I am very fond of the Old Masters, but—I must again admit—modern painting is something of a closed book to me."

Bruno didn't think an artistic conversation promising. And he recalled that Matthew Tresilian had died when the real Luke was too young to remember him. His first hazy plan to horrify the old man with scandalous anecdotes of his supposed father's Bohemian life and morals couldn't really be brought off. Deciding, therefore, to switch to direct action at once, he stood up and strolled to the chimneypiece, where lay Luke's abandoned packet of cigarettes. He managed, he thought, to impart a really maidenly modesty to the move. "You don't mind, sir, if I smoke myself? Or if I begin getting out of these beastly clothes?"

"By no means." Lord Burntisland sounded only faintly surprised. He did, however, make as if to rise. "But I must be off to bed myself."

"Oh, do stop a minute or two, sir." Bruno's demurely respectful manner was unflawed. He put down his unlighted cigarette, strolled over to Luke's bedroom door and threw it open. "It's fun having one of the college's distinguished guests as a visitor. And I've just got back from such a boring dinner." He slipped out of his dinner-jacket and waistcoat and tossed them gracefully through the bedroom door. "Rugger toughs. I can't think why they asked me." He tugged off his black tie and dropped his braces over his hips. He wriggled out of his shirt and vest and chucked them after the other things. Then he went back to the chimneypiece, picked up the cigarette, and went over to Lord Burntisland. "I wonder, sir," he said, "if I might have one of those matches?"

Lord Burntisland produced the matches with a slightly unsteady hand. "Then you are not yourself," he asked, "given to athletic pursuits?"

Bruno lit his cigarette, returned the matches, and took a single step backwards. "I do a little fencing, from time to time," he said. "Have you ever fenced, sir?"

"Yes, indeed. I took considerable pleasure in it as a young man."

Lord Burntisland was eyeing Bruno, stripped to the waist, as it was perfectly proper to eye a young man whose athletic pursuits—as he had called them—were in question. Nevertheless Bruno observed with satisfaction that the old man was uneasy and agitated. "And I do some Judo," he said. "Did you ever do that?"

"No, no—nothing of the kind."

Lord Burntisland was struggling to rise, and Bruno saw that this queer diversion was almost over. "I could show you a thing or two there," he said.

"I have no doubt of it." Lord Burntisland managed an odd laugh. "But it would have to be at a less unholy hour." He appeared to be obtaining an uncertain balance on groggy knees. Bruno debated whether to step forward and offer him his naked arm. He decided against this. He decided against any gesture at all. And he decided against uttering another word. He waited until Lord Burntisland was more or less firmly on his feet, and then he looked at him. It was one of his enigma acts, and he brought it off perfectly. He saw the pupils of Lord Burntisland's eyes dilate, and a faint flush—which might have been anger or fear, or both—come into his cheeks. Moreover he was trembling all over, so that Bruno thought with a sudden wild alarm that he might drop down dead. But nothing dramatic happened. Lord Burntisland's body stiffened again, he looked at Bruno— he very decidedly looked at Bruno—in his turn, and then gave a nod the curtness of which answered to the grimness of his eye. "I have detained you too long, Mr Tresilian," he said. "Good night."

Bruno hastened across the room to open the door. He carried with him the most virginal of airs, an expression of innocence unflawed. It would add to the joke if the old man had to decide that anything else had been entirely the work of his imagination. "Good night, sir," he said. "I do hope you sleep well."

He watched Lord Burntisland down a couple of steps, and then shut the door. He was alone once more in Luke's sitting-room, and the next event on the programme was undoubtedly Satanic laughter. Only it didn't come. Instead he felt apprehensive and depressed. What if the old man complained to Leech, or to the Provost himself? It would mean, surely, Bruno's being chucked out of the college on his ear.

But that was nonsense. The whole joke—apart from impersonating Luke, which was something Lord Burntisland could have no suspicion of—had been cunningly created out of confused and fugitive impressions. The old creature would certainly keep his disturbing experience to himself.

Bruno went into the bedroom and collected his scattered clothes. He returned to the sitting-room and his glance fell on the photograph of Luke's Rugger Fifteen. He went over to it and put his tongue out at Luke—Luke sitting cross-legged and knobbly-kneed in the front. He did this to cheer himself up rather than out of any malice, for his spurt of hostile feeling against Luke had quite evaporated. He turned out the lights and made his way down to his own rooms. On the staircase he dropped his dress tie and had to stoop for it. Suddenly his evening's humiliation, which his evening's later performance had blotted out for a while, was back with him. "Damn!" he said aloud, as he moved downstairs again. "Oh, damn, damn, *damn*!"

It had been a marvellous joke—he told himself, trying to rally. And it certainly could do Luke no harm—Luke, whom he wasn't sure that he wasn't rather fond of. Nevertheless the sense of an evil act went downstairs with him. "Oh, *damn*!" he repeated, as he recklessly banged behind him the door of his own room.

CHAPTER TWENTY-SIX

LUKE WOKE UP in the small hours. He had been dreaming that he was for some reason impersonating Bruno.

This was surely a most unusual dream, and as his mind swam into an awareness of his body lying in the still unfamiliar Landreth guest-room he wondered whether the dream had culminated in some nightmarish twist which his coming awake had swiftly censored. His heart was thumping suspiciously, and his pyjama jacket was damp over his shoulders. But that might mean no more than that it had been a football dream—a childish and almost humiliatingly innocent form of creation to which his unconscious mind was obstinately prone.

Then he remembered the college kitchens. His dream had begun there. It was quite usual to visit the kitchens, because they were housed in arched and vaulted mediaeval chambers which visitors liked to see. And there was a mediaeval painting of cooks and scullions too, uncertainly traceable on a cracked and smoke-blackened wooden panel, to which one usually drew attention. But Luke, in his dream, hadn't come to the kitchens because he had visitors. He had come because he was hungry, and in the hope of finding food. Of course one never really went to the kitchens for such a purpose; one went to the buttery. But here he had been, driven by an urgent hunger, and surrounded by tables piled with stuff to eat. But whenever he stretched out a hand there was something mysteriously wrong and unsatisfying about what it came upon, so that he wandered on, oppressed less and less by anything that was quite simply physical hunger, and more and more by an unnameable need which was an obscure anxiety as well.

The dream—Luke thought as he gave a tug at the bedclothes —had been of rather a tiresome kind. Nevertheless, as usual when he woke up from anything of the sort, he was keen to get off to sleep again on the chance of catching up with the dream and seeing how it developed next. He was interested in dreams. He had a theory that Freud had got dreams absolutely wrong, but so persuasively that the proper study of them had been at a standstill ever since. He had once dreamed that he had explained his opinion to Freud, and that Freud was impressed and promised to think the whole matter over in this new light. Freud had added that, as it happened, he was then engaged in a study of conceit in dreams, and that if Luke would allow him he would make a few notes there and then. Luke, awakening unchastened, had judged this such a clever dream that he made a short story out of it. Unfortunately he tried to do this in the manner of Kafka, and it hadn't been a success.

But now, for a time, he didn't manage to go to sleep again. Instead, he found himself remembering, in a fragmentary way, some farther phase of his dream. As he did so, he again became aware that his heart was thumping—thumping in a way that no memory from the dream as yet explained.

He had turned to the grubby old mediaeval painting in the kitchens and had found himself, without surprise, looking at something quite different. For the college possessed a very great painting, and this was where it hung. It was Leonardo's Virgin of the Rocks. But it was only for a moment that he took it for granted. For, even as he looked, the painting somehow became three-dimensional, and he himself was impelled to move into it. He had moved past the Virgin and into the pre-human world of rocks and waters before which Leonardo had disposed her. It was as if the college kitchens had broken down from vaulted, man-made chambers, such as the real kitchens were, into arched passages that became cavernous, tortuous, narrow, slippery with slime as he advanced, and then into an endless system of sewers such as Nature herself might construct painfully through aeons of geological time were Nature in any need of sewers. A dark tide pulsed through them. They were at once unutterably alien and identical with the cavities of Luke's own heart. So that he knew that in his heart there was a darkness—there in his heart that throbbed at an accelerating tempo, as one's heart will do if one climbs a steep hill in desperate and mounting excitement, thrusting one's body up and up against the pull of gravity. It was at this point that the dream had sharpened its focus on the issue of his, Luke's, identity, and of some threat to it which was also a dreadful promise.

He knew that, with this, the whole tone of the dream had changed. But that was all he could remember. And, this time, he wasn't wanting to sink down into sleep again and have another look. But he knew, with a swiftly mounting anxiety, that he was now going to do so, all the same. For he was involved with the kind of dream which half returns the dreamer to a waking consciousness and then pulls him back again. He realized that his mind was like a horrifying sadistic toy which sometimes came into his dreams, and with which, in fact, he had once played as a child : a manikin in a phial almost filled with fluid. You pressed a diaphragm and your captive slowly, helplessly sank; released it and your captive rose as slowly until its head just broke the surface. You allowed a brief breath and the torture again began. It was in this fashion that Luke was sinking and rising and sinking through the dark waters of his dream. He had a helpless knowledge that this would indefinitely continue; that again and again he would struggle upwards into the darkness of the bedroom, sink down into the answering darkness of a primordial place. When his head did break surface, and he sensed that he was lying warm and snug in a material darkness, even although his body was ready for more sleep and indeed demanding it, his will asserted a contrary impulse. But down he went again—and now he had penetrated far into the hinterland of Leonardo's painting. He was approaching a place where some release, some revelation would be granted him; where this intolerably mounting tension and anxiety would be broken. But what he was to be shown was a forbidden thing.

He found himself using his mind like flailing arms to keep himself up, to keep himself awake. He tried orienting himself in space, in the real space of this upper darkness. He had the sensation, nocturnally familiar but always uncanny, of lying in a room the door and window of which had inexplicably passed through a looking-glass in relation to the line of his own supine body. The door ought to be *there*, surely. And the window *there*. He made an effort to remember the room as he had gone to bed in it. And instantaneously, as by one of those optical tricks which Mrs Landreth had explained in some of his father's paintings, it turned inside-out, disposing itself round about him as it ought to be. Through *that* wall, he now knew, was Mrs Landreth's room. And through *that* wall was Hatty's.

239

At this last waking realization he sank again, dropping now through deeper and deeper waters of sleep, and dropping quite helplessly this time because his hands were in his pockets. Leech was beside him, Leech wrapped in his gown so that he looked like a cloaked Virgil sinking with Dante through Botticelli's or Blake's Inferno—only the gown he drew around his shoulders wasn't really there. It was now that Luke understood—as he dimly remembered he had understood before in this dream that was for ever repeating itself—that he must submit to the rules of the nether world. One of the rules was that you must pretend to be someone else if you wished to escape from anxiety, escape to your need and desire. So now, with a shameful sense of cunning, he said to Leech—as he had said before yet was somehow now saying for the first time—"Yes, I am Bruno Landreth."

And at once the kitchens were full of whispering and peeping scullions waiting to watch him doing what he could now do. Here in the kitchens that broke down ino caverns, labyrinths, stark phallic rocks and dark uterine waters, here in Leonardo's dawn world, a world without human sorrow or joy, without divine Grace, he was making love, at last he was making love, to Hatty. And around him the scullions were whispering more loudly and had been transformed : they had become *voyeurs*, old *roués* out of a Forain etching. Only there was nothing doing for them. The entertainment wasn't on. Hatty was in his arms, but in this dark region she was not merely Hatty, but Hatty's mother too. She smiled up at him—almost with one of Bruno's enigma smiles —from the bed as broad as a battlefield that had swum into being beneath her. And then her smiles were tears. And she was Hatty again.

Silently and in a searing, childish sorrow, Hatty wept and wept. He knew why. And he knew that her burden of wickedness was nonsense; that he could strip it from her as easily as he could her schoolgirl's absurd tunic and hat. He had the strength for that and far more, because his heart was pure. He thought he knew what he must do. He stood up and ripped the clothes from his own body—clothes which were not his but Bruno's. He tossed them over his shoulder and they vanished into air. And all the scullions vanished. The whole dark place was gone. He dropped to his knees beside Hatty and kissed her.

Only Hatty wasn't there to be kissed. In his arms there lay, instead, a Leech who had become a naked and decrepit hag. The hag was pressing her wrinkled breast to Luke's breast. Luke strained away from her, conscious through panic as he did so of a chill, compulsive clutch at his bowels and reins. But the hag's hands were amorously in his hair. She was, he realized, combing his hair. She was, he realized, cutting it. He had just strength to speak. "Who are you?" he asked. "Tell me who you are."

She cut another lock and held it for a moment in her withered fingers. "I am the truth of the matter," she said. "I am the truth about human love." And she drew the lock of Luke's own hair slowly down the length of Luke's naked spine. He was suddenly wide awake, with a body wildly throbbing and a mind appalled.

He lay quite still, humiliated but calming himself, taking dismissively the measure of the lumber that had been flying around in the rag-and-bone shop of his unconscious mind. He didn't much have to inquire into Hatty being Hatty's mother too. Probably she had been Lucilla as well in bits he didn't remember. That came simply from Bruno's talk. He didn't much have to inquire into the stuff about girls being wooed by lovers who were brothers as well. That too was Bruno's sense of quiet family fun. To hell with it. His own job was to straighten things out.

Luke stretched himself in the bed and—already sleepy again— straightened his rumpled pyjama jacket. He turned over cautiously after this tiresome dream. But perhaps such dreams were designed by the Life Force—having lately read Shaw, he rather believed in the Life Force—to tip you off as to just what you sat on top of. Perdita wooed by Florizel wanted a bank for love to lie and play on. Donne and his girl had a bank of violets; they sat, they engrafted hands, all day the same their postures were and they said nothing all the day. But beneath all four of them that other world had whispered. Did the existence of that other, nether world render finally tragic every exploration of love?

There was no answer. Luke had closed his eyes. He slept dreamlessly through the dawn.

PART FOUR

CHAPTER TWENTY-SEVEN

Cᴴᴬᴿᴸᴱꜱ Rᴏꜱᴱ ᴘᴏᴜʀᴇᴅ himself out a glass of Jane Landreth's sherry. It was one of the few ritual informalities that he spontaneously allowed himself—even when, as now, he had been bidden to the most casual of family lunches. "How did it go?" he asked. And seeing Jane in an abstraction, he added, "I mean the Tresilian private view this morning."

"Everybody I spoke to was tremendously struck. And so was the Press crowd yesterday. I went to that too."

"Got your notice in?"

"Early this morning."

There was a silence. Rose, puzzled, consulted his glass. "Was that nice lad there?" he asked. And again had to add, "The son, I mean. Luke."

"Oh, no—or I hope not. He said he was going to go at a quieter time. He's back in Cornwall, fortunately."

Now Rose positively stared. "Has it been difficult about Hatty? And are you sure you were nice to the boy?"

"Yes, I think it was a little difficult, perhaps. And of course I was nice to him. In fact, I kissed him."

"My dear Jane! Wasn't that rather sealing the possible maternal relationship? I thought you felt the young people's romance was best muted for a time."

"There was nothing maternal about it."

"Jane!"

"When I was saying good-bye to him it just came over me that he was extremely charming. It was something that might happen between any two people of somewhat discrepant years. Between you and Lucilla, for example."

Rose set down his glass. It was a long time since Jane had been what he used to call outrageous. He remembered, down a vista of his own staid years, that it was something he had greatly liked. But he wasn't sure he liked it now. "Did the young gentleman respond?" he asked, and flushed at so false a note.

"Look!" he went on, grabbing at a genuine one. "The picture is quite absurd, for a start. You must have had to stand on tiptoe. Unless you stole up to him by surprise, while he was sitting smoking his big, manly pipe."

"Yes, I can see the picture. But you must remember, Charles, the dreadful people I move among. They're not a bit B.M. In fact, they are casually and innocently kissing each other all the time."

"This boy knows nothing of that."

"How right you are. He was much disconcerted. More so than I'd have expected. I thought—" Jane broke off, frowning. "I *thought* that I thought it the mildest of gaieties; the lightest of possible ways of suggesting that we did agree tentatively to adopting him."

"In other words, that it was maternal after all. You've got yourself into a muddle, if you ask me."

"Yes, Charles." Jane was provokingly meek.

"And you see where it leads you. You have to be glad this decent lad is out of London, because you've behaved—"

"Rubbish!" Unexpectedly and rather harshly, Jane laughed. "I merely said I was glad he wasn't at the private view. But, of course, you haven't heard. You see—" She broke off as a telephone-bell rang in a corner of the room. "Damn!" For a moment Jane Landreth was very like her son Bruno. "It's that bloody paper hounding the thing. You bet it is."

This language, too, made Charles Rose stare. Nevertheless he sat down with an air of effacing himself while his hostess picked up the instrument.

"Yes," Jane said. "This *is* me." She listened for some time. Rose was every now and then obliged to comprehend incoming words and phrases, but maintained an inner propriety by refraining from trying to string them together. "Nonsense!" Jane said.

"But it's true!" The voice at the other end was now agitated, raised and inescapable. "The old devil himself. A personal instruction. It's a thing he doesn't do once in a twelvemonth. That chap Roundhay sent it round in his boss's own hand."

To Rose, although so blessedly remote from the hideous world crackling in the receiver, this could not be other than intelligible. Jane's weekly operated under remote control, the Press lord who owned it commonly leaving it to its own obscure devices. But he could dictate when he wanted to. It sounded as if he were doing so now.

"It has nothing to do with me," Jane was saying. "It's not the sort of purpose for which I go to such things."

"But Jane, dear"—the voice was anxiously reasonable—"there was nobody else covering it for us."

"That may be. But you can get the facts from any of this evening's rags. And make what you like of them. Only they have no place in a professional notice written by an art critic."

"That's not Roundhay's view."

"Then Roundhay can have me sacked. It's as simple as that."

"Jane"—now the voice was urgent—"will you let me fudge up a few rotten lines and tack them on at the end of your piece?"

"Absolutely not."

"Jane—do think."

"I'm thinking. Dogs don't eat dogs. But, if anything of the sort happens, I'll find somebody to print a letter."

"But, Jane, the old devil—"

"The old devil can go to hell." Jane paused, and had an inspired afterthought. "And I'll go to Rome. Good-bye." She banged down the receiver and turned to Rose. "Charles," she said, "would you, at a pinch, lend me a couple of thousand pounds?"

"Yes, of course." Rose contrived to get a moment's genuine amusement out of this being remotely an uncertainty. "But what on earth is it all about?"

"It's about a disagreeable and ludicrous incident at the affair this morning—I mean at the Tresilian show. There was an H. R. H. opening it, you know. Well, almost before he'd left—"

Jane was interrupted by the banging of an outer door. A moment later, Hatty tumbled into the room, flushed and panting. "Have you heard?" she said, and flung a midday paper down on a table. "Some horrible old man has been filthy about Luke's father's pictures. I hope they put him in gaol."

"They're more likely to put him in a mental hospital, I imagine." Jane had become instantly composed. "But it's probably not important. That sort of freakish thing does sometimes happen."

"There's a banner headline." This time, and as she pointed

247

at the paper, Hatty addressed Rose. She did so accusingly, as if planting him squarely in a context of horrible old men. "It's too obscene."

"Is that what somebody has been saying about the paintings, perhaps?" Rose, whose intelligence seldom lingered on the outskirts of a problem, was no longer puzzled. "About the last ones, no doubt?"

"Yes. Somebody I've heard Mummy talk about. A lord. Lord Burntisland."

"Good lord! *That* lord." Now Rose really was shocked. He turned to Jane. "He actually made a scene on the spot?"

Jane nodded. "A very painful one. At first, I think, he didn't mean to. It was in front of a painting which is called, rather obscurely, 'A Kind of Avarice'."

"I know it. It belongs still to the Tresilian estate, and has never been exhibited. But I did once have a glimpse of it. In a grotesque way, this begins to make sense."

"Possibly so. It was surprising that old Burntisland was there at all—although I heard somebody say he'd given some sort of promise to Lady Madrona. Anyway, he was restraining himself. But then—and it seemed quite involuntarily—he said something out loud. He appeared, in a queer way, to hear himself doing it. And then he went off the deep end. Sodom and Gomorrah. I decided instantly that he was mad."

"And did the assembled notables decide that too?"

"There was a great deal of confusion. He was persuaded to leave. But it has become public, as you see. I suppose it must run its course as a sensation."

"It will certainly do that." A new voice spoke, for Lucilla Landreth had entered the room. She too carried a newspaper— neatly folded. "And there's been rather a staggering sequel since. I'll tell you about it when I've had a drink." With faint amusement, Lucilla watched Charles Rose dive for the sherry decanter. "It's awkward, but at least I think Sir Hector's all right. He's blessedly furious at the moment, and says that his wife's been insulted, to say nothing of the exalted gentleman who opened the show. Not that this old lunatic didn't behave rather correctly, in a queer way."

"Correctly!" Hatty had suddenly gone quite pale with anger.

"He wrote to Ruth Madrona—it was something I haven't

felt entitled to divulge even in a family way—to say that he must withdraw his agreement to attend in any sense as her guest. Then he wrote to the secretary of the gallery asking for a card for himself in his capacity as the president of some council or other that dishes out moral welfare."

"And they sent it!" Hatty was aghast.

"It would have been most injudicious not to," Rose commented briskly. "And they no doubt thought he was just another eccentric peer doing his stuff."

Lucilla nodded. "Just that. But he seems to have gone on doing it. The police turned up in the gallery just an hour later."

"It's not possible, Lucilla." This time Rose sounded almost impatient. "That sort of thing never moves in such a fashion. It would take days—"

"Two elderly and respectable men in plain clothes. I don't know how they got cards. But one of the gallery's young men recognized them. He says they're the feelthy pictures squad. Connoisseurs in dubious photographs and picture postcards. They walked round peaceably and left."

Rose decided on a further glass of sherry himself. "I wonder," he asked, "whether ever before—"

"Yes, years ago there was a small fuss somewhere over a late Tresilian. One of those occasions upon which a city councillor, or a person of that sort, takes exception to a painting on loan to a local gallery. But it faded out, and nobody remembered anything about it. As for the police visit coming with improbable speed, there's no doubt that a certain amount of spade-work has been going on. Sir Hector has been telephoning like mad, and I think he's begun to see a pattern in it."

"A pattern?" Jane asked. "That seems a very odd expression. Surely it's just a question of some sort of morbidity in Lord Burntisland suddenly bubbling up?"

"Not unassisted."

Rose gave a sudden exclamation. "Yes," he said. "I believe I see. Burntisland has been trying to start a campaign to clean up certain kinds of advertising. A fellow at my club told me not long ago that the old chap was becoming obsessed with the theme. And his crusade would be a great nuisance in some quarters if it really got under way. I suspect that somebody has neatly side-tracked him—diverted his energies, you might say, into a neighbouring field. Don't you remember, Jane, an occasion on which he revealed himself as not at all sympathetically disposed to anything that could be called the modern movement in painting?"

"I do. It was at that curious Madrona soirée—when you and I had our lovely long chat behind the Chinese screen, and Lucilla was equally wonderfully entertained by old John Alabaster."

"I don't recall quite all that. But you've got the occasion. Arthur Roundhay was there. Yes, by Jove, he was! And I'm not sure that Burntisland didn't reveal himself as having a particular allergy towards Matthew Tresilian."

"There was a young man from the N.G.," Jane said. "Justin Somebody, who knows about Baciccia. He told me some vaguely uncomfortable story about Burntisland and a Tresilian."

Lucilla had opened her newspaper and was looking at the headline. "There's been nothing so outrageous," she said, "since Alfred Munnings tried to instigate a prosecution of Stanley Spencer. It must be stopped."

Rose nodded. "No doubt. But these things are less easy to stop than start."

"Sir Hector will do his best. He's bound to. He practically sponsored this Tresilian exhibition. And, as I said, I think he's sound on it. I think he'll stick it out."

"Perhaps he may, Lucilla. But I rather doubt his being the right man for the job. May I speak disrespectfully of your employer?"

"No, of course not. Or not after asking me."

"Very well. I'll say something about Burntisland instead. We see him as a dotty old man being unscrupulously egged on to make a fool of himself. At least that's the picture we're in process of building up. But there's rather more to him than that. Of course he doesn't know what painting is about; his innocence there isn't a bogus and sophisticated innocence, like old Bernard Le Mesurier's. But as a citizen he's tough and rocky, and he has the most inflexible standards for people as well as policies. He may be taken in by an astute journalist like Roundhay, who has abruptly turned up on him more or less from nowhere. But he won't be impressed by anybody he has already weighed and found wanting. And I'd be very surprised to hear he hasn't got

Madrona in that category. The arts Madrona will advance in this matter will make no impression on him. So what will happen then?"

"Charles is forming a bad habit," Lucilla said. "He asks questions to which he proposes to supply the answers himself. It's a terrible portent of middle age."

"When Madrona's arts don't work"—Charles Rose had managed not to be disconcerted—"it will be his instinct to use some sort of big stick. Burntisland's years are now rather burdensome. There are no doubt plenty of people prepared to call him gaga—as we ourselves, indeed, have been doing in rather a facile way. And a vulgar newspaper campaign can boomerang very awkwardly. Burntisland must be aware of all this, and Madrona may try exploiting it. It's my guess that he would find his adversary not at all the man to yield ground under pressure of that sort."

"In fact," Jane said, "the only impact upon Lord Burntisland will be made by somebody he respects."

"Or is prepared to respect. Quite so."

"The Professor of the History of Art at Oxford." Hatty spoke rapidly and rather surprisingly. "The President of the Royal Academy. The top man on the Arts Council. Another old man in the House of Lords who pontificates on arty matters. That sort of official standing is what counts with a retired statesman, or whatever this horrible old man is."

Charles Rose nodded, rather with the air of an academic dignitary admitting some young person to a new grade or degree. "Just that, Hatty. The alternative would be sudden and impassioned appeal at a personal level. It's a pity that Matthew Tresilian hasn't left a widow in reduced circumstances."

"Oh, hullo." The door had opened rather quietly, and Bruno Landreth had come into the room. He wore a subdued air. "Hullo, Charles," he said. His glance fell on one of the newspapers. "Quite a sensation, isn't it?" he asked of nobody in particular. "Some eminent Victorian having a field day in the vicinity of Bond Street, apparently." Bruno seemed to have decided on conventional elegance for this vacation; like the Madrona boys, he even had a bowler hat. "Luke will be upset," he said, and drifted towards the drinks. Then, with an air of conscious temperance, he drifted away again. "Of course, it's a pretty foul show."

"You don't say so," Hatty said. Brother and sister gave each other—the others remarked—one of their uncomfortable long stares. "It's a good thing it's an old man," Hatty added, suddenly childish. "Otherwise, Luke might have socked him."

"This Lord Burntisland *is* an old man?" Bruno looked round, as if seeking confirmation at large. "Really an eminent Vic? I was just guessing, of course." He turned to his mother. "What about food?" he asked, a shade rudely. "I'm famished." Again he looked round quickly, this time with a deftly apologetic smile. "Sorry," he said. "Is it a council of war?"

"If we feel directly concerned," Rose said with what Jane thought of as his endearing assumption of paternal severity, "it's because Tresilian's son is a friend of yours—and now, indeed, a friend of your family's. We've been wondering whether anything can be done to smother this unfortunate affair."

"It looks bloody like it, I must say." Bruno tapped the newspaper. "They're going to run it for all it's worth. That's clear enough. And I suppose this old man can make speeches in parliament. Does anybody know just what has made him tick?"

"Not really." Rose shook his head. He was now treating Bruno carefully as an equal in conference. "But it does appear that when he came to this exhibition he already had a thing about Tresilian. Somehow, you might say, he'd taken against the name."

"How very odd!" If Bruno had looked momentarily perturbed, the effect was immediately obliterated by a cheerful smile. "Perhaps he had a nasty experience with a Tresilian in the woodshed when he was a kid. Or something of that sort." Bruno turned to his mother. "What's this picture like? I mean the one Burntisland particularly created about at the exhibition."

"It's never much good describing pictures," Jane said. Something in Bruno's manner disturbed her. "And I'm going to mash the potatoes."

"Bruin does that," Hatty said. "It's one of the things he *can* do."

"Yes, of course." Surprisingly, Bruno moved with alacrity towards the kitchen. "It wouldn't," he asked, "be a picture called 'A Kind of Avarice'—with two faces and a background of stalactites and stalagmites? Luke once told me about that one as being the most disturbing of the lot."

Jane nodded. "That's it."

"It sounds pretty inoffensive, even if a bit mad."

"A large public will certainly think it a bit mad. They'll call it surrealistic, which it's not. It's highly conceptual, although in a bafflingly elusive way. The background of stalactites and stalagmites isn't exactly a background, and it isn't exactly these things either. It's a kind of framework or broad margin, filled with a minutely depicted vision of a pre-organic world—or the next thing to that. Perhaps lichens have arrived, but the first flowers haven't bloomed and the first lizard hasn't crawled. It's what somebody's called Hard Primitivism : the Garden of Eden after Darwin's had a go at it. But that, as I say, is only a surround. As the composition moves inward all these forms, painted with a Pre-Raphaelite minuteness, lose distinctness, turn ambiguous, take on elusive suggestions of animal life. If the thing were done the other way, with the precision at the centre and the indefinables on the periphery, it wouldn't be nearly so strange, because actual human vision works more or less like that. Charles, am I getting it right?"

"As I remember the picture, I think you more or less are."

"As it is, the centre of the composition is something that has withdrawn into invisibility."

"Just a luminous haze?" Hatty asked.

"Not in the least. It's a highly organized three-dimensional passage. One's mind hovers on the verge of interpretation in figurative terms, but just can't make it. One feels that one is refusing to grasp something, or that the concept of graspability is an illusion."

"It doesn't *sound* like a good painting," Bruno said. "But what about the two heads?"

"They peer out from among your stalactites on either side of the painting. They are identical heads, as in a fresco when a cartoon has been reversed. And they are locked in each other's gaze. That's emphasized by making their line of sight a dead horizontal, bang across the centre of the canvas."

Bruno, who seemed to have forgotten about the potatoes, shook his head. "It continues to sound an atrocity," he said.

253

"But, of course, I'm prepared to believe it's tremendous. The question is, though, what does this old man believe about it?"

Charles Rose nodded. "Quite so. And I suppose that this enigmatical affair—and particularly the elusive core of it—has been operating like a Rorschach blot."

"What's that?" Hatty asked sharply.

"Rorschach inkblots are fortuitously shaped blobs and splashes used by psychologists. People are asked to interpret them, and do so according to what's going on inside their own heads. And here's what has happened in the case of our unhappy peer. He's looked at 'A Kind of Avarice' and read it in terms of some rather improper and wholly unacknowledged interests in his own unconscious mind." Rose turned to Jane. "If the old man could be persuaded that this is the situation—and he must be, after all, a highly intelligent person—I suppose it's possible he would drop the thing?"

"The newspapers mightn't drop it. Or the police, whose effective bosses are capable of any absurdity in this field, once they get started on it. And in any case, Charles, I'm not quite certain that your analysis covers the situation."

"The analysis in terms of a big, complex Rorschach blot?"

"Just that. After all, a late Matthew Tresilian *isn't* a Rorschach blot. It's a late Matthew Tresilian."

"Not a neutral sort of thing," Lucilla said. "However enigmatic, it's designed to have a positive potency. That must go for every highly evolved work of art."

"No doubt. But, my dear Lucilla, no work of art, however highly organized, exists simply as a closed system. It leaves the spectator an astonishing amount of work to do, and really a very striking liberty of interpreting. Experimental psychology in the field has been making that very evident."

"The potatoes!" Bruno said suddenly. "I'm as hungry as hell." He disappeared into the kitchen.

"I don't see that this sort of talk is going to take us anywhere," Hatty said. "Not in routing this old man and clearing Luke's father's pictures. And I suppose *somebody* must lay the table." She too vanished.

"And now the grown-ups can talk," Jane said. "And have another quiet sherry."

Lucilla reached for the decanter. "Bruin always knows," she

said. "It amuses him to watch us fighting the Demon Drink. Charles?"

"Thank you, I've had my second. And I'm busy wondering what factor your mother thinks is missing from my analysis of this absurd but rather damnable affair."

Jane held out her empty glass towards her daughter. "Evil," she said. "Simply that."

Rose was startled. "Evil?" he repeated. It was as if this was something he hadn't heard of.

"We're taking it for granted, aren't we, that this old man has gone off the rails, has moved from reality towards delusion? And so he has, in a way. Tresilian's last paintings don't hide indecencies, or not in the way Burntisland, if we've got him right, imagines. He's looking at these things as if they were like the pictures we can remember—you and I, Charles—in the children's magazines. Turn the forest upside down, and find bears and bicycles hidden in the branches. Of course that's nonsense. But it doesn't end the matter. You say that Burntisland has been worrying about advertisements?"

"I believe so. Using scenes mildly suggestive of impending fornication to recommend the charms of Bodger's Chocolates. That sort of thing. A real enough issue, in its way."

"In its way. Is it right or wrong to persuade boys and girls that it's masculine, or that it's alluring, to smoke Bodger's, or anybody else's, cigarettes? Right and wrong aren't all that difficult to get clear. But, in a way, poor old Burntisland, in addressing himself to the art of Matthew Tresilian, is coming nearer to reality and not getting farther away from it. Art has as little to do with right and wrong as ever poor Oscar could have asserted. But it's full of massive intimations of good and evil."

"Yes," Rose said—a shade reluctantly. "I suppose it is. So are you going to tell me that some of those last paintings of Tresilian's are—objectively and quite apart from the blottesque theory—indefinably sinister?"

"Yes, indeed. Precisely that."

"Evil?"

"Aware of it. Very. Perhaps that's what won't come into focus at the centre of the canvas."

"Haven't I heard you"—Lucilla asked—"say that in his last phase Tresilian was probably influenced by Zen Buddhism? I don't see that evil can be squared with total elusiveness, and what-not. Error can be. But not evil."

"Very well. I drop Zen, if I have to. Perhaps it's only a critic's fashionable gimmick. But I don't drop the idea that Burntisland, looking at those pictures, was in contact with something he had a right to be disturbed by."

"My dear Jane"—Rose was momentarily impatient—"that's common ground. Everybody knows those last paintings are strangely disturbing."

"Very well. But, in that case, I mean something more. On the one hand, the notion that the paintings are depraving or corrupting or in any way the province of the police is nonsense. But, on the other hand, they are the work of a man conscious of some pretty dark area, or areas, of human experience. If old Lord Burntisland has been frightened and horrified by them—and I suppose he genuinely has—then he hasn't been utterly making a fool of himself."

"He's certainly making a fool of himself if he wants them condemned or suppressed."

"Not, perhaps, from his point of view. He probably believes that the function of works of art is to soothe and edify. And Tresilian's paintings disturb him deeply. He interprets that deep disturbance in your blottesque way, if you like, by projecting illicit images upon those rather invitingly enigmatic compositions. So there's an obvious question. Just how contagious is such behaviour likely to be?"

"It's not easy to forecast, Jane. Two or three days from now, people may be beginning to forget that someone called Lord Burntisland had an embarrassing aberration in a West End picture gallery. Alternatively, other old men may be queueing up with their own quota of denunciation, in which case we shall be in for one of those Philistine field-days our countrymen love to indulge in from time to time. It's very absurd, but I can't see it as tragic. Some of the paintings might have to be withdrawn from public exhibition. There might even—granted an extreme of the preposterous—be some sort of prosecution. But no magistrate nowadays would venture to order the destruction of such things. They'd be perfectly safe."

"Well, I suppose that's something," Lucilla said. "But an outcry would make us cut a pretty figure in the world."

"Quite unimportant." Rose was indisposed to give any countenance to this idea. "There's been nothing of the sort in England since 1929. Even the French have art-and-morality rows almost as frequently. Personal hurt is the only consideration worth worrying about, and Burntisland himself is the man chiefly at risk there. But of course there's the boy—Hatty's boy, as we seem to be thinking of him. Would he mind?"

"Very much," Jane said. "Luke doesn't remember his father, but he's in a very real relationship with him, all the same."

"Then that *is* a rather damnable slant on the thing. But I suppose the boy isn't an utterly sensitive plant?"

"He is sensitive, but not utterly or merely so. He doesn't mind plenty of mud on the rugger field, so he oughtn't to mind a little in Bond Street. Or is that crude? I'm trying, Charles, to match your rather robust note."

"A robust note?" Rose glanced at Jane almost suspiciously. "Ah, if we want to hear that sound in the affair we must get hold of my friend Delver, the American who is so indefatigably pursuing Matthew Tresilian's life and presumed literary remains. I'm sure that Delver, although with a foreigner's proper diffidence, will make *this*"—and Rose tapped the newspaper—"the occasion of a quite splendid letter to the *Times*."

"I wonder if he witnessed this morning's shocking scene," Jane said.

"I'm sure he didn't. Delver has gone down to Cornwall to tackle the relatives."

"Meaning Luke?"

"Luke somewhere in the north, and possibly Luke's half-sister somewhere in the south. In between, he'll make further notes on a derelict industrial landscape by way of elucidating the genesis of the juvenile Matthew Tresilian's sense of form."

"He hasn't gone after any living Tresilians before?"

"No. He appears to have his own technique for worming himself into a subject. And he's lucky as well as pertinacious. It seems he really has found a body of writing by Tresilian. Only it's in private hands, and he hasn't yet been allowed a comprehensive view of it."

"Even if he's merely proved to himself that it exists, surely, he must be jubilant."

Rose shook his head. "Actually, I'd call him puzzled, or even troubled. But as I've had no more than a word or two with him lately, I can't tell why."

"Perhaps," Lucilla said, "Matthew Tresilian isn't coming out quite as Professor Delver thought he would."

"Anything of that sort would certainly upset Delver very much. As so often with American scholars, an ingenuous temperament underlies his shrewdness and competence. I'd almost say that a hero-worshipper lurks beneath the research-worker. He has an image of Tresilian which he'd be slow to relinquish."

"Let's go in to lunch." Jane rose and moved towards the dining-room. "I think it possible your professor will make his trip in vain. Luke won't be keen on him."

"Why not, if his father is in some way very real to him?"

"Again, perhaps, hero-worship. Or no, not quite that. Luke possesses something of his father's—definitely one of the writings your American wants to get hold of—which he feels rather private about."

"Something to his father's credit?" Lucilla asked.

"Oh, decidedly. A sort of posthumous confidence—call it a sacred confidence—which Luke doesn't feel the time has come for publishing or divulging. He told me a little about it, but perhaps that's all I should say."

"Then we won't go on being curious." Rose held open the door. "But Delver will. I hope the boy sticks to his own view of such a matter. But what about the daughter by the first marriage?"

"I believe your professor will get even less out of her. She's much older, and sounds not at all impressionable. In addition to which she has married, so to speak, back into the people, and wants nothing to do with the world her father made his career in. And in addition to *that*, she has a husband oppressively given to religious enthusiasm."

"It sounds," Lucilla said, "as if the derelict industrial landscape will be Professor Delver's best buy."

Rose nodded. "I wish Delver well, but I'm not sure I don't hope you're right."

Lucilla looked at him curiously. "On any particular hypothesis or assumption?"

"Lord, no! On the vaguest and most general grounds in the world."

CHAPTER TWENTY-EIGHT

Having placed himself where he could keep an eye on the vestibule of his club, Sir Hector Madrona was able to lay down his newspaper with delicate ostentation as his guest came in.

"My dear Roundhay," he said, "how good of you to find the time. For how busy you must be!" He shook hands with benignity. "How busy thinking up—shall we say the next thing? Or possibly you have young men—scouts, as it were—for that department of your activities? Or even one of those wonderful new machines?"

"Ha ha," Roundhay said. He contrived to make a word rather than an ejaculation of this. "Ha ha ha."

"But let them take your coat." Madrona's smile might have been that of a man who, all unexpectedly, has been paid a deft compliment by a pope or emperor. "And forgive me while I enrich our poor book with your name." For a moment he turned aside in the interest of this ritual observance. "I hardly like to suggest," he went on, "that we linger over a preliminary drink?"

"My day's damned tight."

"Ah, to be sure. And I have to confess that my own engagements are not wholly foolish and inconsiderable. So we'll go straight in to lunch. This way, my dear fellow." Madrona led the way down a corridor. "Indeed, I've been told"—he spoke as if continuing an intimate talk, and at the same time with the effect of a sudden discharge of bland venom—"I *think* I've been told that your proprietor requires to see you every day?"

"We usually have a talk on the telephone." Roundhay was unruffled.

"Indeed—the telephone?" Madrona was courteously curious. "I'd heard that you wait upon him—a good, old-fashioned idiom that, is it not?—at some club-house when he has finished a round of golf. It's curious the stories that get about. Would you, I wonder, be moderately comfortable here? No—on this side. It's

the less draughty of the two. Oysters? Capital." Madrona began
to scribble an order. "If we then have the saddle of mutton you
—who look to be under no sort of doctor's orders, my dear chap
—might bring your well-known connoisseurship to a carafe of
the claret. I'm told that, for a wonder and just at present, it's
not at all bad." He sat back abruptly. "Those official hand-outs,
saying that the discussions were conducted in a relaxed and informal atmosphere: there's something in it, wouldn't you say?
So I'm delighted to get hold of you."

"You certainly have a tolerable turn of speed." Roundhay said
this with an air of bluff approval.

"It comes of having a good many interests to consider."
Madrona's air was, in turn, entirely self-depreciatory. "They
brought me your early edition almost as soon as I got back from
the gallery. And I put in quite an active hour, as a matter of fact,
before I had the good luck to contact you. But I must apologize.
There's an idea that iced water is poured the moment one sits
down. Only it doesn't seem actually to happen. You are of
American origin, are you not?"

"Nothing of the sort," Roundhay said. He was genuinely
nettled. "I was born in the West Riding."

"How intensely interesting!" Madrona might have acquired
some important accession of knowledge. "And how curiously mis-
conceptions get about. As slanders and libels also do."

"Ah," Roundhay said.

"I know you will wish me to be quite frank. What has happened offends me in three ways, Roundhay. First, it offends me
as a man of honour. You'll forgive my saying this so-little Anglo-
Saxon thing. But one's remoter ancestry sometimes speaks."

"Humph," Roundhay said. The sound might have been
designed to conjure up a vision of the remoter ancestors of Sir
Hector Madrona as tugging a primitive plough among another
man's vines.

"I sponsored the Tresilian exhibition largely because of the
intense interest which my wife always took in his work. She did
much for him, if the truth be known. I can't quite rid myself of
the feeling that she has been insulted."

"Nothing could distress me more than any such idea." Roundhay was prompt. "I have the greatest respect and admiration for
your wife. She's a most charming and accomplished woman. I

shall take very good care that her name is not associated in the remotest way with—um—the matter in hand." Roundhay sat back. He had the appearance of a man justifiably confident that he isn't to be caught out on ground like *that*. Perhaps his adversary agreed, for he went on at once to his second point.

"I come next to Tresilian's own reputation. He's a great English painter—one of the very greatest. It is grossly offensive to me—as you will find, Roundhay, that it is to other not totally inconsiderable persons concerned for the arts—it is, I say, grossly offensive to me that he should be made, wantonly and absurdly, the target of a vulgar newspaper stunt. You may feel"—and Madrona produced his blandest smile—"that my phrase is ever so slightly a stiff one. May I, however, repeat it? A vulgar newspaper stunt."

Roundhay swallowed an oyster. He hadn't the least air of one swallowing an insult at the same time. "And I think," he said cheerfully, "that you mentioned there being a third consideration in your mind?"

"Decidedly there is. And here indignation is reinforced by anxiety."

"Oh, I don't think they could prosecute *you*."

"You misconceive me." This time, Madrona's smile revealed two teeth not hitherto in evidence. "What's in question now is my friendship—a very old-established friendship—with Lord Burntisland. I am deeply sorry that he has fallen ill—"

"Ill?" Roundhay looked astonished. "I'm told he appeared quite all right this morning. He certainly seems to have been in very good voice."

"It's perfectly clear, Roundhay, that his behaviour today is the consequence of nervous aberration. It will almost certainly be followed by a serious breakdown. I don't mind telling you that I've been in touch, only half an hour ago, with a top man at that sort of thing. He doubts whether you could find a single one of his neighbours in Harley Street to guarantee Burntisland against senile dementia for a twelvemonth."

"My dear Madrona, I don't propose to try to find anything of the sort. It would be damned expensive, for one thing."

"I hope the claret is right? I suspect them of sometimes using a carafe that has been brought distinctly above room-temperature. That is unjustifiably hazardous, to say the least. But what was I speaking of? Ah, yes—precisely that. Unjustifiable hazard."

"I don't think I follow you."

"Your proprietor would do well to take that view. What are called 'sensations' no doubt bump up circulation, and consequently advertising revenue, for a while. But some, I imagine, are not worth the risks attending them. Flagrant contempt of court, for example."

"That has nothing to do with the case."

"I merely instance it. Would you care for a little more redcurrant jelly? But, as I was saying, poor Burntisland, who is so clearly failing badly, is simply not a good buy. Encourage him to go on fussing about Tresilian's last paintings and all sorts of embarrassments may result for you. And there's another thing, you know, Roundhay." Madrona was now softly reasonable. "People just aren't going to be all that interested in Matthew Tresilian—not for more than a day or two. We all know that art ought to be for the people. But it's a regrettable fact that the people just aren't for art. Whether or not there's something smutty in a few paintings by someone they've never heard of until your papers begin shouting his name, they're going to feel they couldn't care less, one way or another. Don't you agree with me?"

"Oh, yes indeed!" Roundhay seemed surprised that this could be questioned. "Mind you, I think Tresilian will last a *little* longer than you suggest. But consider him as a trailer, Madrona. Fascinating vistas open up."

"A trailer?"

"Or a lead-in. When the public gets tired of modern art as smutty—and I'd give that three weeks, myself—its interest may fairly readily be directed to modern art as a racket. Compared with that, Tresilian is a mere bagatelle."

"I see." Madrona swiftly corrected himself. "Or rather, I *don't* see. What would conceivably be in your mind, I wonder, under the head of modern art as a racket?"

"Quite a lot. And, I may say, it's in the mind of Burntisland too. His interest in the subject is widening. As a matter of fact, he and I have been studying it together. He feels that there is a public scandal not only in the mere currency and acceptance as works of art of paintings and objects that are actually mere rubbish, but also in the enormous sums of money that are paid for them—and nowadays often paid for them out of public funds."

"So you are going on to *that*."

"Oh, most certainly. Decadent art."

"I suppose you're aware that the very term 'decadent art' was more or less invented by Adolf Hitler?"

"No, I hadn't heard that." Roundhay looked across the table at Madrona with something of Madrona's own blandness.

"He put paintings on bonfires, just as he put books."

"We certainly don't intend anything like that. But we might —if the thing really gets happily under way—*exhibit* pictures. And all those queer objects too."

"Hitler was again before you there."

"Was he, now?" Roundhay actually managed an impudent imitation of Madrona's gratified curiosity. "Well, he had something there. Ridicule, you know. We might even crack the market in the stuff. That would be rather an amusing thing to do. That's where the old boy—my proprietor, as you're pleased to call him —comes in. He has a famous sense of humour, has he not?"

"You realize that a great deal of damage might be done?"

Roundhay made an apologetic gesture. "My dear fellow, I know that you happen to have invested heavily in the things."

Quite suddenly, Sir Hector Madrona was a genuinely angry man. "Have you any dim notion, Roundhay," he asked softly, "of what are called orders of magnitude? Do you imagine that my pocket would be materially affected if my collection—and I see you're thinking of my collection : my collection and my wife's—were wiped off the slate tomorrow? As a matter of fact, and just for your pitifully muddled record, I'm giving my entire present collection away."

"I've heard a rumour to that effect." Roundhay finished his mutton with evident appreciation, and allowed his glance to stray to the Stilton on a neighbouring table. "But there are other considerations besides the cash ones. For example, and as I was saying, ridicule."

There was a moment's silence. "I hope," Madrona said in a level tone, "that you'll join me in a morsel of cheese? Were we to choose the Stilton, which isn't bad, we might even venture on a glass of port."

"I'd be delighted." Roundhay made a positively gracious

gesture out of this acceptance. "At present, you know, and roughly speaking, the public has agreed to gape. But take an example. If we buy—I mean, if the nation decides to buy—that affair the pundits are talking about—"

"What affair?"

"Well, it's something by some French fellow, and about the size of a house. The name escapes me, but the production looks like an immense magnification of my grandmother's patchwork quilt. If we buy it, the public, as at present disposed, will dutifully queue up and gape. But just a very small push, just a firm, insistent emphasis on somebody's getting away with the equivalent of successful bank robbery—"

"We seem to be straying a long way from the point at which an old man has produced—unfortunately upon a rather public occasion—a pathological reaction to something he's not equipped to make head or tail of. Except, Roundhay, that that too could be made to look ridiculous. I repeat that you're playing with edged tools."

Roundhay made a vague, easy gesture. "Don't we all do that nowadays? But perhaps I oughtn't to have entertained you, in my guileless fashion, with this possible shape of things to come. For the moment, and for some little time ahead, Tresilian and the notion of either lurking or blatant indecency in works of art will make all the going."

"Our talk, at least, has been a most interesting one." Madrona had returned to his familiar manner. "It's within your knowledge, no doubt, that the habit of collecting modern works of art is fairly widespread among tolerably influential people?"

Roundhay was now looking at another side-table, on which there were several boxes of cigars. "We go ahead," he said, "without fear or favour. We are a kind of searchlight, you know, sweeping every quarter of the realm. And every stratum too, however influential. You must come and see my room sometime. The idea's rather neatly embodied in it."

CHAPTER TWENTY-NINE

An early and light luncheon had left John Littlejohn with the time and inclination to take exercise. Not until two o'clock would the bells of St Mary's Church clang out their summons to Congregation in the Sheldonian Theatre. When that happened the surrounding streets would be thronged for a time with dons hastening or sauntering, each according to his temperament, to the university's deliberative assembly within the recently refurbished splendours of Sir Christopher Wren's building.

This time, Littlejohn thought, there would be a big crowd. The dignitaries would be decidedly outnumbered by the nobodies. For the university retains curious vestiges of democratic control. Almost anybody capable of holding down a job in it can weigh in on these occasions, and can debate and subsequently impose a flat veto upon some specific measure which the wisdom of the dignitaries has prompted them to propose. "*Non placet*", the small fry shout. "*Fiat scrutinium*", the presiding dignitary solemnly pronounces. And if the small fry have it in the resulting division—well, that is that. An odd disposition of things, Littlejohn—who was very much a dignitary—thought. But it does give scope for manoeuvre from time to time.

Spring was now far advanced. Upon the foliage of the High Street's few but artistically crucial trees dust and petrol vapour had been discernibly at work. Already—Littlejohn noticed, pausing on Magdalen Bridge—there were punts on the river. Soon—but for how brief a space!—the undergraduates in their touching ephemerality would be back for the Summer Term. And then the deep enchantment of the Long Vacation would settle upon the quads.

In the middle of Magdalen Bridge Littlejohn continued to pause. The Provost's perambulation was not entirely recreative. That was not his way. Full before him now rose certain buildings —red brick or even Redbrick—which an adjacent college had recently erected. They spoke, Littlejohn thought, volumes. Really blessed volumes. From these volumes Littlejohn filed certain phrases upon his tongue.

Of Oxford as of London, Littlejohn thought, the skyline is dramatically changing. And, as it does so, the pressures and counter-pressures are, at the lowest, fascinating. Dons are inherently conservative. And, equally, they are inherently Philistine. It is a thing chiefly to be remarked—he added grimly to himself—among some of those who give themselves airs of taste. The speculative intelligence—it comes down to this—is radically inimical to the imaginative and aesthetic. The thing is evident in the current architectural chaos. It has long been evident in those university disciplines that march, willynilly, along with any manifestation of the creative mind. Consider—Littlejohn told himself—the university's senior *littérateurs,* steeped since childhood in an education conceived precisely as Addison or Johnson conceived education, who so ludicrously back the wrong horses in every department of the contemporary and developing artistic or literary scene. Consider—Littlejohn here looked at his watch and turned back towards Catte Street.

Oxford's skyline changes, and another such change was to be discussed and contested this afternoon. John Littlejohn was not, any more than was his adversary, Philip Leech, a university politician. His own college remained the focus of his activities. But all this of new buildings—whether they should be soaring or squat, "modern" or Tudor pastiche—bore very directly on some of his own immediate concerns and policies as he had inherited them from his predecessor, Lambert Gilstrap. The development of what might be called anaesthetic attitudes in the university at large would be bound to affect the climate of opinion in his own college.

And the plain truth—he told himself, quickening his pace—was that Leech had been gaining ground for some weeks. Among the junior Fellows it was beginning to be whispered that a tide had turned. Littlejohn simply sensed this, for none of his supporters had ventured to put it to him baldly. What had produced this change of balance, or at least the threat of it, he found it hard to say. Perhaps it was the elemental genius of Leonard Benton Curry, and the building he proposed to erect within the shadow of the college's principal pride : Nicholas Hawksmore's slender neo-Gothic tower. Or perhaps it was the very scale of

Sir Hector Madrona's proposed benefaction. However this might be, there was no doubt that Leech was coiled to spring. One further hinted shift in the sway of power and he would judge the moment come actually to do so.

And that was why today's answering struggle at a university level was important—important as well as fascinating in itself. Was the place to have another and yet nearer approximation to a sky-scraper? You simply could not tell how these things would go. Some obscure natural scientist—myopic, one would suppose, in point of any vision beyond his isotopes—might, in the teeth of his own interest, rise and sway the assembly with quotations from Matthew Arnold. Or a reclusive old person, whom one would suppose unattracted to any sort of construction other than in Greek or Latin verse, might rise with a vibrant demand for a whole dozen sky-scrapers soaring up from Christ Church Meadow or the University Parks.

It was at this point in his reflections that Littlejohn turned a corner and almost ran into Leech. Leech was hurrying, just as he was. But Leech was hurrying in the opposite direction. More-over, while Littlejohn was in cap and gown Leech was in hat and overcoat.

For some reason which he could by no means identify, Little-john was strongly and disagreeably struck by this fact. That Leech did not propose to be present at Congregation was cer-tainly surely all to the good, since his vote and voice would cer-tainly be exercised in the wrong interest. That aesthetic considerations and the demands of taste should have any claim to hold up the development of facilities for teaching and research was a proposition against which the Pro-Provost could be guar-anteed to throw all his weight. If a sky-scraper was needed for furthering the intellectual life of the place, a sky-scraper ought to go up tomorrow. It didn't matter if it was out of scale with the dreaming spires. If the dreaming spires were any good what they were dreaming of was the university's getting on with its job in the future as it had done in the past. That, assuredly, was the line that Philip Leech would develop.

But he wasn't going to be present to do so. Littlejohn walked on, frowning. As he walked, a realization of just what had dis-composed him rose up in his mind. It rose up simply in the physical image of Leech as that had appeared a minute before.

Leech's attire and Leech's expression had been equally significant. His expression had been that of a man who *is* going to spring, and his attire that of a man who proposed to take the 2.19 p.m. to London, presumably for the purpose of doing so.

Littlejohn's mind had just operated in this virtually intuitive manner when he turned another corner and came upon a newspaper poster freshly displayed. The *Oxford Mail* was announcing to anybody that was interested :

London
Picture Gallery
Sensation.

A jangling of urgent bells interrupted Littlejohn's scrutiny of this announcement. For a moment he hesitated to feel for a coin in his pocket. The *Oxford Mail* is a most respectable publication; nevertheless Littlejohn felt that a mild indignity must attend the Head of a House's hurrying into Congregation with his nose in a newspaper. Quickly, however, he overcame so unworthy a self-consciousness and made his purchase. A glance sufficed, so that a moment later he was conversing, civilly if abstractedly, with the Master of Balliol. Or was it with the President of Trinity? Afterwards, he couldn't clearly remember. And certainly sky-scrapers had gone out of his head. Philip Leech, he reflected, must have succumbed to the time-consuming habit of tuning in to the B.B.C.'s One O'clock News. On this occasion, it had paid off. For a moment Littlejohn had the wild thought that he might catch the 2.19 himself. Then, at a measured pace, he entered the Sheldonian Theatre.

CHAPTER THIRTY

THAYNE DELVER FINISHED his book just as the small, residual train ran into Padstow station. This was convenient. It meant, in a sense, that one phase of his inquiry had been concluded just as another was opening.

He had now read all the later novels of Mary Emeleus. Doing so not for their intrinsic merits but for such hints of Matthew Tresilian as they might contain had proved to be both an irritating exercise and not a particularly rewarding one. Two or three times he had noted passages which he felt might well be by Tresilian's hand. None of them had possessed the dramatic quality—the curiously "fictional" quality, as he had thought of it—of that episode in *Glory Ann Barn* in which an artist had come upon the body of his son. But each had contained something that he sensed as authentically Tresilian rather than Emeleus.

He was conscious of how erratic such subjective judgments might be. It was partly because of this that he had ended up in a state of irritation with Miss Emeleus. In the past few weeks the lady had been of no further help. She had proved to him that she possessed a substantial body of Tresilian's papers, and she had continued to name a totally unrealistic figure as the sum she was prepared to accept for them.

If anything, his impatience had been increased rather than diminished by the fact that he now had on the credit side of his research two independent and important finds. Inquiry in a weekly journal had produced, first, a short critical essay on the German Expressionist painter Emil Nolde, the manuscript of which had somehow passed into the possession of a dealer with whom Tresilian had been associated; and, second, an even shorter autobiographical fragment in which Tresilian recorded some of his earliest recollections, and which was owned by the widow of an obscure painter who had been a contemporary of

Tresilian's at the Slade. Of neither of these could the authenticity be in doubt. Moreover, insubstantial though they were, they did, to Delver's sense, vindicate the hunch that had brought him to England. Matthew Tresilian had written, and Matthew Tresilian had been able to write. The assurance of this made more calamitous the destruction during the London Blitz of the painter's correspondence with Aidan Marrot. It made more infuriating the mercenary attitude of Miss Emeleus.

Delver walked down the platform of Padstow station. There wasn't much bustle in evidence, and he supposed that the season for Cornish holidays hadn't begun. Not that there seemed much reason why it shouldn't have. The shallow estuary of the Alan sparkled in sunshine and there was a fresh warmth in the air, so that he found himself wishing he were making more than a flying visit. At the same time, a mood of impatience was growing in him. As he skirted a slumbrous little harbour, he caught this up for review. Something as much in the temper as the tempo of his quest had changed. It was as if a sleuth, he thought, were taking over from the scholar. He was out to solve any mystery hanging over Matthew Tresilian's life.

That there *was* something of a mystery had been an implication that the Emeleus woman, whether deliberately or not, had contrived to convey. Probably it *was* deliberately : and this by way of inflating the value of her wares. She possessed—he thought, his irritation returning—the unscrupulous practical alertness that often underlies aesthetic pretension. For example, if she had been employing delaying tactics it might well be on the calculation that the coming Tresilian exhibition might enhance the value of what she had to market.

But the exhibition wasn't coming. It had come. This was the very day—Delver suddenly remembered—on which it was due to open up. At least it was the day of what, in England, they called the private view.

Delver found that he had come to an abrupt halt—an action not particularly incommodious in the streets of Padstow—and was confronting blank dismay. It seemed probable that his present pilgrimage would be in vain. And that he should have neglected to consider this again pointed to a change of attitude. Matthew Tresilian's daughter—the daughter by his first marriage —had made no response to a letter. She had made no response to a second letter which had politely suggested some misadventure to the first. But the son by the later marriage, now a college boy, had replied to a similar letter at least politely although without much enthusiasm. The politeness conceivably deserved better than an unheralded call. Yet that was what Delver had committed himself to in Padstow now. He had committed himself—he now for the first time clearly saw—to frontal assault upon a Tresilian. And in doing so he had neglected the probability that young Luke Tresilian would, upon this very date, have gone off to the opening of the Matthew Tresilian Memorial Exhibition.

Sobered but not undeterred, Delver made his way through Padstow's early afternoon sunshine. Luke Tresilian lived with his guardian Dr Dolben, a retired country doctor, at an address in this small town with which Delver had provided himself. All that was now required was to seek directions from a policeman if the place ran to one—England, he realized, was so law-abiding that its constabulary was thin on the ground—or at the post office if it did not. But first, and by way of controlling a certain interior breathlessness, he would simply stroll around.

His stroll, as it happened, brought him straight where he wanted to be. The name stood at the end of a terrace of tall, grey houses, narrow-fronted and bow-windowed, and each with a stunted cast-iron balcony over its front door. Up there, he thought, bathing trunks would dry, children's buckets depend, and jellyfish decompose throughout the advancing holiday season. The houses were of that order. But the one he sought stood, at least, at the end of the row, with an extra set of bow windows at the side, and the further distinction of owning a species of glasshouse or conservatory built into a residual triangle of garden beyond these. Even so, it seemed an undistinguished setting for his first encounter with a live Tresilian.

There was to be another encounter first. For in the small front garden an old man had straightened up from a flower bed and was looking at the approaching stranger with attention. It was a scrutinizing glance which had the appearance of picking up some significant piece of information at once, and this in turn seemed to satisfy the old man that it was proper for him to continue to look. Delver, whose impulse had been to walk on and do a little more thinking, felt constrained to stand and speak. "Pardon me," he said. "Am I correct in thinking that Mr Luke Tresilian lives here?"

"You are indeed correct." The old man, who was in the shabbiest of clothes, spoke in what Delver supposed to be an old-fashioned West Country accent. But it was clear that he was not (as one might have supposed) the gardener, but an educated man. It was equally clear that Delver's question had been entirely the expected one.

"And is Mr Tresilian at home?"

"No." The old man continued to look steadily at Delver. "I'm afraid he's not."

"And didn't I know it!" Delver allowed himself a gesture of vexation. "He'll be at the opening of his father's exhibition in London."

"By no means. He tells me that he distrusts any enterprise that requires new clothes. At the moment it's Luke's favourite remark. I'd say it comes from a book."

Delver could have named the book: it was E. M. Forster's *A Room with a View*. But he recalled some joke about the informativeness of the American academic classes, and refrained.

"Luke," the old man went on, "intends to see the paintings at the end of his holidays. I hope he hasn't negligently broken an appointment with you?"

Delver, being far from obtuse, didn't miss a faint irony in this. "I guess not," he said. "I came down on the chance, sir. My name is Thayne Delver, and I'm a student of Matthew Tresilian and his work."

"Ah, yes." The old man emerged from behind his small garden bed and opened the stunted iron gate which had separated him from the road. "I'm Dr Dolben, and Luke's my ward. Won't you come in? Luke mayn't be far away. He cut himself some sandwiches and went off after a bird."

"A bird?" To Delver this seemed odd.

"Perhaps one not commonly to be remarked in these parts. I have little information in such matters. It's Luke's joke that my interest in ornithology ceases with the pterodactyls. And that's fair enough. Fossils are rather a thing of mine—my chief thing, as a matter of fact, since I retired from practice." Dr Dolben was now mounting a dwarfish flight of steps with the evident intention of conducting Delver into his house. He talked easily as he did so, but with the distinguishable air of a man thinking at the same time. "Would you by any chance," he asked, "take an interest in the early crustaceans?" He paused attentively while Delver disclaimed this. "A pity," he said. "Were such an interest yours, I venture that my Trilobites would hold your attention." He opened a front door which seemed to consist mainly of random fragments of dismally hued glass. "But Luke, of course, may return at any time. Something may come into his head and he may drop the bird—I speak figuratively—and come home at suicidal speed on his bicycle. To get it down. Luke's a writer."

"Say! Is that so?" Delver was much struck.

"Indeed, yes. Were we now to go up to his room—which we can't, of course, do, since he's absent from it—we should find writing all over the place."

"That interests me a lot. What kind of writing would it be?"

Dr Dolben laughed gently. "At the moment, it's chiefly a perfectly enormous letter every day. Which is very nice. For it means—doesn't it?—that the boy's in love. And I tell no tales out of school. You'll know it the moment you set eyes on him. At least I think you will. I should. You see"—Dr Dolben had led the way into a shabby and untidy room which still harboured the faint smell of a surgery—"I've had hundreds of lads as patients in my time, and it has always been something I've known at once. Nine times out of ten, there's been nothing but blessing in it. Not that broken hearts and hard cases don't turn up. How much I hope that nothing of the sort will come Luke's way. He has necessarily had rather a lonely life. I ought to have done better. I'm fond of the lad. But I don't know that it has ever much obtruded itself as a fact between us. Won't you sit down?"

Delver sat down. He was aware that confidence had been offered as inviting confidence. Dr Dolben did not strike him as wholly a simple man. "But Luke," he said, "must be rather young to be thinking of marriage? I don't know very much about the Tresilians. But at least I have the dates."

"The dates?" It was with some sharpness that Dr Dolben said this.

"The year of Luke's birth, and so forth. I hope the girl's at least of the right age?"

"Even younger than Luke is—which I suppose is well enough. But I'm not sure the thing goes quite right. They are London folk, and sophisticated as Luke is not. The mother's a writer on artistic topics—a Mrs Landreth. She seems to have disconcerted Luke in some obscure and, no doubt, trifling way. But then there's a brother, who's a college friend of Luke's. And he seems to trouble the waters at rather a deep level. How does that strike you?"

"I can't say it conveys much to me." Delver had been startled by a sudden concentration in Dr Dolben's steady gaze. "But the young man seems to tell you quite a lot. May I ask whether you have been his guardian ever since his father's death?"

"I have."

"Then perhaps you were a close friend of Matthew Tresilian's? You must just forgive my curiosity, sir. But any contact with Tresilian is a great find for me."

"So I'd conjecture. It's true that I was a fairly close friend of Tresilian's. Otherwise I should scarcely have taken on a charge so onerous to a bachelor as the wardenship of an infant. But I must disappoint you, nevertheless. Tresilian and I had no meeting place in the arts. We scarcely spoke of his work, and I scarcely ever saw it. Unhappily, I have no feeling for such things. So there's really no particular in which I could be of help to you."

"But I'm interested in the man in his private as well as his artistic character."

"His *private* character!" These words came from Dr Dolben with the largest surprise.

"Well, call it his personal character." Delver was nettled. "Dash it all, the lives of the great painters and poets and musicians do get written, you know."

"Oh, yes—of course." Dr Dolben, with no appearance of changing ground, was instantly reasonable. "You are going to write a biography of Tresilian. Well, that's most interesting. I'd be delighted to write down some of my memories of him and transmit them to you. But Luke, you know, can hardly do anything like that. I'm blessed if I see what you can get out of him."

"I realize that he can have no memories. His half-sister—isn't she called Mrs Crinnis?—is the person to whom I must go for that."

There was a moment's silence while Dr Dolben appeared to consider this proposition. "Ah, yes," he said. "But I don't know that it would really be worth your while. She's far from approachable, I believe. Her marriage has been a factor. It has taken her away from—well, from interests like yours. She must be said to have turned away from her family and its past."

"She certainly doesn't answer letters." Delver caught himself wondering whether he had lacked guile in making this honest complaint.

"I doubt whether she would answer the doorbell, either. If lighthouses have doorbells, that is. She has married, you may say, into lighthouses." Dr Dolben accompanied this faint joke with a smile in which Delver seemed to detect some exercise of the will. "Luke would be more your man, if only he had been born ten or fifteen years earlier."

"That's true. But you'll readily understand, Dr Dolben, that I'm interested in documents, as well as reminiscences. There's been some reason to suppose that Matthew Tresilian had notable powers as a writer. And almost the first fruit of my research has been to uncover a couple of manuscripts that confirm this. So far, however, I've traced no letters—"

"He can hardly have corresponded with a son much too young to know his ABC."

"I'm not blind to that. But I have to consider that Luke Tresilian may at least have a line on some specimens of his father's writing. As for letters, sir, what about yourself?"

This abrupt approach brought Dr Dolben to his feet, apparently with some intention of stirring a fire that turned out not to be there. He sat down again. "Matthew," he said, "must have sent me a good many letters in his time. I preserved none of them."

"None of them!" Delver felt an impulse almost of anger. Under the stress of such an emotion, he knew, one ought to risk nothing. Nevertheless he took a risk now. "Was there something to hide?" he asked.

If Dr Dolben was angry in turn—as he well might be—he gave no sign of it. His next words were spoken with particular mildness. But this, Delver had to admit, only contributed to their devastating effect. "God bless my soul!" Dr Dolben said. "You're as good as asking me whether Matthew Tresilian did something disgraceful. As it happens, I can tell you straight out that he did not. But what astonishes me is that, to your sense, as it seems, we might as well be talking of Holbein or Claude. To me,

I must say, it's relevant that Tresilian was my personal friend —and that I've even brought up a son of his who, incidentally, is just about to join us now."

At the end of this forthright speech Dr Dolben had nodded towards his bow window. Delver turned in time to see a young man, large of limb and flushed of face, vault from a moving bicycle, and at the same time give the machine a deft flick which sent it through the front gate, across the lawn, and neatly into a privet hedge which was thus instantaneously accommodated to the purpose of a bicycle rack. Luke Tresilian then took the dwarf steps four at a time, so that at three bounds he was through the front door. It seemed impossible to tell whether urgent literary inspiration was the occasion of this performance, or whether here was simply his customary manner of getting around.

"Luke, come here a moment!" Dr Dolben's summons was shouted through a closed door. And Luke entered at once. "This is Professor Delver—I hope I have his title correctly—who has come to pay a call on you. He's interested in your father. So perhaps you've heard of him. I haven't."

Delver wasn't troubled that this last remark failed to sound wholly cordial. He was studying Luke Tresilian, and it was his first impression that the boy—who had shaken hands agonizingly and produced a crisply English greeting—would never have educed any spontaneous conjecture that he was an artist's son. There was a lot of him but he wasn't gigantic; you would have credited him with a singularly untroubled soul; and there could be no doubt about his distrusting new clothes. Yet in his dress there was a considerable effect of style, particularly in the angle of the old deerstalker, plainly a prized possession, which he had forgotten to remove from his head. You could only call him very English. Yet the essence of him, Delver reflected, would have been entirely at home on Delver's own Pacific campus. In fact he was in the habit of hailing Luke Tresilians every day: boys full of engaging *élan* and cheerful ignorance, honourably ambitious of playing for the Huskies or the Bears.

It suddenly struck Delver that, if he was sizing up Luke, Luke was decidedly sizing up him. And the result had declared itself in a flicker of mischief on the boy's face. But it couldn't in any degree have been called an oafish mischief; in fact it had a quality that Delver found quite mysteriously attractive. It wasn't only attractive, it was exciting as well. And in a further instant he knew why. In repose, Luke Tresilian's face suggested not much more than the satisfactoriness of being young, healthy and disposed to see a good deal of interest in things. When animated, it held something that reminded you whose son he was. That was it. This pleasant boy was indeed Matthew Tresilian's son. The fact declared itself, for a start, simply at the level of what might be called the family photograph. The Tresilian features—known to Delver alike by way of the camera and of Augustus John's portrait of his fellow painter—were there, and would accent themselves with the maturing years.

If this discovery induced in Delver a mood of sober respect in the presence of the young man—and it did so even to a point of incongruity—it induced too an enhancement of the impatience that had recently been growing in him in relation to his whole Tresilian enterprise. Here in Luke was the man's son, and here in Dr Dolben was confessedly the man's intimate friend. These contacts had been made. If they proved perversely evasive—and in Dr Dolben there had been at least a hint of something of the sort—he would feel ill served by them.

"It's my idea," Dr Dolben was saying to Luke, "that you should take the Professor to your room. Talk to him—or let him talk to you. Then bring him down again. Mrs Julian will give us a cup of tea before he has to take his leave of us."

"Yes, of course," Luke said. "I'm afraid it's right at the top of the house, sir. But come on. I'll lead the way."

And with these words the young man did decidedly lead the way, so that by the time Delver had got to the foot of the final flight of stairs Luke was waiting for him solicitously at the top of it. "I've this whole storey now," he explained as his visitor caught up with him. "Two rooms and my own shower and bog. It's fearfully grand. You get nothing like that in college." He flung open a door. "Do come in." He stood back and then followed Delver into the room. "Oh, God!" he said. "I didn't know it was in quite such a mess."

The large attic room was certainly untidy. There was a big table with a typewriter, a girl's photograph and a litter of papers. There were more papers all over the floor. There were books, some open and some shut, on most of the chairs. Over the chimneypiece there was a watercolour by Matthew Tresilian, and beside it stood a rudely rifled packet of chocolate biscuits. There was a bookcase that seemed mainly devoted to Thomas Hardy. Apart from this, the walls of the room were entirely clothed with photographs of birds. These had simply been pasted to the wallpaper. They ranged from small, blurred squares, much faded, such as a seven-year-old boy might have secured with a box Brownie, to some rather large and finely achieved studies of wild fowl in flight.

"Isn't it frightful?" Luke said. "Let me clear up a bit." He began hastily collecting the papers on the table and sweeping them into a drawer. It was absurdly evident that his concern was less to tidy up than to conceal whatever species of literary activity was going forward. "But do sit down, sir." He seized a chair and tipped it so that its quota of books fell to the floor. "That's Virgil," he said. "I've a date with him in the rather near future. You'll find this one quite comfortable."

Delver sat down. "I see," he said, not very brilliantly, "that you're keen on birds."

"Well, yes. I've been after birds this morning, as a matter of fact. Redshanks."

"Would that be a rare sort of bird?"

"Lord, no!" Quite inoffensively, Luke was amused by this question. "The British subspecies, *Tringa totanus britannica,* is all over the place. It's increasing, too. But, you see, this is the one tip of England where it hasn't yet been found nesting. So I'm going after that."

"That's most interesting." Delver, who was no field naturalist, felt himself in the presence of erudition. "Would you be considering, Mr Tresilian, taking up a career as an ornithologist?"

"I've never thought of that. But there are some birds I'd like to go and study. After taking Schools, I mean, and when a little money comes in." Luke kept his eyes away from the table with its photograph. "Perhaps with one other person. To Bikini."

"Bikini?" Delver was surprised. "That sounds kind of macabre to me."

"It is, in a way. It's where the nuclear tests have hit the fauna, all right. Do you know about the turtles? They can still lay eggs—although probably they'll be sterile eggs—and they still make their way painfully inland for the job. But the radio-activity has destroyed whatever mechanism they had for finding their way back to the sea. They plod round and round in the sand till they perish. And just when they do *that*—when *in articulo mortis*, as I expect Virgil says—they *think* they've reached the ocean. They die performing swimming motions instead of crawling ones. There's something to think of in that. Still, the really fascinating thing is some of the birds. They've learnt to go underground, like the people in your Pentagon. Bring them up and they burrow down again. And there are millions of eggs that will never hatch. But, you see, even so, the skies are still dark with wings. Myriads of live birds, after all. We've had a damned good try at total extinction, but haven't quite succeeded. So we give the place's name to a sexy kind of bather. Thanatos and Eros. I honestly think I could write something on it. But I have another plan as well, quite a different one. I want to go to Fez."

"Ah, Fez. There would be plenty of sand there too. But no turtles."

Luke Tresilian laughed, as unaffectedly as if this were really a good joke. "I'm certainly talking rot," he said. "And it's not what you've come for. But I don't see how I can help you. I tried to explain that in replying to your letter. In coming to Padstow you've wasted your time, I'm afraid."

"Dr Dolben must have known your father well. I've had some hope of gathering information from him. But I didn't feel I was getting on too well with him while we were waiting for you to get back. He didn't seem prepared to be communicative."

"I'm not surprised." Luke had cleared another chair and sat down. "Of course he knew my father ages ago—I think when he himself had his first medical practice at a place called Lancraddock. But he's never talked much about that time. Still, he can't be your only resource. I expect you've been getting around quite a number of people who knew Matthew Tresilian. He's not exactly ancient history yet."

"I've picked up a few trails. For instance, Mary Emeleus, the novelist. She was a friend of your father's at one time."

"She was his mistress."

"Well, yes." Delver was rather startled. "But one goes delicately in mentioning such things to relations."

"You needn't do any going delicately with me. Not about anything that my father was ever connected with. I know quite well that Mary Emeleus lived with him for a time. It was before he met my mother. Of course, everything changed after that."

"No doubt. And do you know, Mr Tresilian, that your father did a certain amount of writing—very distinguished writing?"

"Of course I do! Why, I've—" Luke checked himself. "Have you found any of it?"

"Just lately, I've found a little. And I know the whereabouts of quite a lot. It's in the possession of Miss Emeleus."

"But this is tremendously exciting!" Luke had jumped to his feet again. "Is it wonderful?"

"I can't tell you, except for very limited stretches of it, and in a rather odd and special way. Miss Emeleus is sitting on her manuscripts, hoping to get an absurd sum of money for them. So, for the moment, I'm looking elsewhere. Mr Tresilian, would *you* have any writing by your father?"

There was a moment's silence, and then Luke spoke very clearly. "Yes," he said. "I have. But you're out of luck again. I'm sitting on what I have too, although not with the same motive."

Not for the first time under Dr Dolben's roof, Delver felt angry. "Since you haven't yet come of age," he said, "I think it possible—"

"Please put anything of the kind out of your head." Luke was a different person from the boy who had been blundering cheerfully about the room a few minutes before. "I've got the facts from the trustees. There are questions of copyright, it seems. But my manuscript itself is as much my property as *that* is." Luke had pointed to the watercolour over the chimneypiece. "Sketch for Lyonnesse No. 3."

"Of course I accept that, Mr Tresilian." Delver was shocked by the inept plunge he had taken. "But why do you want to keep your manuscript private?"

"I think that was my father's idea. He wanted me to have it, and he wasn't opposed to its being given to the world one day. But not in the lifetime of his children."

"If the document's a purely personal one—and I have independent knowledge that your father did from time to time put himself on autobiographical record—then that's a very understandable point of view. I won't say it doesn't make me mad.

The sooner the world knows everything about your father the better. Great men demand great candour."

"Candour? There's nothing to be candid about. Not if you mean stuff about coming clean with the frailties of the great. What I have of my father's is about strength, not frailty." Luke hesitated. "I say!" he said. "That sounds terribly pompous. Let me tell you just what it is that I possess. It's the story of my father's marriage to my mother. Shortly after that marriage, you know, they were both dead. And there wasn't any child but me. There wasn't time for one. So the whole thing's private, if anything is. Don't you see?"

"I see your point of view." Delver didn't like these words as he uttered them. They were lacking in grace. "Of course," he went on doggedly, "your father's second marriage isn't wrapped in utter privacy even without your document. There's a certain amount on record, after all. And I've had a good deal more from Miss Emeleus. She remained in your father confidence, it seems. And she took me a little into hers."

"Really?" Luke Tresilian seemed far from offended at his visitor's developing the matter in this way. "I don't in the least mind talking about it, you know. It's just my father's chronicle —the actual flow and texture of his writing as he tells of the thing—that I've no fancy for seeing being pawed over by reviewers and people. Or even scholars. You *do* understand?"

Delver understood. He understood, too, that he liked this young man almost to an extent that might get in the way of a substantial part of the project to which he had dedicated himself. "You are the judge," he said.

"Thank you." Luke had flushed suddenly. "And there's another thing. It's rather queer. It's just, you know, that, in a way, the story's too *much* a story. Don't you agree?"

"I guess I don't know about that. It was certainly romantic." For some reason that he couldn't arrive at, or wouldn't arrive at, Delver felt a curious alarm.

"There's that silly crack about truth being stranger than fiction. But here it is. Glimpsing my mother in Spain. Following her into Vichy France. Knowing she was in dire peril there. You know it was like that?"

Delver nodded. "I'm sure it was. There was no Jew in Europe who stood outside that shadow."

"Jew?" Luke was puzzled. "My mother wasn't a Jewess. Not that I wouldn't be proud if she had been. She was of a Polish aristocratic family. They'd been desperate patriots for generations. That's why she was booked for trouble."

"I see," Delver said. But he didn't at all see. He only felt. And what he felt was something like panic.

"I think I'm a snob, really," Luke said cheerfully. "I must be. Because it does mean something to me—just that of my mother's being an aristocrat. But perhaps it's not snobbery, either. It may be that I have—and, you know, I honestly think I have—a little of my father's slant in me. A novelist would call that bit of the story a value—just a small value. My parents' coming, I mean, from classes so very far apart. And, in a way, it's terribly *like* a novel. It might be suggested by *The Rainbow*. And the rest of the story might be suggested by something almost like a thriller. For think of it! Out of France into Switzerland. And then into Bavaria."

"Bavaria?" Delver said. "During the war?"

"Yes! And bringing her out virtually through the barbed wire. A woman who knew she mightn't have a score of months to live. To go after a dying woman—and bring her out to life, and to *making* life." Luke Tresilian's voice had suddenly trembled. "Even Mary Emeleus—who seems to me to have a pretty acrid kind of mind, if her books reflect it—even Mary Emeleus must have been moved as she told you *that*. And she did tell you? She knows the whole thing?"

"She told me a certain amount." Delver believed he spoke steadily. But he was extremely disconcerted by this further evidence of Matthew Tresilian's fondness for providing autobiographical record with imaginative embellishments.

"But I'm going to sit on it," Luke said. He spoke easily again. "On the manuscript, I mean. Actually, I've told the story only once. To a girl I know. And, perhaps, a little of it to her mother. I didn't know about Miss Emeleus's knowing. And I'm not sorry, sir, that she told you. I mean, I'm glad it *was* you, and not some chap who might go and do a cheap write-up of it. I'd find that rather a bore. You do see?"

Delver, thus a second time appealed to, thought that he did see, and he said so without qualification.

"So I'm terribly sorry," Luke went on. "That I can't, that is, be of any use to you. But perhaps my guardian will manage something. And you ought to try Faith."

"Faith?" Delver was momentarily at a loss.

"My half-sister, Faith Crinnis. I told you her address in my letter. And said, you remember, that she's not at all on-coming. Quite oddly not, as a matter of fact. Still, if you went and tackled her—and it's only an hour's run to the south coast—you might get something to the point. I've a notion that she had rather a precocious interest in our father as an artist, and knew quite a lot. But it all failed her later on." Luke paused. He seemed anxious not to leave a sense of having rebuffed a man who admired his father. "Yes," he said. "You never know. She might surprise you."

CHAPTER THIRTY-ONE

For some weeks I've been gaining ground, Philip Leech told himself as his cab dodged through Victoria Gate. No more than inches. But even a small maintained momentum is useful when the chance comes. And it has. This is it.

He glanced out at Hyde Park and remarked it to be in the height of spring. The grass was green and unjaded; the aristocratic sport of equitation was proceeding through a sunlight dappled by burgeoning leaves; the Serpentine would presently disclose humbler persons messing about in boats. There was much to be said for keeping one or another of the parks between oneself and the West End or the City. Regular exercise could be obtained while going about one's daily occasions. As he remembered it, Lord Burntisland's spare figure suggested that sort of hygienic pedestrianism.

Dismissing external nature from his regard, Leech sank into brooding reflection. His chance had come—his reward for holding on—but he couldn't pretend that the manner of its coming pleased him. On the seat beside him was a paper he had bought at Paddington. He didn't need to glance at it again, and he didn't want to. He had seen at once—as soon as he got beyond the headline, as soon as he observed the topic to be taken up again on an inner page—that there was more in the whole thing than the sudden aberration of an elderly industrialist and statesman. Whoever was behind the stunt—for it wasn't possible to name it in one's private mind as other than that—could scarcely have counted on Burntisland's behaving precisely as he seemed to have behaved that morning. But *something* had been counted on : after one fashion or another, the first shot in a campaign. Leech had got faint wind of this even in the decorous news bulletin from the B.B.C. And he was sure of it now. However dubious the waters in which he proposed to fish, there were strong currents in them—currents upon which, with a little deft steering of his own, Littlejohn and all his miserable crew might be floated into oblivion.

Leech frowned darkly—not at the Albert Memorial, now appearing on his right hand, but at a certain confusion and facile picturesqueness in the image he had been elaborating. Plainly put, Burntisland's demonstration could be discerned as the planned start of a rumpus over much more than any supposed indecencies in those indubitably enigmatic last Tresilians. Not that *that* would be let drop; there would be lots more about it in the immediate future. But the nonsense would be so contrived as to broaden out into organized exploitation of the resentment which the vulgar can always be made to feel before anything incomprehensible to them. That was it.

Leech picked up his paper, folded it tightly, and thrust it into an affair on the door of the taxi that seemed designed for rubbish. It was rubbish he was going to exploit. He had to face that. He cared nothing for contemporary art. But he frequently met intelligent persons who declared themselves to take pleasure in it, and he judged it reasonable to conclude that it possessed affinities, not readily identifiable, with the accepted art of the past. He was prepared to let Picasso and Tresilian alone, just as he was prepared to let Courbet and Manet alone. Outcry against the first pair was no doubt as idiotic as outcry against the second. He was prepared to let the whole lot alone—so long as whatever trivial gratifications they afforded were not inflated and then obtruded in places where only the intellect should have any status at all.

At this moment—Leech thought, grinding his body into a corner of his cab—Littlejohn was in the Sheldonian Theatre, that incommodious but doubtless highly artistic structure devised by Sir Christopher Wren, making a speech designed to hold up the scientific development of the university on the score that modern buildings would mar the delicately feminine contours of Oxford as observed from Boars Hill. Yes—Leech said to himself—I have actually heard these words uttered. Now I am trembling with rage at the memory of them. Anything, *anything* is justifiable that will swamp such balderdash under the obliterating ridicule it deserves. Gilstrap and his Tresilian, Littlejohn and his projected load of lumber from the fellow Madrona, that outrageous project to abridge our necessary expansion in order to make room for a grotesque squashed corkscrew of a picture gallery : these things have to be killed because they are absurd expressions of something in itself not absurd but dangerous.

Face it, Leech said to himself, as the taxi left the park and nosed its way uncertainly through South Kensington. You are proposing to use this old man. You are proposing to use him as an instrument, and that is a grave thing to do. It will do him no good to continue questing with those hounds. You saw how old he is. You told yourself he was a rigid type, the kind that may crack rather than crumble. Your designs are nothing to his advantage. Nothing at all.

They can't regard him as wholly reliable, Leech added to himself, pressing into his subject. This morning's incident gave them a splendid start. But it's quite possible they may now think it better to go it alone. They may drop Burntisland without dropping the stunt, in which case he'll have little power to continue making himself heard, even if he wants to do so. That's not certain, of course. They may plan quite a continuing role for him. But alternatively, he may himself be having second thoughts. He's rather a distinguished old person, with at least the remains of a first-class mind. It's not necessary to suppose that he won't recognize something thoroughly vulgar and spurious as soon as he has closely to hob-nob with it. He may walk out on it, even if they want to keep him prominently in.

And for me, of course, the point is that he's a key person. He's Pro-Chancellor of a Scottish university. He made us a speech at that dinner which impressed the majority of my colleagues a good deal. *His* campaign would carry weight with them, whereas they wouldn't be impressed by a leash of journalists in a cheap paper. Contrariwise. So I have to keep Burntisland on the job, and on the job in its larger dimensions. Matthew Tresilian in himself won't take us far—although, if the last Tresilians were to be removed from the present exhibition, the college might become uneasy about having even a next-to-last Tresilian on its great staircase. It might be possible to carry the point that it should be removed for a time. As Pro-Provost I've power to do it myself, and get indemnity afterwards. That in itself would be a sharp reverse for Littlejohn. But the crux is the Madrona Collection. Get that under public attack as utterly bogus and absurd, and the main battle is won. We reverse our decision, decline the whole benefaction, and send Leonard Benton Curry and all his works packing.

The taxi had come to a halt in a square on the fringes of Chelsea. It was the sort of locality behind the regular façades of which a great deal of proliferation by way of simple fission had been going on; expensive flats, small offices, deformed maison-nettes, attic studios, together with miscellaneous mere dens and lurking-places, all contributed to a general effect of disgrace and departed decorum. But a few of the houses evidently re-tained more than a superficial integrity, and Lord Burntisland's was one of these. It was uniformly and sombrely painted, sombrely and more or less uniformly curtained, from basement to roof. As Leech paid his fare, he remarked two men to be lounging on the pavement, one being equipped with a camera. Two further men, similar in appearance, were just being turned away from Lord Burntisland's front door. Indeed, the slamming of this barrier coincided rather dishearteningly with Leech's driver's stretching out a backward-reaching hand and similarly closing the door of his cab. Leech, however, mounted the steps and rang the bell.

The door was opened again almost at once—but only to the extent permitted by a stout chain—by an old woman. She was evidently a retainer of high antiquity. Conjecturing that her face had once been freckled and her hair red, Leech concluded that she had been imported from North Britain in her employer's earlier years. "Is Lord Burntisland at home?" he asked politely.

"His lordship is *not* at home." The old woman spoke with satisfaction. But then she took a good look at Leech. "His lord-ship," she said, "regrets that he is unable to receive visitors."

"I'm not surprised. Leech glanced backwards at the group of reporters still on the pavement. "But I'll ask you to take him my card."

The ancient parlourmaid—for that was presumably her condi-tion—was sufficiently impressed at least to take the card and peer at it. "Well," she said, rather unexpectedly, "you're frae a respectable place. But what are you for?"

"I beg your pardon?" Leech was unprepared for so radically philosophical a demand.

"What might your business with his lordship be?"

"Ah, I see. But you and I need not, I think, discuss that.

Simply be so kind, my good woman, as to take your master my card."

This manner of address plainly came to the old woman as an agreeable waft from the past. "But wha' am I to dae?" she asked, in a deepening Doric and with some suggestion of senile agitation. "I canna' let ye in tae wait. But it's no decent tae—"

"Never mind that." Leech was concealing a great deal of impatience, and it was with satisfaction that he now saw the old woman withdraw. Two of the men on the pavement, observing him thus left kicking his heels on the doorstep, advanced upon him as if with some conversational or other intent. Leech turned and looked at them, at the same time wrapping himself in so large a darkness that they thought better of their proposal and turned away. And then the old woman had come back.

"If ye'll please to step by," she said, unchaining the door. Leech entered and found himself in a cavernous hall. It was compounded of Turkey carpeting, chocolate-coloured paint, and massive bronze objects—these last preponderantly human, substantially unclothed, and frozen in gestures which seemed part athletic and part inspirational. From the ceiling there depended a chandelier which had been muffled in a linen bag. "His lordship," the old woman said in a tone of reverence, "is in his library." She led the way up a gloomy staircase—on which the carpet, Leech noticed, was protected by the superimposition of some sort of calico runner. Suddenly she paused and turned, and Leech realized that she was in a state of discomposure. "But he's no' richt!" she said in a new voice. "Who could tell if it wasna' me? Whatever's happened, sir, he's no' richt the day!" For a moment she looked at Leech, her original distress for the moment swallowed in the sense of the enormous impropriety her thus speaking to him had represented. "If ye'll but come up," she said hurriedly, and began to climb again. Her ancient bones, Leech fancied, could be heard to creak as she did so.

"Dr Leech! Good afternoon." Lord Burntisland was standing courteously at the head of his staircase, and now he shook hands. "I couldn't think of denying myself to you—although, as it so happens, I have been having a somewhat tiring day, and have still much work on hand." Burntisland paused on this, which was clearly intended to give his visitor a notion of the length of time his call might properly last. "But at least—if Janet will be so good—we can take a cup of tea together. Come this way."

Leech, led down a corridor, had a surprised glimpse, through an open door, of a shadowy drawing-room groaning under swathed and shrouded furniture. It was like an Arctic landscape. And Burntisland was aware of what he had noticed. "I must explain," he said in a dry voice, "that my wife's health does not permit her to live with me. It has been so, indeed, for many years. My establishment is therefore a restricted one. But everything remains in readiness, should things change for the better."

Leech ventured only a murmur; he saw that, behind this communication, there lay matter of an order not to be met with sympathetic remarks and polite hopes. And he now looked quickly round the room into which he had been led. It was lined with heavy-looking books in even heavier-looking Victorian bookcases. On the chimneypiece were two further gesturing nudities : female, frigid, and executed in the same marble as the structure they perched on. Between them hung a large reproduction of a painting which Leech uncertainly recalled as by Luke Fildes : a bearded doctor fighting death at the bedside of a child of the good poor. This had a massive oak frame and appeared to have been printed in brown gravy soup.

All this Leech more or less approved. Such surroundings and such treasures were satisfactorily remote from the world of Provost Littlejohn, Sir Hector Madrona, and Leonard Benton Curry. But their proprietor was less reassuring. Lord Burntisland couldn't, perhaps, in any clinical sense be called disturbed. But, like his parlourmaid Janet, he was agitated. He settled Leech in a chair, but he didn't himself sit down. Instead, he walked restlessly and in spite of evident fatigue about the room. And the room wasn't merely lined with old books. It was littered with new ones. It was littered, too, with colour prints and photographs.

"There's so much that it's essential to get up." It seemed to have escaped Burntisland that Leech's call stood in any need of explanation. "And now, of course, having taken the first step so decisively this morning, it all has to be mastered very quickly. Fortunately they brief me very well. They possess what can only be termed archives. It is quite astonishing. And Roundhay is a remarkable man."

"Roundhay?" Leech asked.

"But there's the inconvenience of the other group. They have reporters outside my house now, hoping to get something unguarded out of me. Roundhay has explained all that. Roundhay is a remarkable man."

"I'm sure he is," Leech said—and noted this ominous repetitiveness.

"The other people will be out to pan us. I believe that to have been Roundhay's expression. So one must take no false step. And certainly I was right to make a start with—" Very oddly, Burntisland rotated his craggy head in air, as if vainly seeking for something. "Yes," he said, "—with Tresilian." He had been walking away from Leech; now he made a spasmodic turn towards him. "It began with the painter Tresilian. The corruption. Those areas of—of dubiety in his pictures. They are a deliberate invitation to foul thoughts, to impure imaginings. I see that clearly. I see that *vividly*. Only"—Burntisland gestured towards the scattered books—"there has been much ingenious sophistry produced about that sort of thing. And it's necessary to know about it. I'm not quite certain that Roundhay has adequately taken that point. We must be well equipped, we must be impregnable, on the purely intellectual plane. I have colleagues in the Lords who favour modern art. They will cite authorities—academic authorities, my dear Dr Leech, from your own world. I must be able to meet them on their own ground."

"Do you think that is really wise?" Leech was startled to find how uneasy he had himself become. "Surely it's a matter of the public conscience, even of the public sense of humour." He made a wary pause. "The sort of stuff, for instance, that Hector Madrona collects and would pass off as significant. Don't you think it vulnerable to mere laughter?"

"Laughter?" Burntisland might never have heard the word. And, for the moment, he might never have heard of Madrona. "It was started," he said, "by—by Tresilian. But I had no idea how far it had gone. I don't want to shock you, Leech. But just look at these photographs."

Burntisland had pointed to a pile of photographs on a table. Leech rose obediently to study them. He turned over three or four—and desisted, much startled. They were obscene affairs of the kind which one hears of people being gaoled for peddling. Each was stamped on the back with an index number and the name of a newspaper. Roundhay's archives had no doubt supplied them. "They're abominable," Leech said. "But are they entirely relevant?"

"They are deliberately created to rouse lustful imaginings. Some of them"—Burntisland's voice rose a pitch—"would even rouse unnatural imaginings. Tresilian started it."

"But surely—"

"And, of course, other degenerate painters as well. Roundhay has a great deal of evidence. Only, as I was saying, he doesn't entirely realize the ingenuity of their apologists. Roundhay's extremely capable. And his moral concern is wholly admirable. But he's not an intellectual man." Burntisland fished restlessly among a pile of books on another table. "Did you ever hear of alternative perspective figures?"

"I think not."

"One of these books is on the psychology of perception. It has some discussion of phenomena of the kind. Tresilian exploited a number of such devices. I was in contact with them, I have discovered, in the very first painting of his that I saw. I don't know what can have happened to that particular book." Burntisland made a baffled gesture. "There are so many of these books. Many of them are abstruse or even recondite."

"Has Roundhay provided the books as well as the photographs?"

"No, no—it's something that I have felt it necessary to take up myself. I find that there are large areas of speculation on the visual arts about which I've been entirely without information." Burntisland moved towards the pile of photographs, thought better of this, moved indecisively back towards the books. "For example, there's the very considerable labour of interpretation which the spectator has to perform, it seems, before *any* picture. There are innumerable ambiguities in any conventional representation upon a plane surface of the appearance of a three-dimensional scene. We learn to choose between them on a principle of internal consistency." He picked up a volume and leafed vaguely through it. "No doubt you with your enviable academic leisure, Dr Leech, are familiar with the work of Professor Gombrich. I've derived from it a new sense of the *active* role we are called upon to play in the reception of a work of art. There are numerous philosophical implications. As it happens, I've always a little kept up my philosophical reading. I find, for example, that *Gestalt* is by no means a closed book to me."

"Most interesting," Leech said. He had been right to credit this old man with a respectable intellectual endowment. But this was showing signs of operating in a manner very little to the point. "Yet aren't these investigations," he went on, "diverting you from the course you've set yourself? You began, after all, with something quite different."

"Is that so?" Burntisland looked bewildered. But then he nodded. "Ah, yes," he said. "I recall what you mean. In the first instance what was in my mind was the regulating and purifying of public advertisements. That's certainly true. I recall it very clearly. But these graver matters have supervened. Notably this serious scandal of exhibiting the last Tresilians." Suddenly he turned and faced Leech. "You have the man's son in your college," he said.

"To be sure we have. He might be called one of the last Tresilians himself." Leech, as often, thought poorly of this trifling remark as he made it. "He's a very decent—"

"Exactly. I am much shocked that you should maintain him in residence. Indecent proclivities are surely an intolerable menace in a society of young people."

Leech was astounded. "My dear Lord Burntisland," he said, "you misheard me. I was going to say—" He stopped. To continue was pointless, since Burntisland was not listening to him. Instead, he was prowling strangely about the room. And then he halted by the pile of photographs, his hand swept over them, and they lay scattered on the floor. He swung round towards Leech, and Leech had a sudden, fantastic awareness that Burntisland was about to *shout*.

"Abomination!" Lord Burntisland shouted, and collapsed into a chair.

Leech felt for his hat—which, with an old-fashioned propriety, he had brought with him into the room. He had the impression that Burntisland had not *heard* himself shout; that here had been a weird freak of momentary dissociation. No doubt it tied up with what seemed to have been the equally weird manner in which he had launched his campaign that morning. The old man was in some degree deranged; he was no ally to choose, short of desperation; Roundhay—whoever Roundhay might be—was welcome to the whole of him. Leech's had been a fool's errand.

Unfortunately it wasn't now possible to make a quick getaway. Burntisland's performance had coincided with the ancient parlourmaid's entering with a tea-tray. Moreover, Burntisland had begun to talk again, and in something like a rational manner.

"I feel that I must make a disclosure to you," he said. "It is unpleasant and distasteful, but a duty that I positively owe you, connected as it is with the occasion upon which I was the guest of your colleagues and yourself. In brief—" Burntisland paused. "And yet I am in two minds." He touched his forehead. "I might almost say that I am in some bewilderment. Let me pour you out a cup of tea, and take a moment to recollect myself."

"Thank you," Leech said. He was far from clear that he wasn't bewildered himself. The tenor of Burntisland's remarks made it look as if he proposed to make some charge of moral obliquity against young Tresilian. Leech, who had perforce spent many years in the observation of undergraduates, knew this to be nonsense. If Burntisland was going to embark on anything of the sort, it could only be another facet of what was beginning to look like a lurking madness. The old man had allowed his dislike of Matthew Tresilian's painting to reflect itself in some delusion about Matthew Tresilian's son.

"But I think not." Burntisland had poured the tea with an approximation to composure; he was visibly making a big effort to regain command of a situation which had been slipping away from him. "To go further would, curiously enough, be in some sense a breach of hospitality. I must ask you to forget my last remarks. I must ask you to put them utterly out of your mind." Burntisland paused, and Leech had the uncomfortable impression that there had hovered over his craggy features a momentary look in which there was something almost frightened and almost cunning. But now Burntisland rose stiffly from his chair, the more ceremoniously to offer his guest a plate of bread and butter. Then he walked across the room again, and with a creaking of bones stooped and gathered up the scattered photographs. "Clumsy of me," he said, with a dry casualness. He roughly squared the prints and slipped them into a drawer. "Do you know," he asked, closing the drawer and turning round abruptly, "that there's a considerable trade in obscene cinematographic films? Roundhay has shown me several on a screen. Roundhay presses me hard." He frowned. "He briefs me, I ought to say. He's a remarkable man. And the films are known as blue films." He sat down again, and again touched his forehead. "I don't know why. There's doubtless a reason. But it escapes me. Dr Leech, let us address our minds once more to the Tresilian exhibition."

"Certainly," Leech said. He continued to feel that Burntisland was no sort of safe buy. But he would now hear the old man out.

"My first determination has been to have it closed. That would be my wish. Yet we must avoid the slightest suggestion of repressive action."

"Ah," Leech said.

"It may therefore be more politic simply to insist on the withdrawal of the patently offensive last paintings. That would finish Tresilian, anyway—at least among men of sound conservative principles."

"I think it would," Leech said. He was prepared to be cautiously interested again. It was, after all, men of sound conservative principles that he had to activate himself. "But, of course, that would only be a first step. There's the issue—to my mind the equally important issue—of sheer imposture and absurdity in modern art. Everybody hopes that you will address yourself to that."

"I agree that it is something I have felt strongly about." Burntisland's glance went to the pile of books. "Yet I have misgivings. I doubt whether I am the man to lead any sort of attack or exposure. It should be a younger man. As I said before, one ought to know one's ground. That has always been my prime tenet in the conduct of business. I am a little uneasy about deserting it now."

Leech ignored this. "Let us consider another example," he said. "Let us consider Sir Hector Madrona's collection."

"Madrona?" Burntisland's features darkened. "I don't care for him."

"I'm interested to hear that." Leech really was interested now. The existence of some current of feeling between Burntisland and Madrona might be useful—so useful as to compensate for the hazards of alliance with one demonstrably far gone in senile eccentricity. "As you know, Madrona is proposing to present us with the greater part of his present treasures, and with a grotesque gallery for their exhibition, into the bargain. I'm much opposed to accepting the offer, partly because I suspect a substantial proportion of the collection to be booked for the lumber room within a generation. Briefly, it's full of pretentious rubbish." Very slightly—Leech reflected—he was here going against his conscience. An uninterested agnosticism represented his actual critical position. But he was beginning once more to see possibilities in Lord Burntisland. He ought at least to explore a little farther.

"For my own part, I entirely agree." Burntisland nodded his head with a slightly tremulous vigour. "I've seen the things. And I find it hard to believe that in *these*"—and he pointed at his recently acquired books—"there will be found anything to vindicate them. Still, however, there is the duty of keeping some sort of open mind."

"No doubt," Leech said, and the more shortly because aware that Burntisland was in this, for the moment, teaching him his scholar's business. "But what I should like to see is simply a little robust ridicule cast on the whole thing. I should like to see Madrona's masterpieces laughed out of court—and, incidentally, out of the only spot where my college has room for its own legitimate expansion. That, frankly, is my position. And I think much could be done. My pupils tell me that satire is much in vogue among the young. Fun might be made of Madrona in one of the burlesque entertainments which I understand to have become popular in London. That sort of thing. People are very sensitive to ridicule—particularly the Governing Bodies of Oxford colleges."

"Is that so?" Burntisland didn't show much sign of going very far with his visitor in these speculations. "I would not myself associate light diversion with grave abuse of the high and inspiring mission of true art."

"And there's another thing." Leech had taken swift and contemptuous note of this outbreak of twaddle. "I've been looking into Madrona's situation rather carefully. I'm not sure that it's not a delicate one."

"Delicate?"

"Precisely that." Leech settled back more confidently in his chair. The old man, as he had remarked to himself earlier, retained the vestiges of a good brain. A subtle approach to the problem in hand might not be wholly beyond him. "Madrona has not only been a collector of contemporary art for many years. He has also been a dealer."

"A dealer?" Burntisland interrupted sharply. "Do you mean any more than that he has frequently parted with some purchases to make room for others?"

"That has no doubt been a factor." Leech was nettled. "But there's been money in it. Madrona has generally got much more than he paid. And some of his sales have been to governmental institutions and agencies. And he sits on the boards and committees of a good many of these." Because he was now being subtle according to plan, Leech gave his host the benefit of a subtle smile. "You follow me?"

"You surprise me, Dr Leech. I wouldn't touch such an approach to the problem. I've told Roundhay so. He, I may say, has been there before you. You and he could, of course, get together. But I have never done anything like that."

"Lord Burntisland, I hardly think you can understand—"

"I understand very well, sir." Because Lord Burntisland was now angry, it was the more apparent that he had been much under the weather during most of the preceding conference. "Anybody with any financial sense—which, no doubt, is seldom a classical scholar's affair—would know that there's nothing but nonsense in the imputation you have in mind. I don't like Madrona, and I'd distrust many of his business operations. But his private fortune is one of the largest in this country. He might buy pictures for six pounds and sell them for six thousand till the crack of doom, without perceptibly improving his financial position. He might, of course, accept large sums for objects he had paid little for, and knew to be worthless, simply out of a perverted sense of humour. As it happens, he has no sense of humour, perverted or otherwise. You are out of your depth, Dr Leech, just as Roundhay is. *Ne sutor ultra crepidam.*"

The pallor with which Leech had received this unexpected castigation was deepened by the crashingly forthright Latin in which it ended. After this humiliating miscalculation, it was satisfactory to remark that Burntisland was once more in a state of painful agitation.

"It's my instinct to withdraw." Burntisland had set down his teacup with a trembling hand, and his breathing appeared awkward. "I don't say that I shall do so. I think I shall not do so. A vigilant regard, Dr Leech, *must* be paid to the problem of the morality of art. One ought not to shrink from it. Yet, being entered upon the field, it is too easy to press forward with violence and self-will. This has struck me in Roundhay, although he is so excellent a man. I fear I express myself badly. I have had a tiring day. I am not confident that Plato, for example, approached these matters sufficiently in the spirit of art."

"The spirit of art?" Leech repeated. He was again struck by Burntisland's liability to decline into twaddle.

"Perhaps it's again a matter of the shoemaker and his last. The processes of artistic creation are evidently much perplexed. They are highly intricate. And we don't—you and I—very clearly understand what we're meddling with. As a result, we may achieve mischief where we don't intend it."

"These are considerations to which due weight must, of course, be given." Leech glanced curiously at Burntisland. He was conscious of a passing sympathy for him. It was sad to see a man of ability letting his mind thus decline from sense to nonsense. Whether the old man remained any use at all was very doubtful. Nevertheless Leech felt that he ought himself, at least for a little longer, to hang on to the possibility. For in this affair there were surely glittering prizes. If the persuasion grew that Matthew Tresilian had ingeniously concealed unspeakable depravities in his final enigmatic paintings, then the people who had spread even that blameless Tresilian over the great staircase would find themselves awkwardly placed. And if—what was really an entirely different issue—the more bizarre varieties of contemporary art could be brought under sustained attack and ridicule alike at the popular level of the man Roundhay and among persons of influence in the country : why, then—Leech thought—Littlejohn and his absurd tie-up with Madrona would be done for. Littlejohn might even have to retire, departing into the outer darkness represented by the headship of some dingy quasi-governmental institute on the fringes of Whitehall.

Huddled in Lord Burntisland's large library chair, Philip

Leech made his gesture of wrapping an invisible gown round himself. Having acknowledged all this, he had to acknowledge, too, that he was not entirely at peace with his own conscience. The notion that some large and unapprehended mischief might be occasioned by prowling round aesthetic productions other than in what Burntisland called the spirit of art was—he knew—mere balderdash. But specific mischief to Burntisland himself was another matter. His backers, or exploiters, were—he had used the very phrase—pressing him hard. The process had even extended to exposing him to "blue" films. Leech himself had never seen such a film, and he thought he could name more than one reason for his declining to do so if invited. But this unfortunate peer, whose mainspring seemed to be a creditable if muzzy public spirit, was being harassed and distressed by a great deal that was probably entirely new to his experience. Already he was behaving oddly—as, for example, when he had cried out in that surprising manner. If he continued on the path marked out for him by Roundhay he might well land up, as the young men said, right round the bend.

"Then what do you think?"

The question had come from Burntisland suddenly and in a new tone, so that Leech was startled by it. This rocky old person had made something like a direct appeal. And—rather awkwardly—what Leech did feel was quite clear to him : Lord Burntisland ought to pick up a few light novels and depart for the Riviera. But, in that case, this whole promising campaign would probably fizzle out. Roundhay and the newspapers concerned would simply write it off, and think up something else.

Placed in this dilemma—and conceivably, he thought, you might call it a moral dilemma—Leech compromised. "In the first place," he said, "I feel the issue should not be approached in too intense a spirit. I do, of course, sympathize with your feelings about the last Tresilians. I've no doubt that there's something pretty far wrong with them. I favour bringing pressure to bear in such a manner as will result in their being quietly withdrawn from the exhibition. Informed persons"—Leech had a brief vision of his assembled colleagues—"will take due note. Beyond that, I'm not in favour of pursuing the matter violently in terms of indecency, obscenity, pornography, grave moral damage to the young, and so forth. Fundamentally, of course, I'm with you there too. But we must choose our own battlefield, or our own *first* battlefield. The ludicrousness of wealthy men being fooled into paying large sums of money, and persuading others to pay large sums of money, for objects which common sense sees to be the product of imposture or mere madness : it's here that I discern our most promising line."

"I see."

But it was plain that Burntisland didn't see; it was plain, even, that he had let his mind drift away. And when he next looked directly at Leech it was with a new reserve, and at the same time with a return to formal courtesy. Leech flushed. His mental habit—which was pretty consistently perceptive—told him at once that, essentially, he had been written off by this rocky old person.

"I shall do my duty," Lord Burntisland said. And he immediately added, "May I give you another cup of tea?"

"No, thank you." Leech got to his feet. "I'm afraid I have trespassed upon your time for too long."

"By no means." Burntisland had also risen; this son of the manse—Leech reflected—was at his most seignorial. "I have had a great deal of satisfaction in our talk. Would you care, by any chance, to join me in a short constitutional?"

Leech hesitated before this unexpected question. The proposition didn't attract him in the least. There was no getting further with Burntisland at the moment. And what had prompted the suggestion was a stiff graciousness that Leech, who thought of Burntisland as a man of the people, took no particular pleasure in. Still—and once more—it might be as well to hang on. "Thank you," he said. "I should enjoy it."

"You are probably going to Paddington? We'll take a cab to Kensington Gate, and stroll across the park. I am fond of that, but I find that I like to have company." The strains and stresses of his situation appeared momentarily to have departed from Burntisland; he was continuing to speak with a polite urbanity. "And I can take a cab back. The walk both ways might be a little too much for me."

With a final glance at Luke Fildes's intent physician, Leech followed his host from the room. Once more they went past the shrouded drawing-room behind its open door. And, although the corridor was carpeted, it was as if their footsteps were echoing in some empty, resonant place. Fate had not dealt kindly with Burntisland, it was clear, on the side of the domestic affections. And the same inscrutable power was not dealing kindly with him now. The unknown Roundhay was using him for an essentially ignoble end. Leech himself was, or had been, proposing to use him for a morally unimpeachable end—but (as he had earlier told himself) it was still a matter of *use*. And as the two men now stood on the kerb, waiting for the cab which had been called by the ancient Janet, Leech was visited by an obscure sense that —somehow, somewhere—there had been something more. He compared the Burntisland of this afternoon's visit with the Burntisland who had dined in college only a few weeks before. And it seemed to him that here, now, was a man against whom some evil stroke had been directed.

The cab drew up and they climbed inside. Preparing himself for an unprofitable half-hour, Leech dismissed this last speculation from his mind. It was fanciful. And he had no taste for fancies.

CHAPTER THIRTY-TWO

Acting upon impulse, Delver had walked back to the main street of Padstow and hired a car. It was now making good speed with him across a Cornwall agreeably unrolling beneath clear spring sunshine. But on this occasion he paid little attention to Matthew Tresilian's county, or to the problem of how its subtleties of contour and colour, its contiguities of Stone Age and Steam Age, might be conjectured variously to inform the canvases of the painter. It was the writer that occupied his mind. Tresilian's writing—chief end and bourne of this English journey—had become something more than mere mirage on the horizon. Delver now knew that if he but got his mouth to it he wouldn't taste sand. Nor could he question the quality of what waited : its sparkle and sharp coldness. What seemed doubtful was rather, one might say, the flow of the spring, the unexpected terrain it had elected to irrigate.

Delver frowned at the back of the cloth cap of the rural character driving him. In plain terms, whatever autobiographical writing of Tresilian's survived must be regarded as likely to contain an element of fiction. And of rather irresponsible fiction. Tresilian seemed to have been far from diffident about deceiving people. His story about coming by chance upon the body of his own son was an invention, but he had let Mary Emeleus believe in it. She, in turn, had used this semi-fiction in her own straight fiction, but had so used it while supposing it to be true. And—since she had never, for some reason, come across the incompatible brute fact of the case—she supposed it to be true still. On Tresilian's part this performance had been, to say the least, an odd one. Perhaps it could be subjected to some simple psychological analysis. Delver felt that it could. But, for the moment, his only keen sense was that he didn't like it.

Then there were the circumstances surrounding Tresilian's second marriage. These, in the unadorned and doubtless authentic version known to Mary Emeleus, were striking enough in themselves. They were also creditable to Tresilian. In wartime Spain he had come upon a woman in desperate plight. Not only had she been destitute and of a persecuted race; she had been, it seemed, *une mourante* as well. He had got her into Portugal, married her, and made her the mother, before her death, of a healthy male child. It seemed a good sort of history. Mary Emeleus herself, although not romantically inclined, had been unable to represent it as otherwise.

But this history Tresilian had proceeded to embellish in an autobiographical document seemingly prepared as a memorial or heirloom for the woman's son. He had embellished it cleverly but recklessly with an adventure-story element, well calculated to thrill a schoolboy, but uncomfortably vulnerable (surely) to any dispassionate adult intelligence. In this version the "woman from a Warsaw ghetto" had become a countess or the like, and her rescue had been accomplished only by a raid within the frontiers of Hitler's *Reich* itself. This was the story that Luke Tresilian believed now. It was a story, moreover, that clearly meant a great deal to the kid.

For the second time that day, Thayne Delver, facing his developing research project, felt an impulse akin to panic. What had heaved itself up in front of him during the past few weeks was, in essence, an obliquity in Matthew Tresilian. And Delver's established sense of the man held no provision for accommodating such a thing. He found himself almost wishing that he hadn't let the interrelationships of the arts start him on this particular trail. Tresilian *had* possessed a talent for writing. There could now be no doubt about that. But just how he had used it, just how he had comported himself with his pen when taking an hour or two off from his pencil, mightn't be all that creditable to the total stature of the man.

At this point in his meditation, it came to Delver that there was a truth he must face with a cold eye. It was even conceivable that a knowledge of certain ways in which Tresilian had exploited the art of writing would lead to a diminution in the regard in which his painting itself was held. If the matter were to turn out in this way then he, Thayne Delver, would in fact have involved himself in what the outside world might regard as a small and comic instance of the operation of dramatic irony. He would have set out to bring about one state of affairs, and have proved, all unwittingly, to have brought about its opposite.

But this was a portentous view of the matter, and at least nobody would be hurt in more than their vanity when the curtain came down. And he mustn't himself now shrink from working the thing out. To begin with, that simple psychology was easy enough to supply. Tresilian had twice tinkered with the integrity of what he was about—that, at least, was the stiff way of expressing the thing—and on each occasion his motive was distinguishable. The story of finding the body of his son dead beside his battery was straightforward compensatory fantasy. John Tresilian's real end had been miserable, and had been on the fringes of being shameful as well. His father had provided him with an imaginary one, and had then handed the result to a former mistress with the evident implication that she might shove it into a work of fiction if she wanted to. Delver had owned frequent professional occasion to study the artistic character. He acknowledged to himself that it had its moments of baffling him still.

Broadly, you might say that, in the affair of his son John, Matthew Tresilian had employed the resources of art simply to make things more comfortable. In the affair of the second marriage, correspondingly, he had employed them to make things more edifying or inspiring. It was very odd—but that, clearly, had been his motive. He had embellished the truth with a number of fictitious accretions designed to make an impact upon the adolescent boy into whose hands he proposed that the narrative should come.

It seemed to Delver that these had been wrong things to do. They had been wrong, rather than merely freakish and unstable. Matthew Tresilian had used artistic endowments to non-artistic ends. This was a violation of art, and eventually of other things as well. John Tresilian was dead, but his memory wasn't honoured in the obscure trick that had been played with it. Luke Tresilian was alive, and it was shocking that something incontinent in his father's fancy should have left him, for family legend, a hodge-podge of fact and fiction. The unadorned truth of the matter, should it ever come to him, wouldn't in fact kill him. But the element of deception in the story would at least needlessly cheapen what was authentic and good in it.

But Delver's present job lay elsewhere. A new facet of Matthew

Tresilian's personality fell to be entered on the record. What new scrutiny of his art—he asked himself again—might it precipitate? Delver recalled some remarks murmured to him by old John Alabaster to the effect that Tresilian had come to own a dangerous facility in hazardous improvization, a power to turn failure into success by some sudden stroke of craft or imagination —but a power in the use of which he had not always been able to avoid overreaching himself. The old fellow had said something like that. And perhaps there was a relation—

Delver's thought was checked at this point. His automobile was coming to an undesigned and distressed halt. The engine had coughed and faltered; now it faded out. The driver, after several ineffective janglings of his starter *in situ*, climbed sulkily from his seat, muttered darkly something about the feed, and flung open his engine. Delver looked at his watch. He knew that, quite soon, he would become impatient and annoyed, for he had a national intolerance of mechanical contrivances that refuse to work. But he got out of the car with the conscientious intention of once more admiring the Cornish landscape. He noticed at once that the sunshine had departed; he noticed presently that the prospect before him showed as a singularly bleak one. There was a certain amount of what he supposed to be gorse. Apart from this, the landscape might be adequately described simply by saying that there were a lot of big stones lying about. Only in a slight depression straight ahead there stood some abandoned manufactory, with round about it a straggle of cottages and a couple of byre-like chapels. He couldn't, from where he stood, distinguish much of the place. But he knew what its more detailed face would present, since one such village was like all the others, and he had already seen a good many of them.

The driver was now blowing noisily through a piece of narrow, curved tubing he had removed from his engine. Delver hoped this technical manoeuvre would be successful, for he now much wanted to move on. The sky was darkening. There was a sultry sort of storm coming up. And he suddenly saw all this region—which he had formerly romanticized as young Matthew Tresilian's nursery of significant form—as inimical and sinister: lonely, decayed, poverty-stricken, graceless, horribly narrow and mean. It occurred to him to wonder what these people, the people who had to stay put in these hamlets, precisely did with themselves. There wasn't much sign of employment. On Sundays they sang hymns. He had a notion, perhaps picked up from novels, that at other times they were much occupied in spying upon each other through small, oppressively curtained windows.

Delver had taken a turn down the road. He now walked back towards his car, and was relieved to hear its engine running again. He realized that a disenchantment with the region he was traversing must have been in some way building up in him. Tresilian's children—the children of the first marriage—had been abruptly despatched to the depths of Cornwall, he remembered, at some early stage of the war. He wondered whether anything in their earlier experience had much prepared them for that plunge, as it must have been, into rural isolation. The boy was now dead; the girl, whom he was about to visit, had apparently chosen a life as narrow as could be conceived. On the other hand, Luke Tresilian clearly enjoyed being a young Cornishman. But he was a young Cornishman who had steered himself firmly to Oxford, acquired acquaintances and a girl friend in London, and formed cheerful designs upon Bikini and Fez.

These reflections occupied Delver as he got under way again, and from Luke Tresilian he was led to speculate on Luke Tresilian's guardian. Dr Dolben had not been oncoming about his early association with Matthew Tresilian, or about himself in any way. Delver had, indeed, casually heard the name of the place where Dolben had practised at that time, and it would be perfectly possible to find out more. Yet finding out about the undistinguished living seemed morally a different thing from finding out about the illustrious dead; it persisted in being different even when the illustrious dead remained the sole reason of one's feeling any curiosity at all.

But here, nevertheless, there rose before him a fresh phase of what must be called his investigation. For the sea now lay below, livid and motionless beneath this darkening sky. On a rocky promontory, littered with granitic debris, the short, stiff thrust of the lighthouse, its two adjoined cottages, and the irregular wall of whitened stone surrounding it, showed like a *graffito* scrawled rudely and indifferently on turf and water. Somewhere there must be at least a cart-track down to the place. But only a footpath was in immediate evidence, striking off from a tiny group of cottages immediately ahead. And Delver was prompted to speak quickly. "I guess I'll walk down from here," he said. "If you come back to pick me up in an hour's time it's not likely I'll keep you long."

He walked past the scatter of cottages and noticed that not all were tenanted. The last building was a chapel, and he paused to read the word "Bethsaida" in almost obliterated characters above the door. The pool of healing. The fountain filled with blood. His mind took a dip into its own well-furnished store of information on English Nonconformity. He had a great respect for that whole tradition, but it had certainly left some forlorn and dismal things around. He climbed a stile—an affair of stones so massive that it would surely still be there to nego-tiate when the bodies rose from the Bethsaida's graveyard at the Last Trump. He dropped down towards a cove and then climbed again. The lighthouse was directly before him.

There was no sign of life about the place, and no sound. Or rather, he realized, there *was* a sound, which he could only hope was not a human one. It was a high, thin vibration on the very frontier of hearing, like a cry of despair carried on a single un-varying note from far away. Presumably it emanated from some engine or similar mechanism. But he found it disturbing. He found the whole little complex of buildings, compact in their hard, white purity of paint and polish, very much that. It was something he didn't want to break in on. He had a curious im-pulse to withdraw.

He compromised, partly as recalling that he hadn't thought out any effective approach to Matthew Tresilian's daughter. He compromised by walking straight on. He ought to have thought ahead during the run from Padstow. He would give a few minutes to thinking ahead now.

Bypassing the lighthouse, he dropped down and climbed up again, on a track that was no more than a few scratches from nailed boots upon stone. Once or twice he paused to look at the ominous sea. Within an hour it had become no Cornish sea he knew, either from nature or from Tresilian's pictures; it seemed not a sea at all, but a great flat grey slab that might have been bolted down over some dangerously eruptive thing. And the sky was like a single blind eye above it. These were morbid images. They might have developed farther in Delver's imagina-tion. But suddenly he was over the brow of the headland he had been climbing and was standing on the verge of the cliff. Before him was a spectacle by which he was at first startled and then appalled.

On either hand the cliff swept round in a small circle of dark rock, so that his first impression was of looking down a well—a well in which water no more than sullenly glinted, terrifyingly far below. Only when he looked ahead, and saw how the sea flowed into the cove as if through the narrow neck of a dull green jar, did the perspective of the place come true, and the unnaturally remote surface rise up to within a measurable hundred feet of where he stood. But it was an impressive spot—and now a fearful one. Here and there the dizzy verge broke down into delusively practical-seeming paths. One of these, only a few paces away, dropped for some yards without danger, suddenly became no more than a narrow ledge overhung by smooth rock and itself overhanging empty space, and then ended upon a platform—as long and as broad as a hearth-rug of moderate size—of invitingly green turf. To this hazardous perch a young child had unbelievably strayed. In a moment Delver saw why. Now disregarded at the terrified child's feet was a brightly coloured ball.

It was the sort of sharp, fantastic crisis that finds a man at once. Delver knew that he had to get straight down to the child, who was cowering a safe enough couple of feet from the brink. He had to get to the child and then decide what to do next: whether to stay down there and shout for the help that wasn't likely to come until folks starting hunting, or to risk bringing the child up. It didn't occur to him to note that he went without hesitation. He just went.

But, perplexingly, he was forestalled. A woman had appeared from nowhere, and she was going swiftly down the first and unhazardous part of the path. He had seconds in which he could do no harm by startling her. So he called out urgently.

"Stop, please!"

The woman halted and looked back. She was young—perhaps no more than in her early thirties—and it occurred to him, even in this horrible moment, that she was dressed with a sort of old-fashioned charmlessness at odds with the figure beneath the clothes.

"Stop, please," Delver repeated. "Come back. I'll go down and fetch the child. I'm a climber as it happens. That isn't a pretty place. But to me it doesn't mean a thing."

The woman looked at him steadily, so that he wondered just how obtrusively lacking in the appearance of a mountaineer he was. She had a curiously still face.

"Stay where you are," she said. "When I've got to him—then we can decide what to do next. It may be best that you get men and ropes. So wait." Her voice seemed not to come from a person conscious of crisis, or even of any untoward thing. And this was a chilling rather than a steadying circumstance. She had turned away and was walking on. Now she was at that frightful place. She turned towards the sinister overhang of rock—intelligently but not expertly, he thought—and moved unfalteringly round its ugly angle. She was safely on the small plot of grass with the child.

It was half the struggle achieved. What followed was a sequel so horrible that for long it was going to numb his brain when he looked back on it. The boy—for it was a boy—stared at the woman and panicked. He backed away towards the abyss. And she acted as if this were an expected thing. In an instant she was between the boy and the verge, had seized him and was holding him to her. He blindly struggled.

Delver found himself round the deadly place without consciousness that he had reached it in long strides. Presumably he had used the same technique of pressing his belly to the rock. He seized the boy just as the boy broke free, and dragged him back from the edge. "All right," he said. "Quite all right. We keep still till the youngster calms down."

"Yes." She had dropped to her knees beside him and was holding the boy's vainly thrashing legs. "We must stay until people come, I think. I shall be missed—in time. I often walk this way." She spoke, he noticed, with a Cornish intonation but like an educated person, so that he was fleetingly reminded of Dr Dolben. "Look out!" she cried.

It was her first accent of alarm, and one abundantly justified. With a queer tearing sound—as of cattle, he thought, cropping grass—a small part of the plaform on which they stood had broken away and vanished. He was conscious, by the sudden strange acuity of an utterly irrelevant sense, of the smell of bruised thyme. And a tiny noise came up from far below.

Delver looked at the boy, judging his weight, his strength. He wondered with what sort of blow the child could be stunned and made inert. But it seemed an impractical course. He took him by the waist and reckoned that, at least for a crucial couple of minutes, he could hold him firmly in the crook of one arm. "I'm afraid you'd better follow," he said to the woman. "We can't be sure an inch of this is safe."

A couple of paces took him to the rock, and to an instant realization that the child simply could not be carried round it. There was no possible way of balancing himself with such a burden. But now the child had gone still. And the child, he saw, had only to walk. That was why he had got where he had. He was so small that the overhang was no impediment. So there was only one thing to do. Delver set the child gently on his feet. "Go ahead," he said. "Up to the top. I'm following." And the child moved forward obediently. Delver knew that, if the child stumbled, he would have to reach out for him; the motion would be futile and fatal, yet he would have to make it. But the child turned the corner unfalteringly. Without looking back, he stumped prosaically upon his short legs up the short, secure path. And now, for the first time since he had accepted danger, Delver rashly looked down. The remote, grey-green water was faintly marbled by submerged rocks, and in the vacancy a single gull sank, pivoted and rose. Delver felt sudden terror—a terror which had less to do with the thought of falling to instant death than with the sheer, potent thrust upon his senses of a fully three-dimensional world. Very strangely, he found himself exercising a professional skill, willing the horror to project itself upon a plane surface, willing it to come flat and safe, approximating all the soar and plunge and far recession to the harmless world of monocular vision. He thought, absurdly, that he was learning something about painting. And then he was round the overhang, and the woman had instantly, coolly, followed him.

He wondered how long all this had taken to happen. Probably no time at all. He looked back and down at the deadly place. No more of it had fallen away. The ball was there still.

The woman was standing with her hand on the small boy's shoulder. He found it difficult to speak. "Your child's none the worse," he managed to say.

"He is no child of mine." The woman took her hand from

the boy's shoulder and tapped him on the back. "And now go home," she said. "I shall speak to your mother. Go home at once." The child walked away. As he did so, sounds came from him for the first time, and Delver supposed for a moment that he was sobbing. But the sounds were meaningless and idle; their emotional content was nil. "Yes," the woman said. "He's simple. Normal children hereabouts learn of such dangers as they toddle."

"Then somebody has been uncommonly careless, if you ask me."

"Yes." She spoke indifferently and looked at him indifferently. Yet there existed between them the strong, ephemeral intimacy that springs from a physical peril shared. "I suppose you are the American professor?" she asked.

"I'm Thayne Delver," he said. He realized that he had somehow known this to be Tresilian's daughter. But, important as the moment was, his gaze didn't readily leave the small boy aimlessly walking down the path before them. There was nothing irresponsible in the child's dismissal, since the way back to the scatter of cottages above the lighthouse was safe enough. But something in the temperature of the thing troubled him.

"These are lonely places," Faith Crinnis said. "There is carelessness because there is hopelessness, I suppose. Hopelessness and misery and evil. Cornwall is like the human mind as I once read of it in some book. We walk about up here. But underneath is a whole subterraneous world of pits and shafts and workings where people's lives were lived out a long time ago. And there are communications with that world still. We don't know what's there. But something is there. And sometimes it rises up from millions of years back and commands us."

Delver was startled. He was startled by the perception that the woman had been more affected by this adventure than her manner so far had suggested; that in a minute she had said more to him than normally she would have been constrained to in a year. He was startled that she possessed such book-learning as this manner of looking at things implied, for he had got her in his head as entirely submerged in the folk. And he was startled by her articulateness. Yet, after all, she was Matthew Tresilian's daughter. She was Luke Tresilian's half-sister—and Luke, if not largely sophisticated, had a natural grip on words.

"But," Delver said, "you have made your life in Cornwall, haven't you?"

"Our lives are made for us, I suppose." They had dropped down the narrow path in single file, and now they could walk on towards the lighthouse side by side. The child had disappeared. "Yes," Faith Crinnis said, "of course they're made for us. But between sleeping and waking a whole life can be made or unmade." She walked on in silence, and when she spoke again it was in a new voice. "Why have you come here?" she asked. "You're uninvited. I made you no sign."

"I'm very well aware of that, Mrs Crinnis. But I came down to Cornwall to see your half-brother——"

"Was that without an invitation too?"

"Well, yes—it was. But Luke had at least corresponded with me. And today he agreed that I really ought to try to see you some time. You must know a lot, he said, and might surprise me."

"Luke said that? But I think it is I who am surprised by you. You are a professor. But you push in like some common man with things to sell."

"I guess I'll do no more pushing after *that*." Delver had come to a halt—by the little gate, he realized, that led up a short, straight path to the lighthouse and its cottages. "Only I must just apologize. Your father's genius means a great deal to me. So I want to find out all I can about him." He paused. "It's right that I should, you know. I must give you notice I shall stay on the job. Only without, I assure you, intruding on your privacy again."

She had heard him in silence. "And is there anywhere else in Cornwall," she asked, "where you hope to search things out?"

He thought the phrase was odd, but he had to answer honestly. "I might go back to Gwennap, your father's birthplace, although I doubt whether there is more than what may be called atmosphere to be picked up there. But there's another place I've heard of : Lancraddock. It's where Dr Dolben once practised. The idea has come to me that at one time your father may have had a kind of retreat there. But now I think I'd better go, Mrs Crinnis. And I apologize again for vexing you."

"I think you had better come in." Faith Crinnis was looking at him gravely, while with one hand she opened the little gate.

"Perhaps I've been wrong. And I think we shall be undisturbed. My husband said he was to be down at the siren."

Delver followed Tresilian's daughter silently up the path. Her change of front surprised him and made him uneasy. He glimpsed, indeed, as for the first time, the full measure of a discomfort that had been, from several directions, closing in on him. In this very instant he would have turned back if he rationally could.

But now they were inside. They were in a small living-room that gave curiously little sign of being lived in. It was bleak and white and sparely furnished, and it was tidy in a fashion making him think of a ship's cabin at the moment of a captain's inspection. If there was any sort of individual note, it sounded austerely in the framed religious texts on the walls.

"Please sit down," Faith Crinnis said. And Delver sat down on one of two hard chairs set before a deal table. Through a window straight in front of him he noticed how dark the sky had now become. But the room seemed to generate its own clear, hard light. You couldn't, he thought, hide anything in such a place. "You are right," she was saying, "about Lancraddock. My father had a cottage there at the time of his second marriage. Luke was born in it."

"And it was there, perhaps, that you and your brother John were sent to be out of the way of the Blitz?"

"No, that was elsewhere. Grimmer. Bleaker."

Delver remembered that this was something about which Mary Emeleus had told him. "A place called Malcar?" he asked.

Faith Crinnis seemed startled. "Yes," she said. "Malcar. A miserable place. We felt something unaccountable in our father's arrangement of the thing." She looked steadily at Delver. "Ought you not to be taking notes?" she asked.

There was something sardonic about this before which his discomfort grew. "Mrs Crinnis," he said, "I don't feel happy about how we're getting along. You seemed to make it clear you didn't want—"

"But I said I saw that to be wrong. You want to fill in the background of your study of my father with some account of his life, some impression of his personality. And that's quite right." Faith Crinnis was speaking slowly and carefully. He saw that she was making a great effort which was partly of a straight intellectual kind. For a long time, he supposed, she had done little talking of this sort. Yet it wasn't this alone that was building up such a sense of strain in the small room. "Only I must be sure of something," she was going on. "The time hasn't come for a whole book about my father's life. I can see the sort of man you are : trained for work of that sort and clever at finding things out. If you pressed on and on—as I think you've thought of doing —then you might come upon things that it's not at all important for the world to know, but which would hurt some people who are still alive. This must often be the case. Surely that kind of interest can wait?"

It was a swiftly definitive moment. For Delver's conscience told him that in one part of his project he was defeated. He was a scholar, not a journalist, and he had to respect the private life when it asserted itself as firmly as this. Yet, just for a moment, he didn't give in. "Are you thinking," he asked, "of matters which can fitly be made public later on, or matters which, if not inquired into now, will probably fade out of the record for good?"

She shook her head, and he saw that he was going to get no direct reply. "You might ask me questions," she said. "About my father, I mean. I was nearly twenty-two when he died. Only remember, please, the point I've made from the first. My life's as you see it. I've no place in the world in which my father lived. And it's only in order to give you the small help I now see to be right that I'd make any attempt to think back into it." She gave him her steady look. "But always on that condition I made."

"I agree to it, Mrs Crinnis. And let me add this. Nothing about your father's life based upon any research of mine will reach print without having been submited to you. So may I, upon that understanding, ask a few questions now?"

She nodded, but this time without looking at him. Her gaze was upon the window, and he wondered whether she was now expecting her husband's return. "Well?" she said.

"I'm interested in what you tell me about your father's continued association with Cornwall, and his sending you and your brother John here during the war. Did you say you found something unaccountable in it?"

"Perhaps I did." She frowned, as if feeling that here was not a relevant line of approach. "We were too old to be turned into evacuated children, and John was soon to be taken into the army. There was a blindness in it."

Delver found himself thinking, surely inconsequently, of Tresilian's last paintings, which seemed to explore the world of a man to whom only peripheral vision was left. But he recalled his mind from this. "Did you know Mary Emeleus?" he asked.

"My father's mistress? We may just have met."

"It must have been when that association was forming that you and your brother were sent to Cornwall. Did it seem so bleak and grim, do you think, because of some sense of relegation?"

"Relegation?" She clearly neither understood the word nor cared for these questions.

"You might have been jealous."

"Yes, I see. And so might John." She spoke indifferently now.

"And I think that both your brother and yourself, by that time, must really have been developing—well, as I guess the children of a well-known painter in London would develop. With intellectual and artistic interests. So it must have been a big change. You must have felt yourselves back where—"

"Perhaps so." Faith Crinnis's voice now had a trace of bitterness—which didn't, however, make much impression on the curious strained deadness that was her predominant note. "You are very acute. Yes—I suppose so. Clogs to clogs in three generations, don't they say? Not that we wear such things down here." She seemed to brace herself before saying anything more, and the squaring of her shoulders and lifting of her breasts recalled to Delver his first impression of her on the cliff. She was still almost young, and the mere lines of her figure spoke of something that ought to have been with her and, somehow, wasn't. "It wasn't good for John," she said. "When he needed things, you see, he needed them desperately. We were very close to each other. I suppose our father thought we would keep each other amused. Then the war did take John. He was—" she hesitated. "He didn't come through it, you know."

"Did you realize that your father did a good deal of writing, and that some of it professed to be autobiographical while really taking odd liberties with fact?"

"No—or rather, yes." For the first time, Faith Crinnis seemed conscious of having to take a grip of herself. "Yes," she repeated. "It was a curious application—or, perhaps, misapplication—of a secondary power which your father undoubtedly possessed. Your brother—I mean your half-brother Luke—quite certainly cherishes an example. It's a narrative of your father's second marriage. And—I think beyond doubt—it's fictionalized in the way I have been describing."

"Fictionalized?" She spoke sharply.

"Not in the essentials, Mrs Crinnis. I don't think that was your father's way."

"I see." Faith Crinnis had taken a deep breath. "I'm certain Luke believes—"

"Sure. That's the point. And it worries me." Delver had a sudden sense that it was his business to be reassuring. "In a way, I might say I've been ahead of you. I mean, about the season for a full-scale biography not having come. There's no question but that Luke possesses a narrative of your father's that isn't quite the truth. And he sets an equal store on the parts that are romancing and the parts that are not. Well, that's an awkward thing. Too awkward to handle with comfort. I felt, let me say, something like panic when it broke on me. And I'm prepared to call it a day. For the present. By which, Mrs Crinnis, I mean for my time."

"You mean that you drop that side of your interest in my father?"

"I do. But I don't relinquish him as the great English painter of his age. Were you much about his studio as a girl?"

Throughout this interview Faith Crinnis had been standing beside the chimneypiece of the small room. Now, with a sudden suggestion of acute fatigue, she sat down. "Well, yes," she said with a faint smile. "And I was interested. But it's all sadly vague now to me."

"You wouldn't have any vivid memory or impression of his working methods?"

"Pulling chestnuts from the fire. Improvising—isn't that the word?—improvising his way out of a scrape." Momentarily, Faith Crinnis had become animated. "He'd have been confident and rash, and the whole composition would be wrong. And then a brilliant stroke would come to him. Of course it didn't always work."

"I've heard something like this from others." Delver felt a momentary relief in the air, and felt it as something he shared with Tresilian's daughter. For his own part, it was simply that he was back where, after all, his major interest lay. "But I wonder—" He broke off, having heard a door open behind him.

"My husband," Faith Crinnis said. "Alfred, this is Professor Delver."

Alfred Crinnis was much older than his wife : a grey, haggard man, with dark eyes and a sombre air. He was carrying some small but heavy piece of apparatus in both hands, and was now shutting the door behind him with his shoulder. Delver stood up. Some greeting appeared necessary, but Crinnis seemed not disposed to take the initiative. So Delver spoke in his own form. "I'm very pleased to meet you, Mr Crinnis," he said.

"Peace be with you." Crinnis set his apparatus down on the table. There was a pause which Delver felt to be awkward.

"Professor Delver," Faith Crinnis said, "is interested in my father's paintings."

"Then he'll have heard the tidings of them. Aye, it will be because of that, maybe, that he has come to you."

"Tidings, Alfred? What do you mean?"

"Your father's vanities, Faith, have been denounced—denounced before the face of the people as profaneness and an abomination." Crinnis's dark eyes were glowing fiercely. Delver, although he had no notion of what the words were about, found himself expecting some tremendous commination. Instead, Crinnis crossed over to his wife and laid a hand on her shoulder. "Aye," he said. "It was on the five o'clock news. Some great lord in London has seen evil things in them. Your father, child, was but one among many makers of lewd and evil images. But I took you from among them, even as a bird from the snare of the fowler." He turned to Delver. "These matters are none of ours," he said. "But every night my wife and I search the Scriptures. We pray for all sinners—aye, and confess ourselves among them. For God has set our iniquities before Him, and our secret sins in the light of His countenance."

Delver glanced cautiously at Faith Crinnis. Her relationship to her elderly husband was an enigma to him, but he could at least see that she found no meaning in a vision of life centred in the Old Testament. A sort of still weariness had descended on her, and she seemed even to be without curiosity about whatever had really happened in London. It was otherwise with Delver himself. There must have been some incident, he supposed, at the opening of the Tresilian exhibition that morning, and he was eager to hear about it. He doubted, however, whether he would gain accurate information from this fanatical lighthouse-keeper. He must get away, and find out. In any case, it was now much his instinct to get away. He had virtually given Faith Crinnis his word to drop the biographical side of his research. This was uncomfortable in itself, since it implied that there had been aspects of Matthew Tresilian's life vulnerable to a hard look. But far more sharply uncomfortable was the household—if household it could be called—which he had rashly intruded upon.

It wasn't that there was nothing alive between this ill assorted couple. Something there certainly was, although he could neither identify the passion or emotion nor tell whether its operation was a reciprocal one. On challenge he would have said that duty, affection, loyalty were in the room, but that at play against them was some wholly incommensurable force which he had no view of and could give no name to. In any case, he was just plain anxious to get away.

He was about to speak whatever words would most directly serve this end when he saw that Alfred Crinnis, still standing with his hand on his wife's shoulder, had fixed upon him from across the narrow table an extraordinary intensity of regard. And now at least he was in contact with something he could give a name to. What looked at him through Crinnis's eyes was suspicion. In its present bearing it was perhaps no more than a fleeting and puzzled suspicion. Its intensity came from some sizeable reservoir of the same stuff, stored under pressure quite some way down. That was it, Delver told himself. The look he was getting from Alfred Crinnis was like a fierce jet of steam forced through some tiny orifice. He was considering whether the man's mania perhaps extended a good way beyond religious topics—whether this was the true explanation of what he so much didn't like in the air—when the man spoke, gently and almost sanely, yet without any change of what was disturbing in his eye.

"A Lord Burntisland," Crinnis said. "One that has been among the rulers and governors of the land. He it is that has called for judgment against the vain and amatorious imaginings of Faith's father. It would be because of that that you have come?"

"Not at all. I know nothing about it. I study the work of great artists, Mr Crinnis. I'm employed to do so by a university in my own country. To me, Matthew Tresilian's paintings are good and pure. A man who denounces them as amatorious must have a dirty mind or a tormented one."

Crinnis shook his head. "I have seen such paintings," he said, "in ungodly prints. They seem meaningless at first, but there is a nether darkness about them. Their makers have envied God's creation, tearing it apart in their hearts, making riddles and monsters from the shards. And I ask, how long shall the wicked triumph, how long shall they utter and speak hard things? They break in pieces thy people, O Lord, and afflict thine heritage."

"I can't admit that it's like that at all," Delver said. Few accomplishments were more tedious, he was thinking, than a large command of the Scriptures exploited to stir up bees in a man's bonnet.

"Whether good or evil," Crinnis said, "neither my wife nor I knows anything of these things. We are simple people, without skill in them. So why should you come here?"

"Professor Delver has been interested in my father's life, and in his family." Faith Crinnis spoke wearily but swiftly, as if there were something in the drift of her husband's mind that she was prompted to deflect. "It happens, Alfred, with people who have become famous. But the professor will not go on with that part of his work. He has promised me."

"And why should that be?" Crinnis had turned on his wife in such a fashion that she started back from him and turned pale. It was as if, Delver thought, she had made some decisive error at the end of a long, exhausting game. "Let thy light—" Crinnis began. He broke off, and raised his voice. "Let thy light—"

"Stop!" Faith Crinnis had raised her voice too. For the moment it was commanding. "I will not listen, Alfred, to these mouthings out of your horrible Bethel. I will not listen to them again. You say we are simple people. Then speak like the simple man you used to be."

There was a moment's silence. Delver had reached for his hat. Whatever was now present in this room, he had no standing before it. Humiliating though it was, he must simply scramble out. Hastily he spoke into the silence, uttering whatever words occurred to him.

"How will you be going?" Crinnis asked briefly.

"By now there will be a car waiting for me on the road."

"I'll see you to it." It seemed to Delver that in Crinnis's eyes, now again searching his face, those fissures giving upon a fathomless suspicion had widened, so that he wondered whether there lurked in him the mind of a paranoiac. But the man was picking up with steady hands the piece of apparatus from the table before him. "First, I'll put this where it belongs," he said, and left the room.

Delver heard Faith Crinnis draw a deep breath. He moved awkwardly towards the outer door. Through the window he could see a sky now so louring that he began to put on the light overcoat he had been carrying over his arm. She came up to him hesitantly, as if to help. "You say," she asked, "that you saw Luke today?"

"Earlier this afternoon. I have come straight from Padstow."

"They say he has grown very tall. Does he look as if he has outgrown his strength?"

"I'd say not." Delver shook his head. This was an anxiety, he reflected, rather touchingly of the common people. "He looks a very healthy kid to me."

"Did you feel that he's happy?"

"Happy?" Delver found this second question obscurely disturbing. "I guess so. He's looking forward to quite a lively life, I'd say. And I rather gathered he has a girl friend, which probably helps a lot."

"That." Her face had changed. "Thank you," she said, and drew back as her husband returned to the room. "Good-bye." She made no offer to shake hands.

Delver found himself outside the lighthouse cottage and walking up the path with Alfred Crinnis beside him. "So it was to find out about my wife's father," Crinnis asked, "that you came into these parts?"

"That was the idea."

Crinnis made no rejoinder. The two men walked on in a silence which Delver found himself possessed of a strong instinct not to break. But, at the same time, it was an oppressive silence. And perhaps it was something in the tremendous sky which presently made that oppression unbearable. "I suppose you knew him?" Delver heard himself ask.

"Knew him?" Crinnis seemed to have passed broodingly out of contact with what was being said. Then he nodded. "Yes, I knew him. And he had cunning in his bones. So, mayhap, have all such artificers of illusion and lies. But Tresilian would weave cunning over cunning till he snared his own foot."

Delver was again strongly prompted to silence. He had come eager to make contact with these people. Now he only wanted to get away from them.

"And he was a Gwennap man," Crinnis said. "Woe unto that evil and adulterous city, for the Lord seeth into the darkness of its heart."

Delver felt suddenly revolted by this maniacal talk, more revolted by it than he was amused at the notion of Gwennap as a city, adulterous or otherwise. But now they had climbed the massive stone stile, and his car was only twenty yards off. This time, he broke silence only with the vague idea of getting away on some lighter note. "But at least," he said mildly, "Tresilian seems not to have gone back there. Nor back to St Ives, for that matter. He tried other places in Cornwall : Lancraddock, where he had a cottage; and Malcar, where he sent his children during the war."

"His children?" Crinnis seemed not to understand.

"The children of his first marriage. Your wife and her brother John."

"Not Malcar."

"Yes, Malcar." Delver, with freedom before him, was unreasonably irritated. "I've had it from both—"

"None ever spoke to me of Malcar."

There was a moment's silence. Delver's driver was climbing sulkily from his seat. But Alfred Crinnis was immobile. Delver looked at him and sensed disaster; looked again and saw that the man's eyes were now chasms. He tried to speak to the madman. Then he tried, ineffectively, to make some restraining movement. For, without a word, Crinnis had turned and walked away. Delver's driver said something about the lateness of the hour. Crinnis reached the stile, and for the second time that afternoon it came to Delver that he must go to the help of Matthew Tresilian's daughter.

But Crinnis walked on, now visible and now invisible on the undulating road. When he grew small in the distance it would still have been impossible to think of him as a man moving aimlessly. He was on a journey to some goal.

Delver shivered, for it was chilly here by the car. The day which had begun in late spring sunshine was fading out between an unearthly sea and sky : a sea and sky, Delver thought, charged with the impossible darkness of the very last paintings of Christopher Wood. And against this tremendous background stood the lighthouse, still weirdly white.

CHAPTER THIRTY-THREE

ALREADY LUKE'S ROOM was again littered with books and papers. And Luke sat thumping on his typewriter.

> *Nor did the wisest wizard guess*
> *What would bechance at Lyonnesse*
> *While I should sojourn there.*

That's been my favourite poem for a long time. I used to chant it like mad. But it's no longer apposite. Nothing bechances in Lyonnesse now, and radiance rare and fathomless exists only in a London flat. Darling. But I shall return with magic in my eyes in only three days.

Hardy's tremendous. Like him, and you'll never fall for one or another sort of fashionable bosh. This morning I did that daily hour on Virgil, who's an Establishment figure, if ever there was one. Still, he's not like Horace, who was clearly one of what Bruno calls the Vile Old Men. After Virgil I went back to Hardy: The Dynasts. *Because I was going to have a date later with some birds, I was struck by a little piece about birds. It's at Albuera—"in a few hours to be the sanguinary scene of the most murderous struggle of the whole war." And then in come the birds. "The birds in the wood, unaware that this day is to be different from every other day they have known there, are heard singing their overtures with their usual serenity."*

Think, Hatty, of those bloody lucky Napoleonic birds. The nations begin bashing at each other, but the birds carry on with their usual serenity. I suppose the birds on Bikini carried on with their usual serenity, too. Oh my, weren't the silly little bastards sold! Still, even there the same job of just being alive is in hand again. I told the American professor that.

Lord, I haven't mentioned him. His name's Delver, and he came and went only a couple of hours ago. He turned up without notice—which didn't much please my guardian—and on the hunt for information about my father. He's to be the great *Tresilian* authority, I gathered, so I'd have expected him to be in on the opening of the exhibition this morning. But here he was. I felt a bit awkward. It was like having a don not knowing his place and coming into your rooms. But he was very nice. And so I felt curmudgeonly as well, having nothing either to tell him or sell him. But I told him quite clearly I was sitting on what of my father's I have. And I said he should go and see *Faith*. I know she doesn't want to see him, but it couldn't do any harm. She might be the better of a shake-up. She lives in a shell with a husband who goes in for *Jehovah's Witnesses* or something. I've never got anything out of her at all.

Hatty, we go on singing, you and I, with our usual serenity, and take a chance with the darkening scene. It's literally darkening here, at the moment. I've never seen such a strangely ominous sky. But *WHO IS SO SAFE AS WE, WHERE NONE CAN DO TREASON TO US, EXCEPT ONE OF US TWO?* Who discovered this kind of love? That each can say everything, and the other want to hear it all. That we can share the whole universe in its minutest parts so passionately. Did I tell you my tutor disapproves of the new fashion for all-glass buildings in Oxford because it impedes undergraduates in two of their most important activities: love-making and saying their prayers? Whimsy and How-understanding-I-am. But he has something, all the same.

Three days. And then thirty thousand. We can have thirty thousand without quite living to be centenarians. I've just worked it out. It's taken the last minute to posting time, because I'm not good at maths. *I LOVE YOU*.

LUKE

PART FIVE

CHAPTER THIRTY-FOUR

THAYNE DELVER WALKED slowly up the steps of the British Museum. He was so lost in thought that he failed to notice Charles Rose, walking up the steps beside him. Rose, although he too appeared preoccupied, was less unobservant. "Good morning," he said. "You're back among the early birds."

For a moment Delver seemed to take this literally, for his glance went from Rose to the pigeons. The hour was certainly early; the sun had barely edged round the Iron Age Gallery and the Department of Ethnography; there was still a chill in what Rose liked to think of as Smirke's stylophilous colonnade. But the well-intentioned feeding of the feathered pests was already going forward. It seemed as if some people brought packed breakfasts as well as packed lunches to the Museum.

"And here's a pretty kettle of fish," Rose went on. Seeing Delver again look round in a kind of abstracted bewilderment, he added : "In this Tresilian business, I mean."

Delver came to a halt in the portico. "You've heard something?" he asked.

"Heard something!" Rose stared. "I suppose anybody who buys a newspaper has done that. And it's coming to an absurd crisis this afternoon. As it happens, I'm due to be in at the death."

"The death?" Delver seemed to be emerging with difficulty from a state of painful literal-mindedness. "I guess you're talking about the row at the exhibition. Of course I've seen about that. But I'm not up with the developments."

Rose was puzzled. "Then is there something else," he asked, "that one ought to know about on the Tresilian front?"

"Well, yes—there is. There sure is." Delver hesitated. "And I'd like to talk to you about it. If you have the time."

"Come to my room now." This, Rose thought, was scarcely the same confident Delver whom he had first re-encountered a few weeks before. It looked as if the arts had been misbehaving and failing to interrelate themselves as they should. "Of course I've time. And there's something I'd like to have your opinion on."

As if they had an old and established habit, they turned left and walked through the Roman Gallery. The emperors and matrons, constrained to stand like flunkeys in menial files, asserted in retaliation an oppressive silence; among them the unknown patrician boy who was also Bruno Landreth seemed to meditate some deft and unobtrusive mischief. They turned right by the Capitoline Venus, frozen while declaring the lucid and unmysterious sensuality of Greece, and passed once more through the muddled dynasties of Egypt, the confused and gloomy pantheon of Osiris and Isis. Before a representation of these two divinities, cut in lateral relief on a tomb, Delver came momentarily to a halt. Then he walked on abruptly. "Isn't it here"—he asked with an odd effect of thrusting something out of his mind —"that there's a bellowing hippopotamus?"

"Yes, in blue faience. But I prefer the really comical one in the Louvre. It has water weeds painted all over it." Rose glanced curiously at his companion. "My favourite thing of that sort here is a polychrome glass fish. I believe it dates from about 1370 B.C."

"Do you know, I think this is a depressing kind of place, Rose. D you walk through it every day?"

Rose's surprise grew. "Well, I commonly take one devious route or another. The direct access to my department is from Montague Place. But one learns quite a lot by simply drifting around."

Delver said nothing more. He didn't speak until they were in Rose's room. This, although evincing the basic lack of amenity everywhere achieved by Her Majesty's Office of Works, was rather lavishly provided by its occupant with objects worth looking at. But Delver, as he sat down, showed no curiosity. "Say," he said quickly, "—do you begin. Tell me about this guy Burntisland that the London newspapers are full of. Does all the ballyhoo add up to a real threat to the paintings?"

"Most decidedly it does. And the amazing thing is how quickly it's grown. They've had several strokes of pure luck, of course. Such as the Afro-Asian gent."

"For heaven's sake! Who's he?"

328

"I call him that because I've no idea where he hails from. He's been holding an exhibition in a picture shop in the West End. He was billed as inspired by Indian temple sculpture—and you know what some of that's like. I'd judge it more likely he began simply from the illustrations in some textbook of gynaecology. He took them over, blew them up, schematized and convoluted them, and the result was a sort of semi-abstract art that you had to wonder whether or not you were bringing a dirty mind to. Only you didn't have to wonder very hard. Only the other day, a metropolitan magistrate found the job not too hopelessly difficult. An instructed eye, of course, could see no possible relationship between such rubbish and the last Tresilians. But the case has certainly given a fillip to the other side."

"The other side?" Delver's mind seemed still to be struggling with something else. "You're really in on this?"

"I was a not very active member of the committee that got the exhibition going. Now I do feel drawn in. One can't—one simply can't—let such things happen. They've presented virtually an ultimatum, you know. We face it, as I mentioned, this afternoon. An actual confrontation with old Burntisland. And they've made a clever move there. He's heavy metal, in his way. He knows no more about art than a Hottentot, or rather he knows a great deal less. But there's something estimable about him. They've been pushing him damned hard."

Delver looked up from an unseeing inspection of a Bokhara rug. "You keep on talking about *they*," he said. "Will you tell me just who *they* are?"

Rose shrugged his shoulders, a gesture he wasn't at all addicted to. "Small-time newspaper people running a stunt? A powerful proprietor deviously pursuing a vendetta? One can take one's choice. But it's a fellow called Madrona who's perhaps the chief target. He's a great patron of modern art. And he's extravagantly wealthy. That may help us. Only I wish I could feel sure that, when it comes to a showdown, Madrona has what it takes. I don't really see him standing up to Burntisland, if Burntisland stays the course."

"Why shouldn't he stay the course?"

"He's old. And they've been driving him hard, as I said. Persuading him that in every conceivable way London is a sink of iniquity. Not a nice change of diet for a respectable old person.

329

Physically or nervously, he may crack up. But it's not a thing to bank on. I tell you I don't like the state of the case, Delver. And now, only this morning, those confounded Oxford dons have made it worse. Their action has been utterly ludicrous. But it reads damned awkwardly, all the same."

"Jesus Christ!" Delver, although preoccupied, was plainly startled by the direction of this new indictment. "What has Oxford got to do with it?"

"As you know, there's a college there that has one of the finest—and certainly the largest—of the middle-period Tresilians. Nobody in his senses could see in it what some not quite lunatic people are now imagining they see in the final things. But it's been removed from view."

"Removed? You mean to say that the Fellows—"

"One Fellow. The vacation isn't over yet, and the dons are dispersed. The Tresilian has been removed by one of them, Philip Leech, acting on his authority as a Pro-Provost. He's reckoning on our being beaten here in London, and on his therefore getting retrospective approval for his action from his Governing Body. Obviating an occasion of scandal—some rubbish of that sort."

"Why on earth should this Leech do such a thing?"

"College politics. He's dead set on killing his Provost's party, which has gone rather out on a limb in the direction of the arts. Madrona comes in again there. He wants to give the college —his own old college—his collection of modern paintings, complete with a gallery to house them. Leech thinks it isn't the function of Oxford colleges to go in for that sort of thing. Perhaps he has something in that. He thinks that if Madrona can be discredited as having pushed a painter of dirty pictures in Tresilian he can then be further discredited as the owner or donor of a great deal of mere rubbish. The Provost and his party will be routed, and the college recalled to its proper intellectual pursuits. Although I'm an art historian like yourself, Delver, I see some sense in Leech's position. But I won't forgive his taking down that Tresilian. And I wish I could be sure he hasn't been egging on poor old Burntisland in a ruthless and even unscrupulous way, just as that damned newspaper has." Rose paused, glanced at Delver, and was again aware of being puzzled. "I suppose," he said, almost accusingly, "you've *seen* the exhibition by this time?"

"Yes. I saw it Wednesday."

"Then you can give me the opinion I want from you. Setting all this nonsense of Burntisland's and the rest aside, what is your opinion of Tresilian as a painter now? You've never seen anything like so much of his work in one place before. How does your verdict go? Is he still the great English painter of his age?"

Delver was silent. He was looking at the Bokhara rug again. This time he appeared to be studying it.

Rose laughed—a shade impatiently. "I'll give you a lead," he said. "Just *my* lead. I say Yes."

"I guess that's how I suppose I feel." Delver produced this dubitating credo slowly and with a frown. "You've never felt, I take it, that there was a kind of blindness in him?"

"A blindness!" Rose was astonished. "Wouldn't that be a pretty stiff disability in a painter?"

"Or say a recklessness. Perhaps he was prone to going ahead in an unconsidered way, knowing that he had a brilliant power of extemporizing a solution when things got sticky. He *was* clever, you know. Think of that early mastery of all those optical tricks. Perhaps he was too clever. Perhaps he lacked, in a last analysis, the responsibility and integrity of a great artist. And the discipline not to overreach himself, not to go one better and too far."

"Well, I'm blessed!" Rose's was much more than a rhetorical astonishment. "I'd call that the voice of the opposition—of the rational opposition, that is, as distinct from Burntisland and his crowd. Do you realize how much you're changing ground?"

"Am I?" Delver asked the question out of what came to Rose as a deep bewilderment. "Perhaps so. But I haven't yet given the whole exhibition a fair spin. I spent most of my time with the final things. In a way, I think I found them comforting."

"Comforting? That's an odd word. And particularly odd as applied to the last Tresilians. I find them disturbing, I frankly confess. Not in Burntisland's naïve sense, which I take to be of copulating couples and worse lurking in the design, like concealed faces in children's puzzle pictures. But rather—"

"I'm not so sure. I'm not so sure of what images aren't forcing themselves upon the canvas in devious ways. What I am pretty sure of is that these last paintings are *not* vitiated by the sort of irresponsibility, the sort of disabling cleverness, I've been speaking of." Delver looked at Rose very seriously. "Their integrity is absolute. And for twenty years God alone knew what evil thing they confront, or declare to be not confrontable. Unfortunately God hasn't continued keeping the knowledge to himself." Delver got to his feet, and restlessly walked the length of the room. "I've been in Cornwall again," he said.

Rose felt no disposition to treat this as a *non sequitur*. "Well?" he asked.

"But that's not where to begin, I guess." Delver seemed again to be fighting bewilderment. "You ought to know that I've found out quite a lot about Matthew Tresilian's writing." He laughed shortly. "About what brought me to England, that is."

"Then I suppose I must congratulate you."

"Thanks a lot." Delver made a wry face. "And I was right, you know. He *could* write. Only he used his power in some darn queer ways. For example, he wrote some very authentic wartime reminiscences. Then he shoved in what was in fact a spurious account of the death of his own son, and gave the result to a former mistress to stitch into a novel if she wanted to."

"That certainly sounds a shade odd."

"He made a second marriage in romantic and rather creditable circumstances. Then he seems to have written, once more, a jazzed up account of the whole affair. What is one to make of that?"

Rose smiled. "Nothing more, surely, than that writing wasn't his main job, so that he took it rather lightly. It's true you're reporting activities that seem insensitive or in poor taste. But artists are queer cattle, after all."

"But his writing was an artist's job. He couldn't stop being an artist, could he, simply by laying down his brushes and taking up a pen? I'm troubled, for a start, by the notion of his having made a wrong use of artistic power. I remember our talking about something of the sort."

"And I remember your declaring that Tresilian's shade was going to smile upon your biographical researches. Whereas—" Rose broke off. Some small impatience had prompted him to this mildly tart speech. He was startled by the sharp distress it appeared to have occasioned. "I'm sorry," he said. "There must be something I haven't got hold of—and something that isn't just a question of a dead painter's artistic integrity."

"There is." Delver had ceased pacing the room. He was now standing between two large portfolios and looking straight at Rose. He had the appearance of one who has placed himself in a dock.

"Listen, Rose. I was in Cornwall Tuesday. I saw the children : Luke Tresilian and Mrs Crinnis. Wednesday I went to the exhibition. I saw the last Tresilians. Almost all of them, I suppose. Yesterday I was in Cornwall again. They sent me back there."

"I don't follow," Rose said. "Who sent you back there?"

"Those last paintings did. Or the pain and evil I sensed in them."

"I see." Rose made this rejoinder as a matter of colloquial convention. He was feeling that he very much didn't see. All that he saw was, once more, an unfamiliar Delver. Pain and evil, he reflected, belonged to a class of terms not hitherto prominent in the technical vocabulary of the Professor of the Interrelations of the Arts. "Do you mean," he asked, "that if you hadn't gone to Cornwall on Tuesday you might have missed this quite fresh perception on Wednesday?"

"Just that. It doesn't sound sense—but just that. To begin with I saw the boy, Luke. He's a pretty normal sort of kid, perhaps with a streak of what got Matthew Tresilian where he did. I liked Luke, although he hadn't much to offer me. He told me to go right ahead and see his sister. His half-sister, he was meaning. She's Mrs Crinnis, and her husband looks after a lighthouse. So I went to the lighthouse."

"Like Mr Ramsay and his children." Rose didn't know why he had made this idiotic literary joke. It could only, he supposed, be an impulse to sidestep the advance of something he didn't care for. Certainly a disturbing tension was tightening its grip on Thayne Delver. And now Delver was disconcerted rather than amused. "I'm sorry," Rose said. "Go on."

"I encountered this Mrs Crinnis in unexpected circumstances, over which I won't waste time. They gave me a kind of temporary standing with her, without which I'd never have seen the inside of that lighthouse. Or rather of one of the cottages tacked on to it." Delver made this correction conscientiously. "I wish to hell I hadn't."

333

"Did you meet Mr Crinnis?"

"Sure I met Mr Crinnis. He's a religious fanatic, and his home-chat comes straight out of the Bible. No harm in that. But there was something between him and his wife that I couldn't get at. For that matter, that one or another of *them* couldn't get at. Or couldn't *quite* get at. Or had never consciously acknowledged having got at. Christ! I just couldn't fix the thing. I can't convey it to you, Rose. But there I was, pursuing what you call with your damned English irony my biographical researches, and with all hell beginning to heave beneath the floor as a result."

"Hell? My dear chap!"

"Or beginning to breathe, say, just for a start, through some tiny crack or fissure. And it might have closed up again—if I hadn't spoken out of turn. Isn't that your phrase?"

"My phrase?" For a moment Rose didn't realize that he was being appealed to on a point of English idiom. "Oh, I see. Do you mean that you're blaming yourself about something?"

"It isn't as if I hadn't been warned. Listen. I'd picked up a piece of information—a small, harmless piece of information—from a woman called Mary Emeleus. She'd told me other things, too."

"The novelist?"

"Yes. I haven't given you an account of that, and needn't now. But there was this small thing—you might call it about the least significant thing she came out with. Well, I happened to reveal my knowledge of it when talking to Tresilian's daughter—when talking to her alone. It troubled her. So, as I say, I'd been warned. Then why, in God's name, with this heave at my feet and smell in my nostrils, and knowing that my only wisdom, before I couldn't tell what, was to quit while I could, did I come out with the thing again in my last thirty seconds with the woman's crazy husband?"

Rose found himself wishing that he could credit Delver with a melodramatic streak. Being unable to do this, he could only look at him gravely and in silence.

"It was no more than the name of a place in Cornwall, Rose. Malcar. The place where Tresilian sent his children—not that either was any longer a child—to be out of the way of Hitler's bombs and rockets. Crinnis had never heard of it—never heard of it, I mean, in that connection. And the mention of it took him over the horizon pretty well as if he had been a rocket himself. But at least it *was* over the horizon. I was afraid, you see, that he was going to attack his wife. Not that I hadn't seen he was fond of her. Which made the whole thing more ugly and ominous." Delver came forward from his odd position between the portfolios and sat down squarely in front of Rose. "Have you any notion," he asked, "what I'm talking about?"

"You're talking about having inadvertently stirred some old memory, or prompted some dormant suspicion, in this man Crinnis. Some infidelity, or supposed infidelity, I take it. And it's certainly unfortunate. It's a queer consequence of your entirely harmless and honourable curiosities, my dear chap. But are you not making rather a lot of it, taking it rather hard?"

"I've been to Malcar. There comes a point with curiosity at which you just can't stop off. Not that it was disinterested curiosity any more. Partly—and as I've said—it was what I felt before those last Tresilians a couple of days ago. Partly it was the thought that, if I could find out, I could perhaps help. I went to Malcar—as Crinnis had done."

"Crinnis had? You mean when he disappeared over the horizon?"

"Just that. It became very clear that he'd been there. I was going round in his footsteps, more or less."

"What sort of a place is this Malcar?"

"God-forsaken, I'd say, beyond any spot in England. Of course, that may have been what you'd call a subjective impression. I was there, after all, with the imagination of disaster obsessing me."

"The imagination of disaster? You're using the most damnably strong language about all this." Rose looked at Delver's face, and his uneasiness grew. "Don't you need to distance this awkward affair a little, get it in a longer perspective?"

"It has it's own long perspectives. I've been peering down them. I've been hunting in hiding places many, many years deep."

"Well—it's your job, I suppose." For a moment Rose tried to hold an astringent note. "How did it feel?"

"Not *like* my job. Not like my job as I've always regarded it : harmless and honourable, as you say. I'd shed the luxury of being a scholar, Rose. I was a low fellow rummaging in a hotel register, or kneeling at a key-hole. Figuratively, that is. A private eye, but no glamour."

"My dear man! And you felt you had to?"

"In a queer way, it was the only honourable course left to me. Finding out. Collecting the gossip of old women. Gossip, I suppose, that in a few years would have mumbled itself away into silence."

"And you managed that? I'd have supposed they'd have kept it for each other, your old women."

"They'd had Alfred Crinnis to loosen them up."

"Can what you've come upon ever have the status of more than gossip? Would it be verifiable?"

"Probably not." Delver paused. "They didn't even remember the names, those old women. It was just something happening that doesn't happen all that infrequently in such isolated places, it seems. We've been brought up, you know, you and I, on a Wordsworthian view of rural society. I noticed, by the way, that Luke Tresilian's favourite writer is Hardy. He had a row of his books in his room. You get something a bit different in Hardy."

"No doubt." Rose was unenthusiastic before this digression.

"But not all that different. When he was an old man, Hardy said that if he'd told the truth about village life no one would have stood it."

"I don't see—"

"I think I'm only saying that it must have been the spirit of that inbred, direly poor community, yet further closed down on by the war, that brought the thing about. Or that gave the last fatal prompting."

Rose shifted in his chair, like a canoeist who sees rapids ahead. "But nobody," he asked, "has really put two and two together except yourself?"

"Myself and Crinnis. Rose, I'm desperate! I feel I must do something. And yet there's nothing I can do."

"If I'm to go by the tone you're speaking in, I don't think there is, except to pray that Crinnis will get the right answer from his Bible. And that may be to lock away in his heart whatever it is he's come upon. You'd better do the same. Except that, if you trust me, it might be a good idea to speak the thing out now. It will grow a little less enormous, perhaps." Rose spoke quietly. "This sort of affair isn't my line, any more than it's yours. But we both know that there's nothing to be said for making a to-do about the face of evil."

"I guess you're right there."

"Whom does this thing most affect?"

"I'd say the boy, Luke Tresilian."

"He is the son, not of Matthew Tresilian, but of Matthew Tresilian's daughter Faith?"

"Yes. And his father was Matthew Tresilian's son John."

There had been a long silence. It was broken by Rose.

"And this man Crinnis," he asked, "knew nothing?"

"Perhaps he knew that his wife was Luke's mother. Perhaps it was an acknowledged, or unacknowledged, secret between them. But the full truth was utterly unknown to him. I'm sure of that."

"He may have had some brooding, almost unconscious, notion of *something*?"

"Yes."

"I don't quite see why the mention of this place Malcar—"

"Nor do I. But it was something that had been concealed from him. And he's mad, you know—I'm sure of that—with the kind of madness that flares up in fantastic suspicion. Only what he actually dug up at Malcar happened to be sober history. Village history. Folks' memory of the brother and sister who had behaved in such a way that there could be small doubt about the trouble when it came. And who then vanished."

There was silence again, while Rose seemed to cast round for speech. "No doubt it's foolish," he managed, "to think of such things as happening only in Jacobean plays. But still—" He broke off, and the silence resumed itself.

"You see," Delver said presently, "they'd been growing up in London. And suddenly they were pitched into that back-of-beyond."

"Yes."

"And pitched, you might say, into their own racial past. And it had happened as a kind of relegation, and because of their father's sexual involvement with another woman. And soon the boy would be taken away to the war. All these things. Of course, there must have been some underlying intensity or perversity of relationship between the children to give the thing a start."

337

"One supposes so," Rose said. He looked almost irritably at Delver. "Tresilian might have arranged something simpler, mightn't he, when this untoward family affair broke on him? He might have found a husband for his unfortunate daughter. Or simply backed her in having an illegitimate baby by some man unknown. It was happening often enough at that time—as at all times—heaven knows."

"He had his habitual impulse, I suppose one must say, to contrive a *tour de force* in the face of disaster."

"My God!"

"Think of that Polish second wife. A foreigner, and with only a year or two to live, and owing him, after all, a debt of gratitude. Having her, Tresilian needed only seclusion for the two women, which I suppose his retreat at a place called Lancraddock provided, and a doctor, whom he had in the friend who is now Luke's guardian and who was then in practice there. He took a dizzying risk when he wrote up an improved version of the whole fiction as a legacy for the child. But he would have got away with it, if only he hadn't died famous." Delver laughed forlornly. "In the fullness of time, a pious biographer came along."

"It was certainly the literary elaboration, the artist's touch, that was novel." Rose judged unwholesome Delver's disposition to dwell upon the hazards of research among the recently dead. "I don't know how it may be in America. But, in the pretence you've stumbled on, Tresilian got a start from what is common enough among the English agricultural poor. Children whose actual begetting might bring in the police are quietly fixed up with less embarrassing parentages. There's plenty of collusion. Nobody *wants* the police—including the police. People feel, I suppose"—Rose tried slightly hardening his tone—"that it's a matter for God, and not for the magistrates. It was only in this century, I think, that what these two near-children did became an indictable offence at common law. Which doesn't mean that a vast horror doesn't attend it. Tresilian was almost freakishly clever when the crisis came along. But it shook him, all the same."

"It certainly did that." Delver seemed momentarily to emerge from his deep personal distress. "We *know* about the final paintings now. They're the record of how the thing really came to him. He had to paint what it's like to be able to see only what can't be looked at. You remember he called one of them 'A Kind of Avarice'?"

"He often gave his works bizarre titles. It was a fashion."

"Yes—but it isn't without significance, that one. It comes back to me. Some mediaeval philosopher—might it have been Thomas Aquinas?—describes incest as just that. The hoarding within an unnatural compass of what should be as out-going as charity."

"It's an interesting way of looking at it," Rose said. "But a little on what one may call the scholastic side."

CHAPTER THIRTY-FIVE

Aᴀꜰᴛᴇʀ ʙʀᴇᴀᴋꜰᴀꜱᴛ Lᴜᴋᴇ had gone upstairs to pack his
trunk. The occupation set him first chanting, then whistling, and
finally singing. It was because he was making this cheerful row
that he didn't at the start hear what was going on below. But
he did presently hear a man shouting, and when he had paused
to listen for a moment he decided it was a sound he didn't like
at all. So he shot downstairs in a hurry. The disturbance was
coming from the room Dr Dolben still called his surgery. Luke
walked in.

Dr Dolben was sitting at his desk. What struck Luke about
him at once was that he appeared to be ten years younger than
he had been half an hour before. He was as Luke remembered
him when he was still in practice and some pretty formidable
occasion had suddenly presented itself. He was sitting very still
in his chair, intently watching the man who seemed to have
broken in upon him. The man looked like a tramp of the
strangest and wildest sort. His clothes were torn and muddied as
if he had been through hedges and ditches. He was shouting
again—and now he was making a movement towards Dr Dolben
that Luke didn't care for.

"Shall I chuck him out?" Luke asked.

Dr Dolben didn't turn his head. He still watched the man
fixedly. "Luke," he said, "leave the room."

Luke hadn't received so stern a command for years. He might
even have turned round to obey, if the tramp hadn't made
obedience impossible by a sudden leap that barred his path.
There was something about this that disconcerted Luke still more.
And in a second he knew what it was. A scrum-half puts in a
lot of time calculating just how human bodies can move in a
given situation. And the tramp, who was an elderly man,
oughtn't to have been able to move like that. The tramp was
in possession, for the time, of some uncommon source of
energy.

340

"Is he mad?" Luke asked. "Shall I tackle him?"

"Stay still." Dr Dolben spoke in a low voice. He hadn't, as yet, once glanced at Luke. "He'll be mad, all right, in no time now. Meanwhile, he's making a start with raving. He's talking nonsense. Remember that." He raised an arm, and pointed a steady index-finger at the tramp. "Quieten down," he said. "Your shouting will alarm my neighbours. They'll call the police. And off you'll go. So be silent."

And, for a moment, the man was silent. Or he was silent except for his breathing. It was deep and stertorous. There might have been a great animal in the room.

"You had better have something in writing, hadn't you?" Dr Dolben asked. He reached for a writing-pad and a pencil. "One ought always to have that. So I'll write it all down."

Momentarily the man seemed uncertain and bewildered. The pencil moved rapidly. Dr Dolben talked at the same time. "Of course, you did right to come," he said. "We must have a full explanation. That's only reasonable. And you're a reasonable man. And a godly man. Truths are revealed to you."

The scribbling was finished, and Luke was aware that the pad had been slanted towards him. Standing by his guardian's desk, he glanced down and read:

Faith's husband, Alfred Crinnis. Wild delusions. Get out and send the police. *Don't return yourself*. You exacerbate him. *Go now*.

Luke glanced at the window. He could get through it easily enough. But it seemed a bad plan. He couldn't possibly leave his guardian with a madman. Dr Dolben was forgetting that he was eighteen and pretty tough.

"No," he said. "Use the telephone. I can hold him off. I can knock him out."

"You child of sin!"

Luke stiffened, less at the man's words than at something new in his voice. He spoke loudly, but it wasn't a shout. Rather the voice rang out with a strange authority.

"On your knees!" the man said. "The whore your mother is on her knees."

341

"Luke," Dr Dolben said quietly, "I promise you that this man is on the brink of absolute insanity. I've had such cases. In a matter of hours, of minutes, he'll be in a coma. And any world he wakens to later will be a world of utter delusion. It's a matter of uncontrollable chemical changes taking place in his brain."

"These shall stand upon mount Ebal to curse," Crinnis said, "Reuben, Gad, and Asher, and Zebulun, Dan, and Naphtali." Luke saw that something was happening to Crinnis's eyes, and that his complexion was altering strangely. He saw, too, that his guardian was watching these things. "God shall pour down rain upon the sinners," Crinnis said, "snares, fire and brimstone, storm and tempest : this shall be their portion to drink." His body began to twitch. "For lo," he said, "the Lord is come out of his place to visit the wickedness of such—" He broke off. He was finding difficulty in articulation. "Wickedness?" he said. "Child of no common wickedness. Child of abomination. Child—"

"Stop !"

Dr Dolben had spoken in such a tone as Luke had never heard. It held Crinnis up—and now the man was swaying on his feet. Luke had a moment's grotesque vision of a face prepared for shaving, and saw that there was foam welling from the man's mouth. And the man spoke through it, hoarsely, in a whisper.

"Deuteronomy, twenty-seven, twenty-two," Crinnis whispered.

For a second Crinnis's eyes were full on Luke, and then he had spun round and fallen rigidly across a chair. Luke sprang forward and tried to ease him into it. And as he felt the man's body in his arms he experienced the first distinguishable emotion that this nightmarish scene had roused in him. It was of momentary extreme terror. "His body," he said. "Something's happened to it."

"All right, Luke. It can be manipulated." Dr Dolben came forward, and together they somehow managed to arrange Crinnis in the chair. Dr Dolben then raised the inert body's right arm, and composed it queerly in an attitude of salute. Crinnis held the pose like a statue. "Yes," Dr Dolben said, and gently lowered the arm, "a cataleptic trance is well in the picture. He'll have nothing to say for himself for some time, if ever, poor chap.

Which is a relief, after all that raving and religious mania. Luke, you might just fetch—" Dr Dolben paused, as if he hadn't quite quickly enough thought of what Luke might fetch. "You might just fetch some warm water, would you? There's nothing I can do, but we might as well sponge his face. And I'll call the ambulance. The mental hospital's our friend's next berth."

Luke found that he had fetched the water before any real thought about all this came to him. What first struck him was the fact of his being more dazed than even the oddity of the thing need have made him. But then, although the thing was surprising as well as odd, he wasn't surprised. This made him realize that an event had happened of a kind, of a size, before which surprise doesn't operate. And the lack of surprise was making him feel that the thing was a fact he had always known, or at least always suspected. But this wasn't so. The thing had been utterly unknown to him.

Luke put the bowl of water down on Dr Dolben's desk and understood—now, in this instant, for the first time understood— what the thing was that the man, in effect, had said. Faith was his, Luke's, mother. He, Luke, was Faith's illegitimate child.

Luke pressed out the small sponge that he had brought and handed it to Dr Dolben. "Is it true?" he asked. "Is it true that Faith's my mother?"

Dr Dolben wiped the foam from Crinnis's immobile face with a steady hand. He seemed like a man who has made up his mind and is being careful not to hesitate. "Yes, Luke," he said. "That is true."

Luke had a confused impression that his own face was being sponged. He was feeling the hot tears. And he heard his own sobbing. He didn't try to crush these things. He let them happen for what was probably a long time, his strong limbs curled like a child's in a corner of his guardian's sofa. Then he sat up. "But why?" he cried passionately. "Oh, but why? Why was I robbed of her? Why had I to be taken from her? It's stupid, stupid, stupid! My father—" He caught, through eyes that were dry again, Dr Dolben's expression, and he paused, bewildered. "My grandfather," he said, "—but he was mad, mad! He was a great artist, wasn't he? And invented lies—lies and lies and lies—to cover up so—so simple a thing as an illegitimate baby!" His voice dropped. "He wrote it all down—nonsense, utter nonsense —and left it me as my dearest possession. The world's mad. This man's only joining in." He looked up at his guardian. 'Sir," he said, "What have you to say?"

"Your grandfather did it for the best." Dr Dolben was feeling for words. "Matthew Tresilian was a much older man than I, but he was my closest friend. And I say he did it for the best. We must think no evil of him. And we must take things slowly, Luke. There's a lot to be thought about." This time, Dr Dolben did hesitate. "I have to think. And I no longer do it quickly. Wait, please wait. Ah! There's the ambulance."

Luke didn't hear this. He was on his feet, and glaring at Crinnis : Crinnis, who seemed like a dead man. He pointed. "And I've never seen him before," he said. "That's the measure of how I've been kept from her. And what will he have done to her, the filthy lunatic? I'm going to her now."

"Luke—"

"I'm going to the lighthouse. I can find it, can't I? I'm going to take the car. You can't stop me. It would be wrong."

"Very well. Perhaps it would be wrong. Get the car out. But I must come too." Dr Dolben turned back to his desk—and Luke, through all his passionate absorption, saw that he was no longer younger, but much older; that he was a tired old man. "I need only write a note and say a word," Dr Dolben said. "Five minutes. And perhaps when driving over we can—" He broke off, and sat down heavily. "Perhaps I can think."

Luke saw no need to think. He wanted simply to take advantage of the fact that, with only two on board, the small new car for which they had recently exchanged their lumbering old one had a splendid turn of speed. Ten minutes later Dr Dolben, had he not been preoccupied, might have been reminding him that he had only just ceased to be a learner-driver. But Luke knew that he could take corners as if on his bicycle. He knew that, once up on the moor, he could go very fast indeed. Unless the madman had done some fearful thing, there was no reason why the sinful folly of eighteen years should not be ended within the hour.

They drove, then, in a trance of speed. Eventually Dr Dolben spoke. He spoke with immense effort, as if he had some dire thing to communicate. "We'll need petrol," he said.

They stopped at the first garage, and were attended to by a small, dark man with malicious eyes. Luke was large and fair, and would have acknowledged that his own gaze was candid to the point of idiocy. But now, simply encountering this unknown man, he was made suddenly conscious of a darkness in his own blood. It was a feeling—obscurely racial, he supposed—that sometimes came to him on the lonely, upland places. After he had read his first memorable books—*The King of the Golden River* and *Puck of Pook's Hill* and *The Hobbit*—he had begun to build this feeling into his own private myth of Lyonnesse. The myth told, in part, of a dark, secret people, driven by fair and blue-eyed conquerors deep underground, and toiling in their subterranean galleries at an evil undermining of the land, so that finally they achieved catastrophe, and the ocean rolled over all the broad fields and pastures between Scilly and what thus became Land's End. Luke in this fantasy was a child of the conquering race who felt the ominous pioneering as a faint pulsation of the earth. But nobody believed him. One day he heard the sound of picks and shovels coming from a cavern. He entered, and there the dark people were. After that the myth grew cloudy. Perhaps he had been subjected to some potent and terrible initiation. For, although he escaped, it was to carry some of those people's darkness for ever afterwards within him.

Now, at the garage, the man took his money silently, and went back into his prosaic dwelling as if into a cave. They drove on. But the small encounter, and the recollection it prompted, had changed Luke's mood. He was urgent for knowledge, desperate for clear thought. The monstrous wrong came up on him again as owning dimensions that required a largeness of explanation he couldn't get a glimpse of.

"But *why*?" he flung at his guardian. "It's been too unnatural! When did—when did she marry that man?"

"In 1949, I think."

"Earlier, before I was born, did she have any sort of religious mania, as the man has now?"

"I don't think so."

"It's senseless. And why didn't I ever see the queerness of it? Hardly ever to have met her, although she was supposed to be a half-sister, over years and years!"

345

"They were a long time overseas, remember. Crinnis kept something called the Wurlee Light. In Flores Straits."

"Damn Flores Straits." Luke gave a vicious but controlled jab at the accelerator. "They've been at this place on the south coast for three years. And I've never been there once. In all that time I've seen her only once—at some meaningless family funeral. It was unnatural. And yet I never gave a thought to it. I did write to her from time to time. But nothing came of it. I ought to have seen there was *something*."

"A half-sister, with whom one has never lived, needn't be much in one's thoughts, I suppose."

"And everybody lied to me. Explicitly or implicitly, they lied. *You* lied." Luke, although still driving very fast, for a moment turned his head to glance at his guardian. "But it's nonsense!" he cried in a kind of despair. "You're not that sort of person. Not a bit. *Why*?"

Dr Dolben looked grey now, as well as old. The mad ride might have been making him sick. "Luke," he said, "there's nothing to be said that's for me to say. Or not yet. Wait. It's for her to speak first." He paused. "When I've prepared her."

Luke gripped the wheel. "I go straight to her," he said. "Nothing comes between me and that. Nothing." Hazardously, he put out one hand and touched his guardian's arm. "Not even you."

Dr Dolben made no reply; it was as if there were a point he had no mind to concede. They were near the south coast now, and in a maze of narrow, high-banked lanes. Luke drove with a strange certainty, as if the route had been long in his dreams. Quite suddenly, the lighthouse lay below them. Beyond the green turf running up to it, its dead white buildings and squat tower showed like some large graveyard memorial in an uncouth taste.

"There's a track on the right," Dr Dolben said. "I think the car will take it."

They bumped down a track between steep banks, and the lighthouse disappeared. When it became visible again it was quite close. And Luke cried out in horror. "They've brought that man —they've brought Crinnis—back here!"

There was certainly an ambulance before the lighthouse, and

two or three men were standing round it. For a second Dr Dolben didn't speak, and when he did his voice, for the first time, was not wholly controlled. "No," he said. "It isn't that. That's not the Padstow ambulance." He waited until the car had come to a halt. "Luke," he said, "I think that, after all, you'd better let me go in first. It's a medical emergency, I suppose. I'll send out a message, or come back at once."

"Very well." Luke had a long habit of respecting his guardian's proposals, and with an effort he continued this habit now. "But quickly." He was staring at the ambulance. Its doors were open, and it was empty. "Please."

Dr Dolben climbed from the car and swung open a little gate. Luke was conscious of somebody coming down a path to meet him. He himself, having promised, waited. He sat and looked stonily at the ambulance. His long limbs were cramped in the miniature car, and he felt that it had the dimensions of a coffin. He shifted his position. He still kept his gaze from the lighthouse, but it now fell on the garden wall, close by the ambulance. He saw that there was a stretcher propped against this. It was dripping with sea-water. It had been set up like that to dry.

He was aware of not being able to tell how time was passing. But his heart had begun to thump, and he thought confusedly that if he counted its beats it might help. He tried to hear the sea, but heard only a gull crying—that and a single high, faint note which also seemed to come down from the air.

Dr Dolben was back. He was standing by Luke's window; he had put a hand through it and taken Luke by the arm. "You can come in now," he said. "But, Luke, first I must tell you. There's nothing can be done."

"She's dead?"

"Yes."

Again a gull cried, and there was the same strange sound in the air.

"Did Crinnis—"

"No, no, Luke. Nothing about Crinnis. It's supposed that she met with an accident. Only a few hours ago. It must have been an instantaneous death."

Strangely, Luke's heart had stopped pounding, and his mind had come quite clear. He wasn't aware of much that could be called feeling, except of horror before the thought that perhaps

347

this thing was going to be emotionally null and meaningless to him. "Tell me," he said.

"It seems that, some days ago, she rescued a child from a dangerous place on the cliff. The child had gone down after a ball. The ball remained. They suppose that, very rashly, she went after the ball again this morning. She never reached it. It's there still."

Luke had climbed from the car. It was a relief to stand up straight, and now something in him made him stand up very straight indeed. "But of course that's not true," he said. "She killed herself. Didn't she?"

"It won't be supposed so. She saw to it that the ball would prevent that."

A bitterness that took him by surprise broke from Luke. "Lies to the end," he said.

They were walking up the little path, between loops of white-painted rope or cable. Dr Dolben stopped and took Luke's arm. He glanced round, as if anxious that they should have one more exchange in private. "I don't know how it would have worked out," he said, "or that it could have been other than painful and baffling. But now it can never happen : a meeting on that new ground. You must accept it like that, Luke, and let be. The story belongs to the past, and now there can be no sequel to it. What you had best bring to it is charity, acceptance, silence."

Luke felt for a moment only an inexplicable chill before these words; then he tried to struggle with the sense of them. "Do you mean," he said, "that I should go on calling myself the son of the man who was really my grandfather; that I should live out the rest of my life under those false colours? That just doesn't come to me as right or natural. And I must see her. I'm going on."

Dr Dolben said nothing more, and they went inside in silence. There was a policeman and another man—perhaps a doctor—in a small, bleak room. Nobody spoke, and now Dr Dolben simply pointed to a door on the right. Alone, Luke went through it. He was in a bedroom which was almost entirely occupied by a big bed. On this the dead woman lay.

For a moment he was conscious of something he had read about : the peacefulness and dignity of death. Then the horror of feeling nothing gripped him in earnest. He had an impulse to kneel down and pray, to kiss the cold forehead from which somebody had combed back the wet hair. He refrained from these acts because he knew they would be wrong. One fishes, dredges, drags for a drowned corpse, but not for one's own emotions. He stood dry-eyed and quite still. And slowly feeling came to him. It was of an immense desolation.

The big bed in the small room gave him the sense of an unnatural place; it was like a tomb in which, for a long time, rites not proper to a tomb had been celebrated. He looked around as if for something to hold on to, something familiar to him in other rooms as well. On the walls there was nothing but some sort of religious text, and this he didn't want to read. But at one side of the bed stood a small table. There was an open book on it, set down covers uppermost, as if his mother had been reading only minutes before, and had put it aside before dropping off to sleep. He looked at the spine, and saw that it was *Barchester Towers*. And suddenly his mother seemed to be with him in a whole new dimension, as if he had turned from a photograph to the identical scene focussed in some stereoscopic device. His sense of desolation grew, but it had turned from something chill here in the room to a warmth in his own heart and a sharp, hot pricking in his eyes. He dropped on his knees and wept. There was a taste of salt in his mouth. His tears were mingling with the cold sea water she had brought with her to her bed.

He got up to go. For he saw that his guardian had spoken the stern truth when he said there was nothing that could be done. The figure on the bed could receive no word of loyalty, listen to no argument, lighten no bewilderment. And it was not for him to cry aloud what one now dead had held secret for eighteen years. Charity, acceptance, silence: Dr Dolben had been right.

Yet for a moment he paused, irresolute. The extreme strangeness of what had been done, the inexplicability of a deception so monstrous, rose up again before him like a terror. Hardly knowing what he did, he walked round the big bed. There was another little table. There was another book. It was a Bible. All Crinnis's words came back to him; they seemed to take resonance as if in some vast, empty place. He picked up the book and turned the leaves.

Genesis, Exodus, Leviticus, Numbers, Deuteronomy.... He turned a final page and read:

Cursed be he that lieth with his sister, the daughter of his father, or the daughter of his mother. And all the people shall say, Amen.

Luke closed the Bible, and put it down. The inexplicable had been explained. He walked out of the room and out of the cottage, disregarding someone—he didn't know whom—who spoke to him as he went past. There was a high, thin note in the air. This time he thought it might be the wind in the grasses, for there was a little wind coming up. He walked away from the car, the ambulance, the lighthouse. He walked with no purpose in his mind, with scarcely a consciousness that he was skirting a rocky cove, following the ghost of a path that dipped and climbed.

He was standing still, looking down into a tremendous chasm at the bottom of which lay the sea. He thought vaguely that he hadn't known there was anywhere a gulf as deep as this. Then some small, bright thing stirred and caught his eye. It was the ball, perched on the verge of a part-crumbled, grassy ledge, to which one could climb down by a hazardous path. The ball quivered and shifted slightly; presently the rising wind would touch it and send it into the sea. He looked again and took the measure of the hazard: the path curved round an almost impossible place. Without any sense of motivation he went down the path and seriously studied this. There was an overhang which his height made additionally awkward. He lifted each foot in turn to examine the soles of his shoes; it doesn't do, he remembered, to have been treading on bluebell leaves before tackling rock. Then he went forward and negotiated the deadly spot with care. He reached the ledge, picked up the ball, and tossed it into space. It seemed to go down at first slowly and then very fast, like a free-falling object in a film. He didn't see it hit the water. He didn't see it float. The vestigial strip of turf shifted under his feet. He moved back to the overhang, and rounded it with absolute concentration upon the precision of his movements. When he had reached safety he walked away. He had done something entirely meaningless, he supposed. He hardly supposed that any action would again have meaning for him.

For what might have been a long time he continued walking. He seemed to get nowhere in particular, so that he wondered whether, in a small way, he was walking as lost people do in a desert, or prisoners in a yard : round again and round. But at his feet there were wild flowers : Milkwort and Stonecrop and Thrift and Sea Lavender. He stooped and gathered the faintly scented Thrift, the Sea Lavender miraculously thrusting out in tiny blue flames from the leafless scapes. When he had gathered what he wanted he looked round him collectedly, oriented himself, and walked back to the lighthouse. The small garden was as bleak as the cottage beyond it. It seemed too neat to allow of anything's being grown there. Only in the angle of a wall Nature seemed to have broken through, airborne, in a scattering of Sea Campion. He stopped to gather a few of the drooping flowers and add them to the others. Then he entered the cottage and walked through to the dead woman's room. He looked at his mother for the last time, laid the flowers on the bed at her feet, picked up the Bible, and came out again.

There was only an old woman in the living-room. She was putting a kettle on the stove, and had an air of settling in; he supposed that she had been summoned from the village to keep vigil by the body. She looked at him curiously, but said nothing when he didn't speak. The ambulance was still outside, but there seemed to be nobody else about. He guessed that his guardian, and perhaps others, were looking for him, and had missed his return. He felt this to be fortunate. He took a notebook from his pocket, tore out a page, and scribbled a note to Dr Dolben. He left this on the table, and beside it the Bible, open at the twenty-seventh chapter of Deuteronomy. And then he went out again into the open air.

There was some stir at the cottage next door, and he guessed that a replacement for Crinnis was being moved in. The stretcher still stood against the wall, but now it was almost dry. The ambulance, he thought, would provide Dr Dolben with transport.

Luke got into the car and drove away. His mind—what there was of it—was trying to remember about trains. He had very little idea of what the day had done to him. A numbness that seemed simply physical was coming over him. His whole body felt as his lower jaw did when the dentist had plugged it full of anaesthetic. Still, he could drive the car. And he had a train to catch. Otherwise, he would have to spend another night in Lyonnesse. And he did know that he wanted never again to do that.

CHAPTER THIRTY-SIX

"SHALL WE NOT wait any longer?" Jane Landreth asked. "Luke must have been delayed. We can make another pot when he comes."

Hatty nodded and stood up. "Very well," she said. "If Bruin promises not to eat the whole cake."

Bruno, who was making a great show of industry with Thucydides, nodded indulgently, and Hatty went into the kitchen. There had been a wholesome change, Jane thought, in the relations of her two younger children lately. Bruno's Finals were now only seven weeks away, and if he was less than previously inclined to provoke Hatty to equivocal combat it was perhaps because he was taking his work really seriously at last. But more significant was the fact that Hatty had simply got free of her brother; she responded to him or ignored him as she chose. And of this happy if belated exodus from the nursery Luke Tresilian was undoubtedly the guide and occasion. Any troubles into which Hatty's romance had run during the first days of the Easter Vacation appeared to have been dissipated through the agency of the ceaseless correspondence which the young man had been carrying on with her throughout the succeeding weeks. And now, at any minute, he was turning up again.

"Just what are my young friend's plans, Mum?" Bruno had closed his book like one who expects his tea and is willing, at the same time, to give a few minutes to merely domestic occasions. "Isn't there some question of a childish exam?"

"That's tomorrow. He should be here any time now, and he's staying for an early supper. He'll go to Oxford on the nine-five, cope with his Latin in the morning, and then come back here for the inside of a week until term begins. He'll run around with Hatty, I suppose, and see his father's pictures quite a lot."

"I wonder what he thinks about the row over them. I suppose it's still going on?"

"It most certainly is. There's some sort of meeting taking place now. Charles Rose is there, and so is Sir Hector, presumably with Lucilla in attendance. Lord Burntisland is presenting himself, and putting a case to the committee."

"I suppose this old dotard Burntisland is just a figurehead?"

"So we were inclined to think. But we were wrong. He's converted some eminent people to his point of view, and it's only his personal authority that makes the idiotic case against the final Tresilians pretty formidable. What he'll really be putting to Madrona and the rest is an ultimatum. If they don't withdraw that whole section of the exhibition at once, he'll be compelled to make representations to the law officers of the Crown. And it's probably true that he could get a prosecution started."

"How very silly."

"Yes, of course. But he's said to have got a real bee in his bonnet about Matthew Tresilian : something with the character of a personal animosity."

"Now, I wonder how that can have come about?" For a moment there hovered on Bruno's face an expression his mother hadn't seen for weeks : his celebrated wicked smile. But it faded away almost unborn, and it struck her that he was perhaps working not only steadily but actually too hard. Something almost pinched appeared at times in his delicate features. "He wouldn't," he asked, "by any chance come here?"

"Whatever are you talking about?" Jane looked at Bruno in surprise.

"Burntisland isn't likely to roll up on us?"

"What an odd idea ! Why ever should he?"

"Well, there's our tie-up with Madrona through Lucilla. And you're chums with Charles Rose. And you've been writing letters and things to the papers defending the pictures. Burntisland, being a bit cracked, might take it into his head to come and present an ultimatum to *you*."

"I can't think of anything less probable." Jane felt puzzled and obscurely disturbed. "You haven't ever met Lord Burntisland, have you?"

"Of course not. What could be less probable than *that*?"

"Tea up !" Hatty had stuck her head through the kitchen door. As she did so, the telephone bell rang. Her face brightened, and she hurried into the room. "That's Luke," she said. "Explaining himself, the idiot." She picked up the receiver, listened for a moment, and then held it out to her mother. "Charles Rose," she said briefly. "Come on, Bruin. Kitchen tea. You can butter some toast." She hustled her brother from the room before her, and firmly shut the door. It was very much a point with Hatty now that Charles Rose and her mother were the most devoted of elderly lovers.

"Hullo, Charles—is that meeting over?"

"My dear Jane, it hasn't begun. Burntisland hasn't yet turned up. Nerve-war, I suppose. So I can't get away. And there's something I wanted to have a word with you about. Something I was told this morning."

"Then go ahead." Jane couldn't remember Charles's ever before having spoken as he was speaking now—with an odd, staccato effect suggesting considerable agitation.

"Are you alone?"

"Quite alone. The children—Bruno and Hatty—have just begun a kitchen tea."

"Well, it's about Hatty, in a way. Is there still anything in that business of her being interested in Tresilian's grandson?"

"Son," Jane corrected. "Luke."

"But, you see—" Charles appeared to check himself. "Well, is there?"

"Yes. And Luke should be here any minute."

"It might be really serious?"

"Decidedly. Charles, whatever have you got in your head?"

"It's this. I'm afraid there may be rather a scandal about the Tresilians."

"Good heavens, don't I know it? Aren't you in the middle of it at this moment?"

"Not that, at all. It's a matter of something very distressing, very painful, in the family history. There's a madman going about with a dreadful story."

"You mean, something he's invented?"

"No, I'm afraid not."

"Then what story, Charles?"

"Jane, that's the awkwardness. I'm simply not entitled to tell. It's nothing that any rational mind could think of as to the discredit of this young man. And it may well be hushed up. It's precisely the kind of thing that *ought* to be hushed up. The point is that it may reach the boy, and it's something that would rather upset him. So I've felt I simply had to indicate the general situation. If he turns up, I mean, in what's obviously a disturbed state—"

"Charles, pull yourself together! What do you imagine I can do about it if you can produce only this mystery-mongering? Can't you trust me?"

"Yes, of course." Charles Rose now sounded acutely distressed. "But I must think. It *is*, believe me, a matter of high confidence. And certainly I could say nothing over the telephone, except to forewarn you of possible trouble. You see—" He broke off. "Jane, I'm frightfully sorry. They're calling me. Perhaps Burntisland's come. Or perhaps they're proposing to give him up. I *will* think. And I'll come and see you. Good-bye."

There was a click, and Jane realized that Charles had simply rung off. It was incredible. She put down the receiver, puzzled and alarmed. She knew that, during the last few days, Charles had been developing a single-minded concern for the vindicating of the Tresilian pictures. That something totally different had suddenly got him into such a state as he had just exhibited was mysterious. Composing herself, she returned to the kitchen. She had barely sat down when the telephone rang again.

"*That's* him!" Hatty jumped to her feet, and for a moment there flashed over her face a vivid happiness. "His train was late. It's to say he's coming." She ran from the kitchen, closing the door behind her.

Jane poured three cups of tea. Bruno glanced at her, and then stared. "Mum," he asked, "is anything wrong?"

"Wrong? Of course not." Jane was angry that she should have betrayed her perturbation. "I wonder if Hatty remembered to make up Luke's bed for tomorrow? It would be entirely like her to forget."

They were both silent. Through the closed door they could just hear Hatty's voice. Suddenly it rose to urgency, and then became inaudible. They heard the receiver put down. A full minute passed before Hatty returned to the kitchen. "Luke's not coming," she said in a strange voice.

"Good Lord!" Bruno put down his tea-cup. "Can't the poor boy face it?"

"*Get out!*"

Hatty had hurled the words at her brother with a savage

passion that brought him to his feet. He caught a glance from his mother, and suddenly, like a frightened child, hurried from the room.

"Hatty, is Luke ill—or hurt?"

Hatty looked at her mother for a moment as if without recognition. Then she slowly shook her head. Her face was drained of colour. She was like a person who has been hauled out of debris, physically unharmed but in a state of deep shock. "No," she said. "No. He just said he couldn't come. I asked him if he was injured or ill. He said no. I asked him where he was, and he didn't seem to know. Then he said yes, that he was here in London. He said—" Hatty's voice faltered, and then took on a desperate strength again. "Mummy, he said he found he couldn't be in a room with people."

"I see." Jane was silent for a moment, bracing herself. She knew that she must manage confidence, calm, a strong support that wasn't obtrusive solicitude or sympathy. "Did he talk as he normally does?"

"No. I only just knew it was him. I asked him what was wrong. I said to tell me—*to tell me*. He didn't say anything. He didn't seem able to."

"And then?"

"I told him that, if he wasn't hurt, it was all right. I told him that, as long as he was alive, nothing could be wrong between him and me. *That it was all right.*"

"Did he reply?"

"Yes, with one word. It was like a battle in him." Hatty had raised her head, and her mother saw that a faint flush had returned to her cheeks. "He said *Darling*."

There was a moment's pause, and Hatty flung herself into her mother's arms in a bewilderment of tears.

CHAPTER THIRTY-SEVEN

"Ah, Rose—we thought you might have left us." Sir Hector Madrona had turned away from the big window through which he had been nervously scanning the square. His features expressed their customary gratified surprise. But this was so plainly not Madrona's mood that the effect was uncomfortable. "It's quite intolerable," he said. "And, if you ask me, it's something that the fellow Roundhay's put him up to. It's as good as saying that he has us where he wants us, and can come when he pleases."

For a moment there was silence. The half-dozen men sitting round the table looked at one another gloomily. Then John Alabaster spoke. "I think not. I doubt whether Burntisland would consider tactics of that sort quite becoming. He may have underestimated the time required for some other meeting." Alabaster looked round maliciously. "Say, with the Director of Public Prosecutions."

Madrona returned to his own chair. "Miss Landreth," he said, "please go and ring up again. Get any further information you can. Whatever the reason, it remains outrageous that we should have to hang around like this."

Lucilla Landreth left the room. "But need we?" John Littlejohn asked. "Our policy is determined upon : absolute refusal to compromise in any way. In my view we ought to write to Burntisland to that effect, and let him do what he pleases. We have counsel's opinion, and an impressive list of expert witnesses. A successful prosecution's almost unthinkable."

"That's all very well." Somebody had spoken in a frayed and irritable voice from down the table. "But there would be grave scandal in the mere fact of a body such as ours being brought into court in such a matter. Whatever the verdict, it would be known that the Attorney-General and lord knows who had considered there was a reasonable case against us. That sort of thing isn't healthy. We've our grant to consider. And I've been far from supposing, as Dr Littlejohn seems to do, that our policy is determined upon. I understood we were to feel our way with Burntisland at this meeting."

"What makes the whole attack so formidable," Rose said, "is its two-pronged character. Moral indignation is being whipped up against the Tresilians and a number of other things : some innocent, some not. But, at the same time, there's a very deft exploitation of what can be represented in contemporary art as merely ridiculous. If I may say so, Madrona, it's a pity you published that rather sumptuous catalogue of your collection some time ago."

"They've been very funny about it." Alabaster spoke with unconcealed amusement. "And they've got hold of your proposal to pack it up and send it to our friend Littlejohn here in Oxford. There's rather a good joke about that in Roundhay's rag only this morning."

Madrona had flushed and then turned pale. "To my mind," he said, "the sense of our meeting has certainly not yet been determined. I regard the main issue as something of an open question still. We haven't, remember, been asked to shut down the whole Tresilian exhibition. All that's required is that we should unobtrusively remove the final things. There's scope for negotiation—which is precisely why we're supposed to be meeting Burntisland now." For a fraction of a second Madrona hesitated. "As I see it, we must ask ourselves this : if we agree to removing the controversial paintings, can we get a guarantee that the whole disgraceful campaign will be called off?"

There was an uneasy murmur, and then silence. Rose and Alabaster glanced at each other like men confirmed in a shrewd guess. And then Lucilla Landreth had returned to the room.

"I haven't got much more," she said. "But I spoke to a parlourmaid. She confirms the time Lord Burntisland left home. He told her where he was going—which is, apparently, his habit. And he said he would walk part of the way, and then probably pick up a cab."

"I begin to think it likely," Rose said, "that he's been taken ill. It's the simplest explanation of his non-appearance. Nothing merely casual would have stopped him. I'm sure of that. All the evidence is to the effect that he's been giving himself to this whole wretched business to the point of sheer obsession."

"Illness is certainly far from improbable." Alabaster, who for many years had borne the appearance of something temporarily released from a shroud, spoke with pleased emphasis. "Burntisland's of no age to speak of, but he strikes me as being far from a good life."

"Ought we to ring round the hospitals?" Madrona asked on a note of hope.

"No, Sir Hector." Lucilla spoke firmly. "There may have been an accident, but Lord Burntisland couldn't possibly remain unidentified for five minutes. He'll be carrying various papers; and his tailor, for that matter, is most unlikely not to have sewn his name into his suit. They'd ring up his house, and then we'd get a message at once. I've fixed that."

"Of course," Littlejohn said, "we must very much hope that nothing of the sort has occurred. It would be most distressing. But it would put an end to this nonsense, if you ask me."

"You don't think," Alabaster asked, "that Roundhay and his crowd of gutter-scribblers would simply carry on?"

"They might try, but they'd be stopped." Charles Rose spoke briskly. "They thought to have the edge on Burntisland, but in fact he has the edge on them. He has convictions, even if they're muddled ones. They have nothing of the kind. With Burntisland out, the whole thing would lose drive and flop. The issue would be dead and forgotten within a week."

Madrona looked at his watch. "Half-past," he said. "I think we can only—" He broke off at a discreet knock on the door of the committee-room. A commissionaire came in, caught Lucilla's eye, and beckoned. She crossed the room, spoke to him briefly and returned. She had a small piece of pasteboard in her hand.

"It's from Lord Burntisland," she said unemotionally. "His visiting card. Handed in by a taxi-driver, with instructions that it should be given to Sir Hector." She put the card down on the table before her employer. "There seems to be a message, scribbled in pencil, on the back."

There was a tense silence. Madrona was fumbling agitatedly for his spectacles. "What the devil," somebody asked, "does *this* mean?"

"At least," Rose said, "it means that he can't come—or won't come."

"But I'm almost unable to read this!" Madrona was peering

at the back of the card. "I didn't know he had such a wretched scrawl."

"Burntisland?" Littlejohn asked. "Nothing of the sort. He writes a good, firm hand."

"Then he certainly *has* had—" Madrona paused. His expression changed. He rose to his feet with what must have been his best board-room manner. "Gentlemen," he said, "I will simply read Lord Burntisland's message. *'I find myself unfit to pursue the matter at issue between us, and I withdraw from it herewith.'* He adds what appears to be his signature. Gentlemen, how right we were to remain absolutely firm."

There was a murmur of excited comment, and then Littlejohn made himself heard. "Unfit?" he said. "That's it. We were right. He's ill."

"Unfit?" Alabaster repeated. "Doesn't it strike you as rather an odd word?"

But Littlejohn wasn't listening. He had turned to Rose. "I must be getting back to Oxford," he said. "Do you know that one of my colleagues, simply because he has some technical superintendence of our domestic affairs during the vacations, has had the hardihood to remove—"

"Yes, I've heard about that." Rose, who was not feeling jubilant, had no disposition to listen to the Provost.

"Well, he's cooked his own goose, all right," Littlejohn said grimly, and looked round for his hat and coat.

Madrona was still on his feet. "There can be no doubt," he said, "that we have weathered this storm. Certain matters will still, of course, need tactful handling. But I hope I am not immodest in suggesting that the committee can now safely leave them to me."

There were murmurs of somewhat perfunctory approval. Without waiting for its formal close, the meeting was breaking up.

"It's all over," somebody said to Charles Rose. "And no harm done."

CHAPTER THIRTY-EIGHT

LUKE CAME OUT of the telephone kiosk, walked up a ramp, and found that he was in Piccadilly Circus. His mind had gone blank again when Hatty asked him where he was. But he experienced no difficulty in recognizing his whereabouts now. In fact it was only when he tried to get back beyond his train journey that he came upon a complete void—his memory closing up like a sea-anemone when you poke at it in a rock-pool. The important thing was not to let his knowledge of his own identity slip. As long as he knew he was Luke Tresilian, as long as he resisted the voice whispering to him that he was no longer that, he could cope with whatever came along. But if he lost his grip here, he would simply wander around until they took him to some hospital.

He crossed Piccadilly and walked down Lower Regent Street. He had some sort of aim in doing this, but he had no idea what it was. It had been in the train that he became aware of something wrong. It was when the young man and woman came into the compartment and he found that he himself at once wanted to move to an empty one. There was something wrong with a feeling like that. And another trouble had followed. He had looked round for his baggage and discovered he had none. He had tried to think where it could be, with the result that he saw at once that his memory wasn't right. He couldn't remember where he lived. Presumably he must live in a house, and of this house he tried to conjure up a visual image. Nothing would come. What had happened in his head was only freakish, he had thought at first, and not really important. But when he had found an empty compartment he sat wondering about the feeling he had had when the people entered the other one, and wondering whether he might not be forgetting other things as well as the look of the house he lived in.

Now, walking through London, he reached Waterloo Place and turned towards Trafalgar Square. There was a statue of George the Third on a horse, much like one of London's mounted police-men getting in the way of the traffic. He recalled a tremendous bit in *The Dynasts* about George the Third when insane. His memory had no difficulty with things like that. He could even be pretty sure that he had been reading Hardy's drama only a few days ago. And here was the National Gallery. He had come this way because of the National Gallery.

Luke felt a stab of the terror that had been coming on him, like a toothache, every now and then. If you did forget who you were, if you believed the voice whispering that you had become somebody else, then you would be like the mad king. The attend-ants, as Hardy's stage-direction said, would have to hold you. He told himself he had better face it : he was in a funk about perhaps going mad. It was almost as if he had brushed up against madness lately and been scared by it.

But now he looked at the National Gallery and knew that his coming here was because of this threat of losing his identity, this strange fear that he was not Luke Tresilian but somebody else. And it was a fear, surely, that he had known once before. Only, as a recollection, it hovered in his mind in so unstable and dreamlike a way that it seemed possible it was only in some dream that he had encountered it. Luke had no sooner thought of this than he knew why he had come to the National Gallery. It was to see Leonardo da Vinci's Virgin of the Rocks.

As he walked up the final flight of steps inside the building, he realized in what a mess his mind must be. He realized this be-cause, quite suddenly, a small, contrasting area of what seemed complete clarity had turned up in it. Just because he was Luke Tresilian he possessed a kind of status in this impressive place. The third of his father's Lyonnesse paintings hung in its farthest room. He must go there first.

The White Mermaiden was just as he remembered. But that was natural, because he owned one of the sketches for it, and that kept it in his mind. There was a bench in front of the painting, and he sat down like an old man who has had a tiring day. He thought of the rooms in college to which he was going back. They were quite clear to him. There was the photograph of the Piazza della Signoria, and the bear Ambrose, and the injudi-ciously-purchased tobacco-jar. He felt tranquil and happy. But something told him that this was a dangerous feeling, that it was connected in some way with the slipping process he had to avoid, that it was like allowing yourself to fall asleep in the snow. He had to recover something he had lost, something that required facing up to. And he had to find the Virgin of the Rocks.

He discovered the right room, but turned first to the wrong wall and found himself facing a couple of nudes. Correggio's Venus was posed with a bold *déhanchement* like a Hindu dancing-girl's; Bronzino's squatted in staring flesh, and Cupid, like a lover, was cupping her left breast with his hand—the nipple nipped in the cleft of two fingers. Luke found that he was neither pleased nor amused by these performances. In fact they were producing the same sort of sick feeling as the young man and woman had done on the train. He turned away in a hurry and found the Leonardo. He looked at it and remembered, as if from aeons back, his dream. The college kitchens had been in the dream, and Leech, and Bruno Landreth. That was where the business of a threat to his identity had come in. In some fashion he had *been* Bruno. And he had made love—

Instantly, Luke remembered everything. It was all in his mind at once, like a life history in a drowning man's.

He remembered the madman Crinnis, whose madness had been the truth. He remembered who his mother had been, and how she had died. He remembered who his father had been. He realized that intermittently he had been forgetting these discoveries and everything that surrounded them. He knew that there were medical terms for his condition when forgetting : amnesia, hysterical fugue. He understood why, in the railway carriage, he had found a man and a woman together to be something he couldn't take. He understood what had constituted the particular impossibility of going to the Landreth's and seeing Hatty and Bruno together.

Luke seized upon this last reaction—the reaction that had necessitated the ghastly telephone call—and tried to wrestle with it in its full unreasonableness. *This* brother and sister, he knew, hadn't got round to sleeping together; their behaviour amounted to little more than tormenting their mother with perverse nonsense. Only it was nonsense which, to his own present sense whether sick or sane, horribly mimicked the thing that couldn't be looked at : the blur in the centre of Matthew Tresilian's last paintings.

Bruno and Hatty were innocent enough, and so was he. Only innocence isn't armour. Gazing at the Leonardo, Luke felt that he had dragged this last truth from the painting's farthest recesses. So far as this day's dire story went, he himself was innocent, however much other darknesses harboured in his heart. Perhaps it would be better for him had he committed, wittingly or unwittingly, some dreadful deed : killed his father, married his mother, offended the gods by an overweening pride. It's comparatively easy to expiate one's own sins. To expiate the sins of others is the job of the saints.

He wasn't a saint. For one thing, he *had* a great deal of pride. And essentially it wasn't pride in being a reasonably decent citizen or in having the germ of a talent that might grow. It was pride in his eighteen years and his six feet, his speed with a ball and his steadiness on rock. His pride began with his body, which was what had been given him to be alive with. And it was his body that was dishonoured in what had been revealed to him.

With the Leonardo still before him, he saw that something deep in human evolution was going to make this inescapably his conviction, and that in the very irrationality of the conviction lay all its pain and power. Here was the heart of his plight. He had no *reason* to be so much as upset. He had nothing for which to blame himself. There was no particular in which he had failed of his own inches, so that he could promise himself to try harder next time. His health, his fortune, his strength of mind and imagination such as they were : these were unimpaired. He knew very well that he wasn't even going to be saddled with an ugly story or an ugly name. The very dreadfulness of the fact, the peril of uttering it, would prevent the ramblings of Alfred Crinnis's darkened mind from ever being carried out into the world. What he faced was something quite different, too primitive to be amenable to reason, as arbitrary as a phobia or a dreadful neurosis, about which nothing could be done except perhaps by people who took off the top of your head while you lay on a couch and who then paddled about with its inside for years. Perhaps the horror would wear itself out, as phobias, if you were lucky, were said to do. At least there might be, as with mental illness, remissions, spells of forgetfulness and ease. But always the horror would be liable to appear again, as unpredictably as a sadistic gaoler wandering a prison.

Luke turned away from the Virgin of the Rocks. As he did so, in the now nearly empty gallery, he met the gaze of an old man who was himself turning away from a picture, Raphael's Ansidei Madonna.

It was Luke's first impression that the old man was one of those down-and-out types—tramps or solitaries or destitute eccentrics—who seem to come into the National Gallery primarily for warmth and shelter, but who are often seen, nevertheless, in absorbed contemplation of the pictures. Then he saw that he had been judging wholly by the old man's expression and bearing, and that about these there was something so haggard and fugitive and broken as to render unnoticeable for the moment the fact that his clothes declared him to be of quite a different condition. He might, Luke thought, be a retired judge. Or he might—and this would account for something strikingly wrong with him—be a financial magnate whose affairs had suddenly folded up.

But Luke was in no state to speculate idly about anyone, and he would have turned away at once if something else hadn't strangely and instantly declared itself. He had never seen the old man before, and the old man had almost certainly never seen him. They were totally unknown to each other. Yet this was in some indefinable way an encounter. And, in fact, the old man was going to speak. He was going to speak, although—and this, with an equal strangeness, Luke was aware of—there was nothing he wanted to do less. For the old man was looking at him almost with horror and fear : almost, it came to him, as he himself must have looked at the young couple in the railway carriage. It was as if Luke belonged to a species suddenly revealed as dangerous. But, at the same time, there was something utterly different in the old man's face as well. And what this was declared itself in his tone the instant he did speak. For he spoke gently and out of a kind of compassion. "Forgive me," he said, "but can I be of any help to you? You seem distressed . . . ill."

Luke was staggered. It just hadn't occurred to him that he might be looking differently from what he ordinarily did. And what made the words more startling still was their being spoken by somebody, as Luke now clearly saw, who was himself in some state of desperation.

"Thank you," Luke said awkwardly. "I think I'm all right. It's just that I've had a bit of a shock. But it was some time ago. This morning, in fact. So I'm getting better." For a second he hesitated before saying what, queer as it was, he now felt he must say. "But could *I* help *you*?"

The old man moved his head oddly, and Luke saw that he had made a kind of bow. The gesture carried an enormous dignity that made the old man's broken state appear more evidently. "Thank you," he said. He began fumbling with the buttons of his overcoat, and then stopped as if the effort was too much for him. Luke somehow guessed that he had been trying to reach his watch, and his next words confirmed this. They were spoken in a new and hoarse voice. "Do you happen to know how soon they will turn us out?"

Luke stiffened. For he had heard something he had lately become acquainted with : a note of quite irrational fear. "Oh, not for ages, I think," he said cheerfully. "I've an idea it's one of their late nights."

"Then perhaps we might sit down. The National Gallery is, of course, an inspiring place. It's a great thing to be surrounded by masterpieces. I would venture to advise you to cultivate the habit of frequenting it." The old man might have been striving to recapture a dead life. "You are young, and must forgive me if I seem impertinent. But of course, it's a tiring place, curiously tiring. Perhaps, as I say, we might sit down."

"What about getting a cup of tea, sir? I think the cafeteria downstairs may still be open." Luke moved swiftly forward, for it had seemed to him that the old man was swaying on his feet. "Can I give you a hand?"

"No!"

Luke stopped in his tracks. This time, he was more startled still. For the old man had recovered himself and taken a swift backward step, like one retreating from a chasm. "I'm sorry," Luke said. "Perhaps—"

"I shall be glad of your arm." It seemed to Luke that the old man had made some immense effort of the rational will. "On floors like these a person of my years is the better for an umbrella or walking-stick. But, of course, one leaves that with the attendant downstairs. One has to do that, you know. Thank you. I am grateful for your support. It would all have been different, I suppose, if only sons had been granted me."

Luke was a long way from finding any reply to this, and they went down the steps in silence. At a little window the old man recovered an umbrella. They went down another flight. It was still possible to get tea. Luke brought the cups to a corner table. There was nobody else in the room except a group of German students. The old man drank his tea slowly. Taking a good glance at him, Luke wondered whether he ought to do something about getting a doctor. The old man was fumbling at his overcoat again. "This button," he said.

"Don't worry." Luke consulted his own watch and told him the time. "But perhaps, sir, when you've had a rest, I'd better get a taxi to take you home."

"Home?" The old man frowned. "I am Lord Burntisland," he said suddenly.

Luke had a fugitive sense that this name meant something to him. But what it was eluded him. "My name's Luke Tresilian," he said.

Lord Burntisland gave a slight bow, as a man who receives politely information of no moment. "And you live in London?" he asked.

"No, sir. I don't come here very often."

"There are moral dangers." Lord Burntisland put his cup down with an unsteady hand. "I must warn you. It is my duty. Particularly in—" He broke off in agitation. "I missed an appointment this afternoon," he said. "On a grave matter. I shall never keep another."

Luke too put his cup down. He had a sense that something was coming that it wasn't for him to cope with. "Perhaps," he said, "I ought to get that taxi? Won't they be expecting you at home? Is there anybody—?"

"You mean my wife?" Lord Burntisland's voice was suddenly harsh. "I have a wife. She has been in a madhouse these forty years."

Luke was silent, appalled. A madwoman. And this old man was surely deranged. And, that morning, there had been Crinnis. And he himself was only holding on. He had entered a world that was like some horrible old play.

"You see," Lord Burntisland was saying, "I have been rather hard-pressed. I ventured upon unfamiliar ground. It's very dangerous. Because of the old, impure desires. And so I am earnest to give you this warning. Particularly about the public parks. A moment of insanity, and an irreversible thing has taken place."

Luke was again silent. A horrible nausea was upon him, as if the tea had concealed some filthy draught. He wanted to get up and go away. But he couldn't—not if this old man needed him. "But it wasn't," he prompted gently, "really anything very much?"

"They simply walked away."

"They?" Luke asked.

"The two young soldiers." Lord Burntisland appeared to regard this as self-evident. "But there might have been a policeman, you know. Fortunately there was not." Very horribly, something like cunning momentarily streaked the dignity which the old man so largely preserved. "But a colleague of mine in the—" Lord Burntisland checked himself, and Luke wondered whether he was going to faint. "But an acquaintance was passing." The look of cunning had returned, reinforced by an air of senile calculation. "So I don't quite know where I am."

Luke stood up. "Tell me, please," he said, "how you live. Is it with relations, or just with servants?"

"With servants. They are very respectable elderly women."

"Have you a doctor, sir? One you can absolutely trust?"

"Sir Thorold Buttery in Harley Street. Curiously enough, I have several times of late considered seeing him. On intimate matters which you will forgive my not mentioning to you." Lord Burntisland struck Luke as now verging upon some state of real mental confusion. "Buttery is widely regarded as being in the best consultant practice."

"Then that's where the taxi had better take you, sir."

"I think, perhaps, you are right." Lord Burntisland made a gesture as if he wished Luke to sit down again. "But I have been remiss," he said. "We have been talking about my own affairs. Whereas it was a feeling that all was not well with you that prompted me to address you."

"We mustn't bother about that." Luke was more moved than he would have believed possible. This wretched old man, with

369

his squalid disaster or near-disaster upon him, was doing more than endeavour to pick up some accustomed attitude of benevolence and courtesy. He was regarding Luke across a great distance, but with a genuine wish to help in the trouble he had divined. Luke, after all, hadn't been prancing round the National Gallery with straws in his hair. Lord Burntisland was primarily a lonely old man in search of a son—and perhaps the chance wasn't entirely meaningless by which he had obscurely reached out to Luke, who had that day so strangely lost a father : it was almost as if they had come momentarily together at the prompting of a mutual need. Only it happened that nature had given Lord Burntisland a double dose of interest in young men who might stand in a filial relation to him. And it was this, plus heaven knew what ill-chance, that had betrayed him. There was nothing to be done but get him to his doctor.

Fortunately they had no sooner reached the kerb than a taxi came along. Lord Burntisland gave the Harley Street address and climbed in, but not before he had shot an apprehensive glance around him. Yet he was clearly a commanding man, so that Luke felt like a pain in his own body the pathos of what had happened.

"Good-bye, sir," Luke said. Despite being so much younger, he held out his hand. "I do hope you'll be all right again soon."

It was a lame remark. But Lord Burntisland, as he shook hands, gave a faint, pleased smile. "Thank you. I think you said your name was—?" He frowned as if in perplexity, and made a gesture at once dismissive and baffled. "But no matter. You have a family—a father and mother?"

"No. My father died a long time ago." Luke spoke steadily. "My mother died much more recently."

"Then moral dangers are all the more earnestly to be considered. I would again urge you occasionally to visit the works we have lately been studying." Lord Burntisland spoke with an authority that struck Luke as being, in his circumstances, both comical and touching. "Particularly the Old Masters, when addressing themselves to the sublime subject of the Holy Family. I am not myself a believing Christian, but I have never failed to find inspiration in them. They will recall to you, my dear lad, the sanctity of the home that you look back upon : and

may you never forfeit the right to make that retrospection un-
ashamed. Forgive me. An old man must sometimes claim the
privilege of speaking in a serious manner to his younger friends.
Good-bye."

Luke had a last glimpse of Lord Burntisland's face, craggy
and haunted, as the taxi moved into the stream of traffic. He
found himself thinking of the turtles on Bikini, returning to their
swimming motions when hopelessly lost in sand. This old man
was hopelessly lost—or at least he believed himself to be that—
and involuntarily he had been going into a routine appropriate
to his former condition. For he was the sort of old man who
made speeches at school prize days and had a line in lay sermons
for boys' clubs. So here, Luke told himself, is something to
notice about catastrophe. You leave part of yourself perplexingly
on the farther side of the chasm.

He turned away, retracing his route to Piccadilly Circus. The
Bakerloo line would take him to Paddington. The final stage of
his day's journey was before him.

By the time he got to Oxford there was at least no longer
anything wrong with his memory, or not in a big way. He
knew just who he was, and he knew that he would never again
take refuge from that knowledge by putting on any sort of mad
turn. Anything he now did—and he had no notion what he
might do, since his future had taken on such a vagueness as
scarcely to seem a future at all—he'd do in his right mind. As
for the present, it was only in minor matters that he was a bit
hazy. A kind of obstinate inattention to what should properly
be attended to seemed to be his line. For instance, he didn't
bother to recall why it was so late when he arrived at college.
He just gave a kick at the gate, said good-evening to the porter
when admitted, and walked off to his rooms. Perhaps the man
was surprised to see him without so much as a suitcase. He
didn't bother about that either.

He climbed his ill-lit staircase without noticing whether or
not it was deserted. He was thinking about something he had
never experienced—not to speak of—but which had often
haunted his imagination. It was waking up as if to another
ordinary day and then remembering it wouldn't be that because
something had happened the day before, or a week or a year

371

before. You'd committed a dreadful crime, or lost your wife and children in a hideous accident. The point was that this sort of waking up could happen again and again. The mind coming out of sleep was so made that such a realization could return again and again and again with all its pristine force through a long lifetime. It was a little like the torture of the manikin in the phial he sometimes dreamt about. Climbing the final narrow flight of stairs to his rooms, Luke told himself that this sort of evident senseless cruelty in the nature of things was what had set upon Thomas Hardy's face the expression recorded in Augustus John's portrait. It was odd that he himself had managed to square an unbounded admiration of Hardy with a fatuous persuasion that the nature of things was in general rather nice. He was now looking at a door above which was written, still in very fresh white paint, *Mr L. Tresilian*. It ought to read, he thought, *Mr L. Tresilian: cheerful moron*. The college hadn't known or noticed. But Fate had. That was why Fate had taken a lethal kick at him.

He turned on the lights and looked round. The room seemed to stand awkwardly and hesitantly before him, like a person re-encountered after an interval, who doesn't know whether any intimacy had been started up with you or not. Of course it was quite unchanged, except—Luke noticed with a minute start of memory—that a packet of cigarettes had been taken from the chimneypiece and thrown down, open, on the table. Perhaps his scout had felt in need of a fag.

The thing to do was to take possession again. You did that by sitting down. So Luke sat down. And at once his consciousness was flooded with the horror that alone now had meaning for him. It was as if his body was something he couldn't too quickly take soap and water to and wash away from himself for ever. And he saw that he had been right in feeling that he wouldn't again go wrong in the head. The horror was irrational, but it was an essentially sane Luke Tresilian whom it was going to seek to hunt down and destroy. Always he was going to be kept sentient while the torment went on. Digging his finger-nails into his hands, he told himself that he wasn't a savage out of *Totem and Taboo* or *The Golden Bough*. But it was like telling yourself in mid-channel that sea-sickness is a purely nervous phenomenon. He tried to fix his mind on his mother. He remembered that he had stood by her dead body that morning, and felt before it—as soon as he had felt anything at all—nothing but awe and tenderness. Perhaps he could conquer this sheerly pathological horror if he could only hold on to facts like that. Perhaps he could even write it out of himself (for aren't writers said to shed their sicknesses in books?) in some imaginatively disguised form. But Matthew Tresilian, he remembered, had done something rather like that. Luke realized something new. He himself would never again want to write anything.

And he *couldn't* think of his mother. The image wouldn't stay fixed. Instead, he saw only the old man in the National Gallery. It wasn't, perhaps, odd that Lord Burntisland should thus crop up in his mind again. For in the train he had remembered who Lord Burntisland was; why the name had rung some sort of bell in his head. Lord Burntisland was the person who had been making a fuss about the exhibition. Perhaps, Luke fleetingly thought, the excitement of that hadn't been too good for so old a man. The odd thing, however, was that Lord Burntisland seemed suddenly to be in the room with him now, almost like a ghost or a presence. It didn't make sense, since he could certainly never have been here in the flesh. But Luke was mountingly uneasy. It was almost as if the breath of some fresh evil had touched him.

He went into his bedroom and washed, and then he went downstairs again. He told himself that this was because he ought to get something to eat. He was much too late for whatever dinner might be going for undergraduates at the tail-end of the vacation, but probably he could get something in the buttery. There were voices when he got into the quad : the rather noisy voices of robust men who have dined generously. And just such men were streaming out of Hall. They were in dinner-jackets, and here and there among them was a don wearing a gown as well. Luke remembered having been told about this. It was the annual Gaudy, when old members of the college came up for the night and pretty well took the place over. Most of them would be very decorous. A few would be disposed to make a binge of it.

Luke threaded his way against this crowd, and found himself not liking it. He felt dispossessed and awkward. Being a bit hazy, he wasn't even sure that he was entitled to his own rooms for the night. And he didn't like the way some of the men glanced at him as they went past. He even put a hand to his hair and then to his tie, to make sure he was reasonably tidy. He went up the great staircase, for that was the way to the buttery. He made one turn on it, and realized that something had happened. What this was, although entirely a matter of the eye, came to him as an event instantly draining the air of sound. Guests were still coming out of Hall, and still talking loudly. But there was an utter silence, all the same. And at the heart of it lay the perception that the Tresilian had vanished. Where it had hung there was a blind expanse of stone.

Luke found himself responding to this discovery in two quite distinct ways. He knew at once that the disappearance of the painting was connected with the nonsense that had been going on in London. It was something to be angry about and contemptuous of, but it wasn't more than that. This, actually, was his first response. His second was to be overwhelmed by the thing's shattering impact as a sudden brutal symbol of absolute loss. Up till now he had been conscious only that the day had brought him a burden that it wasn't easy to call supportable. It came to him now that the day had also robbed him of something upon which he had built rather too much of his hope and his pride. The blank stone before him was like the wall of a dungeon, asserting total deprivation as his lot.

He saw that somebody who had also been looking at the wall was now looking at him. It was Leech. Leech had come out behind the last of the guests. He had paused to look at the empty wall just as he had used to pause to look at the painting : as if darkly measuring something formidable that he was up against. And Luke, although not much in a condition to notice things, did notice that Leech had never before appeared to him so broodingly withdrawn and absorbed. One would have said an undergraduate was the last thing he would notice. But now he had certainly noticed Luke. And his face had changed as he did so.

"Tresilian, are you all right?"

Leech had walked up to Luke and spoken sharply, almost harshly. Luke, to his horror, realized that the challenge was justified. For he had actually been leaning on the balustrade of the staircase in a feeble way, much as if a knee or elbow had

374

got him vigorously in the wind. He drew himself up stiffly. "Yes, thank you sir. I'm quite all right."

"You've come up for that Latin tomorrow? You mustn't let it worry you, you know. It's quite elementary."

"I'm sure it is. And it isn't worrying me at all."

"I noticed you looking at the wall." From harsh, Leech's voice had become uncertain, almost embarrassed. "I am entirely responsible for the removal of your father's painting. It seemed to me best, in view of the public debate which certain aspects of his work have recently prompted. I've no doubt you understand me. And equally I've no doubt"—Leech's tone went grim again—"that it will be restored to its position almost immediately. Such will be the Provost's wish, and to that, of course, we shall all defer."

"I see." Luke wasn't interested in what this was about. He was conscious only of how the disappearance of the painting had rocked him. Almost, it had renewed the day's worst threat : the threat to his identity. But at least he was a Tresilian—rather exceptionally so—and as a Tresilian he must say something to Leech now. "I think, sir," he said, "it was a poor idea. I mean, taking the picture down. Just because some newspapers were screaming. It doesn't seem to me the idea of a place like this."

"There have been factors you can know nothing about." Leech snapped this out in his most magistral manner. But, even as he did so, his face flushed. "Nevertheless, Tresilian, I wish to offer you an apology. This incident has plainly affected you strongly, and I'm very sorry for it. You are the painter's son, and I acknowledge that I acted without sufficient consideration of what was due to you as a member of the society."

"Thank you, sir." Luke didn't try to make this more than conventionally polite. He knew Leech to be an honest man. But this scholars-and-gentlemen-together business didn't convey much to him at the moment.

"My duties of hospitality are almost over. I wonder whether you'd care to drop into my rooms later for a nightcap, Luke?"

This was really startling, the more so as Leech was decidedly not one of your Christian-name-dropping dons. But there was no point in getting into a false position. "Thank you very much,"

Luke said. "But I think I'd rather not. I think it would be a good idea if I got straight off to bed."

"Perhaps that is the wise thing." Leech sounded relieved. "So good luck with the Latin. And good night."

Leech went on down the staircase. Luke let him get clear, and then followed. He had lost interest in trying to get something to eat from the buttery. He didn't seem to find it at all easy to be interested in anything. The quads were full of the old members in their dinner-jackets—men with flushed, relaxed faces, most of them not at all sure how well they knew each other. Luke made his way to his rooms, not much studying them. But on the staircase there was a group of them he didn't like a bit. They were fooling round with a crate of beer. He thought they were a little drunk. He thought they were like undergraduates when a little drunk : pretending, that was, to be drunker than they were. A Gaudy struck him as a macabre idea. The object of the exercise, he supposed, was kidding themselves they *were* undergraduates once more. Most of them must be married, and have children. Luke felt it to be all quite horrible.

He climbed to his rooms, and shut the door behind him. He turned on the small electric fire, for he thought the night had turned chilly. He sat down in front of it. He felt he ought to think. *If a way to the better there be*—he quoted to himself— *it exacts a full look at the worst.* He must take a rational and thinking sort of look at the worst.

He sat for a long time. He told himself he had reached a conclusion. He saw what had happened. Simply, he had come to know a number of things that he hadn't known before. But they hadn't anything to do with him. Who goes with who, the bedclothes say. Who went with who, the bedclothes—if there had been any bedclothes—had said. It had been he who was getting begotten, but the operation was entirely other people's business, all the same. To be revolted, to allow himself to be irrationally stricken like a wretched blackfellow at whom another blackfellow had pointed a bone : this was in fact to judge and condemn, and that was something he had no right to do.

It had come out like this, it was all seeming almost sane and simple, when Luke heard men singing. They must be the men

who had brought in the beer. They were somewhere on the
staircase, probably in the guest set. And they were reviving old
times. Luke knew the tune—if it could be called a tune—perfectly well. He had a notion that the words went by the name of
the Cambridge Boat Song. It was something that Oxford rowing
hearties sang. And these men were singing it now. They were
bellowing senselessly that the Captain's wife was Mabel and
that the First Mate's name was Morgan. Luke wasn't sure at
first whether the words were really coming up to him quite
clearly, or whether he was recreating them for himself in his
head :

> *She had a son*
> *By Colin Lunn*
> *Upon the cabin table . . .*

The men were getting into good voice, so that there was now
no doubt that he was hearing, and couldn't do other than hear,
every word they sang. There were half a dozen verses, and they
went to and fro among them at random, bellowing each one
again and again. But their favourite seemed to be Morgan :

> *Night and day*
> *He used to play—*

Luke recalled that there were times when he had joined in this
obscene rigmarole himself. But now he tried to stop his ears.
He found that he was on his feet and blundering about the
room. He decided that it might be better in bed. He went into
his bedroom, scrambled out of his clothes, and flung open a
drawer in search of pyjamas. There weren't any; he hadn't left
any in college. All he could find was a white cricket shirt, and
he got into this as if it were a nightgown. Down below, the
revellers seemed suddenly to have remembered a new verse. The
stuff was even more inescapable here than in the sitting-room :

> *We marched into Algeria,*
> *To none we were inferior;*
> *The prostitutes*
> *Upon our routes*
> *Grew wearier and wearier.*

377

Luke stood for a moment helplessly in the cricket shirt. He was trembling as if he had just been whipped and was going to be whipped again. Then he flung himself into bed. The action seemed to silence the people below, as if by magic. Somebody, he supposed, had gone in and told them to shut up.

He lay in the darkness for a long time, with his eyes wide open. He tried again thinking over his whole revelation. He remembered there was a way of doing this which showed him that nothing had happened to *him*; that there was a core of him as intact as it had been when he had woken up that morning. But obviously he *wasn't* intact. On the contrary he was like a woman who has been raped, and who is unable to contemplate the slightest manifestation of sexuality without hysteria. It was just too bad, he supposed, that it had taken him that way.

Luke lay in the darkness, until eventually he began to see things. He began to see vivid images that were only partly inside his own head, so that he thought, blessedly, he would presently be asleep—for that was how the end of sleeplessness commonly signalled itself to him. But, this time, he didn't go to sleep. The images took on the character of a closed, compulsive system. They revolved endlessly, as in a primitive, magic-lantern type of toy that he dimly remembered from his childhood. But even the most Freudian childhood—he found himself managing to think—must be innocent of such images as these. Perhaps Hamlet—another bad hysteric—had gone in for them when things got pretty tough at Elsinore.

Time wore on through the small hours, and carried Luke far away from any point at which he could manage the wryest grin into the darkness. This sort of thing *would* send him mad, after all. He had to get away from it. Suddenly he knew how this was to be done. He was, of course, at the receiving end of a savage farce. Anything so ingeniously wicked as what had been done to him could be described only as that. But he was also a serious student, facing at nine-thirty on the following morning a crucial examination. It was his duty to himself to get some sleep. And people very reasonably and properly took sleeping tablets before such occasions. College doctors prescribed or dispensed them. And there was somebody he knew who went in for that sort of thing in rather a big way. Bruno. He had noticed as he came upstairs that Bruno's oak was unsported. It was possible, of course, that one of those ghastly Gaudy people was in Bruno's rooms. But, if not, Luke could go downstairs and simply walk in.

He got out of bed, and turned on the light. He was in such a queer state that the silly business of being clothed only in a cricket shirt quite worried him. But he walked out to the landing, felt for a light that proved to be out of action, and then groped his way downstairs. He went straight into Bruno's sitting-room. If one of last night's singers was in bed in the room beyond and began screaming for his threatened virtue, that would be just too bad. But he saw at a glance that the set was untenanted. It was at once familiar and alien. The Lawrence Toynbee was over the chimneypiece. His heart turned over as he looked at it. If only he could be doing *that* again. In a corner was Bruno's rather mysterious golf-bag, with the clubs shrouded beneath a carefully padlocked hood. He didn't think Bruno had ever been known to play golf. He went into the bedroom and turned on the light. In the drawer of the bedside table, as he had supposed, there was a fat bottle of the things, along with a large, crumpled handkerchief and some lengths of string. He opened the bottle, shook out two pills, and swallowed them. When he had replaced the top he put the bottle back in the drawer. Then he changed his mind, slipped it into the breast-pocket of the cricket shirt, and went back to his own rooms.

But he still didn't sleep. And it was almost useless to try to think any more, since it seemed to be something he could do directedly only for seconds at a time. He was involved in some dreadful process of dissolution that was being intolerably delayed; it was as if his body had been dead for a long time and nevertheless he couldn't get away from it. He found that the bottle of pills was no longer in his shirt pocket. It was in his right hand as his hand lay under the bedclothes. Perhaps the two pills he had taken hadn't sent him to sleep because that hadn't honestly been his idea; perhaps it was with a transparent sort of self-deception that he had started worrying about the examination next morning.

And here he was thinking again, after all. But thinking, he told himself, is what's precisely no good. Not when you've got into a fix like this. If salvation's conceivable, it's only through action. But no action was available to him. None. Except with this bottle.

Luke weighed the bottle in his hand. Doing so, he was reminded of something he'd done that morning. Of an action, in fact. Instinctively and apparently senselessly, he'd gone down that path and round that deadly rock. He'd taken the child's ball in his hand—rather as he had Bruno's bottle now—and he'd tossed it down into the cove. But one doesn't do anything senselessly. Somewhere in the mind, there's always a reason for any action. Or certainly there is for any action taken in crisis.

Luke lay quite still in bed. His room was in utter darkness. He might have been anywhere. He found himself working out in his head *precisely* where he was : just where the useless little fireplace lay, and just where the window. And he was carefully judging the weight of the bottle in his hand.

For that had been it. He hadn't gone round the rock, picked up and thrown the ball, as any demonstration of courage. It had been rather contrariwise. He had been showing himself that courage wasn't involved or required. There had been no danger, simply and merely because he was in command of his muscles and his nerves. They were *his*.

He heard himself take a deep breath. The floor was uncovered except for a mat by the bed. If the bottle came down on it there would be a smash and a mess. But just *there*, in the small window embrasure, was the small window-seat with its small, floppy cushion. The problem, Luke thought, was rather like that of getting the ball into the hands of your stand-off half in a game played at some starless and moonless midnight. But he believed the thing could be done. It *must* be done.

Luke paused in intense concentration, and then tossed the bottle. He listened. There wasn't a sound. It had come down plumb on the cushion. And that's it, he thought. Possess your body, exercise its skill, guard its mysterious potencies, and your body's yours. Only you can violate it. So leave it at that. Leave it at that now, and begin there tomorrow.

Luke felt the fingers of his right hand to be stiff, as if a lot of tension had been gathered there. He began flexing and unflexing them. Before he had done this very often he was fast asleep.

He woke up to a very common waking-up sensation. His last thoughts before going off to sleep hadn't been anything like as wonderful as he'd supposed. Bruno's bottle was on the window-seat, but Luke's having successfully chucked it there no longer had the almost apocalyptic significance it had appeared to have. It hadn't got him anywhere very much. Except, of course, *here*. Morning had come, and here he was. Perhaps that was something.

Rather a lot of morning had come; it was broad daylight in the room. He looked at his watch, and saw that it was twenty past nine. His scout appeared to have slipped up on things. Perhaps he had his hands full with last night's musicians.

Luke got out of bed and wandered about the room. Inattention to things in general still seemed to be his line. He opened the wardrobe. There was nothing in it but his dark suit, and he looked at this without interest. He pulled out some drawers, and came on vests, pants, shirts and socks. He might as well, he supposed, get into some of these things. He pulled out another drawer, which proved to hold handkerchiefs and ties. There was a white dress tie. This improbable possession surprised him. Then he remembered that at Oxford, for some reason, people wore dark suits and white dress ties to take examinations. He remembered that he himself was supposed to be taking an examination in just over five minutes' time.

There was his old safety razor, abandoned when he'd bought an electric one. He shaved and dressed, quickly rather than slowly, but not all that quickly either. He was tired, or for some reason rather torpid. He was also hungry. He looked for some chocolate, which proved to have disappeared. But then he found a packet of biscuits behind some books. He stuffed this in a pocket. He scrambled into his absurd commoner's gown, stuck his absurd square on his head, and ran downstairs. He didn't feel particularly in a hurry. Running downstairs was his habit.

The High Street was almost deserted. Anyone else involved in this business was already at grips with it. But here were the Examination Schools. Above the door there was a gruesome stone-carving of bearded dons conducting a *viva*. He went in. A dingy mosaic owl leered up at him from the floor. He looked at a board, and found the right room. Its doors were still open. Inside there were rows of young men and women sitting at little desks, scribbling, or chewing pens. Luke knew at once that not a great deal had changed since yesterday. He knew this because he found he didn't want to be sitting close to any of these young people. It was just as it had been in the railway-carriage.

"Yes, you may come in. But you have just thirty seconds in which to do so." A woman don had come forward, frowning severely. "Mr Tresilian, I suppose? Your place is over there." She nodded towards a corner of the room. She was a grim, elderly woman, with wisps of grey hair sticking out under her odd black cap. No doubt she was one of the examiners. Luke, simply because he was intimidated, overcame his threatening resurgence of hysteria, or whatever it was, and made his way to his seat. He sat down, and picked up the question paper. He saw, with surprise, that most of it was in Latin. He realized that this surprise was unpromising, and then he remembered that the examination was *about* Latin. It was about *Aeneid* IV and VI. He now looked at some of the Latin with close attention. It conveyed nothing to him. He might never have learnt any Latin at all.

So that was that. His Oxford days were over. Luke sat back and gazed around him idly. The women candidates seemed to consist mainly of black-stockinged legs that disappeared, with very varying degrees of attractivness, beneath short black skirts. He knew that here was a field for wholesome study. But he only wondered whether he could stand up and walk out. He was just going to do this when he saw the woman in charge glaring at him. He was terrified, and stuck his nose into the question paper again, with an air of great concentration.

Solaque culminibus, he read, *ferali carmine bubo....*

He knew about *bubo*. *Bubo* had been leering at him a few minutes before in the hall of the Schools. Luke was, in fact, rather an authority on owls. He had photographed them. What was more to the point, he had dealt faithfully with this particular owl when getting up omens of dreadful import in Virgil.

So now he looked at this piece of Latin again, and it was perfectly clear:

> *alone on the roof-tops the screech owl with its song promising ill often made complaint and drew out its long notes into a wail.*

Mildly surprised at this sudden accession of learning, Luke turned back to the beginning of the passage he was supposed to be translating:

> *Tum vero infelix fatis exterrita Dido mortem orat; taedet caeli convexa tueri ...*

He read the words, and then looked up. Everything had gone curiously silent, and curiously still. It was as if all these people had been frozen as they scribbled. In this timeless moment he saw that there was a job here he must try to do rather well. He took out his pen, and wrote his name: *Luke Tresilian.* He wrote: *Question 1.* Stick close to it, he told himself, but not so as to be too slavish. Don't, for instance, follow all the Latin tenses. And he began:

> *Then, indeed, poor Dido, defeated by the burden Fate had laid upon her, prayed for death; she was tired of gazing on the arch of heaven ...*

Luke wrote for nearly an hour. *So when,* he concluded:

> *So when, beaten at length by sheer misery, she succumbed to madness and resolved to die, in her secret heart she fixed upon the time and manner of her dying.*

Luke put down his pen, and read through his version of Dido's agony. It would have to do; it would have to serve as a kind of requiem.

He realized that it was twenty-four hours since he had eaten anything, and that he was very hungry. He took the biscuits from his pocket and ate them, without any anxious care to minimise the noise involved. The attention of the presiding

lady was attracted. She frowned at him, but didn't try to inter-
fere. Her book of rules, he supposed, didn't authorize any tyranny
of the sort. Having eaten, he searched the paper for another
reasonably promising question. He was badly behind on the
clock. But the paper seemed rather a decent one. He made his
choice, and wrote steadily. He began to think it just possible
that he might get through.